Killashandra

KILLASHANDRA

ANNE McCAFFREY

A Del Rey Book
BALLANTINE BOOKS
New York

A Del Rey Book
Published by Ballantine Books

Copyright © 1985 by Anne McCaffrey

LIBRARY OF CONGRESS CATALOGING IN PUBLICATIONS DATA
McCaffrey, Anne.
Killashandra.
Sequel to: Crystal singer.
"A Del Rey book."
I. McCaffrey, Anne.   Crystal singer.   II. Title.
PS3563.A255K48   1985   813'.54   85-6193
ISBN 0-345-31599-5

Manufactured in the United States of America
First Edition: December 1985
Designed by Ann Gold
10   9   8   7   6   5   4   3   2   1

This book is gratefully dedicated to
Ron and Chris Massey
of the Tidmarsh Stud, and their Arabian friends,
Ben, BC, Racqui, Linda and Winnie

Killashandra

Chapter 1

Winters on Ballybran were generally mild, so the fury of the first spring storms as they howled across the land was ever unexpected. This first one of the new season swept ferociously across the Milekey Ranges, bearing before its westward course the fleeing sleds of crystal singers like so much jetsam. Those laggard singers who had tarried too long at their claims were barely able to hold their bucking sleds on course as they bolted for the safety of the Heptite Guild Complex.

Inside the gigantic Hangar, its baffles raised against the mach winds, ordered confusion reigned. Crystal singers lurched from their sleds, half deafened by wind-scream, exhausted by their turbulent flights. The Hangar crew, apparently possessed of eyes in the backs of their heads, miraculously avoided injury as they concentrated on the primary task of moving incoming sleds off the Hangar floor and into storage racks, clearing the way for the erratic landings of the stream of incoming vehicles. The crash claxon pierced even storm howl as two sleds collided, one to dip over the baffle and land nose down on the plascrete while the other veered out of control like a flat rock skipping across water, coming to a crumpling halt against the far wall. A tractor zipped in to fasten grapples on the upside-down sled, removing it only seconds before another sled skimmed over the baffle.

That sled almost repeated the nose dive, pulling up at the last second and skidding across the Hangar floor to stop just inches away from the line of handlers carrying the precious cartons of crystal in to Sorting. Only a near miss, the incident was disregarded even by those who had barely escaped injury.

Killashandra Ree emerged from the sled, taking as a good omen

3

the fact that her sled had skidded to a halt so close to the Sorting Sheds. She caught the arm of the next handler to pass her and firmly diverted him to her cargo door, which she flung open. She didn't have much crystal, so every speck she had cut was precious to her. If she didn't earn enough credit to get off-planet this time . . . Killashandra ground her teeth as she hurried her carton into the Sorting Shed.

As the man she had pressed into her service quite properly put her carton down at the Hangar end of a line of ranked containers, Killashandra's patience evaporated. "No, over here!" she shouted. "Not there! It'll take all day to be sorted. Here."

She waited until he had deposited her carton in the indicated row before adding her own. Then she strode back to her sled for a second load, commandeering two more unencumbered handlers on the way. Only after eight cartons were unloaded did she permit herself to pause briefly, coping with the multiple fatigues that assailed her. She had worked nonstop for two days, desperate to cut enough crystal to get off Ballybran. Crystal pulsed in her blood and bones, denying her rest in sleep, surcease by day, no matter how she tried to tire her body. Her only respite was immersion in the radiant fluid bath. But no one cut crystal from a bathcube! She had to get off-planet to ease the disturbing thrum.

For over a year and a half, ever since the Passover storms had shattered Keborgen's old claim, she had searched unremittingly for a workable site. Killashandra was realist enough to admit to herself that the probability of finding a new claim as important and valuable as Keborgen's black crystal was very low. Still, she had every right to expect to find some useful, and reasonably lucrative, crystal in Ballybran's Ranges. And, with each fruitless trip into the Ranges, the credit balance she had amassed from her original cutting of Keborgen's site and from the Trundomoux black crystal installation had eroded beneath the continuous charges the Heptite Guild exacted for even the most minor services rendered a crystal singer.

By fall, when everyone else she knew—Rimbol, Jezerey and Mistra—had managed to get off-planet, she had labored on, unable to make a worthwhile claim in any color. During the mild winter, she had doggedly hunted in the Ranges, returning to the Complex only long enough to replenish food packs and steep her crystal-weary body in the radiant fluid.

"You really ought to take a week or two up at Shanganagh Base," Lanzecki had said, intercepting her on one of her brief visits.

"What good would that really do?" she had replied, almost snarling at him in her frustration. "I'd still feel crystal and I'd have to look at Ballybran."

Lanzecki had given her a searching look. "You're in no mood to believe me," and he paused to be sure that he had her attention, "but you will find black crystal again, Killashandra. Meanwhile, the Guild has pressing needs in any shade you can find. Even the rose you so despise." A gleam shone in his black eyes and his voice turned lugubrious as he said, "I'm certain that you will be distressed to learn that the Passover storms destroyed Moksoon's site, too."

Killashandra had stared at him a moment before her sense of the ridiculous got the better of her and she laughed. "I am inconsolable!"

"I thought you might be." His lips twitched with suppressed amusement. Then he reached down and pulled the plug on the radiant fluid. "You'll find more crystal, Killa."

It had been that calm and confident statement which had buoyed her flagging morale all during the next trip. Nor had it been entirely misplaced. The third week out, after disregarding two sites of rose and blue, she discovered white crystal but very nearly missed the vein entirely. If she had not been bolstering her spirits with a rousing aria, causing the pinnacle under her hand to resonate, she might have missed the shy white crystal. Consistent with her long run of bad luck, the white proved elusive, the vein first deteriorating in quality and then disappearing entirely from the face at one point, resurfacing half a mile away in fractured shards. It had taken her weeks to clear the fault, digging away half the ridge before she got to usable crystal. Only the fact that white crystal had such a variety of potentially lucrative uses kept her going.

Forewarned of the spring storm by her symbiotic adaptation to Ballybran's spore, Killashandra had cut at a frenzied pace until she was too hoarse to key the sonic cutter to the crystal. Only then had she stopped to rest. She had continued to cut until the first of the winds began to stroke the dangerous crystal sound from the Ranges. Recklessly, she had taken the most direct route back to the Complex, counting on the fact that she'd be the last singer in from the Ranges to protect her claim.

She had almost cut her retreat too fine: the hangar doors slammed shut against the shrieking storm as soon as her sled had cleared the baffles. She could expect a reprimand from the Flight Officer for her recklessness. And probably one from the Guild Master for ignoring the storm warnings.

She forced several deep breaths in and out of her lungs, dredging sufficient energy to complete the final step necessary to leave Ballybran. On the last breath, she grabbed the top carton and walked it into the Sorting Room, depositing it on Enthor's table just as the old Sorter turned toward the shed.

"Killashandra! You startled me." Enthor's eyes flicked from normal to the augmented vision that was his adaptation to Ballybran. He reached eagerly for the carton. "Did you find the black vein again?" His face fell into lines of disappointment as his fingers found no trace of the sensations typical of the priceless, elusive black crystal.

"No such luck." Killashandra's voice broke on weary disgust. "But I devoutly hope it's a respectable cut." She half sat on the table, needing its support to keep on her feet, as she watched Enthor unpack the crystal blocks from their plastic cocoons.

"Indeed!" Enthor's voice lilted with approval as he removed the first white crystal shaft and set it with appropriate reverence on his work table. "Indeed!" He subjected the crystal to the scrutiny of his augmented eyes. "Flawless. White can so often be muddy. If I am not mistaken—"

"That'll be the day," Killashandra muttered under her breath, her voice cracking.

"—Never about crystal." Enthor shot her a glance from under his brows, blinking to adjust his eyes to normal vision. Killashandra idly wondered what Enthor's eyes saw of human flesh and bone in the augmented mode. "I do believe, my dear Killa, that you've anticipated the market."

"I have?" Killashandra pulled herself erect. "With white crystal?"

6

Enthor lifted out more of the slender sparkling crystal shafts. "Yes, especially if you have matched groupings. These are a good start. What else did you cut?" As one, they retraced their steps to the storage, each collecting another carton.

"Forty-four—"

"Ranked in size?"

"Yes." Enthor's excitement triggered hope in Killashandra. "Forty-four, from the half centimeter—"

"By the centimeter?"

"Half centimeter."

Enthor beamed on her with almost as much enthusiasm as if she had brought him more black crystal.

"Your instinct is remarkable, Killa, for you could not have known about the order from the Optherians."

"An organ group?"

Enthor gestured for Killashandra to help him display the white shafts on the workbench.

"Yes, indeed. An entire manual was fractured." Enthor awarded her another of his beams. "Where are the rest? Quickly. Get them. If there's so much as one with a cloud—"

Killashandra obeyed, stumbling against the swinging door. By the time the crystal was sparkling on the table, she was shuddering and had to cling to the bench to keep upright. It took a century for Enthor to evaluate her cut.

"Not a single cloudy crystal, Killashandra." Enthor patted her arm and, taking up his little hammer, cocked his ear to the pure sweet notes each delicate rap coaxed from the crystal.

"How much, Enthor? How much?" Killashandra was hanging onto the table, and consciousness, with difficulty.

"Not as much, I fear, as black." Enthor tapped figures into his terminal. He pulled at his lower lip as he waited for the altered display. "Still, 10,054 credits is not to be sneezed at." He raised his eyebrows, anticipating a pleased response.

"Only ten thousand . . ." Her knees were collapsing, the muscles in her calves spasming painfully. She tightened her grip on the table's edge.

"Surely that's enough to take you off-planet."

"But not far enough or long enough away." Blackness was

creeping across her sight. Killashandra released one hand from the table to rub her eyes.

"Would Optheria be far enough?" a dry, amused voice asked from behind her.

"Lanzecki . . ." she began, turning toward the Guild Master, but her turn became a spin, down into the darkness which would no longer be evaded.

"She's coming round, Lanzecki."

Killashandra heard the words. She could not understand their sense. The sentence, and the voice, echoed in her mind as if spoken in a tunnel. At the softest repetition, comprehension returned.

The voice was Antona's, the Chief Medical Officer of the Heptite Guild.

Sensation returned then, but sensation was limited to feeling something under her chin and a restraint about her shoulders. The rest of her body was deprived of feeling. Killashandra twitched convulsively and felt the viscous resistance of radiant fluid. She was immersed—that explained the need for chin support and the shoulder restraint.

Opening her eyes, she was not surprised to find herself in the tank room of the Infirmary. Beyond her were several more such tanks, two occupied, judging by the heads visible above the rims.

"So, you've rejoined us, Killashandra!"

"How long have you been soaking me, Antona?"

Antona glanced at a display on the tank. "Thirty-two hours and nineteen rinses." Antona shook a warning finger at Killashandra. "Don't push yourself like this, Killa. You're stretching your symbiont's resources. Abuses like this now can cause degeneration problems later on. And it's later on you really need protection. Remember that!" A mirthless smile crossed Antona's classic features. "If you can. Well, at least put it in your memory banks when you get back to your room," she added, with a sigh for the vagaries of singer recall.

"When can I get up?" Killashandra began to writhe in the tank, testing her limbs and the general response of her body.

Antona shrugged, tapping out a code on the terminal of the

tank. "Oh, anytime now. Pulse and pressure read-out's strong. Head clear?"

"Yes."

Antona pressed a stud and the chin support and shoulder harness released Killashandra. She caught the side of the tank, and Antona handed her a long robe.

"Do I need to tell you to eat?"

Killashandra grinned wryly. "No. My stomach knows I'm awake and it's rumbling."

"You've lost nearly two kilos, you know. Can you remember when you last ate?" Antona's voice and eyes were sharp with annoyance. "No use asking, is it?"

"Not the least bit," Killashandra replied blithely as she climbed out of the tank, the radiant fluid sheeting off her body, leaving her skin smooth and soft. She pulled the robe on. Antona held up a hand to balance her down the five steps.

"How much crystal resonance do you experience now?" Antona poised her fingers above the tank's small terminal.

Killashandra listened attentively to the noise between her ears. "Only a faint trace!" Her breath escaped her lips in a sigh of relief.

"Lanzecki said that you cut enough to go off-world."

Killashandra frowned. "He said something else, too. But I forget what." Something important, though, Killashandra knew.

"He'll probably tell you again in good time. Get up to your quarters and get some food into you." Antona gave Killashandra's shoulder an admonitory squeeze before she turned away to check on the other patients.

As Killashandra made her way up from the Infirmary level, deep in the bowels of the Guild Complex, she puzzled over her memory lapse. She had been reassured that most singers had several decades of unimpaired recall before memory deteriorated, but no fast rule determined the onset. She had been lucky enough to have a Milekey Transition ending in full adaptation to Ballybran's spore, an adaptation that was necessary for those inhabiting the planet Ballybran. That kind of Transition held many benefits, not the least of which was avoiding the rigors of Transition Fever, and was purported to include a longer span of unimpaired memory. In this one instance, she could, perhaps, legitimately blame fatigue.

As the lift door opened on the deserted lobby of the main singer level, not a singer was in sight. The storm had blown itself out. She paused to glance through to the dining area and saw only one lone diner. Pulling the robe more tightly about her, she hurried down the corridor to the blue quadrant and her apartment.

The first thing she did was call up her credit balance, and felt the knot that had been tightening in her belly dissolve as the figures 12,790 rippled onto the screen. She regarded the total for a long moment, then tapped out the all-important query: how far away from Ballybran would that sum take her?

The names of four systems were displayed. Her stomach rumbled. She shifted irritably in her chair and asked for details of the amenities in each system. The replies were not exciting. In each system the Terran-type planets were purely industrial or agricultural, having, at best, only conservative leisure facilities. From comments she had overheard, Killashandra gathered that because of their proximity the locals had seen quite enough of their neighbors from Ballybran and tended to be either credit crunchers or rude to the point of dueling offense.

"The only thing that's good about any of them," Killashandra said with disgust, "is that I haven't been there yet."

Killashandra had thought to take her long-overdue holiday on Maxim, the pleasure planet in the Barderi system. From all she'd heard, it would be very easy to forget crystal resonance in the sophisticated amusement parks and houses of hedonistic Maxim. But she hadn't yet the credit to indulge that whimsy.

Exasperated, she rubbed her palms together, noticing that the thick calluses from cutter vibrations had been softened by her long immersion. The numerous small nicks and cuts that were a singer's occupational hazard had healed to thin white scars. Well, that function of her symbiont worked efficiently. And the white crystal would assure her some sort of an off-planet holiday.

White crystal! Enthor has said something about a fractured manual! Optherian sense organs used white Ballybran crystals and she had cut forty-four from the half centimeter on up in half-centimeter gradients.

Lanzecki had asked her a question.

"Would Optheria be far enough?" The words, remembered in his deep voice, sprang to mind.

She grinned with tremendous relief at retrieving that question and turned to the viewscreen to punch up his code.

"—Killa?" Lanzecki's hands were poised over his own terminal, surprise manifested by his raised eyebrows. "You haven't used the catering unit." He frowned.

"Oh, programmed to monitor that, did you?" she replied with a genuine smile at that reminder of their amorous alliance before her first trip into the Ranges. On her return from the Trundomoux System, they had had only a few days together before Lanzecki was swamped with work and she had to venture back into the Ranges. Since then, she had returned to the Complex only to replenish supplies or wait out a storm. Their reunions had consequently been brief. It was reassuring to realize that he wished to know when she was back.

"It seemed the ideal way to make contact. After thirty-two hours in a tank, you should be ravenous. I'll just join you, if I may . . ." When she nodded assent, he typed a quick message on his console and pushed his chair back, smiling up at her. "I'm hungry, too."

As further reassurance of her unimpaired memory, Killashandra had no trouble remembering Lanzecki's tastes. She grinned as she ordered Yarran beer. Though her stomach gurgled impatiently, she'd had no desire for food in so long that she was as glad to be guided by Lanzecki's preferences.

She was just slipping a brilliantly striped robe over her head when her door chimed an entry request. "Enter!" she called. On the same voice cue, the catering slot disgorged her order. The aroma of the dishes aroused her already voracious appetite.

She wasted no time in taking the steaming platters from the dispenser, grinning a welcome at Lanzecki as he joined her.

"The Commissary has asked me to relay a few well-chosen words of complaint about the sudden fad for Yarran beer," he said, taking the pitcher and the beakers to the table. He seated himself before filling the two glasses. "To your restoration!" Lanzecki lifted his glass in toast, his expression obliquely chiding her for that necessity.

"Antona's already scolded me, but I had to cut enough marketable crystal to get off-planet this time."

"You've certainly succeeded with that white."

"Don't I remember you saying something about Optheria just as I passed out?"

Lanzecki took a swallow of the Yarran beer before he replied. "Quite likely." He served himself a generous helping of fried Malva beans.

"Don't the Optherians utilize white crystal in that multi-sense organ of theirs?"

"They do."

So Lanzecki chose to be uncommunicative. Well, she could be persistent. "Enthor said that an entire manual was fractured." Lanzecki nodded. She continued. "And you did ask me would Optheria be far enough?"

"I did?"

"You know you did." Killashandra hung on to her patience. "You never forget anything. And the impression I got from your cryptic comment was that someone, and the inference was me"— she pressed her thumb into her chest—"would have to go there. Am I correct?"

He regarded her steadily, his expression unreadable. "Not long ago you gave me to understand that you would not undertake another off-world assignment—"

"That was before I'd been stuck on this fardling planet—" She noticed the wicked gleam in his eyes. "So, I'm right. A crystal singer *does* have to make the installation!"

"It was a shocking incident," Lanzecki said diffidently as he served himself more Malva beans. "The performer who damaged the organ was killed by the flying shards. He was also the only person on the planet who could handle such a major repair. As is so often the case with such sensitive and expensive equipment, it is a matter of planetary urgency to repair the instrument. It's the largest on the planet and is essential to the observances of Optheria's prestigious Summer Festival. We are contracted to supply technician as well as crystal." He paused for a mouthful of the crisp white beans. He was definitely baiting her, Killashandra knew. She held her tongue. "While the list of those qualified does include your name . . ."

"The catch can't be the crystal this time," she said as he purposefully let his sentence dangle unfinished. She watched his face for any reaction. "White crystal's active, reflecting sound . . ."

12

"—Among other things," Lanzecki added when she paused.

"If it isn't the crystal, what's the matter with the Optherians, then?"

"My dear Killashandra, the assignment has not yet been awarded."

"Awarded? I like the sound of that. Or do I? I wouldn't put it past you, Lanzecki, to sucker me into another job like that Trundomoux installation."

He caught the finger she was indignantly shaking at him, pulling her hand across the laden table to his lips. The familiar caress evoked familiar responses deep in her groin and she tried to use her irritation with his methods to neutralize its effect on her.

Just then a communit bleep startled her. With a fleeting expression of annoyance, Lanzecki lifted his wrist unit to acknowledge the summons.

A tinny version of Trag's bass voice issued from the device. "I was to inform you when the preliminary testing stations reported," the Administration Officer said.

"Any interesting applicants?"

Although Lanzecki sounded diffident, even slightly bored, the curious tension about his lips and eyes alerted Killashandra. She pretended to continue eating in a courteous disregard of the exchange, but she didn't lose a syllable of Trag's reply.

"Four agronomists, an endocrinologist from Theta, two xenobiologists, an atmospheric physicist, three former spacers"—Killashandra noted the slight widening of Lanzecki's eyes which she interpreted as satisfaction—"and the usual flotsam who have no recommendations from Testing."

"Thank you, Trag."

Lanzecki nodded his head at Killashandra to indicate the interruption was concluded and finished off the dish of fried Malva beans.

"So what is the glitch in the Optherian assignment? A lousy fee?"

"On the contrary, such an installation is set at twenty thousand credits."

"And I'd be off-world as well." Killashandra was quite impressed with the latitude such a credit balance would give her to forget crystal.

"You have not been awarded the contract, Killa. I appreciate your willingness to entertain the assignment but there are certain aspects which must be considered by the Guild as well as the individual. Don't commit yourself rashly." Lanzecki was being sincere. His eyes held hers steadily and a worried crease to his brows emphasized his warning. "It's a long haul to the Optherian system. You'd be gone from Ballybran nearly a full year . . ."

"All the better . . ."

"You say that now when you're full of crystal resonance. You can't have forgotten Carrik yet."

His reminder conjured flashing scenes of the first crystal singer she had met: Carrik laughing as they swam in Fuerte's seas, then Carrik wracked by withdrawal fever and finally the passive hulk of the man, shattered by sonic resonance.

"You will in time, I've no doubt, experience that phenomenon," Lanzecki said. "I've never known a singer who didn't try to push himself and his symbiont to their limits. A major disadvantage to the Optherian contract is that you would lose any resonance to your existing claims."

"As if I *had* a decent claim among the lot." Killashandra snorted in disgust. "Rose is no good to anyone and the blue petered out after two days' cutting. Even the white vein skips and jumps. I cut the best of the accessible vein. With the kind of luck I've been enjoying, the storm has probably made a total bollix of the site. I am not—not, I repeat—spending another three weeks in a spade and basket operation. Not for white. Why can't Research develop an efficient portable excavator?"

Lanzecki cocked his head slightly. "It is the firm opinion of Research that any *one* of the nine efficient, portable and durable," a significant pause, "excavators already field-tested ought to perform the task for which it was engineered . . . except in the hands of a crystal singer. It is the opinion of Research that the only two pieces of equipment that do not tax the mechanical aptitude of a singer are his cutter—though Fisherman does *not* concur—and his sled, and you have already heard section and paragraph from the Flight Engineer on that score. Haven't you?"

Killashandra regarded him stolidly for a few moments, then remembered to chew what was in her mouth.

"Overheard him," she said, with a malicious grin. "Don't try to distract me from this Optherian business."

"I'm not. I am bringing to your notice the several overt disadvantages to an assignment that involves a long absence from Ballybran for what might, in the long run, be inadequate compensation." His expression changed subtly. "I'd rather not be professionally at odds with you. It interferes with my private life."

His dark eyes caught hers. He reached for her hands, lips curved in the one-sided smile that she found so affecting. She no longer shared a table with her Guild Master but with Lanzecki the man. The alteration pleased her. On numerous occasions, during sleepless nights in the Milekey Ranges, she had fondly remembered their love-making. Now, seated opposite the charismatic Lanzecki, she found that her appetite for more than food had been completely restored.

Her smile answered his and together they rose from the little table and headed for the sleepingroom.

Chapter 2

Killashandra pushed herself back from the terminal and, balancing on the base of her spine, stretched arms and legs as far from her body as bone and tendon permitted. She had spent the morning immersed in the Optherian entry of the *Encyclopedia Galactica*.

Once she had got past the initial exploration and evaluation report to the release of the Ophiuchine planet for colonization, and the high-flown language of its charter—"to establish a colony of Mankind in complete harmony with the ecological balance of his adopted planet: to ensure the propagation thereon of the Species in its pure, unadulterated Form." She kept waiting for the fly to appear in the syrupy ointment of Optheria's honey pot.

Optheria was an old planet in geological terms. A near-circular orbit about an ageing sun produced a temperate clime. There was little seasonal change since the axial "wobble" was negligible, and modest glaciers capped both poles. Optheria was inordinately proud of its self-sufficiency in a civilization where many planets were so deeply in debt to mercantile satellites that they were almost charged for the atmosphere that encapsulated them. Optherian imports were minimal . . . with the exception of tourists seeking to "enjoy the gentler pleasures of old Terra in a Totally Natural World."

Killashandra, reading with an eye to hidden significances, paused to consider the implications. Although her experience with planets had been limited to two—Fuerte, her planet of origin, and Ballybran, she knew enough of how worlds wagged to sense the iron idealism that probably supported the Optherian propaganda. She tapped a question and frowned at the negative

16

answer: Optheria's Charter Signers were not proselytizers of a religious sect nor did Optheria recognize a federal church. As many worlds had been colonized for idealist forms of government, religiously or secularly oriented, as for purely commercial considerations. The guiding principle of foundation could not yet be considered the necessary criterion for a successful subculture. The variables involved were too numerous.

But the entry made it clear that Optheria was considered efficiently organized and, with its substantial positive galactic balance of payments, a creditably administered world. The entry concluded with a statement that Optheria was well worth a visit during its annual Summer Festival. She detected a certain hint of irony in that bland comment. While she would have peferred to sample some of the exotic and sophisticated pleasures available to those with credit enough, she felt she could tolerate Optheria's "natural" pastimes in return for the sizeable fee and a long vacation from Ballybran.

She considered Lanzecki's diffidence about the assignment. Could he be charged with favoritism if he gave her another choice off-world assignment? Who would remember that she had been away during the horrendous Passover Storms, much less where? She'd been peremptorily snatched away by Trag, shoved onto the moon shuttle, and without a shred of background data about the vagaries of the Trundomoux, delivered willy-nilly to a naval autocracy to cope with the exigencies of installing millions of credits' worth of black communication crystal for a bunch of skeptical spartan pioneers. The assignment had been no sinecure. As Trag was the only other person who had known of it, was he the objector? He very easily could be, as Administration Officer, yet Killashandra did not think that Trag could, or did, influence Guild Master Lanzecki.

A second wild notion followed quickly on the heels of that one. Were there any Optherians on the roster of the Heptite Guild to whom such a job might be assigned? . . . The Heptite Guild had no Optherian members.

From her ten years in the Music Department of Fuerte's Culture Center, Killashandra was familiar with the intricacies of Optherian sensory organ instruments. The encyclopedia enlarged the picture by stating that music was a planetwide mania on Optheria, with citizens competing on a planetary scale for opportunities to perform on the sensory organs. With that sort of environment, Killashandra thought it very odd indeed that Optheria produced no candidates with the perfect pitch that was the Heptite Guild's essential entry requirement. And, with competitions on a worldwide scale, there would be thousands disappointed. Killashandra smiled in sour sympathy. Surely some would look for off-world alternatives.

Her curiosity titillated, Killashandra checked other Guilds. Optherians did not go into the Space Services or into galactic mercantile enterprises, nor were embassies, consulates or legates of Optheria listed in the Diplomatic Registers. There she lucked out by discovering a qualifier: As the planet was nearly self-sufficient and no Optherians left their home world, there was no need for such services. All formal inquiries about Optheria had to be directed to the Office of External Trade and Commerce on Optheria.

Killashandra paused in perplexity. A planet so perfect, so beloved by its citizens that no one chose to leave its surface? She found that very hard to believe. She recalled the encyclopedia's entry on the planet, searching for the code on Naturalization. Yes, well, citizenship was readily available for those interested but could not be rescinded. She checked the Penal Code and discovered that, unlike many worlds, Optheria did not deport its criminal element: any recidivists were accommodated at a rehabilitation center.

Killashandra shivered. So even perfect Optheria had to resort to rehabilitation.

Having delved sufficiently into Optheria's history and background to satisfy her basic curiosity, she turned to research the procedure necessary to replace a fractured manual. The installation posed no overt problems as the bracketing was remarkably similar to that required by the black communications crystal. The tuning would be more complex because of the broad-frequency variable output of the Optherian organ. The instrument was similar to early Terran pipe organs, with four manuals and a terminal with hundreds of stops, but a performer on the Optherian organ read a score containing olfactory, neural, visual, and aural notes. The crystal manual was in permanent handshake with the multiplex demodulator, the synapse carrier encoder, and the transducer terminal networks. Or so the manual said; no schematic was included in the entry. Nor could she remember one from her days at the Fuerte Music Center.

Dedicated Optherian players spent lifetimes arranging music embellished and ornamented for reception by many senses. A skilled Optherian organist could be mass-psychologist and politician as well as musician, and the effect of any composition played on the fully augmented instruments had such far-reaching consequences that performances and practitioners were subject to Federal as well as artistic discipline.

Bearing that in mind, Killashandra wondered how the manual could have been fractured—let alone have killed the performer at the same time, especially as that person had also been the only one on the planet capable of repairing it. Was there perhaps a spot of rot on the Optherian apple of Eden? This assignment could be interesting.

Killashandra pulled her chair back to the console and asked for visual contact with the Travel Officer. Bajorn was a long, thin man, with a thin face and a thin nose with pinched nostrils. He had preternaturally long, thin fingers, too, but much was redeemed by the cheerful smile that broke across his narrow face, and his complete willingness to sort out the most difficult itinerary. He seemed to be on the most congenial terms with every transport or freight captain who had ever touched down at or veered close to the Shanganagh Moon base.

"Is it difficult to get to the Optherian system, Bajorn?"

"Long old journey right now—out of season for the cruise ships on that route. Summer Festival won't be for another six months galactic. So, traveling now, you'd have to make four exchanges—Rappahoe, Kunjab, Melorica, and Bernard's World—all on freighters before getting passage on a proper liner."

"You're sure up to date."

Bajorn grinned, his thin lips almost touching his droopy ears. "Should be. You're the fifth inquiry I've had about that system. What's up? Didn't know the Optherians went in for the sort of kicks singers like."

"Who're the other four?"

"Well, there's no regulation against telling . . ." Bajorn paused discreetly, "and as they've all asked, no reason why you shouldn't

19

be told. You," and he ticked names off on his fingers, "Borella Seal, Concera, Gobbain Tekla, and Rimbol."

"Indeed. Thank you, Bajorn, that's real considerate of you."

"That's what Rimbol said, too." Bajorn's face sagged mournfully. "I do try to satisfy the Guild's travel requirements, but it is so depressing when my efforts are criticized or belittled. I can't help it if singers lose their memories . . . and every shred of common courtesy."

"I'll program eternal courtesy to you on my personal tape, Bajorn."

"I'd appreciate it. Only do it now, would you, Killashandra, before you forget?"

Promising faithfully, Killashandra rang off. Lanzecki had said there was a list. Were there only five names? Borella Seal and Concera she knew and she wouldn't have minded doing them out of the assignment; Gobbain Tekla was a total stranger. Rimbol had been cutting successfully, and in the darker shades just as Lanzecki had predicted. Why would he want such an assignment? So, four people had been interested enough to check Travel. Were there more?

She asked for a list of unassigned singers in residence and it was depressingly long. After some names, including her own, the capital I—for Inactive—flashed. Perhaps unwisely, she deleted those and still had thirty-seven possible rivals. She twirled idly about in the gimbaled chair, wondering exactly what criterion was vital for the Optherian assignment. Lanzecki hadn't mentioned such minor details in the little he had disclosed. From what she had already learned of the planet and the mechanics of installation, any competent singer could do the job. So what would weigh the balance in favor of one singer?

Killashandra reexamined the list of her known rivals: Borella and Concera had both been cutting a long time. Gobbain Tekla, when she found his position on the Main Roster, was a relative newcomer; Rimbol, like Killashandra, was a rank tyro. When she inquired, she discovered that each of the others had been a redundant or a failed musician. Perhaps that was the necessary requirement. It certainly made sense for the installer to have an instrumental background. She rephrased her question to apply to all thirty-seven available singers. Nineteen fit that category.

Lanzecki appeared reluctant to offer her the assignment but she oughtn't to fault him. She was acutely aware of past concessions from her Guildmaster. She had no right to expect an uninterrupted flow of benefits simply because he chose to share his bed with her. Nor, she decided, would she jeopardize their relationship by referring to the assignment again. Lanzecki might well be doing her a favor by not recommending her. She must keep that aspect of the situation firmly in mind. She might not be thrilled to vacation on the four systems to which her available credit would take her, but that was another string in her deplorable luck. She would get a rest from crystal and that was the essential requirement.

Her reawakened appetite reminded her that it had been some hours since breakfast. During lunch, she'd decide where to take herself. When, refreshed and revitalized, she returned to her labors for the Heptite Guild, she'd find a fresh vein of black crystal and *then* she'd get to the planet Maxim.

Before she could plan her vacation in any detail, Antona rang her from the Infirmary. "Have you eaten, Killa?"

"Is that an invitation or a professional query? Because I just finished a very hearty lunch."

Antona sighed. "I should have liked your company for lunch. There's not much doing right now down here. Fortunately."

"If it's just the company you want while you eat . . ."

Antona smiled with genuine pleasure. "I do. I don't enjoy eating by myself *all* the time. Could you drop down here first? You're still listed as inactive and you'll want that status amended."

On her way down to the Infirmary level, Killashandra first worried then chided herself for fearing there was more to Antona's request than a simple record up-date. It might have nothing to do with her fitness to take on the Optherian job. Nor would it be discreet to imply that she knew such an assignment was available. On the other hand, Antona would know more about the amenities of the nearby worlds.

The medical formality took little time and then the two women proceeded to the catering section of the main singer's floor of the Guild Complex.

"It's so depressingly empty," Antona said in a subdued voice as she glanced about the dimly lit portions of the facility.

"I found it a lot more depressing when everyone else was celebrating a good haul," Killashandra said in a glum tone.

"Yes, yes, it would be, I suppose. Oh, fardles!" Antona quickly diverted Killashandra toward the shadowy side. "Borella, Concera, and that simp, Gobbain," she murmured as she made a hasty detour.

"You don't like them?" Killashandra was amused.

Antona shrugged. "One establishes a friendship by sharing events and opinions. They remember nothing and consequently have nothing to share. And less to talk about."

Without warning, Antona caught Killashandra by the arm, turning to face her. "Do yourself a sterling favor, Killa. Put everything you've experienced so far in your life, every detail you can recall from cutting expeditions, every conversation you've had, every joke you've heard, put everything"—when Killashandra affected surprise, Antona gave her arm a painful squeeze—"and yes, I do mean 'everything,' into your personal retrieval file. What you did, what you said, what you felt"—and Antona's fierce gaze challenged Privacy—"how you've loved. Then, when your mind is as blank as theirs, you can refresh your memory and have something with which to reestablish *you!*" Her expression became intensely sad. "Oh, Killa. Be different! Do as I ask! Now! Before it's too late!"

Then, her customary composure restored, she released the arm and seemed to draw the intensity back into her straight, slim body. "Because I assure you," she said as she took the last few steps into the catering area, "that once your brilliant wit and repartee become as banal and malicious as theirs," she jerked her thumb at the silent trio, "I'll seek other company at lunch. Now," she said, her fingers poised over the catering terminal, "what are you having?"

"Yarran beer." Killashandra said the first thing that came to mind, being slightly dazed by Antona's unexpected outburst.

Antona raised her eyebrows in mock surprise, then rapidly dialed their orders.

They were served quickly and took their trays to the nearest banquette. As Antona tackled her meal with good appetite, Killashandra sipped her beer, digesting Antona's remarkable advice. Till then, Killashandra had had no opportunity to appreciate the viewpoint of a colleague who would not lose her memory as an occupational hazard. Stubbornly, Killashandra preferred to forget certain scenes in her life. Like failure.

"Well, you don't have long to wait for a fresh supply of cluttered minds," Killashandra said at last, blotting the beer foam from her upper lip and deferring conversation on Antona's unsettling advice.

"A new class? How did that privileged information seep out? You are only just out of an Infirmary tank. Well, you won't be allowed to brief them if that's what you had in mind, Killa."

"Why not?"

Antona shrugged and daintily sampled her nicely browned casserole before replying. "You've no injury to display. That's an important part of the briefing, you see—the visible, undeniable proof of the rapid tissue regeneration enjoyed by residents of Ballybran."

"Irresistible!" Antona gave Killashandra a sharp glance. "Oh, no complaints from me, Antona. The Guild can be proud of its adroit recruiting program."

Antona fastened a searching glance on her face and put down her fork. "Killashandra Ree, the Heptite Guild is not permitted by the Federated Sentient Planets to 'recruit' free citizens for such a hazardous profession. Only volunteers—"

"Only volunteers insist on presenting themselves, and so many of these have exceedingly useful skills . . ." She broke off, momentarily disconcerted by Antona's almost fierce glance.

"What concern is that of yours, Killashandra Ree? You have benefited immensely from the . . . selection process."

"Despite my unexpected inclusion."

"A few odd ones slip through no matter how careful we are," Antona said all too sweetly, her eyes sparkling.

"Don't fret, Antona. It's not a subject that I would discuss with anyone else."

"Particularly Lanzecki."

"I'm not likely to get that sort of an opportunity," she said, wondering if Antona knew or suspected their relationship. Or if her advice to remember loves and emotions had merely been a general warning to include all experience. Would Killashandra want to remember, decades from now, that she and Lanzecki had briefly been lovers? "Advise me, Antona, on which of our nearer spatial neighbors I should plan a brief vacation?"

Antona grimaced. "You might just as well pick the name at random for all the difference there is among them. Their only advantage is that they are far enough away from Ballybran to give your nerves the rest they need."

Just then a cheerful voice hailed them.

"Killa! Antona! Am I glad to see someone else alive!" Rimbol exclaimed, hobbling out of the shadows. He grinned as he saw the pitcher of beer. "May I join you?"

"By all means," Antona said graciously.

"What *happened* to you?" Killashandra asked. Rimbol's cheek and forehead were liberally decorated by newly healed scars.

"Mine was the sled that did a nose dive over the baffle."

"It did?"

"You didn't know it was me?" Rimbol's mouth twisted in mock chagrin. "The way Malaine carried on you'd've thought I'd placed half the incoming singers in jeopardy by that flip."

"Did you rearrange the sled as creatively as your face?"

Rimbol shook his head ruefully. "It broke its nose, mine was only bloody. At that it'll take longer to fix the sled than for my leg to heal. Say, Killa, have you heard about the Optherian contract?"

"For the fractured manual? That could pay for a lot of repairs."

"Oh, I don't want it," and he flicked his hand in dismissal.

"Why ever not?"

Rimbol took a long pull of his beer. "Well, I've got a claim that was cutting real well right now. Optheria's a long way away from here and I've been warned that I could lose the guiding resonance being gone so long."

"And because you remembered that I haven't cut anything worth packing—"

"No." Rimbol held up a hand, protesting Killashandra's accusation. "I mean, yes, I knew you've been unlucky lately—"

"Who do you think cut the white crystal to replace the fractured Optherian manual?"

"You did?" Rimbol's face brightened with relief. "Then you don't need to go either." He raised his beaker in a cheerful toast. "Where d'you plan to go off-world?"

24

"I hadn't exactly made up my mind . . ." Killashandra saw that Antona was busy serving up the last of her casserole.

"Why don't you try Maxim in the Barderi system." Rimbol leaned eagerly across the table to her. "I've heard it's something sensational. I'll get there sometime but I'd sure like to hear your opinion of it. I don't half believe the reports. I'd trust you."

"That's something to remember," Killashandra murmured, glancing sideways at Antona. Then, taking note of Rimbol's querying look, she asked smoothly, "What've you been cutting lately?"

"Greens," Rimbol replied with considerable satisfaction. He held up crossed fingers. "Now, if only the storm damage is minimal, and it could be because the vein's in a protected spot, I might even catch up with you on Maxim. You see . . ." and he proceeded to elaborate on his prospects.

As Rimbol rattled on in his amusing fashion, Killashandra wondered if crystal would dull the Scartine's infectious good-nature along with his memory. Would Antona give him the same urgent advice? Surely each of the newest crystal singers had some unique quality to be cherished and sustained throughout a lifetime. Antona's outburst had been sparked by a long frustration. To how many singers over her decades in the Guild had she tendered the same advice and found it ignored?

". . . So I came in with forty greens," Rimbol was saying with an air of achievement.

"That's damned good cutting!" Killashandra replied with suitable fervor.

"You have no trouble releasing crystal?" Antona asked.

"Well, I did the first time out," Rimbol admitted candidly, "but I remembered what you'd said, Killa, about packing as soon as you cut. I'll never forget the sight of you locked in crystal thrall, right here in a noisy crowded hall. A kindly and timely word of wisdom!"

"Oh, you'd have caught on soon enough," Killashandra said, feeling a trifle embarrassed by his gratitude.

"Some never do, you know," Antona remarked.

"What happens? Do they stand in statuesque paralysis until night comes? Or a loud storm?"

"The inability to release crystal is no joke, Rimbol."

Rimbol stared at Antona, his mobile face losing its amused expression. "You mean, they can be so enthralled, nothing breaks the spell?" Antona nodded slowly. "That could be fatal. Has it been?"

"There have been instances."

"Then I'm doubly indebted to you, Killa," Rimbol said, rising, "so this round's on me."

They finished that round, refreshed by food, drink, and conversation.

"Of the four, I think you'd prefer Rani in the Punjabi system," Antona told Killashandra in parting. "The food's better and the climate less severe. They have marvelous mineral hot springs, too. Not as efficacious as our radiant fluid but it'll help reduce crystal resonance. You need that. After just an hour in your company, the sound off you makes the hairs on my arm stand up. See?"

Killashandra exchanged glances with Rimbol, before they examined the proof on Antona's extended arm.

Antona laughed reassuringly, laying gentle fingers on Killashandra's forearm.

"A perfectly normal phenomenon for a singer who's been out in the Ranges steadily for over a year. Neither of you would be affected but, as I don't sing crystal, I am. Get used to it. That's what identifies a singer anywhere in the Galaxy. But the Rani hot springs will diminish the effect considerably. So does time away from here. See you."

As Killashandra watched Antona enter the lift, she felt Rimbol's hand sliding up her arm affectionately.

"You feel all right to me," he said, his blue eyes twinkling with amusement. Then he felt her stiffen and suppress a movement of withdrawal. He dropped his hand. "Privacy—sorry, Killa." He stepped back.

"Not half as sorry as I am, Rimbol. You didn't deserve that. Chalk it up to another side effect of singing crystal that they don't include in that full disclosure." She managed an apologetic smile. "I'm so wired I could broadcast."

"Not to worry, Killa. I understand. See you when you get back." Then he made his hobbledy way into the yellow quadrant to his quarters.

Killashandra stared after him, irritated with herself for her re-action to a casual caress. She'd had no such reaction to Lanzecki. Or was *that* the problem? She was very thoughtful as she walked slowly to her quarters. Fidelity was an unlikely disease for her to catch. She certainly enjoyed making love with Lanzecki, and def-initely he exerted an intense fascination on her. Lanzecki had unequivocally separated his professional life from his private one.

"Rani, huh," she murmured to herself as she put her thumb to the door lock. She entered the room, closing the door behind her, and then leaned against it.

Now, in the absence of background sounds, she could hear the resonance in her body, feel it cascading up and down her bones, throbbing in her arteries. The noise between her ears was like a gushing river in full flood. She held out her arms but the static apparently did not affect her, the carrier, or she had exhausted that phenomenon in herself. "Mineral baths! Probably stink of sulfur or something worse."

Immediately she heard the initial *phluggg* as radiant fluid began to flow into the tank in the hygiene room. Wondering why the room computer was on, she opened her mouth to abort the pro-cess, when her name issued from the speakers.

"Killashandra Ree?" The bass voice was unmistakably Trag's.

"Yes, Trag?" She switched on vision.

"You have been restored to the active list."

"I'm going off-world as soon as I can arrange transport, Trag."

Expressionless as ever, Trag regarded her. "A lucrative assign-ment is available to a singer of your status."

"The Optherian manual?" As Trag inclined his head once, Kil-lashandra controlled her surprise. Why was Trag approaching her when Lanzecki had definitely not wanted her to take it?

"You're aware of the details?" For the first time Trag evinced a flicker of surprise.

"Rimbol told me. He also said he wasn't taking it. Was he your first choice?"

Trag regarded her steadily for a moment. "You were the logical first choice, Killashandra Ree, but until an hour ago you were an Inactive."

"I was the first choice?"

"Firstly, you are going off-world in any event and do not have

27

sufficient credit to take you past the nearer inhabited systems. Secondly, an extended leave of absence is recommended by Medical. Thirdly, you have already acquired the necessary skills to place white crystal brackets. In the fourth place, your curriculum vitae indicates latent teaching abilities so that training replacement technicians on Optheria is well within your scope."

"Nothing was said about training technicians. Borella and Concera both have considerably more instructional experience than I."

"Borella, Concera, and Gobbain Tekla have not exhibited either the tact or diplomacy requisite to this assignment."

Killashandra was amused that Trag added Gobbain to the list. Had Bajorn told Trag who had inquired about transport to Optheria?

"There are thirty-seven other active Guild members who qualify!"

Trag shook his head slowly twice. "No, Killashandra Ree, it must be you who goes. The Guild needs some information about Optheria—"

"Tactfully and diplomatically extracted? On what subject?"

"Why the Optherian government prohibits interstellar travel to its citizens."

Killashandra let out a whoop of delight. "You mean, why, with their obsession for music, there isn't a single Optherian in the Heptite Guild?"

"That is not the relevant issue, Killashandra. The Federated Sentient Council would be obliged if the Guild's representative would act as an impartial observer, to determine if this restriction is popularly accepted—"

"A Freedom of Choice infringement? But wouldn't that be a matter for—"

Trag held up his hand. "The request asks for an impartial opinion on the *popular* acceptance of the restriction. The FSC acknowledges that isolated individuals might express dissatisfaction, but a complaint has been issued by the Executive Council of the Federated Artists Association."

Killashandra let out a low whistle. The Stellars themselves protested? Well, if Optherian composers and performers were involved, of course the Executive Council would protest. Even if it had taken them decades to do so.

"And since the Guild's representative would certainly come in contact with composers and performers during the course of the assignment, yes, I'd be more than willing to volunteer for that facet." Was that why Lanzecki had been against her going? To protect her from the iron idealism of a parochial Optherian Council? But, as a member of the Heptite Guild, which guaranteed her immunity to local law and restrictions, she could not be detained on any charge. She could be disciplined only by her Guild. That any form of artistry might be limited by law was anathema. "There've been Optherian organs a long time . . ."

"Popular acceptance is the matter under investigation."

Trag was not going to be deflected from the official wording of the request.

"All right, I copy!"

"You'll accept the assignment?"

Killashandra blinked. Did she imagine the eagerness in Trag's voice, the sudden release of tension from his face?

"Trag, there's something you've not told me about this assignment. I warn you, if this turns out to be like the Trundie—"

"Your familiarity with elements of this assignment suggests that you have already done considerable background investigation. I have informed you of the FSC request—"

"Why don't you leave it with me for a little while, Trag," she said, studying his face, "and I'll consider it. Lanzecki gave me the distinct impression that I shouldn't apply for it."

There. She hadn't imagined *that* reaction. Trag was perturbed. He'd been deliberately tempting her, with as subtle a brand of flattery as she'd ever been subjected to. Her respect for the Administration Officer reached a new level for she would never have thought him so devious. He was so completely devoted to Guild and Lanzecki.

"You're asking me without Lanzecki's knowledge?" She did not miss the sudden flare of Trag's nostrils nor the tightening of his jaw muscles. "Why, Trag?"

"Your name was first on the list of qualified available singers."

"Stuff it, Trag. Why me?"

"The interests of the Heptite Guild are best served by your acceptance." A hint of desperation edged Trag's voice.

"You object to the relationship between Lanzecki and me?" She had no way of knowing in what way Trag had adapted to Ballybran's symbiont or in what way he expressed sexuality. Trag's respect for Lanzecki was patent but she hadn't thought that such respect required additional outlets. If jealously prompted Trag to remove a rival . . .

"No." Trag's denial was accompanied by a ripple of his facial muscles. "Up till now, he has not allowed personal consideration to interfere with his judgment."

"How has he done that?" Killashandra was genuinely perplexed. Trag was not complaining that Lanzecki had awarded her another valuable assignment. He was perturbed because he hadn't. "I don't follow you."

Trag stared at her for such a long moment she wondered if the screen had malfunctioned.

"Even if you just go to Rani, it will not be far enough away or long enough. Lanzecki is long overdue for a field trip, Killashandra Ree. Because of you. Your body is so full of resonance he's been able to delay. But your resonance is not enough. If you're not available, he will be forced to cut crystal again and rejuvenate his body and his symbiont. If you have a real regard for the man, go. Now. Before it's too late for him."

Killashandra stared back at Trag, trying to absorb the various implications—foremost was the realization that Lanzecki was genuinely attached to her. She felt a wave of exultation and tenderness that quite overwhelmed her for a moment. She'd never considered that possibility. Nor its corollary: that Lanzecki would be reluctant to cut crystal because he might forget this attachment. A man who'd been in the Guild as long as he had would be subject to considerable memory loss in the Ranges. Had he learned his duties as Guild Master so thoroughly that the knowledge was as ingrained in him as the rules and regulations in a crystal-mad brain like Moksoon's? It was not Lanzecki's face that suddenly dominated her thoughts, but the crisscross tracings of old crystal scars on his body, the inexplicable pain that occasionally darkened his eyes. Antona's cryptic admission about singers who could not break crystal thrall echoed in her head.

She puzzled at the assortment of impressions and suddenly understood. She sagged against the back and arms of her chair for support. Dully she wondered if Trag and Antona had been in collusion. Would the subject of crystal thrall have come up at that lunch hour even if Rimbol had not arrived?

There was little doubt in Killashandra's mind that Antona knew of Lanzecki's circumstances. And she did doubt that the woman knew about their relationship. She also doubted that Trag would mention so personal an aspect of the Guild Master's business. Why couldn't Lanzecki have been just another singer, like herself? Why did he have to be Guild Master and far too valuable, too essential to be placed in jeopardy by unruly affection?

Why, the situation has all the trappings of an operatic tragedy! A genuine one-solution tragedy, where hero and heroine both lose out. For she could now admit to herself that she was as deeply attached to Lanzecki as he was to her. She covered her face with both hands, clasping them to cheeks gone chill.

She thought of Antona's advice, to put down everything—including love— Killashandra writhed in her chair. Antona couldn't have known that Killashandra would so shortly be faced with such an emotional decision. Which, Killashandra realized with a flicker of ironic amusement, was one to be as deeply and quickly interred and forgotten as possible.

One thing was sure—no matter how long the journey to Optheria, it wouldn't be long enough to forget all the wonderful moments she had enjoyed with Lanzecki the man. She squeezed her eyes shut against the pain of encountering him when she returned, and, perhaps, finding no recollection of her in his dark eyes. Nor feel his lips again on her hand . . .

"Killashandra?" Trag's voice recalled her to his watching presence on the viewscreen.

"Now that I know the ramifications of the assignment, Trag, I can hardly refuse it." Her flippant tone was belied by the tears rolling down her cheeks. "Do you go with him to break the thrall?" she asked when her throat opened enough to speak again.

At any other time, she would have counted Trag's startled look as a signal victory. Maybe if she found someone to sing with, she would also find such a passionate and unswerving loyalty. She must remember that.

"When's the next shuttle to Shanganagh, Trag?" She rubbed her cheeks dry with an urgent impatience. "Tell Lanzecki—tell him . . . crystal resonance drove me to it." As she spun off her chair, she heard herself give a laugh that verged on the hysterical. "That's no more than the truth, isn't it?" Driven by the need just to *do* something, she began to cram clothes into her carisak.

"The shuttle leaves in ten minutes, Killashandra Ree."

"That's great." She struggled to secure the fastenings on the bulging sak. "Will you see me aboard again, Trag? That seems to be your especial duty, rushing me onto shuttles to Shanganagh for unusual assignments all over the galaxy." She was unable to resist taunting Trag. He was the author of her misery and she was being strong and purposeful in a moment of deep personal sacrifice and loss. She glanced up at the screen and saw that it was dark. "Coward!"

She hauled open her door. She decided that slamming it was a waste of a grand gesture. She had just enough time to get to the shuttle.

"Exit Killashandra. Quietly. Up stage!"

Chapter 3

Trag had timed Killashandra's departure well for she and the three crates of white crystal were on board a freighter bound for the Rappahoe Transfer Satellite within four hours of their confrontation. She didn't think about it at the time for she was totally immersed in the strong emotions of self-sacrifice, remorse for her effect on Lanzecki, and a perverse need to redeem herself in Trag's eyes. Even though she had permitted herself to be borne on the tide of circumstance, she kept hoping that Lanzecki might somehow get wind of her defection and abort the mission.

To insure that her whereabouts were known, she rummaged through the shopping area of Shanganagh Base like a mach storm. She bought necessities, fripperies, and foodstuffs, accompanying each purchase with a running dialogue at the top of her voice and spelling out her name for every credit entry. No one could fail to know the whereabouts of Killashandra Ree. After adding a few items of essential clothing to the garments she had stuffed into her carisak, her keen instinct for survival asserted itself in the base's victuallers. She had vivid memories of the monotonously nutritious diet on the Selkite freighter and the stodge supplied by the Trundomoux cruiser. She did have to consider her palate and digestive system.

Sadly, no deferential shopkeeper tapped her on the arm to tell her of an urgent call from the Guild Master. In fact, people seemed to keep their distance from her. A chance glimpse of her gaunt, harrowed face in a mirror provided one explanation—she'd have needed no cosmetic aids to play the part of any one of a number of harried, despairing, insane heroines. At that point her humor

33

briefly reasserted itself. She had often thought that the make-up recommended for, say, Lucia, or Lady Macbeth, or Testuka and Isolde was totally exaggerated. Now, at last having had personal experiences with the phenomenon of losing one's great love through selfless sacrifice, she could appreciate the effect which grief could have on one's outward appearance. She looked awful! So she purchased two brilliant multihued floating kaftans of Beluga spider-silk, and hastily added their fingerlength cases to her bulging carisak, then a travel-case of fashionable cosmetics. She'd nine days to travel on the first freighter and it would only be civil to remedy her appearance.

Then the boarding call for the *Pink Tulip Sparrow* was broadcast and she had no option but to proceed to the loading bay. In an effort to delay the inevitable, she walked at a funereal pace down the access ramp.

"Singer, we've got to get moving! Now, please, hurry along."

She made an appearance of haste but when the Mate tried to take her arm and hurry her into the lock, her body arched in resistance. Abruptly he let go, staring at her with an expression of puzzled shock—his arms were bare, and the hairs on them stood erect.

"I'm awaiting purchases from Stores." Killashandra was so desperate for a last-minute reprieve that any delay seemed reasonable.

"There!" The Mate conveyed frustrated disgust and impatience as he pointed to a stack of odd-size parcels littering the passageway.

"The crystals?"

"Cartons all racked and tacked in the special cargo hold." He made a move as if to grab her arm and yank her aboard, but jingled his hands with frustration instead. "We've got to make way. Shanganagh Authority imposes heavy fines for missed departure windows. And don't tell me, Crystal Singer, that you've got enough credit to pay 'em." Abruptly she abandoned all hope that Lanzecki, like the legendary heroes of yore, would rescue her at the last moment from her act of boundless self-sacrifice. She stepped aboard the freighter. The airlock closed with such speed that the heavy external hatch brushed against her heels. The ship was moving from the docking bay before the Mate could lead her out of the lock and close the secondary iris behind them.

Killashandra experienced an almost overpowering urge to wrench open the airlock and leap into the blessed oblivion of space. But as she had deplored such extravagant and melodramatic actions in performances of historical tragedy, integrity prevented suicide despite the extreme anguish which tormented her. Besides, she had no excuse for causing the death of the Mate who seemed not to be suffering at all.

"Take me to my cabin, please." She turned too quickly, stumbled over the many packages in the passageway and had to grab the Mate's shoulder, to regain her balance. Ordinarily she would have cursed her clumsiness, and apologized but cursing was undignified and inappropriate to her mood. From the pile, she chose two packages with the victualler's logo, and waved negligently at the remainder. "The rest may be brought to my cabin whenever convenient."

The Mate wended a careful passage through the tumbled parcels as he passed her to lead the way. She noticed that the hair on his neck, indeed the dark body hairs that escaped the sleeveless top he wore, were piercing the thin stuff, all at right angles to his body.

This was no longer an amusing manifestation. Just another fascinating aspect of crystal singing that you *don't* hear about in that allegedly Complete Disclosure! It should be renamed "A Short Introduction to what's really in store for you!" One day, no doubt, she would be in the appropriately damaged state to give All the Facts.

The Mate had stopped, flattening himself against the bulkhead, and gestured toward an open door.

"Your quarters, Crystal Singer. Your thumbprint will secure the door." He touched his fingers to a spot above his right eye and disappeared around the corner as if chased by Galormis.

Killashandra pressed her thumb hard into the door lock. She was pleasantly surprised by the size of the cabin. Not as big as any accommodation she had enjoyed on Ballybran but larger than her student room at Fuerte and much more spacious than that closet on the Trundomoux cruiser. She slid the door shut, locked it, and put the packages down on the narrow writing ledge. She looked at the bunk, strapped up to the wall in its daytime position. Suddenly she was light-headed with fatigue. Strong emotion is as exhausting as cutting crystal, she thought. She released the bunk and stretched herself out. She exhaled on a long shuddering sob and tried to relax her taut muscles.

The hum of the ship's crystal drive was a counterpoint to the resonance between her ears, and both sounds traveled in waves up and down her bones. At first her mind did a descant, weaving an independent melody though the bass and alto, but the rhythm suggested a three-syllable word—Lan-zec-ki—so she changed to an idiot two-note dissonance and eventually fell asleep.

Once she got over the initial buoyancy of self-sacrifice aboard the *Pink Tulip Sparrow*, Killashandra vacillated between fury at Trag and wallowing in despair at her "Loss." Until she concluded that her misery was caused by Lanzecki—after all, if he hadn't made such a determined play for her affections, *he* wouldn't have become so attached to her, nor she to him, and she wouldn't be on a stinking tub of a freighter. Well, yes, she probably would. *If* all Trag had told her about the Optherian assignment was true. In no mood to be civil to either the crew or the other three passengers, she stayed in her cabin the entire trip.

At Rappahoe Transfer Point, she boarded a second freighter, newer and less unpleasant than the *Pink Tulip Sparrow*, with a lounge for the ten passengers it carried. Eight were male and each of them, including the only attached man, stood quickly at her entrance. Plainly they were aware that she was a crystal singer. Equally apparent was the fact that they were willing to put scruples aside to discover the truth of the space flot about singers. Three of them desisted after their first hour of propinquity. Two more during the first evening's meal. To have one's hair constantly standing on end seems like a little thing but so is a drop of water patiently wearing away a stone. The bald Argulian was the most persistent. He actually grabbed her in the narrow companionway, pressing her close to his body in an ardent embrace. She didn't have to struggle for release.

He dropped his arms and slid away, flushing and trembling. "You're shocking." He scrubbed his arms and brushed urgently at those portions of his body which had been in contact with her.

"That's not a nice thing to do to a friendly fellow like me." He looked aggrieved.

"It was all your idea." Killashandra continued on to her quarters. *And another singer legend is spawned!*

The female captain of the third freighter, which she boarded at Melorica, bluntly informed her that, under no circumstances, would she tolerate any short term disruption of the pairing in her all-female crew.

"That's quite all right, captain. I've taken a vow of celibacy."

"What for?" the captain demanded, raking Killashandra with an appraising scrutiny. "Religious or professional?"

"Neither. I shall be true to one man till I die." Killashandra was pleased with the infinitesimal tremor of pathos in her voice.

"No man's worth that, honey!" The captain's disgust was genuine.

With a sad sigh, Killashandra asked if the ship's library had much in the way of programs for single players and retired to her quarters, which had been getting smaller with each ship. Fortunately this was the shortest leg of her space hike to Bernard's World.

By the time Killashandra reached the Bernard's World Transfer Satellite, she entertained doubts about Trag's candor. The journey seemed incredibly long for a modern space voyage, even allowing for the fact that freighters are generally slower than cruisers or liners. She'd logged five weeks of interstellar travel and must somehow endure another five before she reached the Optherian system. Could Trag have done a subtle job of recruiting her because no other singer would consider the assignment? No, the fee was too good—besides, Borella, Concera, and Gobbain had been trying for it.

In the orbital position of a small moon, the Transfer Satellite inscribed a graceful forty-eight-hour path about the brilliant blue-and-green jewel of a planet. The satellite was a marvel of modern engineering, with docking and repair facilities capable of handling FSC cruisers and the compound ships of the Exploration and Evaluation Corps, felicitously sited at the intersection of nine major space routes. Fresh fruit and vegetables were grown in its extensive gardens, and high quality protein was manufactured in its catering division: sufficient in quantity and diversity to please the most exacting client. Stores of the basic nutrients were available for five other star-roving species. Additional nodules accommodated small industries and a thriving medical research laboratory and hospital. In the transient quadrant, there were playing fields, free-ball and free-fall courts, spacious gardens, and a zoo housing a selection of the smaller life forms from nine nearby star systems. As Killashandra perused the directory in her room, she noted with considerable delight that a radiant fluid tank was one of the amenities in the gymnasium arc.

Although she was certain that there had been some decrease of the resonance in her body, she ached for the total relief provided by an hour or so in the radiant fluid. She booked the room and, fed up with the reaction of "ordinary" people to her proximity, took the service route to it. She had also decided that she was not going to spend the five weeks on the cruise ship enhancing crystal singer myths. Just then her bruised and aching heart had no room for affection, much less passion. And crystal neutralized passing fancy or pure lust.

If she could reduce the hair-standing phenomenon to a minimum, she intended to adopt a new personality: that of an aspiring young musician traveling to Optheria's Summer Festival, and required by economics to travel off-season and on the cheaper freight lines. She had spent long hours preparing the right make-up for the part, affecting the demeanor of the very young, inexperienced adult and recalling the vocabulary and idiom of her student days. So much had transpired since that carefree time that it was like studying for an historical role. In such rehearsals, Killashandra found that time passed quickly. Now if her wretched body would cooperate . . .

After nine hours of immersions over the course of three days, Killashandra achieved her goal. She acquired a suitably modest wardrobe. On the fifth day on the Bernard's World Transfer Station, in wide-eyed and breathless obedience to the boarding call, she presented her ticket to the purser of the FSPS Liner *Athena*, and was assigned a seat on the second of the two shuttles leaving the station to catch the liner on its parabolic route through the star system. The shuttle trip was short and its single forward viewscreen was dominated by the massive orange hulk of the *Athena*. Most of the passengers were awed by the spectacle, babbling about their expectations of the voyage, the hardships they had endured to save for the experience, their hopes for their destinations, anxieties about home-bound relatives. Their chatter irritated Killashandra and she began to wish she had not posed as a student. As the respected member of a prestigious Guild, she would have been assigned to the star-class shuttle.

However, she'd made the choice and was stuck with it, so she grimly disembarked onto the economy level of the *Athena* and located her single cabin in the warren. This room was the same size as her Fuertan student apartment but, she told herself philosophically, she wouldn't be so likely to step out of character. Anyway, only the catering and lounge facilities differed with the price of the ticket: the leisure decks were unrestricted.

The *Athena*, a new addition to the far-flung cruise line Galactica, Federated, was on the final leg of its first sweep round this portion of the Galaxy. Some of the *oh*'s and *ah*'s that Killashandra breathed were quite genuine as she and other economy class passengers were escorted on the grand tour of the liner. A self-study complex included not only the schoolroom for transient minors but small rehearsal rooms where a broad range of musical instruments could be rented—with the notable exception of a portable Optherian organ—a miniature theater, and several large workshops for handicrafters. To her astonishment, the gymnasium complex boasted three small radiant fluid tanks. Their guide explained that this amenity eased aching muscles, overcame space nausea, and was an economical substitute for a water bath since the fluid could be purified after every use. He reminded people that water was still a rationed commodity and that two liters was the daily allowance. Each cabin had a console and vdr, linked to the ship's main computer bank which, their escort proudly told them, was the very latest FBM 9000 series with a more comprehensive library of entertainment recordings than many planets possessed. The FSPS *Athena* was a true goddess of the spaceways.

During the first forty-eight hours of the voyage, while the *Athena* was clearing the Bernard's World system and accelerating to transfer speed, Killashandra deliberately remained aloof, in her pose of shy student, from the general mingling of the other passengers. She was amused and educated by the pairings, the shiftings and realignments that occurred during this period. She made private wagers with herself as to which of the young women would pair off with which of the young men. Subtler associations developed among the older unattached element.

To Killashandra's jaundiced eye, none of the male economy passengers, young or old, looked interesting enough to cultivate. There was one absolutely stunning man, with the superb carriage of a dancer or professional athlete, but his classic features were too perfect to project a hint of his character or temperament. He made his rounds, a slight smile curving his perfect lips, well aware that he had only to nod to capture whichever girl, or girls, he fancied. Lanzecki might not have been handsome in the currently fashionable form but his face was carved by character and he exuded a magnetism that was lacking in the glorious young man. Nevertheless, Killashandra toyed with the idea of luring the perfect young man to her side; rejection might improve his character no end. But to achieve that end she would have had to discard her shy student role.

She discovered an unforgivable lack in the *Athena's* appointments the first time she dialed for Yarran beer. It was not available, although nine other brews were. In an attempt to find a palatable substitute, she was trying the third, watching the energetic perform a square dance, when she realized someone was standing at her table.

"May I join you?" The man held up beakers of beer, each a different shade. "I noticed that you were sampling the brews. Shall we combine our efforts?"

He had a pleasant voice, his ship-suit was well cut to a tall lean frame, his features were regular but without a distinguishing imperfection; his medium length dark hair complimented a space tan. There was, however, something about his eyes and a subtle strength to his chin that arrested Killashandra's attention.

"I'm not a joiner myself," he said, pointing one beaker at the gyrating dancers, "and I noticed that you aren't, so I thought we might keep each other company."

Killashandra indicated the chair opposite her.

"My name is Corish von Mittelstern." He put his beers down nearer hers as he repositioned the chair to permit him to watch the dancers. Killashandra turned ever slightly away from him, not all that confident of the remission of resonance in her body, though why she made the instinctive adjustment she didn't know. "I hail from Rheingarten in the Beta Jungische system. I'm bound for Optheria."

"Why, so am I!" She raised her beer in token of a hand clasp. "Killashandra Ree of Fuerte. I'm—I'm a music student."

"The Summer Festival." Then a puzzled expression crossed Corish's face. "But they have a Fuertan brew—"

"Oh, that old stuff. I might have to travel off-season and economy to get to Optheria but I'm certainly not going to waste the opportunities of trying everything new on the *Athena*."

Corish smiled urbanely. "Is this your first interstellar trip?"

"Oh, yes. But I know a lot about traveling. My brother is a supercargo. On the *Blue Swan Delta*. And when Mother told him that I was making the voyage, he sent me all kinds of advice"— and Killashandra managed a tinkling giggle—"and warnings."

Corish smiled perfunctorily. "Don't ignore that sort of advice. Fuerte, huh? That's a long way to come."

"I think I've spent half my life traveling already," Killashandra said expansively while she tried to compute how long she ought to have been traveling if her port of embarkation had been Fuerte. She hadn't done enough homework. Though she couldn't imagine that Corish would know if she erred. She took a long sip of her beer. "This is a Bellemere, but it's too sour for me."

"The best beer in the galaxy is a Yarran brew."

"Yarran?" She regarded Corish with keener interest. If Corish came from Beta Jungische, he was a long way from a regular supply of Yarran beer. Killashandra's curiosity rustled awake.

"The Yarran brewmasters have no peers. Surely your brother has mentioned Yarran beer?"

"Well, now, it's possible that he has," Killashandra said slowly, as if searching her memory. "But then, he told me so much that I can't remember half." She was about to giggle again and then decided that, not only did her giggle nauseate herself but it might repel Corish and she wanted to satisfy this flicker of curiosity about him. "Why are you traveling to Optheria?"

"Family business, sort of. An uncle of mine went for a visit and decided to become a citizen. We need his signature on some family papers. We've written several times and had no reply. Now, he could be dead but I have to have the proper certification if he is, and his print and fist on the documents if he isn't."

"And you have to come all the way from Beta Jungische for that?"

"Well, there's a lot of credit involved and this isn't a bad way to go." He enscribed a half circle with his beaker, including the ship as well as the dancers, and smiled at Killashandra over the rim as he sipped. "This Pilsner's not all that bad, really. What have you there?"

She went along with Corish's adroit change of subject and with the beer sampling. Although singing crystal brought with it an inexhaustible ability to metabolize alcohol without noticeable affect, she feigned the symptoms of intoxication as she confided her fake history to the Jungian, whenever necessary embellishing her actual experiences at the Arts Complex. Thus Corish learned that she was a keyboard specialist, in her final year of training, with high hopes that the Optherian Festival would provide her with sufficient data for an honors recommendation. She had credentials of sufficiently high caliber to gain entrance into the Federal Music Conservatory on Optheria where she hoped she'd be allowed to play on an Optherian organ.

"An hour is all I need," she told Corish, blinking in her simulation of advancing inebriation, "for the purposes of my dissertation."

"From what I hear about their precious organ, you'd be lucky to get within spitting distance."

"Even half an hour."

"I hear that only Federal licensed musicians are allowed in the organ loft."

"Well, they'll have to make an exception in my case because I have a special letter from Fuerte's President—he's a friend of my family's. *And* a sealed note from Stellar Performer Dalkay Mogorog . . ." She paused deferentially at the mention of that august personality, who was evidently unknown to Corish, "and I'm sure they'll concede. Even fifteen minutes?" she asked as Corish continued to shake his head. "Well, they'll just have to! I haven't come all this way to be refused. I'm a serious student of keyboard instruments. I won a scholarship to the Federated Sentient Planets Conservatory on Terra. I've been permitted to play on a Mozartian clavier, a Handelian spinet, Purcell's harpsichord, a Bach organ, and a Beethoven pianoforte and—" She hiccuped to mask the fact that she was running out of prestigious composers and instruments.

"So? Which beer do you prefer now?"

"Huh?"

Corish solicitously conducted her to her cabin and arranged her on her bunk. As he drew a light blanket over her, she felt the static leap from her shoulder to his hands. He hesitated briefly, then quietly left.

As Killashandra gave him time to leave her passageway, she reviewed her "performance" and decided that she hadn't dropped from character, even if he had. It was rather nice of him, too, not to have "taken advantage" of her. When she felt secure, she slipped from her cabin and down to the gymnasium level. At that hour, it was empty and she enjoyed an hour's luxuriating in the radiant fluid.

They met the next morning at the breakfast hour, Corish solicitously inquiring after her health.

"Did I fall asleep on you?" she asked with wide-eyed dismay.

"Not at all. I just saw to it that you were safely in your own cabin before you did."

Critically, she held her hands out in front of her. "Well, at least, they're steady enough to practice."

"You're going to practice?"

"I practice every day."

"May I listen?"

"Well . . . it can be quite boring—I have to spend at least an hour on the preliminary finger exercises and scales before I can do any interesting music . . ."

"If I'm bored, I'll leave."

As she led the way to the practice rooms, she wondered if she had slipped up in her characterization. Why else should he be curious enough to want to listen to her practice?

Killashandra was rather chuffed to discover that the old drills came easily to her fingers as she addressed the keyboard with every semblance of true authority. Corish departed after fifteen minutes but she left nothing to chance and played on, making remarkably few errors for someone who had not played in three years.

As she had established her credentials with him, he continued to project the image of an amiable young man on a journey to protect family interests. He sought her out at mealtimes, helped her evade the organizers of team sports, directed her investigations of the caterer's potential with the amused tolerance of the mature traveler, and accompanied her to shipboard activities. On one or two occasions, she had the urge to shock him with her true identity just to see how he might react, but she repressed that whimsy.

Then, after a particularly bibulous evening, when she had taken an extra long radiant bath, she encountered him in the gymnasium. He was sweating profusely, working out against a hefty weight on the apparatus with apparent ease. Stripped as he was for the exercise, Killashandra could appreciate that Corish's lean frame was suspiciously well muscled and fine tuned for his public image.

"I didn't know you were a gymnast!"

"It's only smart to keep fit, Killashandra Ree." He whipped a towel about his shoulders and mopped his face. "Where've you been?"

Killashandra managed a blush of embarrassment, dropping her eyes and affecting mortification.

"I tried that radiant stuff. In the tank," and she pointed vaguely in the right direction. "That blonde girl from Kachachurian was saying that it was good for hangovers!" She kicked at the apparatus base with her toe, eyes still downcast.

"Well, is it?"

"I think it is." She allowed some doubt in her tone. "At least that awful spinning has stopped . . . and the nausea!" She put one hand to her head and the other to her stomach. "I think I may have to go back to Fuertan beer. I could always drink as much of that as I wanted. Or is it something to do with traveling in space? My brother did say something about that . . ." She looked up at Corish. "Isn't this a funny time to be working out?"

"That's how I work alcohol out of my system," Corish said, pulling on his shirt. "I'll see you back to your cabin. You really shouldn't be wandering about the ship at this hour. Someone might get the wrong impression about you."

As Killashandra permitted him to escort her back, she wondered why he was rushing her out of the gym. She felt she had deftly accounted for her presence. And naively accepted his explanation. Safely returned to her cabin, she agreed to meet him as usual for breakfast the next morning, and dutifully went to bed.

Waiting for sleep, she reflected on his extraordinary fitness and the stealth in which he kept it. Could Corish possibly be an FSP agent? It struck her as unlikely that the Federation would choose to send only one observer—an inexperienced one at that—into a planetary society that was being investigated. She chuckled to think that, out of the eighteen hundred passengers and crew on the *Athena*, Corish should attach himself to her. Of course, in her eager-student guise, she might constitute an integral part of *his* shipboard cover. Unless he had been advised of her extra assignment by his superiors. If he was a Federal agent, he would also know the capabilities of crystal singers, and the subtler ways to identify them.

No matter! In her concentrated efforts to recall her days as an impecunious and ardent music student, she had been able to shelve the more recent, painful episode. Seriously now, Killashandra considered Antona's advice to record incidents in detail. Who knew when she might find it necessary to adopt the role of the student again?

Chapter 4

As the *Athena* plunged toward the Optherian primary for the deflected hyperbolic pass that would bring it close to the one inhabited planet of the system, the passengers who were disembarking went through the rituals of leave-taking from their shipboard acquaintances. That strange magic of voyaging which could make total strangers into confidantes and lovers had lost none of its potency in the space age.

As they waited in the airlock for the shuttle that would take them to the surface, Killashandra found herself prattling on at Corish about how they must meet and share their adventures: that they couldn't part and never meet again while they were on the same planet. She'd want to know how he made out with his uncle and she hoped she'd be able to tell him of her success, invading the Optherian musical hierarchy. Of course that sort of chatter was in character with her role. What astonished Killashandra was that she meant what she said.

"That's very sweet of you, Killa," Corish replied, patting her shoulder in a condescending fashion that returned her instantly to her own personality.

"If I don't get a place at the Music Center hostel, I'll go to the Piper Facility," she said, ducking away from his hand as she fumbled with the fastening on the side pocket of her carisak. She tendered the small plastic card distributed by the Facility with its comunit codes. "The Optherian Traveler's Guide says they'll take messages for visitors. You could leave word for me there." She smiled up at him with tremulous wistfulness. "I know that once we leave Optheria, we'll never meet again, Corish, but at least while we're still on the same planet, I was hoping we could stay friends." She broke off, ducking her head and dabbing at her eyes which, on cue, had filled with moisture. She let him have just a confirming glimpse of her teary face, although why she was prolonging their association, she hadn't a notion. One can get too wrapped up in role-playing.

"I promise you, Killa, that I'll leave word at the Piper for you." And Corish put a finger under her chin and lifted her head to his gaze. He had a rather engaging half-smile, she thought, though it wasn't a patch on Lanzecki's. She managed to squeeze out a few more tears on the strength of that comparison. "No need for tears, Killa."

Just then the shuttle clanged against the *Athena*'s side and conversation became impossible with the noise of lock engagement and the excited crescendo of farewells. Then crewmen were officiously directing passengers to move to the port side of the lock. Killashandra was crammed rather tightly between two large men and separated from Corish by another sideways push.

"What's the delay?" one of her cushions demanded.

"They're loading some crates," was the indignant reply. "Must be something special. There're seals and impregtape all over them."

"I shall complain to the Cruise Agent. I was under the impression that people got preference over commodities on this Line!"

As suddenly as it had begun, the press eased off and everyone was shuffling toward the ramp into the shuttle. Killashandra didn't see Corish among the passengers already seated but she couldn't fail to miss three large foam boxes that contained the white crystal, for they occupied the first three rows of seats on the shuttle's starboard side.

"They must be immensely valuable," the first cushion-man said. "Whatever could it be? Optherians don't import much."

"Too right," his companion said in an aggrieved tone. "Why, those are Heptite Guild seals."

The shuttle attendant had taken complete control of seating arrangements, peremptorily filling the rows as he backed down the main aisle. He gestured Killashandra to an inside seat and the two cushions obediently settled in the next two. She caught a brief glimpse of Corish as he passed, but he was assigned a seat on the other side of the aisle.

"Not wasting any time, are they?" the first man said.

"Have none to waste in a parabolic orbit," his friend replied.

"There mustn't have been any outgoing passengers."

"Probably not. Optherians don't leave their planet and the tourist season hasn't really started."

A rather ominous rumbling, issuing from the floor plates, startled them. This was quickly followed by additional metallic complaints, causing further vibrations under their feet.

Two distinct thuds signaled the closing of the cargo bays. Then Killashandra felt the air compress as the main passenger lock was shut and secured. Through the skin of the hull beside her, she heard the snick of the grapple release so she was prepared for the stomach-wrenching motion of the shuttle's falling away from the *Athena*. Her seatmates were not and gasped in reaction, clutching the arm rests as the shuttle's engines took hold and pushed the passengers into the foam of their seats.

The transfer from liner to planetary surface was a relatively short run, though Killashandra's seatmates complained bitterly about the discomfort and duration all the way down. Killashandra accounted the landing smooth but the two cushions found fault with that as well, so she was immensely grateful when the port opened again, flooding the shuttle with the crisp clean cool air of Optheria. She inhaled deeply, clearing her lungs of the *Athena's* recycled air. For all the craft's modern amenities, it had not quite solved the age-old problem of refreshing air without the taint of deodorizers.

No sooner had the first passengers filed into the arrival area than the public address system began a recorded announcement, scrolling through the same message in all major Federated Planets languages. Passengers were requested to have travel documents ready for inspection by Port Authorities. Please to form a line in the appropriately marked alphabetic or numeric queues. Aliens requiring special life support systems or supplies would please contact a uniformed attendant. Visitors with health problems were to present themselves, immediately after Clearance, to the Port Authority Medical Officer. It was the hope of the Tourist Bureau of Optheria that all visitors would thoroughly enjoy their holiday on the planet.

Killashandra was relieved to see that she would be able to present her i.d. in some privacy, for the Inspectors presided in security booths. Those waiting their turn in the queue could not observe the process. She kept glancing to the far right line where Corish should be waiting but he was not immediately visible. She caught sight of him just as it was her turn to approach the Inspector.

Killashandra suppressed a malicious grin as she slid her arm and its i.d. bracelet under the visiplate. The blank expression of the Inspector's square face underwent a remarkable change at the sight of the Heptite Seal on his screen. With one hand he pressed a red button on the terminal in front of him and with the other urgently beckoned her to proceed. Quitting the booth, he insisted on relieving her of her carisak.

"Please, no fuss," Killashandra asked.

"Gracious Guildmember," the Inspector began effusively, "we have been so concerned. The cabin reserved for you on the *Athena—*"

"I traveled economy."

"But you're a Heptite Guildmember!"

"There are times, Inspector," Killashandra said, bending close to him and touching his arm, "when discretion requires that one travel incognito." The hair stood up on the back of his hand. She sighed.

"Oh, I see." And clearly he did not. He unconsciously smoothed the hair back down.

They had walked the short distance to the next portal, which slid apart to reveal a welcoming committee of four, three men and a woman, slightly breathless. "The Guildmember has arrived!" The Inspector's triumphant announcement left the distinct impression that he himself had somehow conjured her appearance.

Killashandra stared apprehensively at them. They had a disconcerting resemblance to each other, not only a sameness of height and build but of coloring and feature. Even their voices were pitched in the same sonorous timber. She blinked, thinking it might be some trick of the soft yellow sunshine pouring in from the main reception area. Then she gave herself a little shake: all were government employees, but could any bureaucracy, Optherian or other, hire people on the basis of their uniform appearance?

49

"Welcome to Optheria, Guildmember Ree," the Inspector said, beaming as he ushered her past the portal, which whispered shut behind them.

"Welcome, Killashandra Ree, I am Thyrol," the first and oldest man said, taking one step toward her and bowing.

"Welcome, Killashandra Ree, I am Pirinio," said the second, following the example of the first.

In unvarying ceremony, Polabod and Mirbethan made themselves known to her. Had they practiced long?

"I am truly welcomed," she said with a gracious semibow. "The crystal? It was aboard the shuttle."

All four looked to her right, left hands rising from their sides at the same instant, to indicate the float appearing through a second portal. Nullgravs suspended float and cartons above the gold-flecked marble floor but proper guidance apparently required six attendants, each wearing an anxious frown of concentration. A seventh man directed their efforts, dancing from one side to the other to be certain that nothing impeded their progress. These citizens of Optheria were reassuringly mismatched in size, form, and feature.

"We four," Thyrol began, indicating his companions with a twist of his hand, "are to be your guides and mentors during your stay on Optheria. You have only to state your wishes and preferences and we—Optheria—will provide."

The four bowed again, like a wave from right to left. The Inspector beside her also bowed. Thyrol lifted one eyebrow and the Inspector, bowing again as he surrendered Killashandra's carisak to Pirinio, formally receded until the portal hissed apart and then closed. Killashandra wondered if the Inspector's euphoria would extend to lesser breeds, those without Guild affiliation, when he resumed his booth in Immigration.

"If you will step this way, Guildmember Ree." Thyrol made another of his graceful gestures.

When she moved to walk beside him, he altered his stride to keep a deferential meter from her. The others fell in behind. Killashandra shrugged, accepting the protocol. Not having to chat with her escort gave her a chance to glance about the shuttle port. The facility was functional and decorated with murals of Life on Optheria: the main attraction of the Summer Festival—the organ—was not depicted. Nor did the vaulted arrivals hall appear to have any catering areas apart from one narrow bank for beverage dispensing. Conspicuous by their absence were curio and souvenir booths. Not even a ticket bank was to be seen. And only one lounge area. At the wide exit, the doors sighed aside for Killashandra and Thyrol, who quickly walked down the wide shallow steps to a broad, intricately patterned apron of flat stones. Beyond was the roadway where the crew had just finished stowing the three foam crates in a large ground effect machine.

Suddenly an arc of light flashed on behind Killashandra and a muted alarm sounded. Guards materialized from inconspicuous booths on both sides of the main entrance and approached the three Optherians of the reception committee who were walking behind Killashandra and Thyrol.

"Please do not be disconcerted, Guildmember Ree." Thyrol waved to the guards and they retreated back into their stations. The arc of light disappeared.

"What was that all about?"

"Merely a security precaution."

"For my leaving the shuttle port?"

Thyrol cleared his throat. "Actually, for Optherians leaving the shuttle port."

"Leaving?"

"This is our vehicle, Guildmember," Thyrol said, smoothly urging her across the flagstone plaza. She allowed herself to be diverted because it was obvious that, whoever *left* the Shuttle Port was first obliged to *enter*: the alarm would work in both directions. But how could the device distinguish Optherians from other humans? No mutation had been mentioned in her perusal of the *Encyclopedia Galactica* entry for the planet: most ingenious for a warning device to differentiate between residents and nonresidents. But surely it got a bit noisy and confusing when Optherians were escorting tourists to the shuttle port. Or was that the reason for this broad flagstone area? She would have to check on FSP regulations about security measures restricting citizens to their planets.

As her vehicle glided forward, the first of the shuttle passengers began to emerge. On cue, fat accommodation buses filed out of the parking area to the flagstone curb. Craning her neck slightly,

Killashandra took due note of the fact that the security system did not respond to the foreigners' exits.

Already the vehicle was climbing out of the valley which contained the shuttle port and the clutter of maintenance buildings. The place looked bleakly ordered and preternaturally neat in comparison to what Killashandra recalled of Fuerte's busy space port. Perhaps when the tourist season started . . . Even the clumps of trees and bushes which softened the harder lines of the buildings had a regulated look. Killashandra wondered how often the plantings had to be replaced. Shuttle emanations had a disastrous effect on most vegetation.

"Are you comfortable, Guildmember?" Mirbethan asked from her seat behind Killashandra.

"Of necessity the shuttle port was placed close to the City," Pirinio took up the conversation, "but is screened by these hills which also absorb much of the noise and bustle."

Noise and bustle, his tone of voice told Killashandra, were the unpleasant concomitants of space travel. "How wise of you," Killashandra replied.

"Optheria's founding fathers planned for every contingency," Thyrol said smugly. "No effort has been spared to conserve our planet's natural beauty."

The vehicle had reached the top of the gap and Killashandra had an unimpeded view of the broader valley below them, in which nestled the felicitous arrangement of pastel colored buildings, domes, and round towers that comprised Optheria's capital settlement, known as the City. From that height, the impressive view drew a surprised exclamation from Killashandra.

"It is breathtaking!" Thyrol chose to interpret her response his way.

Beautiful was a fair adjective, Killashandra thought, but breathtaking, no! Even at that distance something was too prim and proper about the City for her taste.

"None of the indigenous trees and bushes were removed, you see," Thyrol explained, gesturing with his whole hand rather than a single finger, "when the City was constructed, so that the natural, unspoiled landscape could be retained."

"And the river and that lake? Are they natural features?"

"But of course. Nature is not distorted on Optheria."

"Which is as it should be," Polabod added. "The entire valley is as it was when Man first landed on Optheria."

"The City Architect planned all the buildings and dwellings in the unoccupied spaces," Mirbethan said proudly.

"How exceedingly clever!" Killashandra was wearing the contact lenses recommended for Optheria's sunlight and wondered if the planet would be improved, viewed via augmented Ballybran vision. Just then it was very, very, *blah!* Killashandra had to delve a long way for an adequate expression which, tactfully, she did not voice. Would Borella have restrained herself? Would she have noticed? Ah, well, Beauty is said to be in the eye of the beholder! For Optheria's sake, she was glad that someone loved it.

While it might have been laudable of the Founding Fathers to wish to preserve the entire valley as it was when Man first landed, it must have given the architects and construction crews a helluva lot of trouble. Buildings wrapped around copses of trees, straddled brooks, incorporated boulders and ledges. Probably the floors on upper levels were even but it must have been bumpy going at ground level. Fortunately the airfoils of her vehicle were up to the uneven surface in the suburbs but the ride became rather bouncy as they proceeded deeper into the City.

Pausing at the intersection of a huge open square—open except for the many thorn bushes and scrawny trees—Killashandra could not fail to notice that the ground floor of one corner building made uneven arches over repulsively greasy-looking bushes whose thorny branches were obviously a hazard to pedestrians; something was to be said for the curtailment of natural "beauty." She could learn to hate the City quite easily. No wonder some of the natives were restless. Just how did the Summer Festival compensate for the rest of the Optherian year?

Once past the open square, the road climbed gently to a cluster of buildings evidently uninhibited by natural beauties, for they seemed to have an architectural integrity so far lacking in the City.

"It was necessary," Thyrol said in a muted voice, "to add the merest trace of a ramp to ascend to the Music Center."

"I wouldn't have known it if you hadn't told me," Killashandra said, unable to restrain her facetiousness.

"One ought to approach on foot," Pirinio went on in a repressive tone, "but some latitude is permitted so that the audience may assemble punctually." His gesture called Killashandra's attention to the many small switchback paths to one side of the promontory.

Killashandra repressed a second facetious remark which Pirinio's tone provoked. It wouldn't be the installation on Optheria, nor the organ, nor the planet which were hazardous: once again it was the inhabitants. Was she always to encounter such intolerant, inflexible, remorseless personalities?

"What sort of local brew do you have here on Optheria?" she asked, keeping her tone casual. If the reply was "none," she'd book out on the next available craft.

"Well, ah, that is, possibly not at all to your taste, Guildmember." Mirbethan's startled reply was hesitant. "No beverages can be imported. I'm sure you saw the notice in the Port Authority. Our brewmasters produce four distinct fermented beverages: quite potable, I'm told. Spirits are distilled from the Terran grains which we have managed to adapt to Optherian soil, but I've been told that these are raw to educated palates."

"Optheria produces excellent wines," Pirinio said rather testily, with a reproving glance at Mirbethan. "They cannot be exported and indeed, some do not travel well even the relatively short distance to the City. If wine is your preference, a selection will be put in your quarters."

"I'll try some of the brews, too."

"Wine *and* beer?" Polabod exclaimed in surprise.

"Crystal singers are required to keep a high blood-alcohol content when absent from Ballybran. I'll have to decide which is the best for my particular requirement." She sighed in patient forebearance.

"I wasn't informed that members of your Guild required special diets." Thyrol was clearly perturbed.

"No special diet," Killashandra agreed, "but we do require larger intakes of certain natural substances from time to time. Such as alcohol."

"Oh, I see," Thyrol replied, although clearly he did not.

Does no one on this repulsive planet have a sense of humor? Killashandra wondered.

"Ah, here we are so soon," Pirinio said, for the vehicle had swung down the curving drive to the imposing main entrance of the largest building on this musical height.

In orderly fashion but in decorous haste, a second welcoming committee formed itself on the wide and shallow marble steps under the colonnaded portico that shielded the massive central doors of the edifice. Although large urns had been planted with some sort of weeping tree to soften the harsh architecture, the effect was forbidding, rather than welcoming.

Killashandra emerged from the vehicle, ignoring Thyrol's outstretched hand. The Optherian's obsequious behavior could quickly become a major irritant.

She had just straightened up and turned to step forward when something slammed hard into her left shoulder and she was thrown off balance against the vehicle. The fleshy point of her shoulder stung briefly then began to throb. Thyrol began to bellow incoherently before he attempted to embrace her in the misguided notion that she needed his assistance.

For the next few moments total chaos erupted: Thyrol, Pirinio, and Polabod dashed about, issuing conflicting orders. The throng of dignitaries turned into a terrified mob, splintering into groups which fled, stood paralyzed, or added their shouts to the tumult. A flock of airborne sleds reared up from the plateau to hover above the Music Complex, darting off on diverse errands.

Mirbethan was the only one able to keep her wits. She tore a strip from the hem of her gown, and despite Killashandra's protestations that she required no aid, bound the wound. And it was she who discovered the weapon, imbedded in the upholstery of the back seat.

"That's a businesslike piece of wickedness," Killashandra remarked as she studied the asterisk-bladed object, three of its lethal blades buried in the seat back. The one which had wounded her pointed outward, a strand of her sleeve material laid neatly along the cutting edge.

"Don't touch it" Mirbethan put out her hand to prevent such action.

"No fear," Killashandra said, straightening up. "Local manufacture?"

"No." Mirbethan's voice took on a note of indignant anger. "An island implement. An outrage. We shall spare no effort to discover the perpetrator of this deed."

There was a subtle, but discernible, alteration in Mirbethan's tone between her first two remarks and the last which Killashandra caught but could not then analyse, for the rest of the committee suddenly recalled that there had been a victim of this "outrage" and more attentions were showered on Killashandra by the concerned. Despite her protestations, she was carried into the vaulting entrance hall of the main building, and whisked along a corridor, lined floor to ceiling with portraits of men and women. Even in her swift passage she noticed that they all smiled in the same tight, smug way. Then she was conducted to a lift while dignitaries bickered about who should accompany her in the limited space.

Once again, Mirbethan won Killashandra's approval by closing the door on the argument. They were met at their destination by a full medical convention and Killashandra was made to lie on a gurney and was wheeled into diagnostics.

At the moment of truth, when the temporary bandaging was reverently unwound from the injury, there was a stunned silence.

"I could have spared everyone a great deal of unnecessary effort," Killashandra remarked drily after she glanced at the clean, bloodless cut. "As a crystal singer, I heal very quickly and am not the least bit susceptible to infection. As you can see."

Consternation was rampant, with all the medics exclaiming over the wound, and others cramming forward in an attempt to witness this miracle of regeneration. Glancing up, Killashandra saw the very smug smile on Mirbethan's face, so very like the smiles on the portraits.

"To what agency do you attribute such remarkable healing properties?" asked the eldest of the medical people in attendance.

"To living on Ballybran," Killashandra replied. "As you must surely be aware, the resonance of crystal slows down the degenerative process. Tissue damage regenerates quickly. By this evening this minor cut will be completely healed. It was a clean swipe and not all that deep."

She seized the opportunity to slip off the gurney.

"If we may take a sample of your blood for analysis," the elder medic began, reaching for a sterilely packaged extractor.

"You may not," Killashandra said and again felt a wave of incredulous dismay and surprise from her audience. Was contradiction forbidden on Optheria? "The bleeding has stopped. Nor will analysis isolate the blood factor which slows degeneration," she went on with a kind smile. "Why waste your valuable time?"

She strode purposefully toward the door now, determined to end this interlude. Just then, Pirinio, Thyrol, and Polabod arrived, breathless in their haste to rejoin her.

"Ah, gentlemen, you are just in time to escort me to my quarters." And when there were stumbled explanations about receptions and Music Center faculty waiting and the prospect of attendance by the Elders, she smiled gently. "All the more reason for me to change . . ." and she gestured to the torn sleeve.

"But you've not been attended!" Thyrol cried, astonished to see an unbandaged slash.

"Very well, thank you," she said and walked past him into the corridor. "Well?" She swung round to face a throng of very confused people. "Will no one escort me to my quarters?" This farce was beginning to pall.

The corridor, too, had its occupants, mostly in the universal green garb of the medical profession. Therefore, the young man, clad in a dark tunic, his bronzed legs bare to the soft leather ankle boots, stood out among them.

Lanzecki might swear that the Ballybran spore did not confer any psychic enhancement but Killashandra was entertaining severe doubts on that score. She had definitely caught conflicting emotional emanations from Mirbethan, from the other worthies, and now, from this young man—a curious flash of regret, annoyance, interest, and anticipation far too strong to be the casual reaction to a visitor. And flash was all it could be, for Thyrol and Pirinio bore down on her, all apologies for their discourtesies real and imaginary. Mirbethan firmly took her place at Killashandra's right, edging the three men out of position and motioning their guest down the hall. When Killashandra was able to glance back to the young man, he was striding down a side corridor, head down, shoulders sagging as if weighed down by some burden. Guilt?

Then she was swept into the lift, down to the guest level, and into the most sumptuous quarters which had ever been allotted to her. Having agreed to descend to the reception as soon as she had changed gave her time for only the most cursory examination of the apartment. She'd been guided through a large, elegant reception room suitable for formal affairs. A smaller room was evidently to be used as a studio or office. They hurried past two bedchambers, one of them quite modern, before she was ushered into a main room so vast that she had to stifle a chuckle. Mirbethan indicated the toilet and the slightly open closet panel where her clothes had been hung. Then the woman withdrew.

Stripping off the torn garment, Killashandra flicked open one of the Beluga spider-silk kaftans which ought to be suitable for any reception: certainly a foil against the predominantly white or pale colors which the Optherians seemed to prefer. Except for that brooding young man.

Killashandra dwelt briefly on him as she washed hastily. Then she couldn't resist a peek into the other hygiene rooms. One contained a variety of tubs, massage table, and exercise equipment while the third boasted a radiant-fluid tub and several curious devices which Killashandra had never before encountered but which left an impression of obscenity.

Back in the bedchamber, she heard a soft rapping at the door.

"I'm ready, I'm ready," she cried, masking irritation with a lilt in her voice.

Chapter 5

That protocol had become an art form on Optheria told Killashandra quite clearly that if there were no rebellious spirits then the entire population had stagnated. At the reception, every faculty member, their subordinates, then every student, all in order of their rank and scholastic standing, filed past her. Mercifully, handshaking was no longer a part of the ritual. A nod, a smile, a mumbled repetition of the name sufficed. After fifty nods, Killashandra felt her smile fixed in her cheeks and her face stiffened into that mode. With her everfaithful quartette, she stood at the top of a massive double staircase, whose white marble flights curved down into a marbled hall below. The ceiling of the vast reception chamber was so high that the murmuring of the assembled crowd was absorbed.

Killashandra had had a glimpse of tables, laden with patterns of plates whose contents were as precisely placed as the plates were, and with beakers of colored liquids. The assembled scrupulously kept their eyes from the direction of the refreshments. Killashandra guessed that they all knew too well the taste and texture of the reception repast.

There were curious patterns, too, in the reception. Five people would take the right-hand staircase, the next five would descend on the left. Killashandra wondered if a steward in some distant anteroom ticked the people off for left and right. There were never more than ten people waiting to be introduced, yet the flow down the hallway was steady despite its apparent randomness.

Abruptly no more people were making their way to the reception line and Killashandra let her cheeks relax, rotating her head on her neck, wriggling her lips and nose in a very undignified manner in order to ease the muscles. One never knows when one's early training as a singer is going to prove useful, she thought, just as she heard a concerted intake of breath from her quartette. Reorganizing her expression, she glanced up the hall in time to observe the ceremonial approach of dignitaries.

The seven figures who processed—and that was the correct verb to describe their advance—were not differently garbed from the other highly placed Optherians, but they wore their pale robes with an unmistakable air of authority. Four men and three women, each wearing the same slight smile upon their serene faces. Faces, Killashandra would shortly note, that had been carefully adjusted by surgery and artifice to enhance that serenity, for only one of the smiles reached the weary, bored, aged eyes.

Elder Ampris, Killashandra was immensely relieved to discover, was the only one of the Optherian rulers with whom she would have much contact. He was currently responsible for the Music Complex. If there should ever be a Stellarity Award given for Best Character Actor among Planetary Rulers, surely Ampris would win it. But for the disparity of expression between eye and face, Killashandra might have missed that gleam of humor and possibly ignored that spontaneous lifting of the heart that occur when one encounters a kindred spirit. The others, whose names Killashandra promptly forgot, gave her hand one firm shake in welcome, a few words of gratitude for making "so arduous a journey in this moment of planetary crisis," and passed on by, having acquitted their duty. They all waited, without appearing to wait, at the top of the right-hand stair. Then Killashandra felt the almost electric touch of Ampris's hand, looked into his bright and knowing eyes and returned the first genuine smile of the long afternoon.

"We will have time to talk later on, Guildmember. In the meantime, let us gild their afternoon with the gold and scarlet of our presences." His negligent wave took in the whole room, not just the high dignities patiently awaiting the dissolution of the reception line.

Thyrol glanced at Killashandra, her hand on Ampris's arm, then he turned to the nearest Elder woman and offered his arm. No fuss, no confusion, no dithering about altered escorts or who would be left to descend alone: everything was already worked out, planned down to the last detail, including the unexpected.

For, obviously, no one could have expected Ampris to confer such an honor as his personal escort on Killashandra.

Killashandra wondered if the foodstuffs had been minutely measured, for two bites disposed of each of the four small tidbits, five mouthfuls emptied the wine glass. But she was among the lucky minority who had their glasses refilled and were offered additional canapes.

"This will be over soon," Ampris murmured to her, his lips barely moving. "A proper meal will be served us when the lesser orders have dutifully taken their sip and sup and toddled back to the comfort of their routines."

He spoke with neither scorn nor malice: Ampris was stating a fact about the majority of the assembled.

"Having had their rare treat of standing in the same room with a real live breathing Crystal Singer?"

"You are that!" Ampris's gaze returned hers with no trace of guile or evasion but he had a definite twinkle in his eye. "Three minutes after you reached the infirmary, the news of your regenerative powers had seeped to the basements."

"Surely you are not housed in a basement?"

Ampris's bright brown eyes twinkled again. "The seat of all knowledge . . ."

"So you can get to the bottom of things?"

"Of course."

"And a position of maximum security?" Killashandra taunted him. Why shouldn't she start at the top with her covert inquiries?

"Security is never a problem on such a well-ordered world as Optheria." He inclined his head to acknowledge the passing of three of the dignitaries circulating the gathering. "Everyone is secure"—he paused—"on Optheria, each knowing his place and his duties. Security is the foundation of the serenity of spirit which typifies this natural world."

Killashandra could find no mockery in his words nor any special inflection in his voice. No sparkle of amusement lit his eye, no cynical expression molded his face, yet Killashandra heard the denial as clearly as if he had phrased it.

"Someone must have had a momentarily troubled spirit to launch that little star-knife at me."

"An island weapon," Ampris said. "We allowed that settlement too much leeway during the early years on Optheria. Its original colonists were, naturally, of our mind, but before we could reestablish contact with them, they had deviated from the original intent. Optheria was to be an autonomous world: not to consist of autonomous groups." Ampris's humorless voice and manner implied the treatment which had undoubtedly been meted out to the dissenters. "The matter of that outrageous attack on your person will be resolved, I can assure you, Guildmember Killashandra."

"I don't doubt that for a moment."

Ampris searched her face. "On an ordered planet, the unusual is always remarkable."

"Ampris, you may not monopolize our distinguished visitor," said a deep grating voice and Killashandra turned to find herself scrutinized by one of the other male Elders. He had the eyes of a scavenger, bright, dark, piercing. His thin, hooked nose did much to encourage the analogy. His skin had a curious lacquered look, crinkling at the edges of his face from whatever minor shift of expression he permitted. His glance dropped briefly to her left shoulder, as if his gaze could penetrate the silk and examine the healing wound beneath.

"Monopoly has never been my passion, Torkes," Ampris said. "My associate, Torkes, holds the Communications Seat on Optheria. We work closely together in our adjacent disciplines. He maintains that Music is dependent on Communications, and I, of course, take the position that Music is independent and without it, Communications would have nothing to disseminate!"

"But of course!" Killashandra mustered a broad and giddy smile with which she favored both men impartially. Ampris accepted her evasion with a slight smile while Torkes bowed as if her ambiguous reply awarded him the decision. "What sort of a crystal network does your facility use, Elder Torkes?"

"Crystal?" Torkes's piercing stare was affronted. "We have no funds to waste on that sort of technology. Crystal is reserved for musicians!"

"Really?" And Killashandra caught the barest glimpse of the satisfied reaction from Ampris. Torkes seemed totally oblivious to the implication of his statement. "Even when crystal is a very natural—"

"Crystal is not natural to Optheria. Not a native product, you understand. And we must maintain the integrity of our Charter."

"Indeed? Do you not violate that integrity by using alien instrumentation?"

Torkes dismissed her argument with a flick of his bony fingers. "Music is an art form which we were able to bring with us, within the mind. It is intangible—"

"And what is communication, then? Can it be touched? Smelt? Tasted?"

Torkes stared at her so fiercely that Killashandra was made aware of the fact that not only had she dared to interrupt an Elder but she had argued with him. She sensed rather than saw Ampris's intense amusement then, in the next blink of his eyes, when Torkes was faced with the unpalatable realization that a Heptite Guildmember, an invited specialist urgently required by his planet, held equal status with himself.

"Of course," Ampris said, breaking the heavy silence that ensued, "the organ was developed by an Optherian for Optherian purposes and is, in fact, unique to our planet."

"Yes, yes, quite so," Torkes mumbled just as a mellow chime discreetly ended the reception.

Torkes made an adroit escape.

"So, one does not dispute with you Elders here?" Killashandra asked, watching him move off through the throng.

"It is good for us, I assure you," Ampris replied with a chuckle. "Fortunately Torkes is more flexible than he sounds, for when he changes Seats, he becomes totally committed to his immediate responsibility." When Killashandra looked quizzical, he added: "We Elders change our duties every four years, so as not to become too narrow in our understanding of the overview."

"I see."

"Then you are wiser than your years," Ampris said, "for I cannot believe that an administrator who is tone deaf can effectively guide Music: or that an Elder who cannot integrate should have charge of the Treasury. However, the governmental mechanism is so weighty that four years of mismanagement generally produce no more than annoying miscalculations and minor blunders easily corrected. The brilliance of the Founding Fathers of Optheria is once more unquestionably elucidated."

Thyrol appeared, respectfully inclining his upper body at his interruption.

"Elder Ampris, Guildmember Ree, if you will proceed to the dining chamber?"

The beauty of the hall, the elegantly set table and Elder Ampris's earlier comment deceived Killashandra into anticipating a far better meal. Although presented in appealing style, the minuscule portions did not appease Killashandra's hearty appetite. Nor was she offered enough of any one food to make a positive identification of its constituents or savor its taste. The courses were accompanied by beverages which were so bland that the water had more zest to it—and not a brew or a ferment among them. Killashandra's exasperated sigh caught the attention of Elder Pentrom, her right-hand dinner partner.

"Something is amiss?" he asked politely and then stared for a brief moment at her clean plate. He was but halfway through the food on his.

"Doesn't Optheria produce brews, or vintages or something with more taste than these, Elder Pentrom?"

"You mean an *alcoholic* beverage?" he said, as if she had made a particularly obscene suggestion.

Killashandra favored him with a longer look and decided that with his prim mouth, sharp chin, and tiny eyes, no other reaction could have been expected.

"Indeed I do mean alcoholic beverages." He opened his mouth to protest, but before he could utter a word she said, "Alcohol is essential to the proper metabolic function of a crystal singer."

"I have never heard that in all my years as Medical Supervisor of this planet."

"Have you encountered many crystal singers in your career?" Piqued by yet another dogmatic encounter, Killashandra discarded any semblance of tact. These people needed a set-down and she was one in the enviable position of being able to give it with impunity.

"In actual fact, no—"

"Then how can you possibly dispute my statement? Or question my requirements? This," and she waved a scornful hand at the goblet before her, *"bilge—"*

"That *beverage* is a nutritious liquid, carefully combined to supply the adult daily requirements of vitamins and minerals to ensure—"

"No wonder it tastes so revolting. And may I point out that any brewmaster worth his license provides the same vitamins and minerals in a form palatable enough to satisfy the inner man as well."

The Medical Supervisor hitched his chair back, throwing his serviette on the table in preparation for harangue, and suddenly they were the center of attention. "Young woman—"

"Spare me your condescension, Elder," Killashandra replied as she rose gracefully to her feet and glared down at him. She swept the table with a reproving look. "I shall retire to my apartment until such time as my dietary requirements can be met with enough food"—she flipped over her empty plate—" to satisfy my appetite and sufficient alcoholic beverages to keep my metabolism functioning. Good evening!"

In the stunned silence, Killashandra left the room. Doors the size and density of the ones securing the dining chamber did not slam satisfactorily but she had enjoyed her exit so much that she did not miss that part of the finale. In the corridor, she startled minions, lounging against the walls.

"Does anybody know where my apartments are in this mausoleum?" she demanded. When all raised their hands, she pointed to the nearest. "Take me there." When he hesitated and looked anxiously at the door, she repeated her order in a louder and more authoritative tone. He scurried forward, more desirous of avoiding her immediate wrath than courting disfavor of an absent authority.

"Tell me," she asked in a pleasant tone when they had entered a small lift, "is food plentiful on Optheria?"

He cast her a very nervous glance and when she smiled winningly at him, relaxed a little, though he kept as far from her in the carriage as possible.

"There is plenty of food on Optheria. Too much. This year only half the fields may be planted, and I know that early fruit has been left to rot on the vine."

"Then why did I get three mouthfuls at dinner?"

Something approaching levity touched the young man's face. "All the Elders are old: they don't eat much."

"Hmm! That's one explanation. But a good brew or a nice dry vintage would have helped!"

A smile tugged at the young man's lips. "Well, Elder Pentrom was present and he is death on any sort of alcoholic beverage. Says it saps the energy of the young and disrupts thought in the mature."

"And he was my dinner partner!" Killashandra's crow of malice resounded in the enclosed space. "My timing is, as ever, superb! Well, I'm not under his jurisdiction and, if Optheria really needs that organ repaired, the Elders will have to placate me, not him." The young man was obviously shocked. "Tell me," she said in her kindest, most wheedling voice, "you seem to be a knowledgeable fellow, what sort of interesting beverages are produced on this planet?"

"Oh, there are brews and vintages," he assured her promptly and with some pride, "and some rather potent spiritous drinks manufactured in the mountains and the islands—but that sort of stuff isn't permitted in the Conservatory." The lift's doors slid open, and the Optherian bustled out.

"More's the pity." Killashandra strode on down the hallway after her guide. "What do you drink? No, abort the question," and she grinned at his startled glance. "What is the most popular drink?"

"The most popular one on this continent is a brew called Bascum."

"Is Bascum a plant or a person?"

"Person." Her guide was warming to his subject. He indicated they take the left-hand corridor at the junction. "One of the Founding Fathers."

"So his brewery is allowed to function in the face of the Medical Supervisor's displeasure?" Killashandra grinned as he nodded. "I infer from your remarks that there are other popular drinks? Any wines?"

"Oh, yes, the western continent produces some very fine vintages, both white and red, and some doubly distilled liqueurs. I'm not familiar with the wines at all."

"And those islands you mentioned, they go for the spiritous liquors?"

"The polly tree."

"The polly tree?"

"Its fermented fruit makes a brandy which, I'm told, is more potent than anything else in the universe. The polly tree provides foliage for shelter, a fine-grained wood for building, its roots burn for a long time, its bark can be pounded into a fiber which the islanders use for weaving cloth, its pith is extremely nutritious, and its large fruit is delicious as well as nutritious—"

"When it isn't fermented—"

"Exactly."

"And the polly tree only grows on the islands?"

"That's right, and here is your apartment, Guildmember." He opened the door.

"There's no privacy lock on this?" Killashandra had not noticed the lack in her first hurried inspection.

"There is no need for such in the Complex." Her guide appeared surprised at her reaction. "No one would presume to enter without your express permission."

"There are no thieves on Optheria?"

"Not in the *Conservatory!*"

She thanked him for his escort and entered her sacrosanct apartment, closing the door behind her with a sigh of relief. Only then did her eye fall on the table. She exclaimed aloud at the display of bottles of all sizes and shapes, at the beakers, goblets, wine glasses that waited in pristine array on the white cloth. A separate tray offered an assortment of tidbits, nuts, and small wafers. A small chest opened to exhibit chilled bottles and two pottery amphoras.

There was no way the collection could have been assembled and spirited into her apartment in the time elasped since she stormed out of the dining room. Then she remembered her remarks on the trip from the spaceport. Well, Elder Pentrom might be a prissy, dogmatic, abstemious man, but obviously her every whim was someone's command.

Because her guide had mentioned Bascum, her choice among so many finally settled on the neat brown bottle in the cold chest. She flipped the top off and let the mid-brown brew slowly descend into an appropriate beaker. The malty scent that rose to her nostrils suggested good things to come.

"And about time, too," she said, scooping up a random selection of nibbles and sinking into the nearest comfortable seat. "To absent friends!" She lifted her beaker high then took her first sip.

She regarded the brew with respect and delight. "Could Bascum possibly have come from Yarra?" she asked herself. "This might not be so bad an assignment after all!"

Chapter 6

By the time the quick Optherian sunset had finished its evening display, Killashandra had sampled nine beverages, wishing she had someone with whom to share the largesse, especially since there was a prohibition against it. Which brought Corish to mind, and that mythical uncle of his. Unless she could discover how much surveillance she would be having from her discreet quartette—and how easy it would be to outwit it—she didn't want to risk meeting him. Would they think it odd if she left a message in at the Piper Facility? Corish had considerably piqued her curiosity and she was somewhat motivated by a desire to show him that two could play the exploitation gambit.

Someone tapped on her apartment door and, when Mirbethan entered on her permission, Killashandra caught the shade of uncertainty in the Optherian's manner.

"Since you're not accompanied by any priss-mouthed ancients, you are welcome. And if that excuse for a meal is a state dinner here, no wonder you're a lean bunch."

Mirbethan flushed. "Since Elder Pentrom graciously accepted our invitation, we are obliged to cater to his dietary preferences. Didn't Elder Ampris mention this to you?"

"He failed to put me in the know. However, all this," and Killashandra waved expansively at the beverage table's load, "makes up for that deficiency, though solid food would assist my investigations . . ."

"There was no time to show you the catering facility." Mirbethan glided to one of the discreet wall cabinets. Its doors opened on a catering unit. "Alcoholic beverages are not included. Stu-

dents have a distressing aptitude for breaking restricted codes."
Killashandra decided that she merely thought she detected a note
of tolerant humor in Mirbethan's voice. "That is why we have
supplied you with a sampling of the available intoxicants."

"In spite of Elder Pentrom."

Mirbethan cast her eyes downward.

"Tell me, Mirbethan, would you happen to know if Bascum
the brewmaster originated from the planet Yarra?"

"Bascum?" Mirbethan looked up, startled, and confused. When
Killashandra waved the long-emptied bottle at her, she blushed.
"Oh, that Bascum." Now she glided to a second ornate cabinet
which opened into a full size terminal, and a panel in the wall
slid aside to reveal a large screen. She typed an entry as Killashandra made a private wager. "Why, how under the suns did you
know?"

"The best brewmasters in the galaxy hail from that planet. I
haven't sampled everything yet," Killashandra went on, "but I
shall be very well suited indeed if you'll undertake to keep me
supplied with Bascum's brew."

"As you require, Guildmember. But for now, the concert is
about to start in the Red Hall. Only the single manual organ, but
the performer was last year's prize winner."

Killashandra was tempted, but she was a shade hungrier and
drier than she liked to be. "The Elders are present?" When Mirbethan solemnly nodded, Killashandra sighed deeply. "Convey
my apologies on the grounds of travel fatigue . . . and the stress
of metabolic readjustment after the assault and the wound." Killashandra ran the silk up her arm, exposing her shoulder where
only a thin red line gave evidence of an injury.

Mirbethan's eyes widened significantly and then, with a subtle
shift, she inclined a bow to Killashandra.

"Your apologies will be conveyed. Call code MBT 14 if you
require any further assistance from myself, Thyrol, Pirinio, or
Polabod."

Killashandra wished her a pleasant evening and Mirbethan
withdrew. As soon as the door had closed on the woman, Killashandra discarded her languor and made for the catering unit. Once
again, Optherian peculiarities inhibited her, for when she called
up a menu, there was no scrolling of delectable, mouthwatering

selections but a set dinner, with only three choices for the main course. She opted for all three, and immediately the catering unit queried her. She repeated her request and, when the unit wanted to know how many were dining, she tapped in "three." At which point the unit informed her that the apartment was recorded as having a single occupant. She replied that she had guests. Their names and codes were required. She responded with the names of Elders Pentrom and Ampris, codes unknown.

The food was promptly dispensed, two of the meager servings that she had observed in the dining hall. Fortunately the third one was substantial enough to abort the kick that she had been about to bestow on the catering unit.

Once she had solid food in her stomach, she continued her liquor sampling. While not in the least inebriated, thanks to her Ballybran-altered digestion, Killashandra was very merry and sang lustily as she ventured into the hygiene rooms and splashed in the scented water of the bath. She continued to sing, her fancy latching onto a riotous ballad generally rendered by a tenor, as she made her way to the bedroom. A lambent radiance augmented the soft lighting and, curious, she went to the window, observing three of Optheria's four small moons, one near enough for the craters and vast sterile plains to be clearly visible. Entranced, Killashandra broke off the ballad and began the haunting love duet from Baleef's exotic opera, *Voyagers*, which seemed particularly appropriate to the setting.

When a tenor voice joined her on cue, she faltered a moment. Then, despite her astonishment at spontaneity in such a rigidly controlled environment, she continued. *Voyagers* had been her last opera as a student on Fuerte, so she knew it well enough to divert some of her attention from the words. And a fine, rich, well produced voice he had. Might need a bit more support for the G's and A's in the last three measures—she'd be amazed if he could hit the high C along with her—but he had a firm sense of the dynamic requirements and sang with great sensitivity. As the tenor took up the melody, she gathered herself for the taxing finale, delighted to find her singing voice still flexible enough for the dynamics, and the high C. The tenor, with no loss of vibrance, opted for the A, but it was a grand ringing A and she applauded his judgment.

She sustained her note, perversely wishing him to drop but, as it happened, they broke off at the same instant, as if they had had the innumerable rehearsals such inspired singing required.

"'When shall our paths cross again?'" she asked in the recitative which followed that spectacular duet.

"'When the moons of Radomah make glorious the sky with measured dance.'" The invisible tenor also had a vibrant speaking voice, and, better yet, an appreciation of the humor in their impromptu performance for she caught the ripple of laughter in his chanted phrases. Did he also find the words, and the opera, a trifle ludicrous in the austere setting of the Optherian Complex?

All of a sudden, the courtyard below was floodlighted. Figures erupted onto the paving, shouting commands for silence. Before she stepped back from the window, Killashandra caught a glimpse of a figure, in a window directly opposite hers but a story above, withdrawing into the shielding darkness. Soprano and tenor exited the stage while the extras made a diligent and vain search for the conspirators.

Killashandra poured herself a full glass of something which its label identified as a fortified wine. This was an odd music center if impromptu singing, particularly of so high a caliber, was answered by punitive force.

She downed the drink, doused all the lights in the suite and, in the milky light of the moons, sought the comfort of her bed. Despite a wish for sleep, her mind ranged through the scenes of the Baleef opera and the sorrows of the star-crossed lovers. She must remember to ask Mirbethan who that tenor was. Fine voice! Much better than the pimple-faced little oaf who had sung the role opposite her on Fuerte!

Morning chimes, soft but insidious, roused her. She lifted herself on one elbow, saw that dawn was just breaking, groaned and, flinging the light coverlet over her head, went back to sleep. A second sequence of chimes, louder, sounded. Cursing, Killashandra strode to the console, coded the number Mirbethan had given her. "Is there any way to stop the wretched chimes in this apartment? Imagine, having to wake up at dawn!"

"That is the way here, Guildmember, but I shall advise Control that your apartment is to be excluded from the Rising Chimes."

"And all others, please! I will not be ordered about by bells, drums, whistles, shrills, or inaudibles. And who possesses that remarkably fine tenor voice?"

Mirbethan shot Killashandra a startled look. "You were disturbed by it—"

"Not in the least. But if that's the quality of natural musical talent on Optheria, I'm impressed."

"The Center does not encourage vocalizing." Mirbethan's cool denial roused Killashandra's instant hostility.

"You mean, that tenor is a reject from your opera school?"

"You misunderstand the situation, Guildmember. All the teaching centers on Optheria emphasize keyboard music."

"You mean, only that organ?"

"Of course. The organ is the ultimate of instruments, combining the—"

"Spare me the hype, Mirbethan." Killashandra took an obscure pleasure in the shock her statement gave the woman. Then she relented. "Oh, I concur that the Optherian organ is a premier instrument, but that tenor voice was rather spectacular on its own merit."

"You should not have been disturbed—"

"Fardles! I enjoyed singing with him."

Mirbethan's eyes rounded in a secondary shock. "You . . . were the other singer?"

"I was." *File that for future reference!* "Tell me, Mirbethan, if only a few of the hundreds who must study at this Center ever attain the standard required to play the Optherian organ, what happens to those who don't?"

"Why, suitable situations are found for them."

"In music?" Mirbethan shook her head. "I'd think that crystal singing would provide a marvelous alternative."

"Optherians do not care to leave their planet, whatever their minor disappointments. You will excuse me, Guildmember—" Mirbethan broke the connection.

Killashandra stared at the blank screen for a long moment. Of course, neither Mirbethan nor any of the quartette knew of her early background in music. Certainly none of them could possibly know of her disappointment, nor how she would relate that to what Mirbethan had just admitted. If you failed to make the grade at the organ, there was nothing else for you on Optheria? There was no way in which Killashandra would buy Mirbethan's statement that frustrated Optherian musicians would prefer to remain on the planet, even if they had been conditioned to the restriction from birth.

And that tenor had sung with absolute pitch. It'd be a bloody shame to muzzle that voice in preference to an organ, however "perfect" an instrument it might be. Hazardous crystal singing might be as a profession, but it sure beat languishing on Optheria. A sudden thought struck her and, with a fluid stride, she went to the terminal, tapped for Library, and the entry on Ballybran. A much expurgated entry scrolled past, ending with the Code Four restriction. She queried the Files for political science texts and discovered fascinating gaps in that category. So, censorship was applied on Optheria. Not that that ever accomplished its purpose. However, an active censorship was not grounds for charter-smashing, and the Guild had only been requested to discover if the planetary exit restriction was popularly accepted.

Well, she knew one person she could ask—the tenor—if he hadn't gone into hiding after last night's hunt. Killashandra grinned. If she knew tenors . . .

She had breakfasted—the catering unit did offer a substantial breakfast—and dressed by the time Thyrol arrived to inquire if she had rested, and more importantly, if she would like to start the repairs. He tactfully indicated her arm.

"You've apprehended the assailant?"

"Merely a matter of time."

"How many students in this Complex?" she asked amiably as Thyrol led her down the hall to the lift.

"At present, four hundred and thirty."

"That's a lot of suspects to examine."

"No student would *dare* attack an honored guest of the planet."

"On most planets, they'd be the prime suspects."

"My dear Guildmember, the selection process by which this student body is chosen considers all aspects of the applicant's background, training, and ability. They uphold all our traditions."

Killashandra mumbled something suitable. "How many positions are available to graduates?"

"That is not at issue, Guildmember," Thyrol said with mild condescension. "There is no limit to the number of fully trained performers who present compositions for the Optherian organ—"

"But only one may play at a time—"

"There are forty-five organs throughout Optheria—"

"That many? Then why couldn't one of those be substituted—"

"The instrument here at the Complex is the largest, most advanced and absolutely essential for the performance level required by the Summer Festival. Composers from all over the planet compete for the honor and their work has been especially written for the potential of the main instrument. To ask them to perform on a lesser organ defeats the purpose of the Festival."

"I see," Killashandra said although she didn't. However, once she had been admitted through the series of barriers and security positions protecting the damaged organ, she began to appreciate the distinction Thyrol had made.

He had taken her to the rocky basements of the Complex, and then to the impressive and unexpectedly grand Competition Amphitheater which utilized the natural stony bowl on the nether side of the Complex promontory. Some massive early earthfault and a lot of weathering had molded the mount's flank into a perfect semicircle. The Optherians had improved the amphitheater with tiered ranks of individual seating units, facing the shelf on which the organ console stood. This was accessible only from the one entrance through which Thyrol now guided Killashandra. With a sincere and suitable awe, Killashandra looked about her, annoyed that she was gratifying Thyrol's desire to impress a Guildmember even as she was unable to suppress that wonder. She cleared her throat, and the sound, small though it was, echoed faithfully back at her. "The acoustics are incredible," she murmured and, as Thyrol smiled tolerantly, heard her words whispered back. She rolled her eyes and looked about her for an exit from the phenomenal stage.

Thyrol gestured to a portal carved in the solid rock on the far side of the organ console. From his belt pouch he extracted three small rods. With these and his thumb print, he opened the door, the sound reverberating across the empty space. Killashandra slipped in first. As familiar as she was with auditoria of all descriptions, something about this one unnerved her. Something about the seats reminded her of primitive diagnostic chairs which used physical restraints on their occupants, yet she knew that people would cross the Galaxy to attend the Festival.

Lights had come up at their entry and illuminated a large, low-ceilinged chamber. Taking up the floor space in front of the innocuous interlinked cabinets that made up the electronic guts of the Optherian organ were the prominent sealed crates containing the white crystal. Overhead harnesses of color-coded cables formed a ceiling design before they disappeared through conduits to unknown destinations.

Thyrol led the way to the large rectangle containing the shattered remains of the crystal manual.

"How, in the name of all that's holy, did he manange that?" Killashandra demanded after surveying the damage. Some of the smaller crystals had been reduced to thin splinters. In idle wonder she picked up a handful of the shards, letting them trickle through her fingers, ignoring Thyrol's cry of alarm as he grabbed her wrists and pulled her hands back. The tiny cuts inflicted by the scalpel-sharp crystal briefly oozed droplets of blood then closed over while Thyrol watched in fascinated horror.

"As you can see, the merest caress of crystal." She twisted her hands free of Thyrol's unexpectedly strong grasp. "Now," and she spoke more briskly, looking down at the mess in the bottom of the cabinet, "I'll need some tools, some stout fellows, and stouter baskets to remove the debris."

"An extractor?" Thyrol suggested.

"There isn't an extractor built on Ballybran or anywhere else that wouldn't be sliced to ribbons by crystal shards in suction. No, this has to be cleaned in a time honored fashion—by hand."

"But you . . ."

Killashandra drew herself up. "As a Guildmember, I am not averse to performing *necessary* manual tasks." She paused to let Thyrol appreciate the difference. She had done more than enough shard-scrapping on Ballybran to undertake it here on Optheria.

"It is only that security measures—"

"I would, of course, accept your assistance in the interests of security."

Thyrol hastily adjourned to a communication console. "What exactly do you require, Guildmember?"

She gauged the volume of broken crystal in the cabinet. "Three strong men with impervometallic bins of approximately ten-kilo volume, triple-strength face masks, durogloves, fine-wire brushes, and the sort of small, disposable extractor used by archeologists. We have to be sure to glean every particle of crystal dust."

Thyrol's eyes bugged out a bit over the more bizarre items, but he repeated her requirements, and then turned up very stiff indeed when he was subjected to questions by the staff. "Of course, they have to be cleared by Security, but they are to be here immediately, properly geared to assist the Guildmember!" He broke off the connection and, his face blotched with displeasure, turned to Killashandra. "With so much at stake, Guildmember, you can appreciate our wish to protect you and the organ from further depredations. If something should happen to the replacement crystal . . .

Killashandra shrugged. From what she had seen of Optherians, "once bitten, twice shy" described their philosophy. She ran her hand across the instrument nearest her, glancing around at the rest of the anonymous equipment. "This is a more complex device than I'd been led to believe." She turned and presented a politely inquiring expression to Thyrol.

"Well, ah, that is . . ."

"Come now, Thyrol, I am scarcely connected with the subversives."

"No, of course not."

Killashandra diverted Thyrol's attention from realizing that he had covertly admitted the existence of an underground organization by turning, once again, toward the front of the chamber and pointing at the access panel to the keyboard. "Now the actual keyboard is beyond that panel, so the right-hand box houses the stops and voicing circuitry. And is that," she pointed to the largest unit, "the CPU? The induction modulator and mixer must be in that left-hand cabinet."

"You are knowledgeable about organ technology?" Thyrol's expression assumed a wary blankness. For the second time since her arrival, Killashandra perceived intense empathic emanations from an Optherian: this time a strong sense of indefinable apprehension and alarm.

"Not as much about organs as I do about interface techniques, sensory simulators, and synthesizer modulators. Crystal singing requires a considerably wide range of experience with sophisticated electronic equipment, you know."

He obviously didn't or he wouldn't have nodded so readily. Killashandra blessed her foresight in utilizing the sleep-teaching tapes she had copied from the *Athena*'s comprehensive data retrieval system. Her answer reassured Thyrol and the shadow of his fear slowly dissipated.

"Of course there is a double handshake between the program," and he tapped the black case by him, "and the composition memory banks. Composition," and he walked from one to the other, his hand lightly brushing the surfaces, "of course leads directly into the recall excitor stimulator, for that uses the memory symbology of the median individual member of any audience so that a composition is translated into terms which have meaning to the auditors. Naturally the subjective experience of a program for Optherians would differ greatly from the experience a nonhuman would have."

"Of course," Killashandra murmured encouragingly. "And the information from the crystal manual goes?. . ."

Assuming the pose of a pompous lecturer, Thyrol pointed to the various units in flow sequence. "Into the synapse carrier encoder and demodulator multiplexer, both of which feed into the mixer for the sensory transducer terminal network." Beaming with pride, he continued, "While the composition memory bank primarily programs the sensory synthesizer, the feedback loop controls the sensory attenuator for maximum effectiveness."

"I see. Keyboard to CPU, direct interface with manual and synapse carrier encoder, plus the double handshakes." Killashandra hid her shock—this emotion manipulator made the equipment at Fuerte look like preschool toys. Talk about a captive audience! Optherian concertgoers hadn't a chance. The Optherian organ could produce a total emotional override with a conditioned response unequaled anywhere. And a sufficient gauge of the audiences' basic profile could be ascertained by matching ID plates and census data. Killashandra wondered that FSP permitted any of its citizens to visit the planet, much less to expose themselves to full-scale emotional overload at Festival time. "I can see why you'd need many soloists. They'd be emotionally drained after each performance."

"We recognized that problem early on—the performer is shielded from the full effect of the organ in order to retain a degree of objectivity. And, of course, in rehearsal the transducer system is completely bypassed and the signals inserted into a systems analyser. Only the best compositions are played on the full organ system."

"Naturally. Tell me, are the smaller organs amplified in this fashion?"

"The two-manual organs are. We have five of them, the rest are all single manual with relatively primitive synthesizer attentuator and excitor capability."

"Remarkable. Truly remarkable."

Thyrol was not blind to the implied compliment and looked about to smile as the outside door opened to admit the work party. Behind them came three more men, their stance and costume identifying them as security. The work party stopped along the wall while the security trio tramped stolidly down to where Thyrol and Killashandra stood by the sensory feedback transponder.

"Elder Thyrol, Security Leader Blaz needs to know what disposition is to be made of the debris." He saluted, ignoring Killashandra's presence.

"Bury it deep. Preferably encapsulated in some permaform. Sea trench would be ideal," Killashandra answered and was ignored by the security leader, who continued to look for an answer from Thyrol. Abruptly Killashandra's captious temper erupted. She slammed her right hand into the leader's shoulder, forcefully turning him toward her. "Alternatively, insert it in your anal orifice," she said, her voice reasonable and pleasant.

With a wave of astounded gasps sounding in her ear, she made her exit.

Chapter 7

As Killashandra started across the stage to retrace her steps to the Complex, she decided that that was the last place she wanted to go in her state of mind. After all, Trag had chosen her because she could be more diplomatic than Borella. Not that Borella mightn't have handled that security fardle-face with more tact, or effectiveness. However, the Optherians were stuck with her and she with them, and just then she didn't wish to see one more sanctimonious, self-righteous, smug Optherian face.

She strode to the edge of the stage, peered over at the ten-foot drop to the ground, saw the heavy doors at each end of that level and made her decision. She lay at the edge, swung her legs down, gripping the overhang, and let go.

Her knees took the jar and she leaned against the wall for a moment just as she heard the men emerge from the organ room.

"She'll have gone back to the Complex," Thyrol said, breathless with anger. He hurried across the stage, followed by the others. "Simcon, if you have offended the Guildmember, you may have jeopardized far more than you have protected . . ." The heavy door closed off the rest of his reprimand.

Somewhat mollified by Thyrol's attitude and pleased with her timely evasion, Killashandra dusted off her hands and moved toward the clearly marked exit door at the outer edge of the amphitheater. Even the soft sound of the brushing was echoed by the fine acoustics. Grimacing, Killashandra stepped as cautiously and as silently as she could toward the exit. The heavy door had the usual push-bar on the inside, which she depressed, holding her breath lest it be locked from a control point. The bar swung easily out. She opened it only wide enough to permit her egress and it closed with a *thunk* behind her. Its exterior was without handle or knob for reentry and a flange protected it from being forced open—if such a circumstance ever arose on perfect Optheria.

Killashandra now found herself on a long ledge which led to one of the switchback paths she had seen yesterday, though this one was at the rear of the Complex. From that height she had a view of an unpretentious area of the City, to judge by the narrow streets and the small single-story buildings crowded together. Between it and the Complex heights lay a stretch of cultivated plots, each planted with bushy climbing plants and fenced off from its neighbors, and most of them neat. In several, people were busily watering and hoeing in the early morning sunlight. A rural scene served as a restorative to Killashandra's exacerbated nerves.

She began her descent.

As she reached the valley floor, her nose was assailed by the unmistakable aroma of fermenting brew. Delighted, Killashandra followed the odor, squeezing past an old shed, traversing the narrow path between allotments, nodding polite greetings to the gardeners who paused in their labors to regard her with astonishment. Well, she *was* wearing a costume which marked her as alien to Optheria, but surely these people had encountered aliens before. The aroma lured her on. If it tasted half as good as it smelled, it would be an improvement on the Bascum brew. Of course it could *be* Bascum, for breweries were often situated in suburbs where the fumes would not irritate the fastidious.

She reached the dirt road that served as main artery for the settlement, deserted at that morning hour except for some small, peculiar-looking animals basking in the sun. She was aware of being watched, but as that was only to be expected, she continued her inspection of the unprepossessing buildings facing the road. The brew-smell continued to permeate the air but intensified to her right. Common sense indicated that the wide gray structure on the far side of the road some thousand meters away was probably the source. She headed there.

As she walked she heard doors and windows open behind her, marking her passage to her objective. She permitted herself a small smile of amusement. Human nature did not change and anything new and unusual would be marked in a society as dull and repressed as she suspected Optheria's was.

The brew-smell was almost overpowering by the time she reached the gray building. An exhaust fan was extracting the air from the roof, its motor laboring. Although there was no sign or legend on the building to indicate its purpose, Killashandra was not deterred. A locked front door, however, did pose an obstacle. She rapped politely and repeated her knock when it brought no immediate response. Thumping on the door also produced no results, and Killashandra felt determination replace courtesy.

Was brewing illegal in Optheria's largest city? Or could it be brewing without due license? After all, Bascum originated on Optheria and might have a monopoly. To be sure, she hadn't paid much attention to what plants were being so carefully tended in the gardens. Home industry? Thwarting the ever vigilant and repressive Elders?

Quickly she stepped around the building and toward its rear, hoping to find a window. She caught a glimpse of a running juvenile body and heard it raise its voice in warning. So she raced around the corner to find the rear doors folded back on a scene of much industry as men and women supervised the bottling of a brew from an obviously improvised vat. The young messenger took one look at her and fled, ducking down the nearest alley.

"May a thirsty stranger to this planet have a sample of your brew? I'm perishing for lack of a decent glass."

Killashandra could, when she exerted herself, be smoothly charming and ingratiating. She'd played the part often enough. She glanced from one stony expression to the next, holding her smile.

"I'll tell you it was some shock to discover this planet doesn't import anything spiritous or fermented."

"Shuttle got in yesterday," someone in the group said.

"Too early for tourists."

"Those clothes aren't local."

"Nor island."

"I'm not a tourist," Killashandra inserted in the terse comments. "I'm a musician."

"Come to see the organ, have you?" The man's voice was so rich in contempt, disapproval, cynical skepticism, and malicious amusement that Killashandra tried hard to spot him in the hostile group.

"If I can judge by my reception above, that sour lot permits few favors. A body really needs a brew here." Again she fortified her smile with winning charm. And licked dry lips.

Later, in reviewing the scene at her leisure, Killashandra decided that it might have been that unconscious reflex that won her case. The next thing she knew an uncapped bottle was thrust at her. She reached to her belt pouch for the Optherian coins she had acquired on the *Athena* but was curtly told to leave off. Money didn't buy their brew.

Although some had turned back to their job, most watched while she took her first sip. It was rich despite its clandestine manufacture, slightly cool, undoubtedly improved by a proper chilling but superior to the Bascum and almost on a par with Yarran.

"Your brewmaster wouldn't happen to be of Yarran origin?" she asked.

"What do you know of Yarra?" Once again the question was posed anonymously though Killashandra thought the speaker was on her left, near the vat.

"They make the best beer in the Federated Sentient Planets. Yarran brewmasters have the best reputations in the Galaxy."

A rumble of approval greeted this. She could feel the tension ease though the work continued at the same swift pace. Above the rattle of bottles, and the noise of crating the full containers, Killashandra heard a gasping wheeze to her right, on the roadway, and then a dilapidated vehicle, its sides scarred and rusting, pulled up to the open door.

Immediately crates were loaded into it, Killashandra helping, for she'd finished her bottle and wondered how she could wheedle another, others, from them. Thirst properly quenched, she'd find it easier to deal with the reproaches of Thyrol and the others. No sooner had the load bed been filled than the vehicle moved off and another, equally disreputable, slid into its place. Of course this patently unauthorized operation proved conclusively to Killashandra that the population of Optheria had not all stagnated. But how much of a minority did they constitute? And did any of them actually wish to leave Optheria? Some people enjoy thwarting their elected/established/appointed governments out of perversity rather than disloyalty or dislike.

When the third transport had been loaded, only a few crates remained. And the vat and its attendant paraphernalia had been dismantled and reassembled in different form entirely. Killashandra gave the brewers full marks for ingenuity.

"You expect a search?"

"Oh yes. Can't mask brewing completely, you know," said a sun-wrinkled little man with a twinkle in his eye. He offered Killashandra a second bottle, gesturing to the loaded vehicle in explanation of his generosity.

As she inadvertently glanced in the same direction, Killashandra noticed that his workers, each laden with a crate, were disappearing up and down the street and into the alleys. Just audible was an odd siren. He cocked his head at the sound and grinned.

"I'd take that with me, were I you. Won't help you to be found in my disreputable company."

"You'll be making another batch soon?" Killashandra asked wistfully.

"Now *that* I couldn't say." He winked. The siren became more insistent and louder. He began to fold over the doors.

"What's the quickest way back to the City?"

"Over two ranks and then to your left." He closed the last lap of the door behind him and she heard the firm click of the lock.

The vehicle with the siren was moving at a good clip so Killashandra made rapid progress in the direction the brewer had indicated. She had just reached the next parallel road when she heard the sound of air brakes engaging and considerable shouting. She ducked around the corner and was on another deserted block. When she heard the pounding of booted feet, she realized that she might not have time to explain her possession of the illegally brewed beer if she was caught out on the streets.

The first door she approached was locked and her quick rap met with no response. The second door was jerked open just as she got to it. She needed no urging to step into the sanctuary. Indeed, not a moment too soon for the searchers came pounding around the corner and stormed past the door.

"That was a bit foolish, if you ask me," said the woman beside her in a hoarse accusation. "You may be an alien but that

wouldn't matter to *them* did they apprehend you down here."
She gestured for Killashandra to follow her to the rear of the little
house. "You must have some thirst to go roaming about Gartertown in search of a quenching. There are places which legally
serve drink, you know."

"I didn't, but if you could tell me—"

"Not that the hours you can drink are that convenient, and our
brew's superior to anything out of the Bascum. The water, you
know! This way."

Killashandra paused because a crate of the illegal bottling was
sitting in the middle of the floor of the rear room, right by a section
of flooring which had been removed.

"Give me a hand, would you? They might do a house-to-house
if they're feeling particularly officious."

Killashandra willingly complied and, when the crate was
stored, the section replaced, the hiding place was indistin-
guishable.

"Don't like to rush a body's enjoyment of a brew, but . . ."

Killashandra would also have preferred to savor the second bottle, but she downed it in three long swallows. The woman took
the empty and chucked it toward the disposal. With a loud *crunch*
the evidence was disposed of. Killashandra drew her fingers down
the corners of her mouth, and then belched yeastily.

The woman took a position by her door, ear to the panel, listening intently. She jumped back just as the door swung in wide
enough to admit a tall figure.

"They were recalled," the man said. "And there's some sort of
search going on in the City—" He broke off then because he had
turned and caught sight of Killashandra standing in the doorway.

She was as motionless with surprise as he for she recognized
him, by garb and stance, as the young man from the infirmary
corridor. He recovered first while Killashandra was considering
the advisability of dissembling.

"You're making this far too easy," he said cryptically, striding
up to her. Surprised, she saw only his fist before a stunning blackness overcame her.

She roused the first time, aware of a stuffy atmosphere, the
soreness of her jaw, and that her hands and feet were tied. She

groaned, and before she could open her eyes, she felt a sudden pressure on her arm and her senses reeled once more back into unconsciousness.

She was still tied when she woke the second time, with an awful taste in her mouth and the tang of salt air in her nostrils. She could hear the hiss of wind and the slap of water not far from her ears. Cautiously she opened her eyes a slit. She was on a boat, all right, in an upper berth in a small cabin. She was aware of another presence in the room but dared not signal her consciousness by sound or movement. Her jaw still ached though not, she thought, as much as on her previous awakening. Whatever drug they had given her was compounded with a muscle relaxant, for she felt exceedingly limp. So why did they bother to keep her bound?

She heard footsteps approaching the cabin and controlled her breathing to the slow regularity of the sleeper just as an outer hatch was flung open. Spray beaded her face. A warm spray so that her muscles did not betray her.

"No sign?"

"No. See for yourself. Hasn't moved a muscle. You didn't give her too much, did you? Those singers have different metabolisms."

The inquisitor snorted. "Not that different, no matter what she said about alcoholic intake." Amusement rippled in his voice as he approached the bed. Killashandra forced herself to remain limp though anger began to boil away the medically induced tranquillity as she reacted to the fact that she, a member of the Heptite Guild, a crystal singer, had been kidnapped. On the other hand, her kidnapping seemed to indicate that not everyone was content to remain on Optheria. Or did it?

Strong fingers gripped her chin, the thumb pressing painfully on the bruise for a moment, before the fingers slid to the pulsebeat in her throat. She kept her neck muscles lax to permit this handling. Feigning unconsciousness might result in unguarded explanations being exchanged over her inert body. And she needed some before she made her move.

"That was some crack you fetched her, Lars Dahl. She won't appreciate the bruise."

"She'll have too much on her mind to worry about something so minor."

"Are you sure this scheme is going to work, Lars?"

"It's the first break we've had, Prale. The Elders won't be able to fix the organ without a crystal singer. And they've got to. So they must apply again to the Heptite Guild to replace this one, and that will require explanations, and that will bring FSP investigators to this planet. And there's *our* chance to make the injustice known."

What about the injustice you just did me? Killashandra wanted to shout. Instead she twitched with anger. And gave herself away.

"She's coming round. Hand me the syringe."

Killashandra opened her eyes, about to argue for her freedom when she felt the pressure that brooked no argument.

Her final awakening was not at all what she had been expecting. A balmy breeze rippled across her body. Her hands were untied and she was no longer on a comfortable surface. Her mouth tasted more vile than ever, and her head ached. She controlled herself once more, trying to sort out the sounds that reached her ears. Wind soughing. Okay. A rolling noise? Ocean waves breaking on shore line not far away. The smells that accosted her nostrils were as varied as the wind and wave, subtle musty floral fragrances, rotten vegetation, dry sand, fish, and other smells which she'd identify later. Of human noises or presences she had no input.

She opened her eyes a fraction and it was dark. Encouraged, she widened her vision. She was lying on her back on a woven mat. Sand had blown onto it, gritty against her bare skin, under her head. Overhead, trees bent their fronds, one sweeping against her shoulder in a gentle caress. Cautiously she lifted her torso, propping herself up on one elbow. She was no more than ten meters from the ocean, but the high-tide mark was safely between her and the sea, to judge by the debris pushed into an uneven line along the sand.

Islanders? What had Ampris said about the islanders? That they'd had to be disciplined out of autonomous notions? And the young man of the corridor who had assailed her. He had been suntanned. That was why his skin was so dark in comparison to the other onlookers.

Killashandra looked around her for any sign of human habitation, knowing that there wouldn't be any. She had been abandoned on the island. Kidnapped and abandoned. She got up, absently brushing the sand off her as she swung about, fighting her conflicting emotions. Kidnapped and abandoned! So much for the prestige of the Heptite Guild on these backward planets. So much for another of Lanzecki's off-world assignments!

Why hadn't she left a message for Corish?

Chapter 8

Killashandra grimaced as she crossed off yet another week on the immense tree under which she had erected her shelter.

She sheathed the knife again and involuntarily scanned the horizon in all directions, for her polly tree dominated the one elevation on the island. Once again she saw distant sails to the northeast, the orange of the triangles brilliant against the sky.

"May their masts snap in a squall and their bodies rot in the briny deep!" she muttered and then kicked at the thick trunk of the tree. "Why don't you ever fish in *my* lagoon?"

Morning and night she threw in her hook and line and was rewarded by wriggling fish. Some she had learned to throw back, for their flesh was either inedibly tough or tasteless. The small yellowbacks were the sweetest and seemed to throw themselves with selfless sacrifice on her hook.

The bronzed young man had not stranded her without equipment. When dawn had come on that bleak first day, she had discovered hatchet, knife, hooks, line, net, emergency rations in vacuum pack, and an illustrated pamphlet on the resources of the ubiquitous polly tree. She had cast that contemptuously to one side until boredom set in three days later.

For someone who had been as active as Killashandra, enforced idleness was almost a crippling punishment. To pass the time she had retrieved the pamphlet and read it through, then decided to see if she could make something out of this so-universal plant. She had already noticed that many of the tree's multiple trunks had had satellite trunks removed at an early age. Her manual said that these were cut for the tender heart or the soft pith, both

89

nutritious. Was the locals' interference with "nature" one of the reasons for their discipline by the mainland?

And how far away was that mainland? She couldn't even hazard a guess as to how long she had been unconscious. More than a day, at the least. She wished she'd studied the geography of Optheria more closely, for she couldn't even guess at the location of her island on the planet's surface. In her first days, she had prowled the island's perimeter ceaselessly, for there were neighboring ones tantalizingly visible even though they were also small. Hers at least boasted a bubbling spring that flowed from its rocky source mid-island into the lagoon. And, if she could trust her judgment, hers was the largest in the cluster.

Before she immersed herself in polly tree studies, she had swum to the nearest of the group. Plenty of polly trees but no water. And beyond that islet more were scattered in careless abundance across the clear aquamarine sea—some large enough to support only a single tuft of polly trees. So she had returned to her island, the best of a bad lot.

Working with her hands and for a varied diet did not prevent Killashandra from endless speculations about her situation. She had been kidnapped for a purpose—to force an investigation of Optherian restrictions. The FSP, much less her own Guild, would not tolerate such an outrage. *If*—and here her brief knowledge of the Optherians let her down—the Optherians admitted to FSP and the Heptite Guild that she *had* been abducted.

Still, the Elders needed an operative organ by the time of the Summer Festival, and to do that they needed a crystal singer to make the installation. The crystal they had, but surely they wouldn't attempt such a delicate job. Well, it wasn't *that* delicate, Killashandra knew, but the crystal would prove difficult if not handled properly. So, grant that the Optherians would be searching for her, would they think to search on the islands? Would the islanders be in contact with the Ruling Elders about the terms of her ransom? If so, would the extortion be successful?

Probably not, Killashandra thought, until the Ruling Elders had abandoned any hope of finding her within the next two months. Of course, that could throw their timetable off. It would take nearly three months for a replacement Guild Member to reach Optheria, even if the Optherians admitted the loss of the one already dispatched to them. On her own part, she'd be stark raving lunatic if she was left on this island for several months. And if the Optherians acquired another singer to install their wretched white crystal, that didn't mean that they'd continue their efforts to find *her!*

After much deliberation, silent as well as vocal, Killashandra decided that the smart thing to do was rescue herself. Her kidnapper had overlooked a few small points, the most important of which was that she happened to be a very strong swimmer with lungs well developed from singing opera and crystal. Physically, too, she was immensely fit. She could swim from island to island until she found one that was inhabited, one from which she could be rescued. Unless all the islanders were in on this insidious kidnap scheme.

The hazards that she must overcome were only two: lack of water was one, but she felt that she could refresh herself sufficiently from the polly fruit—the tree flourished on all the islands she could see. Too, the larger denizens of the sea constituted a real problem. Some of them, cruising beyond her lagoon, looked deadly dangerous, with their pointed, toothy snouts, or their many wire-fine tentacles which seemed to have an affinity for the same yellowback fish she favored. She had spent enough time watching them to know that they generally fed at dawn or dusk. So, if she made her crossings at midday, when they were dormant, she thought she had a fairly good chance to avoid adding herself to their diet.

Three weeks on the island was long enough! She had a few of the emergency food packets left and they would be unharmed by a long immersion.

Following the directions in her useful little pamphlet, she had made several sturdy lengths of rope from the coarse fiber of the polly tree, with which she could secure the hatchet to her body. Her original clothing was down to shreds which she sewed with lengths of the tough stem into a halter and a loin cloth. By then she had become as tan as her abductor and was forced to use some of the oilier fishes to grease her hide for protection. She would coat herself thoroughly before each leg of her swim to freedom.

Having made her decision, Killashandra implemented it the next day at noon, swimming to her first destination in less than an hour's time. She rested while she made up her mind which island of the seven visible would be next. She found herself constantly returning to the one farthest north. Well, once there, none were far away if she decided she'd overshot the right line to take.

She made that island by mid-afternoon, dragging herself up onto the narrow shore, exhausted. Then she discovered some of the weak points in her plans: there weren't many ripe polly fruits on the island; and fish wouldn't bite on her hook that evening.

Because she found too few fruits, she was exceedingly thirsty by morning and chose her next point of call by the polly population. The channel between was dark blue, deep water, and twice she was startled by dimly seen large shapes moving beneath her. Both times she floated face down, arms and legs motionless, until the danger summoned by her flailing limbs had passed.

She rested on this fourth island all the rest of that day and the next one, replenishing her dehydrated tissues and trying to catch an oily fish. To her dismay, she could only attract the yellowbacks. Eventually she had enough of them to provide some oil for her raddled skin.

On her voyage to the fifth island, a fair sized one, she had her worst fright. Despite the sun's being at high noon, she found herself in the midst of a school of tiny fish that was being harvested by several mammoth denizens. At one point she was briefly stranded on a creature's flank when it unexpectedly surfaced under her. She didn't know whether to swim furiously for the distant shore or lie motionless, but before she could make a decision the immense body swirled its torpedo tail in the air and sounded. Killashandra was pulled under by the fierce turbulence of its passage, and she swallowed a good deal more water than she liked before she returned to the surface.

As soon as she clambered up on the fifth island, she headed for the nearest ripe polly fruit only to discover that she had lost her hatchet, the last packets of emergency rations, and the fish hooks. She slaked her thirst on overripe polly fruit, ignoring the rank taste for the sake of the moisture. That need attended to, she gathered up enough dry fronds to cushion her body, and went to sleep.

She woke sometime in the night, thirsting for more of the overripe fruit which she hunted in the dark, cursing as she tripped over debris and fell into bushes, staggering about in her search until she had to admit to herself that her behavior was somewhat bizarre. About the same time she realized that she was drunk! The innocent polly fruit had been fermenting! Given her Ballybran adaptation, the state could only have been allowed by her weakened constitution. Giggling, she lay down on the ground, impervious to sand or discomfort and fell into a second drunken sleep.

Much the worse for her various excesses, Killashandra awoke with a ghastly headache and a terrible need for water. Number five was a much larger island than her other way stops and she was searching so diligently to relieve her thirst that she almost passed the little canoe without its registering on her consciousness.

It was only a small canoe, pulled up beyond the high tide mark, a paddle angling from the narrow prow. At another time and without her urgent need, Killashandra would not have ventured out on the open sea in such a flimsy craft. But someone had already brought it from wherever they came so it could as easily convey her elsewhere, too. Her need for water diminished by this happy discovery, Killashandra climbed the nearest polly tree and, hanging precariously to the ridged trunk, managed to saw through several stems with her short knife blade.

She didn't waste time then, but threw the fruit into the small craft, slid it into the gentle waves, and paddled down the coast as fast as she could, just in case the owner should return and demand the return of his canoe.

While she no longer needed to wait until noon to cross to the next island in her northern course, Killashandra's previous day's fright made her cautious. She keenly felt the loss of her hatchet. But good fortune continued to surprise her for, as she paddled around a narrow headland, she spotted the unmistakable sign of a small stream draining into the sea. She could even paddle a short way up its mouth and did so, pausing to scoop up a handful of sweet water before she jumped out of the canoe and pulled it out of sight under the bushes. Then she lay down by the water and drank until she was completely sated.

By evening, just before the sun suddenly settled below the horizon in the manner characteristic of tropical latitudes, she stood out on the headland, deciding which of the island masses she would attempt to reach the next day. The nearest ones were large, by comparison, but the distant smudge lay long against the horizon. The water lapped seductively over her toes and she decided that she had fooled around with the minor stuff long enough. With the canoe, a fair start in the morning, and plenty of fruit in her little craft, she could certainly make the big island, however distant.

She had the foresight to weave herself a sun hat, with a fishtail down her back to prevent sunstroke, for she wouldn't have the cooling water about her as she had while swimming. She had no experience with currents or riptides, nor had she considered the possibility of sudden squalls interrupting her journey. Those she encountered halfway across the deep blue stretch of sea to the large island.

She was so busy trying to correct her course while the current pulled her steadily south that she was unaware of the squall until it pelted against her sunburned back. The next thing she knew she was waist deep in water. How the canoe stayed afloat at all, she didn't know. Bailing was a futile exercise but it was the only remedy she had. Then suddenly she felt the canoe sinking with her and, in a panic lest she be pulled down, she swam clear, and had no way to resist the insidious pull of the current.

Once again the stubborn survival instinct came to Killashandra's aid, and wisely she ceased struggling against the current and the run of the waves, and concentrated on keeping her head above water. She was still thrashing her arms when her legs grated against a hard surface. She crawled out of the water and a few more meters from the pounding surf before oblivion overcame her.

Familiar sounds and familiar smells penetrated her fatigue and allowed her to enjoy the pangs of thirst and hunger once again. Awareness of her surroundings gradually increased and she roused to the sound of human voices raised in a happy clamor somewhere nearby. She sat up and found herself on one end of a wide curving beach of incredible beauty, on a harbor sheltering a variety of shipping. A large settlement dominated the center of the harbor, with commercial buildings at the center gradually giving way to residences and a broad promenade that paralleled the beach before retreating into the polly plantations.

For a long time Killashandra could only sit and stare at the scene, rendered witless by her great good fortune. And then not at all sure what her next step should be. To arrive, announcing her rank and title, demanding transport back to the City? How many people had been privy to her abduction? An island weapon had made the first assault against her. She had better go cautiously. She had better act circumspectly.

Yes, indeed she should, she realized as she stood up and found herself without a shred of clothing on her body. Nudity might not be appreciated here. She was too far away to notice how much or how little clothing the happy group on her side of the bay was wearing. So, she would get close enough to discover.

She did that with little trouble, and also discovered abandoned clothing, shirts and long, full skirts of decoratively painted polly fiber as well as undecorated underskirts. So she took several of those, picking from different piles, and a conservatively marked shirt and dressed herself. She also filched several packets of food, spoiling someone's picnic lunch but filling the void in her belly. No footwear had been left on the beach, so she concluded that bare feet would not be distinctive and her soles were sufficiently callused now not to trouble her. The off-white of her underskirts set off the fine brown of her tanned skin.

She tucked her knife under the waistband, then set off on the well-marked path toward the main settlement.

Chapter 9

What Killashandra required most was a credit outlet. She would need more clothing—a proper, decorated overdress—if she was to blend in with the islanders. As well, she needed some sort of accommodation and enough credit to get her back to the mainland or wherever the City was located.

None of the commercial buildings facing the harbor appeared to have credit outlets, though all had intake units. One of them had to, or this planet was more backward than she'd previously thought. Every inhabited planet utilized the standard credit facilities.

She had a bit of a fright, too, while she was making her initial reconnaissance—the sight of herself in a reflective surface. Sun had streaked the top layer of her dark hair almost blonde, had bleached her eyebrows to nonexistence. This, plus the deep brown of her tan, altered her appearance so that she had almost not recognized herself. The whites and the intense green of her eyes with the filtering lenses were emphasized by the tan and dominated her face. The exertions of the last few days had thinned all the flesh which she had acquired with easy living on the voyage. She was as gaunt as if she'd been in the Crystal Ranges for weeks. Furthermore she felt like she had. Why was it, when she was tired, she still felt the crystal surging through her bones?

There was only one other building on the waterfront, set off a little from the others, looking rather more prosperous. A factor's residence? She made for it, having little choice, ignoring the covert glances of the few pedestrians. Was the community so small that any stranger was remarkable? Or was it indeed her lack of the proper attire that occasioned their scrutiny?

She recognized the building's function as soon as she climbed the short flight of stairs to the wide verandah which surrounded all four sides. The smell of stale beer and spirits was manifest, as well as a burned-vegetable odor, pungent and not altogether unpleasant. It was always good to know where the brew was served.

The main room of the tavern was empty and dark and, despite the sea breezes wafting through, stank of a long night's drinking. Chairs were neatly piled on the tables, the floor had been swept and glistened wetly to one side, where mop and pail propped open a door. She gave the room a sweeping glance, which stopped at the reassuring shape of a credit outlet.

Hoping she could make her transaction in private, she glided across the floor on her bare feet. Slipping her i.d. under the visiplate, she tapped out a modest credit demand. The sound of the outlet's whirring and burping was unnaturally loud in the deserted room. She grabbed the credit notes, compressing them quickly into a wad in one hand while she tapped out the security code that would erase the transaction from all but the central credit facility on the planet.

"Ya wanted something?" An unshaven face peered around the half-open door.

"I got it," Killashandra said, ducking her head and making a speedy exit before she could be detained.

While this island town had more in the way of mercantile establishments that catered to fishermen and planters, she had marked the soft goods store in her search for the credit outlet. It was unoccupied and automated so that she didn't need to manufacture explanations to a salesperson. It only struck her then that in none of the shops on the waterfront had she seen human attendants. She shrugged it off as another island oddity. She bought two changes of the brightly decorated, and rather charmingly patterned, outer garments, additional underskirts—for custom apparently demanded a plethora of female skirts—sandals of plaited polly tree fiber, a matching belt and pouch, and a carisak of a similar manufacture. She also got some toilet articles and a tube of moisturizing cream for her dry skin.

The little shop boasted a rather archaic information unit, a service Killashandra needed almost as badly as credit. She dialed first for hostel information and was somewhat daunted by the fact that all the listed facilities were closed until the Season. Well, she'd slept on island beaches for nearly four weeks and come to no harm. She queried about eating places and found that these also were closed until the Season. Irritated because she didn't wish to spend time gathering food in a large settlement, she tapped out a request for transport facilities.

Quite an astonishing variety of ships were available for charter: for fishing, pleasure cruising, and underwater assisted explorations "with requisite official permits. Travel documents are required for passengers or cargo. Apply Harbor Master."

"Which I can't do until I know more about this place," Killashandra muttered as a stately woman entered the premises. "And how many in sympathy with my kidnappers."

"Did you find all you needed?" the woman said in a liquidly melodic voice, her large and expressive brown eyes showing concern.

"Yes, yes, I did," Killashandra said, surprised into a nervous response.

"I'm so glad. We don't have much here yet. No call, with everyone making their own, and the Season not started." She tilted her head, her long thick braid falling over her shoulder. Her fingers moved to check the position of the blossom twisted into the end of the plait. Her smile was luminous. "You've not been here before?" The question was asked in such a gentle voice that it was almost a statement of fact and not an intrusion on Privacy.

"I just came in from one of the outer islands."

"That's lonely." The woman nodded gently.

"Lost my canoe in that squall," Killashandra said and began to embroider slightly. "Came ashore with nothing to my name but my i.d." She flashed her left wrist at the woman who nodded once again.

"If you're hungry, I've fresh fish and greens, and there's whiteroot to make a good fry."

"No, I couldn't," Killashandra began, even as her mouth was watering. When the woman tilted her head again, a broad smile spreading across her serene features, Killashandra added, "But I certainly would appreciate it."

"My name is Keralaw. My man is mate on the *Crescent Moon*, been gone four weeks and I do miss company." She rolled her eyes slightly, her grin twisting upward another fraction of an inch so that Killashandra knew very well what Keralaw missed.

"My name is Carrigana." Killashandra suppressed her amusement; the former owner of that name would be livid at her presumption.

Keralaw led her to the back of the shop, through the storage section to the living quarters in the rear: a small catering area, a small toilet room, and a large living room that was open on three sides, screened against the depredations of insects. The furnishings consisted of low tables, many pillows, and hammocks secured to bolts in the ceiling. Of the modern accoutrements there was only a small screen, blank, with a fine coating of dust and a very primitive terminal. On the one solid wall hung a variety of spears, their barbed heads differing in design and weight, a small stringed instrument, a hand drum that looked well used, four wooden pipes of different lengths and circumferences, and an ancient tambourine, its trailing ribbons sun-faded to shades of gray and beige.

Keralaw led her through this room, out the screened door to the rear and to a stone hearth. Checking the position of the sun over her shoulder, Keralaw altered the arrangement of a mirror and a bright metal sheet to her satisfaction and began to arrange the fish and white root on the sheet.

"Won't be long with the sun right in position. Beer or juice?"

"Island brewed?"

"Best there is." Keralaw's smile was proud. She went to the heavy bushes growing beyond the solar hearth and, pushing them aside, disclosed a dull gray container a meter high and half that wide. Lifting its heavy insulated lid, she extracted two beaded bottles.

"Been a long time dry," Killashandra said, receiving her chilled bottle with considerable anticipation. She flipped back the stopper and took a swallow. "*Whhhhoooee* but it's good." And it was—the equal of a Yarran! But Killashandra stopped herself from making that comparison aloud just in time, smiling instead at Keralaw.

Already the sun was broiling their lunch and the smell was a suitable accompaniment to the taste of the cool beer. Killashandra began to relax. Keralaw tossed the greens into a wooden bowl, slipped two wooden platters to the hearth side, along with two-tined forks and knives with intricately carved handles accentuating the natural dark grain of the wood, and divided the now completed meal.

"That was what I needed most," Killashandra said, closing her eyes in a sincere appreciation for the simple but satisfying meal. "I've been living too long off the polly tree!"

Keralaw chuckled fruitily. "You and your man farming? Or are you fishing for the gray?"

Killashandra hesitated, wondering what cover story wouldn't become an embarrassment later. She also felt a curious reluctance to mislead Keralaw.

Keralaw reached over and touched Killashandra's forearm, just the barest touch, her mobile face suddenly expressionless.

"Don't need to tell me, woman. I been out in the islands and I know what can happen to humans out there. Sometimes the credit ain't worth the agony getting it. I won't pry." Her smile returned. "Not my place to, anyhow. You picked a good day to land on Angel Island. Schooner's making port this evening!"

"It is?" Killashandra picked up the cue to wax enthusiastic.

Keralaw nodded, pleased to surprise. "Beach barbecue and a keg of beer for sure! That's why the harbor's so deserted." She chuckled again, an earthy rich laugh. "Even the little ones are out foraging."

"Everyone contributes to the barbecue?"

Keralaw nodded, her smile wide with anticipation. "How well do you weave polly?" she asked, tilting her head sideways. When Killashandra groaned, Keralaw looked sympathetic. "Well, perhaps you cut and strip while I weave. Chore goes fast in company."

With fluid gestures, she collected a hatchet hanging from a nail under the eaves and a large cariall, which she handed to Killashandra. With a grin and a jerk of her head, she indicated the way.

The expedition suited Killashandra in many ways: Keralaw

could supply her far more information than any terminal, however well programmed, and the little one in Keralaw's shop was intended for tourists and had limited memory. Killashandra could doubtless discover just how closely the Harbor Master stuck to the letter of the law in granting travel permits. Just like the Optherians to need to know who went where and when. Though why they bothered, since their citizens weren't allowed *off* the planet, Killashandra couldn't see. She also needed more general information about the islanders and their customs if she was going to pass as one that evening.

For her purposes, the barbecue couldn't have come at a better time; with everyone relaxed by a full belly and plenty of beer, she could discover more about the islanders' politics and, just possibly, something about her abduction.

By the time they had returned from the polly plantation that evening, both laden with platters and baskets woven at speed by Keralaw's deft hands, Killashandra knew a great deal more about island life, and had tremendous respect for it.

The easygoing gentleness of the style would be abhorrent to the persnickety mainlanders. In the early days of their subjugation of the islanders, the mainlanders had even tried to prohibit the use of the polly tree in their strict adherence to the letter of their Charter. The polly tree itself worked against that restriction, for it grew with such rapidity and profusion that pruning back the plantations was absolutely essential. The casual islander habit of cutting as needed to provide the essentials for daily life prevented overgrowth. The vigorous polly tree would take root on even a square meter of soil, which accounted for its proliferation in the islands.

Killashandra had been hard pressed to cut and strip enough polly fronds to keep up with Keralaw's agile weaving but the crystal singer learned as she watched and, to support her adopted identity, wove a few baskets herself. The manufacture, which seemed to be so easy when one watched an adept, took considerable manual strength and dexterity, which, fortunately, Killashandra possessed. Seeing the clever way in which Keralaw finished off her mats and baskets taught Killashandra the necessary final touches that spoke of long practice.

As they passed a small freshwater lake on their way back, Keralaw suddenly dropped her burden, shucked her clothing, and dashed into the water. Killashandra was quick to follow. Nudity was not, then, a problem. And the soft water was refreshing after the concentrated work of the day.

The tantalizing aroma of roasting meat reached them as they neared Keralaw's dwelling. She rolled her eyes and smacked her lips appreciatively.

"Mandoll's the cook!" Keralaw said with satisfaction. "I can smell his seasoning anywhere in the islands. Porson sure had better catch him a smacker to go with it. Nothing better than long beef and smacker. Oho, but we eat good tonight!" She rolled her eyes again in anticipation. "We'll drop these off," and she swung the tangle of baskets on their string, "and then we get us pretty. A barbecue night's a *good* night for Angel Island!" And she winked broadly at Killashandra, who laughed.

Two barbecue pits had been dug on the beach front. In one a very long animal carcass was slowly turning over the sizzling coals. Four men were good-naturedly attempting to raise a massive fish onto the spit braces, urging each other to greater effort while the onlooking women taunted them for weakness.

Prominently centered on the beach was a long low table, already being laid with garlands of flowers, baskets of fruit and other delicacies which Killashandra couldn't identify. An immensely plump woman, with a most luxuriant growth of hair spilling down to her knees, greeted Keralaw with delight, chattering about the quantity and quality of the baskets and plates, and then fell silent, cocking her head inquiringly at Killashandra.

"Here is Carrigana, Ballala," Keralaw said, taking Killashandra's arm. "In from the outer islands. She wove with me."

"You picked the right time to come," Ballala said approvingly. "We have some good barbecue tonight. Long beef *and* a smacker!"

Suddenly a siren split the air with a hoot that occasioned loud cheers from everyone on the beach.

"Schooner's on the last tack. Be here right quick," Keralaw said and then began smoothing her arm in an absent minded way.

Killashandra cast it a quick look—all the fine hair was standing up. Killashandra rubbed her own brown arms to deflect comment. But Keralaw apparently did not notice the phenomenon.

"Come, Carrigana, we must get pretty now."

Getting pretty meant decorating their hair with the scented flowers that grew on the low bushes under ancient polly trees. There seemed to be a community of possessions on Angel Island, for Keralaw visited several back gardens to find the colors she wanted for her own long tresses. And she had decided that only the tiny cream flowers would do as a garland for Killashandra's head, since Killa's hair was not long enough to braid. Keralaw offered to trim the dried ends, tutting over the exigencies that had deprived Killashandra of so many amenities on her distant island.

Then Keralaw decided that they'd have time to make some wreaths of the fragrant blossoms. Fortunately Killashandra was able to delay starting a wreath until she saw how Keralaw began hers and then the two twisted and tucked the stems in comfortable silence. Eventually, festive sounds drifted back to their ears from the beach and then cheering broke out.

"Schooner's in," Keralaw cried, jumping to her feet, her braids bouncing their floral tips against her waist. She grabbed Killashandra's hand, jerking her up. "Pick yourself a handsome one, Carrigana. Of course, they're all handsome on the schooner," she said with an earthy giggle. "And away in the morning with no harm done, coming or going."

Killashandra followed willingly, clutching her wreaths in her hand, hoping her crude manufacture would not break apart from the jostling.

There could be few sights more impressive than a schooner sailing effortlessly into the beautiful azure waters of a harbor under an evening sky rich with sun-tinged clouds, while colorfully dressed and beflowered people lined the pier and the beach. The odors of a delicious meal permeated the air and all present were happily anticipating an evening spent in joyful pursuits— of all kinds. Killashandra had no wish to resist the enticements so lavishly available and she cheered as hard as the rest of the inhabitants of Angel Island as sailors on the yard arms reefed the sails while the schooner glided toward the pier, and the shoremen waited to secure the lines tossed to them. She jumped about, yelling at the top of her lungs, as everyone else was doing, waggling at arm's length her wreaths, as seemed to be the custom.

Then, suddenly, out of the crowd two men stood apart, grinning

103

at the enthusiastic display but not joining in. Killashandra gasped, clutched the wreaths close to her face and stared, incredulous.

Corish von Mittelstern of the Beta Jungische system, purportedly in search of his uncle, was standing next to the bronzed young man of the corridor who had abducted and abandoned her on a minuscule island in the middle of nowhere!

Even as she reacted to their presence, she saw Corish was glancing about the crowd. Before she could duck, his gaze touched her face . . . and passed on without a blink of recognition.

Chapter 10

Shock rooted Killashandra in the sand. She ignored the surge of the islanders toward the pier, the vanguard already throwing their wreaths about the disembarking sailors. Fury that Corish didn't recognize her—and relief that he didn't—warred in her. To judge by his deep tan, Corish had been in the islands as long as she had. He looked comfortable in the shorts and sleeveless half-vest that the island men preferred, though his was modestly decorated. Not so the one Lars Dahl wore, which was thick with many-hued embroidery.

Common sense quickly tempered her initial strong reactions. She hadn't recognized herself in the mirror, why would Corish or Lars Dahl? Further, neither man could logically have expected to see Killashandra Ree on the beachfront at Angel Island. She relaxed from the tense half-poised stance she had assumed.

"Come on, you'll want to catch a good one," Keralaw said, tugging Killashandra by the sleeve. She paused, seeing the objects of Killashandra's riveted attention. "Lars Dahl is very attractive, isn't he? But he's committed to the Music Conservatory—the first Angel Islander to be admitted!"

"The other one?" Killashandra stood fast, though Keralaw plucked urgently at her to move.

"Him? He's been around the last few weeks. A pleasant enough man but . . ." Keralaw shrugged diffidently. "Come on, now, Carrigana, I want a live one!"

Now Killashandra permitted herself to be drawn, holding her breath as first Corish then Lars Dahl looked toward them. When there was still no sign of recognition from either man, Killashandra grinned, then waggled her fingers at them and brandished the wreaths invitingly. Lars Dahl smiled back, gesturing a good-humored rejection of her offer before he renewed his conversation with Corish.

As Corish did not turn away, she swung her hips in her best imitation of a seductress, and cast one last longing look over her shoulder before Keralaw was hauling her through the crowd toward the approaching sailors.

Joyfully Keralaw deposited her garlands on a lean, brown-black man and, with a half-reproachful, half-apologetic glance at Carrigana, accompanied him toward a distant section of the beach in the gathering dusk. Other couples had the same idea while many more made for the barbecue area and the kegs of beer, and jugs of fermented polly fruit in jackets of woven polly fronds which were now being circulated. Many of the islanders had paired off, and the disappointed drifted back to the imminent feast, all still in the best of good spirits.

"What about garlanding me?" a male voice grated in her ear.

Killashandra turned her head toward the speaker, only far enough to catch the stench of his breath, before she deftly avoided his importunities with a giggle, slipping past a group of women. He paused there and someone less fastidious crowned him. Killashandra continued to glide forward and toward the shadows cast by the polly trees growing above the high tide line. The joyous sensuality of the islanders amused and frustrated her. Crystal resonance was slowly abating, and consequently her body's normal appetites were returning.

Corish and Lars Dahl were still deep in conversation at the water's edge. She was level with them now, though shadowed from their notice and she could observe unobtrusively. She sank to the warm sand, the unused garlands fragrant in her loose grip. Ignoring the happy roistering at the barbecue pits, she concentrated on the two men.

What could be of such fascination to them in the midst of all this jollity? Her original instinct about Corish had been correct: he was an FSP operative. Unless she was fooling herself and his association with the impertinent Lars Dahl was a coincidence. She doubted that vigorously. Did Corish know that Lars Dahl had abducted her? And why? Had Corish taken some covert part in that kidnapping? Had Corish known who she was? Killashandra chuckled to herself, amused by the possibility although everything pointed to Corish having accepted her in the role she had played for him. Then she thought of how her earlier shipmates had reacted to the knowledge that she was a crystal singer. She doubted that Corish was less a man, particularly in his ease on the *Athena*, who would not make the most of his chances.

Keralaw had said that Lars Dahl was the first Angel Islander to reach the Music Conservatory. That explained his presence in the infirmary corridor, and his unconventional clothes, for the islanders appeared to prefer the browns and tans that emphasized their sunned skins. Why had he appeared so unexpectedly in Gartertown? Though he certainly maximized his opportunities. Had the original note of dissatisfaction with Optheria originated in these islands? That appeared logical, now that she had seen the different life styles and standards, and had heard Elder Ampris's disparaging remarks about the islanders' early rebellion against the Optherian authoritarianism.

A shout went up by the long beef pit, and people surged toward it, platters in hand. The aroma was tantalizing and slowly Killashandra rose to her feet. A full stomach was unlikely to improve her understanding of the puzzle, but it wouldn't hinder thought. Corish and Lars Dahl seemed to have succumbed to the enticement as well.

In that instant, Killashandra decided to approach her problem in a direct fashion. Altering her direction, she intercepted the two men.

"You've had your natter," she began, mimicking Keralaw's throaty drawl and speech pattern, "now enjoy. Angel's a good island for feasting." She flung one garland on Corish, the other about Lars Dahl's neck, making her smile as seductive as possible. Before they could respond, though neither removed her flowers, she linked her arms in theirs and propelled them toward the pit, grinning from one to the other, daring them to break away.

Corish shrugged, smiled tolerantly down at her, accepting her impudence. Lars Dahl, however, covered her hand on his arm and, just then, their thighs brushed and she lurched against him, abruptly aware of receiving an intense shock. Startled, she glanced up at Lars Dahl, his face illuminated by the pit fires, his lazy smile appreciating the contact shock they had both felt. His long fingers curled tightly around hers with a hint of possessiveness. His blue eyes sparkled as his gaze challenged her. His arm fastened hers to his smooth warm waist as Killashandra candidly returned his glance. He sidestepped suddenly, pulling Killashandra with him so that she had to drop Corish's arm.

"I've certainly done enough talking," he said, grinning more broadly at the success of his maneuver and maneuvering. "Corish, find yourself another one. You're mine, aren't you, Sunny?"

Corish gave a slightly contemptuous snort but continued on while Lars Dahl stopped, swinging Killashandra into a strong embrace, his hands caressing her back, settling into her waist to hold her firmly against him as he bent his head. The flowers were crushed between them, their fragrance spilling into her senses. With an inadvertent gesture of acceptance, Killashandra's hands slid up his bare warm chest, her fingers caressing the velvet skin, taking note of the strong pectoral muscles, the column of his throat. His lips tasted salty, but firm, parting hers as he settled his mouth against her, and once again the shock of their contact was almost like . . . crystal. Hungrily Killashandra surrendered to his deft kiss, trying to meld her body against the strong, lean length of him. She altered her arms, stroking the silky skin of his hard-muscled back, all her senses involved in this simple act.

They parted slightly, his hands still caressing her, one hand on the bare skin beneath her shirt as she gently stroked his shoulders, breathless and unable to leave his supporting arms. If his embrace had begun as perfunctory, it wasn't now. There was about his grasp a sense of astonishment, wonder, and discovery.

"I must know your name," he said softly, tipping her chin up to look into her eyes.

"Carrigana," she managed to remember to say.

"Why have I never seen you before?"

"You have," she said with a rich, suggestive chuckle, amused by her own presumption, "but you are always too busy with deep thoughts to see what you look at."

"I am all eyes now . . . Carrigana." A slight tremor in his soft tone sent one through her body, as his hands renewed their grip, encouraging her body to conform to his.

Part of her mind recognized the sincerity in his voice while another section wondered how she could make the most of this encounter. All of her didn't care what else happened to either of them if they could just enjoy this one evening. She was so hungry . . . it had been months since she'd made love.

"Not yet, sweet Sunny, not yet," he said, determinedly but gently disengaging himself. "We've the whole night before us," and his low voice lilted with promise. "You'll know I cannot absent myself so soon. And we'll both be the stronger after a good meal"—his laughter rippled with sensuality—"for our dalliance."

She let herself be swung again to his side, his arm tucking hers against his ribs, his warm hand stroking hers as he guided her to the barbecue pits. She had no argument against his so firm decision. Although she murmured understanding, she seethed with abruptly interrupted sensations, forcing herself to an outward amity. Perhaps it was as well, she told herself, as they collected platters from one of the long tables and joined those awaiting slices of roasted meat. She'd need time to recover and buffer herself against the charisma of the man. He was as potent as Lanzecki. And that was the first time she'd thought of the Guildmaster in a while!

What did Lars mean in saying she'd know why he couldn't absent himself so soon? How important was he within the island society, aside from being its first citizen to get into the Conservatory?

Then they were in the midst of the eager diners, with Lars exchanging laughing comments, teasing acquaintances, his rich lilting laughter rising above theirs. Yet he kept a firm grip on Killashandra and she tried to compose her expression against the surprise in the women's faces and the curiosity of the men. Who was this Lars Dahl when he wasn't kidnapping crystal singers?

Once thin slices of the juicy meat had been served them, Lars Dahl escorted her back to the table and they sank to the sand. Lars kept his left hand lightly on her thigh as he filled their plates from the foods displayed in the center of the table: breaded fried fish bits, steaming whiteroots, chopped raw vegetable, large yellow tubers which had been baked in polly leaves and exuded a pungent spiciness. He snagged a jug as it was being passed and filled their cups, deftly pouring without losing so much as a drop. Killashandra was aware of furtive glances the length of the table for Lars Dahl's partner. She looked for Keralaw for her support but there was no sign of her friend. Nor could she discern any animosity in the scrutinies. Curiosity, yes, and envy.

"Eat. I guarantee you'll need your strength . . . Carrigana."

Though she gave him a gleaming smile, she wondered why he had hesitated with the name, as if he was savoring the sound of it, the way he had rolled the *r*s and lengthened the final two *a*s. Was he dissembling? Had he recognized her? He knew she'd been injured by that island star-knife . . .

She almost pulled away from him, startled by a sudden knowledge that *he* had thrown that vicious star-blade at her. She shook her head, smiling to answer his sudden quizzical look, and applied herself to the heaped food. His hand soothed her thigh, the fingers light and caressing.

You sure can pick 'em, Killashandra, she thought, pulled by intense and conflicting emotions. She couldn't wait to roll with him, somewhere in the warm and fragrant plantation, with the surf pounding in rhythm with her blood. She wanted to solve the conundrums he represented, and she was determined to resolve each one to her advantage—and furious that he didn't even recognize the woman he had first injured and then abducted.

Yet, with all apparent complaisance, she sat, smiled, and laughed at his rather clever comments. Lars Dahl seemed to miss nothing that went on about him, and ate hugely. A beaming plump man wearing half a dozen garlands passed about a platter of the black flesh of the smacker fish, nudging Lars Dahl with a lewd whisper for his ear only, while Lars was lightly kneading her thigh, and then the plump man winked broadly at her, dumping a second slice of the fish onto her plate.

She was indeed grateful for the second slice of the smacker for it was succulent and highly unusual in taste, having nothing oily or fishy about it. The fermented polly juice was more subtle than the overripe fruit she had eaten on the island. Lars kept her cup filled, though she noticed that he only sipped at his while appearing to imbibe more freely than the level in his cup suggested.

When she admitted that she could eat no more of the cooked foods, he carefully picked one of the large, dark red melons, and, with one hand—someone called aloud with a quick guess as to where his other hand was—he split it with his knife, glancing expectantly at her. Out of the corner of her eye she had seen another woman so served scoop the seeds from her halved melon. Laughingly she did the same service, settling Lar's half in his plate before taking her own. Then, before she could lift her spoon, he had made a thin slice which he lifted to her lips. The flesh of the melon was the sweetest she had ever tasted, velvety, dripping with juice once the flesh was pierced. He took his first bite on top of hers, his even, strong teeth leaving a neat semi-circle all the way to the rind.

It was not the first time eating had been part of her love-making, but never before so many, even if all the pairings were performing much the same ritual. Or was that why the air was electric with sensuality?

"A song, Lars. A song while you can still stand on your feet."

Suddenly there was the loud roll of drums and tambourine, and applause, while half a dozen stringed instruments strummed vigorously to presage the advent of evening entertainment. Then the applause settled into a rhythmic beat and the feasters began to chant.

"Lars Dahl, Lars Dahl, Lars Dahl!"

Giving her thigh a final squeeze, Lars Dahl rose to his feet, spreading his arms for silence, smiling compliance at the chanters and abruptly the clamor ended, a respectful silence awaited his pleasure.

Lars Dahl lifted his head, a proud smile curving his lips, as he surveyed his audience. Then, taking one backward step, he raised his arms and hit an A, clear, vibrant, beautifully supported. Utterly astounded, Killashandra stared up at him, the half-formed suspicion solidifying into confirmation just as his voice glided down the scale. There couldn't be two tenor voices of similar caliber on one planet. This was her unknown tenor of that spontaneous duet. Fortunately Lars Dahl took the expression on her face as pleasure in his performance. He swung into a rollicking sea ballad, a song as gay, as nonchalant as himself, a song that was instantly recognized and appreciated by his audience.

At the verse, voices joined his in harmony, people swaying to the tempo of the song. Hastily Killashandra joined in, mouthing words until she learned the simple chorus. She took good care to sing in her alto register. If she could recognize his tenor, he'd know her soprano. And she didn't want him to be tipped to her true identity—at least not until morning. Now she relaxed into the music, letting her alto swell in a part singing she hadn't enjoyed since her early adolescence on Fuerte. Suddenly she remembered family outings in the summer in the mountain lakes, or at the ocean shore, when she had led the singing. Was that what Antona had had in mind for Killashandra to keep as enriching memories? Well, there were aspects of even those mellow evenings which Killashandra would have as soon forgot. For her older brothers had always teased her about screeching at the top of her lungs, and showing off and preening herself in public.

Even before this evening, Killashandra had been aware that some melodies seem to be universal, either recreated within a planet's musical tradition or brought with the original settlers and altered to fit the new world. Words might be changed, tempo, harmony, but the joy in listening, in joining the group singing was not: it struck deep nostalgic chords. Despite her musical sophistication, despite her foreswearing that same background, there was no way Killashandra could have remained silent. Indeed, not to participate in the evening would have marked her as antisocial. For the Angel Islanders, singing was a social grace.

Nor was the singing simple, for the islanders added embellishments to choruses and songs, six-part harmonies and intricate descants. Lars Dahl functioned as both stage manager and conductor, pointing to the people expected to rise and sing or perform on their instruments: performing to a high degree of musical competence on such unexpected instruments as trumpet, a woodwind that looked like a cross between an oboe and an ancient French horn, and on a viola with a mellow, warm tone that must have arrived with the early settlers. The hand drums were played with great skill and showmanship, the three drummers executing a whirling dance in time to their intricate rhythms.

Even when the rest of the audience was not actively participating, their attention was rapt, and their reaction to the occasional mistake immediate and understanding. There were songs about polly planters: one sung by two women, humorously itemizing the necessary steps to make one polly plant produce everything needed by their family. Another tune, sung by a tall thin man with a deep bass voice, told of the trials of a man bent on catching an ancient granddaddy smacker fish which had once demolished his small fishing boat with a negligent flick of its massive tail. A contralto and a baritone sang a sad haunting ballad on the vicissitudes of gray fishing and the vagaries of that enormous and ellusive quarry.

"You've dallied long enough, Lars, you and Olav sing it now," a man demanded from the shadows at one point. A wave of cheering and handclapping seconded that order.

Grinning amiably, Lars nodded, beckoning to someone seated to Killashandra's left. The man who came to stand beside Lars had to be related to him for their features were similar, if differently arranged. Though the older man had a thin, long face, the nose was the same, and the set of the eyes, the shape of the lips, and firm chin. Neither man could really be called handsome, but both exuded the same unusual quality of strength, determination, and confidence that made them stand out as individuals.

A respectful silence fell and the instruments began the overture. Killashandra had a good musical memory: she could hear a composition once and remember not only the theme, if there was one, but the structure. If she had studied the score in any detail, she would know the composer and performances, what different settings or arrangements the music had had over the years, and possibly which Stellars had performed it and where.

Before the men began to sing, she recognized the music. The words had been altered but they suited the locality: the search for the lost and perfect island in the mists of morning, and the beautiful lady stranded there for whose affections the men vied. Lars's beautiful tenor paired well with the older man's well produced baritone, their voices in perfect balance with each other and the dynamics of the music.

Nevertheless, at song's end Killashandra stared at Lars in amazement. He had the most outrageous gall . . . until she also remembered that he had been required to sing it, however appropriate it might also be to her circumstances. And Lars Dahl had not had the grace to look abashed.

Why should he? The performer in her argued with her sense of personal outrage. The music was beautiful, and so obviously a favorite of the islanders that the last chorus trailed off into reverent silence.

Then the baritone held out his hand, into which was placed a twelve stringed instrument that he presented to Lars Dahl.

"The Music Masters may not have approved your composition for the Summer Festival, Lars, but may we at least hear it?"

Plainly the request distressed Lars Dahl, for his mouth twitched and he had ducked his head against the compelling level gaze. Nevertheless, he took a deep breath, reluctantly accepting the instrument. His lips were pressed into a thin line as he strummed a chord to test the strings. Lars did not look at Olav, though he could not refuse the older man's request, nor did he look out at the audience. His expression was bleak as he inhaled deeply, concentrating onward to the performance. The rankling disappointment, the pain of that rejection, and the sense of failure which Lars had experienced were as clear to Killashandra as if broadcast. Her cynical evaluation of him altered radically. She was possibly the only one in the entire assembly who could empathize, could understand and appreciate the deep and intense conflict he had to overcome at that moment. She also could approve heartily of the professionalism in him that unprotestingly accepted the challenge of an excruciating demand. Lars Dahl possessed a potentially Stellar temperament.

Despite her proximity to him, she almost missed the first whispering chords which his strong fingers stroked from the strings. A haunting chord, expanded and then altered into a dominant, just like the dawn breeze through the old polly tree on her island of exile. Soft gray and pink as the sky lightened, and then the sun would warm the night-closed blossoms, their fragrance drifting to beguile senses: and the rising lilts of bird, the gentle susurrus of waves on the shore, and the lift in the spirit for the pleasure of a new day, for the duties of the day: climbing the polly for the ripe fruit, fishing off the end of a headland, the bright sun on the water, the rising breeze, the colors of day, the aroma of frying fish, the somnolence of midday when the sun's heat sent people to hammock or mat . . . an entire day in the life of an islander was in his music, colored and scented, and how he managed that feat of musical conjuring on a limited instrument like a twelve-string, Killashandra did not know. How that music would sound on the Optherian organ was something she would give her next cutting of black crystal to hear!

And the Music Masters had rejected his composition? She was beginning to understand why he might wish to assassinate her, and why he had kidnapped her: to prevent the repair of the great organ and, perhaps other less worthy compositions, from being played by anyone. And yet there was nothing in her brief association with Lars Dahl, in this evening's showmanship, even in his reluctant acquiescence to the demands of his island, to suggest such a dark vengeful streak in the man.

When the last chord, heralding moon-set, had faded into silence, Lars Dahl set the instrument down carefully and, turning on his heel, stalked away. There were murmurs of approval and regret, even anger in some faces, a more complimentary reaction to the beauty of what they had been privileged to hear than any wild applause. Then, people began to talk quietly in little groups, and one of the guitars tried to repeat one of the deceptively simple threnodies of Lars's composition.

With a glance to be sure no one was observing her, Killashandra rose to her feet and slipped out of the flickering torch light. Adjusting her eyes to the night, she saw movement off to the right and moved toward it, almost turning her ankle in one of the footprints that Lars's angry passage had gouged in the soft sand.

She saw his figure outlined against the sky, a dark tense shadow.

"Lars . . ." She wasn't sure what she could say to ease his distress but he shouldn't be alone, he shouldn't feel his music had not been appreciated, that the totality of the picture that he had so richly portrayed had not come across to his listeners.

"Leave me—" his bitter voice began, and then his arm snaked out and, catching her outstretched hand, pulled her roughly to him. "I need a woman."

"I'm here."

Holding tight to her hand, he pulled her into a lope. Then, pushing at her shoulder with his, he guided her at right angles to the beach, up toward the thick shadow of the polly grove on the headland, near where she had beached that morning. When she tried to slow his headlong pace, his hand shifted to her elbow. His grip was electric, his fingers seemed to transfer that urgency to her and anticipation began to course through her breast and belly. How they avoided running into a polly tree trunk, or stumbling over the thick gnarled roots, she never knew. Then suddenly he slowed, murmured a warning to be careful. She could see him lift his arms to push through stiff underbrush. She heard the ripple of a stream, smelt the moisture in the air, and the almost overpowering perfume emanating from the creamy blossoms before she followed him, pushing through the bushes. Then her feet were on the coarse velvet of some kind of moss, carpeting the banks of the stream.

His hands were urgent on her and the initial physical attraction she had felt for him was suddenly a mutual sensation. He put her at arm's length, staring down at her, seeing her not as a vessel from which he expected the physical relief, but as a woman whose feminity had aroused an instinctive and overpowering response.

"Who are you, Carrigana?" His eyes were wide with his amazement. "What have you done to me?"

"I've done nothing yet," she replied with a ripple of delighted laughter. No one else had awakened such a response in her, not even Lanzecki. And if Lars had somehow sensed the crystal shock in her, so much the better: it would enhance their union. She had been celibate far too long and he was partly to blame: the consequences were for both to enjoy. "Whatever are you waiting for, Lars?"

Chapter 11

A light, almost tender, finger touch on her shoulder, just where the star-knife had sliced her flesh, roused Killashandra from the velvet darkness of the deepest sleep she had ever enjoyed. She felt weightless, relaxed. Despite her having led an uninhibited private life, Killashandra was inexplicably possessed by shyness, a curious reluctance to face Lars. She didn't want to face him, or the world, quite yet.

Then she heard the barest ripple of laughter in the tenor voice of her lover.

"I didn't want to wake up either, Carrigana . . ."

Loath to perpetuate any lies between them, she almost corrected the misnomer but she found it too difficult to overcome the physical languor that gripped her body. And an explanation of her name would lead to so many more, any of which might fracture the stunning memory of the previous night.

"I've . . . never . . ." He broke off, his finger tracing other scar lines on her forearms—crystal scar (and how could she explain those at this point in a magical interlude)—down to her hands where his strong tapered fingers fit in between hers. "I don't know what you did to me, Carrigana. I've . . . never . . . had a love experience like that before." A rueful laugh that cracked because he couldn't keep it soft enough to match his whisper. "I know that when a man's been troubled, a normal reaction is to seek sexual relief from a woman—any woman. But you weren't just 'any woman' last night, Carrigana. You were . . . incredible. Please open your eyes so that I can see you believe what I'm saying—because it is true!"

Killashandra could not have ignored the plea, the sincerity, the soul sound in his voice. She opened her eyes. His were inches away and she was gripped by an overpowering surge of love, affection, sensuality, empathy, and compassion for this incredible and talented young man. Relief was mirrored in the very clear blue of his eyes: a morning-lagoon-in-sunlight clear blue, as vivid as the sea could sometimes be. Relief and the sudden welling up of tears. With the shuddering sigh that rippled down his body, so close to hers, he dropped his head to the point of her shoulder, just above the knife-scar. When, at length, he confessed that he had caused it, she would willingly forgive him. Just as she was willing to forgive him her abduction, for whatever marvelous reason he might submit. After last night, how could she deny him anything? Perhaps last night had been such a unique combination of emotional upheavals that a repetition was unlikely. The prospect made her smile.

As if he sensed her responses—he had certainly sensed them last night—he lifted his head again, anxious eyes searching her face. She saw that he was not unscathed, for his lower lip was red and puffy as he tried to echo her smile.

Then she chuckled, tracing the line of his mouth with an apologetic finger.

"I don't think I can ever forget last night happened, Lars Dahl." Would she ever find adequate words to record *this* on her personal file at Ballybran? She let her finger drop to his jaw. His grin became more self-confident, and his fingers squeezed hers lightly. "There's one problem . . ." His face tightened with concern. "How long will it take us to recover to try it again?"

Lars Dahl burst out laughing, rolling away from her.

"You may be the death of me, Carrigana."

Once again Killashandra ardently regretted using that particular pseudonym. She desperately wanted to confess everything and hear her own name on his lips, in his rich and sensual voice.

"Like last night?"

"Oh my precious Sunny," he replied, his voice altering from spontaneous laughter to urgent loverliness as he rolled back to her, his hand gently cupping her head, fingers stroking her hair, "it was almost a death to leave you."

That he might be quoting some planetary poet, she discarded as unworthy. Her body and mind echoed the sentiment. Their exhausted sleep had been like a little death, it had overtaken them so completely.

With total unconcern for aesthetics, her stomach rumbled alarmingly. They suppressed a laugh and then let their laughter blend, as they enveloped each other in loving arms.

"C'mon, I'll race you to the sea," Lars said, his eyes sparkling with amusement. "A swim to cool us off." He rose lithely to his feet, offering her a hand.

It was only when the light blanket fell from her body that she realized its presence. And noticed the small basket to one side of the clearing, the unmistakable neck of a wine jug protruding from the lazy stream.

"I woke at dawn," Lars said, hands on her shoulders as he gently inclined forward to kiss her cheek. "The wind was a touch chilly. So I got a few things for us. Could we spend today together and alone?"

Killashandra leaned lovingly against him for a moment. "I feel remarkably unsocial." She wanted nothing more.

"You'll barely look at me!" Lar's voice rippled with amused complaint.

Her hands began to caress him as his were gentle on her arms. Almost guiltily they broke apart. Laughing, they joined hands and pressed through the bushes toward the seashore.

The sea was calm, the waves mere ripples flopping over at the last moment onto the smooth, wet sand. The water was soothing, soft against her body. Finally hunger could no longer be denied and they sprinted back to the secret clearing, patting each other dry, carefully avoiding the sorest spots. That morning Lars had acquired fresh fruits, bread, and a soft savory cheese as well as some of the flavorful dried fish that was an island specialty. There was wine to wash it all down. Lars had also had the wit to 'borrow' from Mama Tulla's wash line a voluminous and comfortable kaftan for her and a thigh length shirt for himself.

They were both hungry enough to concentrate on eating, but they smiled whenever their eyes met, which was often. When their hands touched as they hunted in the basket for food, the touch also became a caress. When all the food had been eaten, Lars excused himself with grave courtesy and pushed through the bushes. Trying to suppress giggles, Killashandra did the same. But when she returned to the clearing, Lars was making a couch of polly fronds and sweetly scented ferns. In silent accord, they lay down, spread the light blanket over their weary bodies and, hands lightly clasped, surrendered to fatigue.

Once again the sensation of light fingers stroking the crystal scars roused Killashandra.

"You were a long time learning to handle polly, weren't you?" he said, his teasing tender.

She sighed, hoping she could somehow, and, with reasonable truth, evade his natural curiosity about her. She daren't risk a full disclosure even in the euphoria which still enveloped them.

"I came from the City. I'd no choice about an island life or an education in polly planting."

"Must you go back to the City?" Apprehension roughened his voice, his fingers tightened on hers in an almost painful grip.

"Inevitably." She turned her face against his arm, wishing it were bare and she could taste the skin covering the strong arms that had held her with such love: which must hold her once again in love, preferably for a long, long time. "I don't belong here, you know."

"I didn't think you did," and his reply was amused acceptance, "once you dropped the Keralawian accent." She warned herself to watch what she said. "Where *do* you belong, Carrigana?"

"Besides in your arms?" Then the honesty of the moment began to close in on her. "I don't really know, Lars." These moments were out of context with any previous part of her life on Fuerte or Ballybran: totally divorced from Killashandra, Crystal Singer. Pragmatically she knew the euphoria would end all too soon but the desire to prolong it consumed her. "How about you, Lars? Where do you belong?"

"The Islands don't actually hold me any more. I've come to realize that over the past few months. And I think that my father recognizes it, too. Oh, I'm partner in an interisland carrier service that's reasonably profitable—useful to the islanders certainly." He grinned. "But three years in the City at the Complex taught me discipline, order, and efficiency and the easy way of islanders irritates me. I can't see me settling in to City life, either . . ."

Killashandra raised herself on her elbow, looking down at his face. The muscles were relaxed but the strength and character in his features were not the least bit diminished.

"Aren't you going to appeal the Masters' decision?" Her fingers traced his clearly defined left brow.

"No one appeals their decision, Carrigana," he said with a contemptuous snort. Then he drew both eyebrows together: her finger followed to caress away his scowl. "They did, damn their souls to everlasting acid, have the incredible gall to suggest that, if I performed a slight service for them, they might reconsider. And like a childish fool, I believed them." Incensed by his memories, he swung to a sitting position, arms clasping his knees tightly to his chest, his mouth in a bitter line. "A real fool but so desperate to have my composition accepted—not so much for my own prestige as to prove that an islander could succeed at the Complex and to vindicate the support the islanders had given me during those years." He twisted his torso around to face her. "You'd never guess what this slight service was."

"I wouldn't?" Killashandra was quite certain what he would say.

"They wanted me to make an assault on a visiting dignitary. Possibly the most important person to set foot on this forsaken mudball."

"Assault? On Optheria? On whom? What visiting dignitary?" Killashandra was astonished at the surprise and concern in her voice, a genuine enough response to Lars's shocking statement.

"You heard that Comgail had died, shattering a manual of the Festival Organ?" When she nodded silently, he continued. "You may not know that the damage was deliberate." It was easy for her to react suitably, for a death involving crystal would not have been painless. "There are a lot of people who believe that they— we," and he grinned humorlessly, admitting to his complicity, "have an inalienable right to leave this planet in order to achieve professional fulfillment. And that right should be enjoyed by more than disappointed composers, Carrigana. This restriction is stagnating intelligent people all over this world. People who have tremendous gifts which have no channel whatever on this backward *natural* mudball.

"So, it was decided to manufacture a situation that would require the presence of an extraplanetary official. An impartial but prestigious person who could be approached to register our protest with the FSP. Oh, letters have been smuggled out but letters are ineffective. We're not even sure that they reached their destinations. What we needed was someone who could be *shown* examples of this stagnation, talk to people like Theach, Nahia, and Brassner, see what they have been developing in spite of strictures of federal bureaucracy."

Lars gave a rueful laugh. "It's rather depressing to realize how little Optheria requires. The founding fathers wrought too well. We're a population expert in making do with the meanest possible natural resources. Good old polly!

"It was Comgail who proposed what had to be done to force the government to bring in a foreign technician. A manual on the Festival Organ would have to be shattered. The Government would be forced to have that replaced in time for the Summer Festival tourists.

"Did you ever realize how dependent the Government is on tourism?" His eyes glinted with malicious amusement. "Theach researched the economics. He can do the most phenomenal computations in his head—that way, there's no written proof of his alienation from the Optheria way of life! That tourist income is absolutely essential to purchase the high tech items which cannot be manufactured here. And without which all the federal machinery would grind to a halt. Even the barrier arc at the shuttleport is fashioned from imported components.

"Mind you, Comgail did not intend to be a martyr. But he didn't draw back when the moment was on him. So the Government was forced to apply to the Heptite Guild for a complete and very expensive new crystal manual. And this is where Comgail's sacrifice becomes relevant; he was also the only technician on Optheria capable of installing the replacement. They'd have to have the services of—at the very least—a highly skilled technician or ideally a crystal singer to make the repair. Once the crystal singer was on Optheria, we'd make sure there'd be an opportunity to present our desperate situation and ask that it be submitted to the FSP Council. A singer has access to the Council, you know."

"Go on, Lars . . ." A nasty suspicion began to form in Killashandra's mind, recalling Ampris's snide remarks about islanders.

He inhaled, closing his eyes briefly against unpleasant memories. "The crystal singer arrived on the *Athena* the day after my audition. Only the Elders weren't sure of her identity."

"That sort of i.d. cannot be forged, Lars."

He gave a contemptuous snort. "I know it, you know it, but you must also know how paranoid our Elders are. And Torkes is now in Communications." Again his words elicited a nodded reaction from her. "Oh, the urgency behind this slight favor was subtly presented to me. A crystal singer is known to have great recuperative powers. A minor scratch would be no inconvenience to a crystal singer but would unconditionally reveal an imposter. Since islanders are known," his voice dripped with sarcasm, "to live primitive and violent lives, accustomed to handling dangerous weapons, it was thought that I was admirably suited to perform this small favor for the Masters, in return for their reevaluation of my composition."

"And did they promise you immunity from reprisal as well?"

"I'm not quite that naive, Carrigana. They did not require a frontal assault. So, I picked a window on the upper storey where I'd have a good view of the arrival. I've been winning competitions with the star-blades since my father first allowed me one. A simple flick and the blade angles at the right trajectory. It caught her on the arm. I think a little higher than I'd planned for she moved just as I had completed the throw." His expression was chagrined and he gave Killashandra a quick defensive glance. "Oh, she was all right, Carrigana. I scooted round to the infirmary the back way and she was walking out of the surgery without so much as a bandage showing." He smoothed her arm reassuringly. "Crystal singers really do heal with unbelievable speed. She seemed more annoyed with her escort than the incident.

"The next morning, of course, I was told that on due reconsideration, the Masters had to abide by their original decision. The omnipotent, omniscient Masters, speaking from their immense and encyclopedic knowledge of all forms of music and their total understanding of the universe and Man's sublimal relationship with the Natural World, do not believe that this facet of Optherian life needs to be celebrated at any point in the year, certainly not during the Summer Festival when off-worlders might possibly hear something evoking a valid Optherian subculture and more original than variations on the usual pre-predigested pap that 'accredited' composers churn out."

"Stupid, insensitive, unimaginative, flatulent fardlngs!" Killashandra's derision was slightly colored by hearing the details of the 'outrageous' attack, and by the realization that her instinct about Ampris's specious assurance was quite valid. "They're so old they've lost the energy enthusiasm requires; they couldn't possibly recognize imagination."

Lars smiled at her vehemence. "So, despite all their promises and assurances, I was given a ticket back to Angel as a reward for my unmentionable service, and told to be out of the City on the evening oceanjet. Guardians were there to be sure I boarded, which I did. After a stroke of incredibly good luck."

He turned his face fully to her then, his lips lightly compressed as if controlling amusement, and the sparkling of his eyes indicated that he had considered confiding in her. As much as she hoped that he might, she wished fervently that he would not. For his honesty would require the similar courtesy from her.

"Lars, I don't mean to be a spoil-sport, but something occurred to me. A star-knife is an island blade, isn't it?"

"Yes . . ." He regarded her, suddenly alert.

"And if an island blade was responsible for wounding the crystal singer—even if it healed rapidly—would that not prejudice her against listening to your problem?"

"A good point. The Elders don't miss many tricks, but that ploy would not have worked. Nahia and Brassner were going to speak for us."

"*Were* going?"

"Yes, I did say that I had a stroke of good luck," and he clasped her hand with a firm grip, his clear blue gaze fixed on the thick bushes. "Nahia and Brassner will now have an even better chance to present our situation." He sounded so confident that Killashandra would have given much to be privy to his plans. "You'll see."

"Since I'm being candid, let me tell you that you've been rather indiscreet confiding in me, Lars. You don't know me—"

"Don't *know* you?" Lars threw back his head and guffawed. He clasped her to him, rocking her in his arms, roaring with laughter. "If I don't, young woman, no one ever will."

"You know what I mean. Who were you talking to last night on the beach? He's not an islander."

"Oh, him? Corish von Mittel-something. No, he's not an islander. In fact, he could be very useful . . ." Lars paused a moment in thought, and then shrugged it off. "He's looking for an uncle. Father asked me to help him, take him on my next swing through the islands. Frankly I don't think the uncle came this far out: doesn't sound like a man who'd want this sort of life style."

"Are you sure this Corish is who he says he is?"

Lars eyed her with some interest. "Father's sent for an i.d. verification. We're not so haphazard as all that in these islands, you know. There've been snoopers before. Father's got a sixth sense about the breed and that Corish tilted it. Oh, he says he came in on the *Athena*, and he sounded as if he'd made the trip on her." Then he added in another tone altogether, "I'm glad you worry about my safety."

He smoothed back her sun-bleached hair, fingering the strands before he patted them in place, his whole face softening as once more he fell in her thrall. Then he relaxed, lying back again, hands under his head, his eyes intent on her face, a very tender smile playing at the corner of his lips. "Anyway, everyone on Angel dislikes federal interference as much as we do. I studied under a master of heresy. My father. The duly appointed harbor master of the Angel Island archipelago and federal representative. If you can't lick 'em, join 'em."

"Your father's the harbor master?"

Surprise registered blankly on Lars's face. "Of course. Don't tell me you didn't know that?"

"I do. I didn't."

"So, if you really insist on going back to the City, you'll have to be very nice to me." He was smiling as he gently reached for her arms to bring her down to him.

"Oh?"

"*Very* nice to me."

"Are you able for it?"

He settled her into the curve of his arm, her head pillowed on his shoulder, his cheek against her hair.

"When you are, beloved." Then he yawned and, apparently, between one breath and the next, fell asleep. For another long moment, Killashandra heard the singing in her blood and for once did not regret its murmur. She repositioned her arm on his chest, placidly noting that the fine hairs across Lars's pectoral muscles stirred upright. Well, they had more energy then he or she did. She closed her eyes and was also claimed by sleep.

Shouts startled them awake: the cheerful calls and laughter of people fishing on the beach. Killashandra couldn't hear what was so exciting, but Lars smiled.

"A yellowback school has been forced into the cove." He embraced her enthusiastically. "Once they've caught what's needed, we'll get our"—he looked about for the angle of sunlight— "our dinner. Hungry yet?"

"Hungry enough to go right out there bold-faced . . ." She made as if to rise, for her belly was almost painfully empty.

He pulled her back flat beside him, kissing her half-formed protest into silence. His eyes were unsmiling as he then gently stroked her cheek.

"My dear girl, with those bruises on you, I'd be hauled up in front of the Island Court and charged with rape."

"What about the marks on you?"

"You resisted my improper advances—"

"And you made enough of those—"

"Precisely what the bruises say. So, since I have a reputation to maintain in this community, we will remain secluded." He emphasized this decision with a gentle kiss. Then he stroked her hair back from her forehead, his fingers lingering in the soft gold-streaked mass. "I don't wish to share you yet, share even the sight of you with anyone. If I believed the ancient tales of witchcraft, sorcery, and enchantment, I'd name you 'witch,' so I would. But you're not . . . though I am completely spellbound . . ." His fingers became insistent, and his expression was an urgent appeal. "D'you think you could possibly bear me . . . if I'm very careful . . ."

She chuckled and linked her hands behind his head to bring his lips to hers.

The fishers were long gone before they finally got around to fishing. Together they waded out through the gentle tide.

"Stay here, Carrigana," Lars directed, "and make a basin of your skirt."

She did, first wringing water from the voluminous folds. Lars was thigh deep in the water when he suddenly bent down and scooping with both hands sent water, and fish, flying at her. She missed the first lot, laughing at her ineptitude, but neatly caught two fish in the second. After three more catches, she had to hold up her skirt lest the active yellowbacks flip out. Lars splashed back to inspect her catch, grinning at his success and her bemusement.

"This one's too small." He released it. "Two, four, six, seven. How many can you eat? Shall I get more?"

Before she could answer, he dove back toward his vantage point, and peered down into the clear water. With one last mighty heave, three big yellowbacks were sent flying in her direction. She cheered when she caught them in her skirt, closing the makeshift net and running awkwardly through the wavelets to the shore before any of the squirming fish could escape.

Helping her secure the bundle, Lars laughingly escorted her back to the bushes surrounding their secluded clearing.

"You clean 'em and I'll get firing, and see what else I can scrounge," he said as he held the bushes back for her to enter.

Gutting fish was not one of Killashandra's favorite chores, but she had finished half the catch before she realized it, washing them clean in the little brook. Lars was back as she slit the last one. In one crooked arm, he held twisted polly fronds that provided a quick hot fire, and another basket swung from his right hand. He found rocks by the stream to enclose their fire, hauled a frying sheet from the basket, and set out oil, seasonings, bread, fruit, and another pot of the soft island cheese.

The quick tropical night had settled upon the island, enclosing them more securely in their clearing as they finished their supper, licking the last of the juices from their fingers.

"Going to be nice to me?" Lars asked, leering dramatically at her.

"Maybe I'll just stay in the islands." Killashandra surprised herself with the longing in her voice. "There's all I could possibly need just for the taking . . ."

"Even me?"

Killashandra looked up at him. Despite his light words, his voice held a curious entreaty.

"I would be a right foolish dolt to consider you part of the taking." She meant it, for quixotic though the man might appear, she sensed that Lars had an unshakeable integrity which she, or any other woman, would have to recognize and accept.

"We could stay in the islands, Carrigana, and make a go of the charter service." Lars, too, was caught in the same thrall which infected her resolve. "Sailing's never dull. The weather sees to that. It could be a good life, and I promise you wouldn't have to hack polly!" His fingers caressed her hands.

"Lars . . ." She had to set the record fair.

He covered her lips with his hand. "No, beloved, this is not the time for life-shaping decisions. This is the time for loving. Love me again!"

Chapter 12

The idyll lasted another full day and into the early morning of the third, during which time Killashandra would have been quite willing to forego all the prestige of being a crystal singer to remain Lars's companion. A totally impossible, improbable, and impractical ambition. But she had every intention of enjoying his companionship as long as it was physically possible. She was haunted by memories of Carrik and, as such traumas can, they colored, and augmented, her responses to Lars.

It was the change in the weather which necessitated their return to society. The drop in barometric pressure woke Killashandra just before dawn. She lay, wide awake, Lars's lax arms draped about her, his legs overlapping hers, wondering what had returned her so abruptly to full consciousness. Then she smelled a change in weather on the early morning breeze. It had not occurred to Killashandra that her Ballybran symbiont would be agitated by other weather systems. And she pushed her sensitivity as far as she could, testing what the change might herald.

Storm, she decided, letting symbiotic instinct make the identification. And a heavy one. In these islands a hurricane more likely than not. A worrisome phenomenon for a reasonably flat land mass. No, there were heights on what Lars had termed the Head. She smiled, for yesterday, in between other felicitous activities, he had given her quite a history and geography lesson pertinent to the island economy.

"This island gets its name from the shape of the land mass," he explained and drew a shape on the wet sands with a shell. They had just emerged from a morning swim. "It was seen first from the exploratory probe and named long before any settlers landed here. There's even a sort of a halo of islets off the Head. We're at the Wingtip. The settlement lies in the wing curve . . . see . . . and the western heights are the wings, complete with the ridge precipice. This side of the island is much lower than the body side. We've two separate viable harbors, north and south, the angel's outstretched hands completing the smaller, deeper one. My father's offices are there, as the backbone sometimes interferes with reception from the mainland. You can't see it from here because of Backbone Ridge, but there's rather an impressive old volcano topping the Head." He grinned mischievously, giving Killashandra an impression of the devilish child he must have been. "Some of us less reverent souls say the Angel blew her head when she knew who got possession of the planet. Not so, of course. It happened eons before we got here."

Angel was not the largest of the islands but Lars told her that she'd soon see that it was the best. The southern sea was littered, Lars said, with all kinds of land masses: some completely sterile, others bearing active volcanoes, and anything large enough to support polly plantations and other useful tropical vegetation did so.

"We were a race apart from the mainlanders, and we've remained so, Carrigana. *They* listen to what the Elders dish up for them, dulling their minds with all the pap that's performed. Islanders still have to have their wits about them. We may be easygoing and carefree, but we're not lazy or stupid."

She had discovered an unexpected pleasure in listening to Lars ramble on, recognizing that his motive was as much self-indoctrination as explanation for her benefit. His voice was so beautifully modulated, uninhibited in its expressiveness that she could have listened to him for years. He made events out of small incidents, no matter that all were aimed at extolling the islands, subtly deprecating mainland ways. He was not, however, an impractical dreamer. Nor was his rebellion against mainland authority the ill-considered antagonism of the disillusioned.

"You sound as if you don't want to leave Optheria even if you are trying to pave the way off for these friends of yours," Killashandra was prompted to remark late that second evening as they finished a meal of steamed molluscs.

"I'm as well off here as I would be anywhere else in the galaxy."

"But your music—"

"It was composed to be played on the Optherian organ and I doubt that any other government allows them to be used, even if the Elders and Masters would permit the design to be copied." He shrugged off that consideration.

"If you could compose that, you have a great gift—"

Lars had laughed outright, ruffling her hair—he seemed fascinated by the texture of her hair.

"Beloved Sungirl, that took no great gift, I assure you. Nor do I have the temperament to sit down and create music—"

"Come on, Lars—"

"No, seriously, I'm much happier at the tiller of a ship—"

"And that voice of yours?"

He shrugged. "Fine for an island evening sing-song, my girl, but who bothers to sing on the Mainland?"

"But, if you get the others off the planet, why don't you go, too? There are plenty of other planets that would make you a Stellar in a pico—"

"How would you know?"

"Well, there have to be!" Killashandra almost screamed in her frustration with the restrictions imposed by her role. "Or why are you trying to crack the restriction?"

"The height of altruism motivates me. Besides, Sunny, Theach and Brassner have valid contributions to make within the context of the galaxy. And once a person has met Nahia, it's obvious why she must be let free. Think of the good she could do."

Killashandra murmured something reassuring since it was called for. She felt an uncharacteristic pulse of jealousy at the reverence and awe in Lars's voice whenever he mentioned this Nahia. Lars had perfectly healthy contempt for Elder and Master alike, indeed all federal officials with the exception of his father. And while he spoke of the man with affection and respect, Nahia occupied a higher position. Quite a few times Killashandra noted a nearly imperceptible halt in the flow of Lars's words as if he exercised a subtle discretion, so subtle that all she caught was its echo. Just as he had stopped short of admitting the abduction of the crystal singer. And, now that she understood his motivation, she marveled at his quick-witted opportunism. Did the others in his subversive group know what he had done? Had they approved of it? And what would the next step be? She could just imagine the furor caused in the Heptite Guild! Or maybe she was supposed to rescue herself? Which she had.

Lars was weather-sensitive, too, for she had only just completed her analysis when he woke, equally alert. With a loving tug at her hair and a smile, he stood up, sniffing at the breeze now strong enough to ruffle his hair, turning slowly. He stopped when he faced in the direction she had.

"Hurricane making, Carrigana. Come, we'll have a lot to do."

Not so much that they didn't start the morning with a quick passage at arms, not the least bit perfunctory despite the brevity. Then they had a quick swim, with Lars keeping a close watch on the dawn changes in the sky.

"Making up in the south so it'll be a bad blow." He stood for a moment as the active waves of the incoming tide flounced against his thighs. He looked southwest, frowning and, dissatisfied by his thoughts, started in-shore, taking her hand as if seeking comfort.

She thought nothing of his brief disappearance as she cleared up the camp site. Lars pushed his way past the bush screen, an odd smile on his face as he came up to her, two garlands of an exceptionally lovely blue and white flower in his hands. "This will serve," he said cryptically, gently draping one around her neck. The perfume was subtly erotic and she stood on tiptoe to kiss him for his thoughtfulness. "Now you must put mine on."

Smiling at his sweetness, she complied and he kissed her, exhaling a gust as if he had acquitted himself nobly.

"C'mon now," and he gave her the basket, slung the blanket with their clothing over his shoulder, and grabbing her hand, led her back through the underbrush.

Though the sun was not yet up over the horizon, there was considerable activity on the beach when they arrived. Torches were lit outside all the waterfront buildings, and torchlit groups of scurrying people pushed handcarts. Bobbing lights on the harbor, too, indicated crews on their way to anchored ships. The schooner was gone but Killashandra had not really expected to find the big ship still at Angel Island.

"Where can they take the boats?"

"Around to the Back. We'll just check to see how much time there is before the wind rises. There'll be a lot to do before we can take the *Pearl Fisher* to the safe mooring."

Killashandra glanced up and down the picturesque waterfront, for the first time seeing just how vulnerable it was. The first line of buildings was only four hundred meters from the high-tide mark. Wouldn't they be just swept away in hurricane driven tides?

"They often are," Lars startled her by saying as they strode purposefully toward the settlement. "But mostly polly floats. After the last big blow, Morchal salvaged the complete roof. It was floating in the bay, he just dried it out and reset it."

"I should help Keralaw," Killashandra suggested tentatively, not really wanting to leave his side but ignorant of what island protocol expected of her in the emergency. Lars's hand tightened on her elbow.

"If I know Keralaw she has matters well in hand. I'm not risking you from my side for an instant, Carrigana. I thought I'd made that plain."

Killashandra almost bridled at the possessive tone of his voice but part of her rather liked the chauvinism. She had too hearty a respect for storm not to wish to be in the safest place during one. Common sense told her that was likely to be in Lars Dahl's company.

Men and women were filing in and out of the tavern. Lars and Killashandra entered and found a veritable command post. The bar was now dispensing equipment and gear which Killashandra could not readily identify. Along the back wall, the huge vdr screen was active, showing a satellite picture of the growing storm swirling in from the south. Estimated times of arrival of the first heavy winds, high tide, the eye, and the counter winds were all listed in the upper left hand corner. Other cryptic information, displayed in a band across the top of the screen, did not mean much to her but evidently conveyed intelligence to the people in the bar. Including Lars.

"Lars, Olav's on line for you," called the tallest of the men behind the bar, and he jerked his head toward a side door. The fellow paused in his dispensations, and Killashandra was aware of his scrutiny as she followed Lars to the room indicated.

However rustic the tavern looked from the outside, this room was crammed with sophisticated equipment, a good deal of it meteorological, though not as complex as instrumentation in the Weather Room of the Heptite Guild. And all of it printing out or displaying rapidly changing information.

"Lars?" A young man turned from the scanner in front of him and, screwing his face in an anxious expression, almost pounced on the new arrival. "What are you going to do—"

Lars held up his hand, cutting off the rest of that sentence, and the young man noticed the garland. He threw an almost panic stricken look at Killashandra.

"Tanny, this is Carrigana. And there's nothing I can do with this storm blowing up." Lars was scrutinizing the duplicate vdr satellite picture as he spoke. "The worst of it will pass due east. Don't worry about the things you can't change!" He gave Tanny a clout on the shoulder but the worried expression did not entirely alter.

Killashandra kept the silly social smile on her face as Tanny accorded her the briefest of nods. She had a very good idea what, or rather whom, they were discussing so obliquely. Her. Still trapped, they thought, on that chip of an island.

"Tanny's my partner, Carrigana, and one of the best sailors on Angel," Lars added, though his attention was still claimed by the swirling cloud mass.

"What if the direction changes, Lars?" Tanny refused to be reassured. "You know what the southern blows are like . . ." He made an exaggerated gesture with both arms, nearly socking a passing islander, who ducked in time.

"Tanny, there is nothing we can do. There's a great big polly on the island that's survived hurricanes and high tides since man took the archipelago. We'll go have a look as soon as the blow's gone. All right?"

Lars didn't wait for Tanny's agreement, guiding Killashandra back into the main room. He paused at the counter, waiting his turn, and received a small handset. "A light one will do me fine, Bart," he added and Bart set a small antigrav unit on the counter. "Most of what I own is either on the *Pearl* or on its way back to me from the City. Grab a couple of those ration packs, will you, Carrigana," he added as they walked out on the broad verandah where additional emergency supplies were being passed out. "Might not need them but it's less for them to pack to the Ridge."

As Lars turned her west, away from the settlement, she caught sight of Tanny, watching them, his expression still troubled. The wind was picking up and the water in the harbor agitated. Lars looked to his right, assessing the situation.

"Been in a bad one yet?" he asked her, an amused and tolerant grin on his face.

"Oh, yes," Killashandra answered fervently. "Not an experience I wish to repeat." How could Lars know how puny an Optherian hurricane would be in comparison to Passover Storms on Ballybran. Once again she wanted to discard her borrowed identity. There was so much she would like to share with Lars.

"It's waiting out the blow that's hard," Lars said, then grinned down at her. "We won't be bored this time, though. My father said that Theach came with Hauness and Erutown. I wonder how they managed the travel permits!" That caused him to chuckle. "We'll know how the revised master plan is working."

Killashandra was very hard put to refrain from making any remarks but, of a certainty, waiting out this blow would be extremely interesting. She might not be getting on with the primary task of her visit to Optheria, but she was certainly gaining a lot of experience with dissidents.

His place was on a knoll, above the harbor, in a grove of mature polly trees. It reflected an orderly person who preferred plain and restful colors. He produced several carisaks which had been neatly stored in a cupboard, and together they emptied the chest of his clothes, including several beautifully finished formal garments. He cleared his terminal of any stored information and when Killashandra asked if they shouldn't dismantle the screen, he shrugged.

"Federal issue. I must be one of the few islanders who use the thing." He grinned impiously. "And then not to watch their broadcasts! They can never appreciate that islanders don't need vicarious experiences." He gestured toward the sea. "Not with real live action adventures!"

The pillows, hammocks, what kitchen utensils there were, the rugs, curtains, everything compacted into a manageable bundle to which Lars attached the antigrav straps. The entire process hadn't taken them fifteen minutes.

"We'll just attach this to a train, grab something to eat and then get the *Pearl* to safety." He gave his effects a gentle shove in the proper direction.

When they returned to the waterfront, Killashandra saw what he meant by train. Numerous personal-effects bundles, all wrapped and weightless, were being attached to a large floater on which families with small children perched. As soon as it had reached capacity, the driver guided it away, along a winding route toward the distant Ridge.

"Catch you next trip, Jorell?" Lars called to the man steering the harbor boat out toward the anchored ships.

"Gotcha, Lars!"

"There's Keralaw," Killashandra said, pointing to the woman who was ladling hot soup from an immense kettle into bowls.

"You can always count on her hospitality," Lars said and they altered their path to meet her.

"Carrigana!" Keralaw paused in serving a family group and waved one arm energetically to catch their attention. "I'd no idea where you'd—" She halted, eyes goggling a bit at the garland about Killashandra's neck, staring at Lars's matching one. Then she smiled. She patted Killashandra's arm approvingly. "Anyway, I put your carisak with mine on the float to the Ridge. Will I see you two there?" Her manner bordered on the coy as she handed them cups from the bag at her side, and poured the hot soup.

"After we've sailed the *Pearl* to the Back," Lars said, easily but Killashandra thought his expression a trifle smug, as if he liked surprising Keralaw. He blew on his soup, taking a cautious sip. "As good as ever, Keralaw. One day you must pass on your secret recipe. What'll Angel do in a crisis without you around to sustain us!"

Keralaw made a pleased noise, giving him a dig in the ribs before she sidled up to Killashandra. "You did better on the shore than I did from the ship!" she murmured, winking and giving Killashandra an approving dig in the ribs. "And," she added, her expression altering from bawdy to solemn, "you're what he needs right now."

Before Killashandra could respond to that cryptic comment, Keralaw had moved off to the next group.

"With Keralaw in the know," Lars said between sips, "storm or not, the rest of the island will be informed."

"That you and I have paired off?" Killashandra gave him a long stare, having now decided what the special blue garlands must signify in island custom. It was presumptuous of him, but then, he was also presuming her acquaintance with island ways. The account, when rendered from her side, was going to be heavy. "You're remarkably well organized here . . ." She let her sentence dangle, implying that she'd been elsewhere to her sorrow.

"Angel's not often in the direct path, and the storm may veer off before it hits, but one doesn't wait until the last moment, not on Angel. Father doesn't permit inefficiencies. They lose lives and cost credit. Ah, Jorell's back. Hang on to your cup. We'll need them later."

The harbor skip waited for them and its other passengers in the choppy waters. Lars bent to rinse out his cup and Killashandra followed suit, before swinging over the gunwales of the water taxi. Willing hands pulled them aboard.

There was a lot of activity on those ships still left in the harbor, but many had already started for the safety of the protected bay. Lars chatted amiably with the other passengers, naming Killashandra once to everyone. The approaching storm worried them all, despite the well-drilled exodus. It was considered early in the season for such a big blow: odds were being given that it would veer west as so many early storms tended to do; relief was felt that neither of the nearer two moons was at the full, thus affecting the height of the tides. The pessimist on board was sure this was the beginning of a very stormy winter, a comment which caught Killashandra's interest. Winter? As far as she knew, she'd arrived in Optheria in early spring. Had she missed half a year somehow?

Then the taxi pulled alongside a sleek-lined fifteen meter sloop-rigged ship, and Lars was telling her to grab the rope ladder that flopped against its side. She scrambled up, almost falling over the life-railing, which she hadn't expected. Then Lars was beside her, cheerfully shouting their thanks to Jorell as he deftly hauled the ladder inboard and began to stow it away.

"We'll rig the cabin before we sail," Lars said, nodding astern toward the hatch.

Killashandra didn't know much about ships of this class but the cabin looked very orderly to her, arranged as it was for daytime use. She went to the forward cabin, and decided that she had been in the top right-hand bunk. She turned back, to approximate the view she would have had, and decided that the *Pearl Fisher* had conveyed her to that wretched little island.

"Update!" Lars said as he came down the companionway, talking to the handset. He listened as he did a cursory inspection of the nearest cupboards, smiling as he turned toward her. "Alert me to any changes. Over."

He put the handset down and, in one unexpected sweep, hauled her tightly into his arms. His very blue eyes gleamed inches above her face. His face assumed the expression of a sex-mad fiend, his eyes wide in exaggerated ferocity, as he bent her backward in one arm, his other hand stroking her body urgently. "Alone, at last, m'girl, and who knows when next we have the privacy I need to enjoy you to good advantage!"

"Oh, sir, unhand me!" Killashandra fluttered her eye lashes, panting in mock terror. "How can you ravish an innocent maid in this hour of our peril?"

"It seems the right thing to do, somehow," Lars said in a totally different tone, releasing her so abruptly she had to catch herself on the table. "Curb your libido long enough for me to make the bed you're about to be laid in." He flipped the table onto its edge, gestured for her to take the other side of the seat unit which pulled out across the deck.

Simultaneously they fell onto the bed, and Lars began his assault on her willing person.

The summons of the handset brought them back to a reality that had only peripherally impinged on their activities. Lars had to steady himself in the lurching ship to reach the handset. He frowned as he heard the update.

"Well, beloved, I hope you're a good sailor, for it's going to be a rough passage around the wing. That storm is hurrying to meet us. Neither a veer nor a pause! Grab the wet weather gear from that cupboard. Temperature's falling and the rain's going to be cold."

Fortunately Lars gave clear instructions to his novice crew and Killashandra coped with her tasks well enough to gain his nods of approval. The *Pearl Fisher* was fitted to be sailed single-handed, with the sheet lines winched to the cockpit and other remotes to assist in the absence of a human crew. Lars beckoned Killashandra to join him in the stern as the anchor was lifted by remote. Another hauled the sloop's mainsail up the mast, Lars's pennon breaking out as the clew of the sail locked home.

The wind took the sail, and the ship, forward, out of the wide mouth of the harbor, which was now clear of all craft. Nor did there seem to have been anyone to notice their delay. The beach was empty of people. The shuttered shops and houses had an abandoned look to them. The tide was already slopping into the barbecue pits and Killashandra wondered just how much would be left on the waterfront when they sailed back into Wing Harbor.

Killashandra found the speed of the *Pearl Fisher* incredibly exhilarating. To judge by the rapt expression on his face, so did Lars. The fresh wind drove them across the harbor almost to its mouth, before Lars did a short tack to get beyond the land. Then the *Pearl* was gunwale deep on a fine slant as she sped on a port tack toward the bulk of the Wing.

It was an endless time, divorced from reality, unlike cutting crystal where time, too, was sometimes suspended for Killashandra. This was a different sort of time, that spent *with* someone, someone whose proximity was a matter of keen physical delight for her. Their bodies touched, shoulder, hip, thigh, knee, and leg, as the canting of the ship in her forward plunge kept Killashandra tight against Lars. Not a voyage, she realized sadly, that could last forever but a long interval she hoped to remember. There are some moments, Killashandra informed herself, that one does wish to savor.

The sun had been about at the zenith when they had finally tacked out of the Wing Harbor. It was westering as they sailed round the top of the Wing with its lowlands giving way to the great basalt cliffs, straight up from the crashing sea, a bastion against the rapidly approaching hurricane. And the southern skies were ominous with dark cloud and rain. In the shelter of those cliffs, their headlong speed abated to a more leisurely pace. Lars announced hunger and Killashandra went below to assuage it. Taking into account the rough water, she found some heat packs which she opened, and which they ate in the cockpit, companionably close. Killashandra found it necessary to curb a swell of incipient lust as Lars shifted his long body against hers to get a better grip on the tiller.

Then they rounded the cliffs and into the crowded anchorage which sheltered Angel's craft. Lars fired a flare to summon the jitney to them, then he ordered Killashandra forward with the boat hook to catch up the bright-orange eighty-two buoy to starboard. He furled the sail by remote and went on low-power assist to slow the *Pearl* and avoid oversailing the buoy.

Buoy eighty-two was in the second rank, between two small ketch-rigged fisherboats, and Killashandra was rather pleased that she snagged the buoy first try. By the time Lars had secured the ship to ride out the blow, the little harbor taxi was alongside, its pilot looking none too pleased to be out in the rough waters.

"What took you so long, Lars?"

"A bit of cross-tide and some rough tacks," Lars said with a cheerful mendacity that caused Killashandra to elbow his ribs hard. He threw his arm about her to forestall further assaults. Indeed they both had to hang on to the railings as the little boat slapped and bounced.

For a moment, Killashandra thought the pilot was driving them straight into the cliff. Then she saw the light framing the sea cave. As if the overhang marked the edge of the sea's domination, the jitney was abruptly on calmer waters, making for the interior and the sandy shore. Killashandra was told to fling the line to the waiting shoremen. The little boat was sailed into a cradle and this was drawn up, safely beyond the depredations of storm and sea.

"Last one in again, eh Lars?" he was teased as the entire party made its way out of the dock and started up the long flight of stairs cut in the basalt. It was a long upward haul for Killashandra, unused to stairs in any case and, though pride prevented her from asking for a brief halt, she was completely winded by the time they reached the top and exited onto a windswept terrace. She was relieved to find a floater waiting, for the Backbone towered meters above them and she doubted her ability to climb another step.

Polly and other trees lined the ridge, making a windbreak for the floater as it was buffeted along, ending its journey at a proper stationhouse. Killashandra had profited by the brief rest and followed Lars's energetic stride into the main hall of the Backbone shelter.

"Lars," called the man at the entrance, "Olav's in the command post. Can you join him?"

Lars waved assent and guided Killashandra to an ascending ramp, past a huge common room packed with people. They passed an immense garage where hundreds of packets resembling some strange form of alien avian life dangled weightless from their antigravs.

There was a storm chill in the air and Killashandra was aware of symbiont-generated inner tension as her body sensed the impending arrival of the hurricane.

"The command post is shielded, lover," Lars said, catching her hand in his and stroking it reassuringly. "Storm won't affect you so much there. I feel it myself," he added when she looked up in surprise at his comment. "Real weather-sorts, the pair of us!" The affinity pleased him.

They reached the next level, predominantly storage to judge by the signs on the doors on either side of the wide corridor. Lars walked straight for the secured portal at the far end, put his thumb on the door lock which then slid open. Instinctively Killashandra flinched, startled by the sight of the storm-lashed trees, and the unexpected panoramas, north and south, of the two harbors. Lars's hand tightened with reassurance. On both sides of the door, the walls were covered by data screens and continuous printout as the satellites fed information to the island's receivers. The other three sides of the command post were open, save for the circular stairs winding down to the floor below.

Olav was on his feet, walking from one display to the next, making his own estimate of the data. He looked up at Lars and Killashandra, noting with the upward lift of one eyebrow the bruised garlands they wore. He indicated the circular stairway and made a gesture which Killashandra read as a promise to join them later.

They crossed the room, Lars pausing to read the displays at the head of the staircase. He made a noncommittal grunt and then indicated that she should precede him. Therefore she was first in the room, grateful that only large windows north and south broke its protection from the elements without, while a fire burned in a wide hearth on the eastern wall. The western wall was broken by four doors, the open one showing a small catering area. But Killashandra's attention was immediately on the occupants of the room, three men and the most beautiful woman Killashandra had ever seen.

"Nahia! How dare you risk yourself!" cried Lars, his face white under his tan as he brushed past Killashandra. To her complete amazement, he dropped on one knee before the woman, and kissed her hand.

Chapter 13

A startled expression crossed Nahia's perfect features at Lars's obeisance. She shot a quick look at Killashandra, managing to convey her embarrassment even as she tried to lift Lars from his knee.

"My friend, this will not do," she said kindly, but firmly. "Only think what effect such a gesture could have on an Elder or a Master—and yes, I do most certainly know your opinion of those worthies. But Lars, such histrionics could damage our goal."

Lars had by now risen to his feet. With a final few pats to his hand, an oblique apology for her public admonition, she withdrew from his grasp, moving past him toward Killashandra. "Whom have you brought with you, Lars?" she asked, smiling tentatively as she extended her slender white hand to Killashandra. "Who wears your garland?"

"Carrigana, lately a polly planter," Lars replied, stepping back to Killashandra's side and taking her other hand firmly in his.

It was one way of apologizing for his effusive welcome of another woman but it was Nahia herself who effectively dissolved Killashandra's incipient hostility. The touch of her hand had a soothing effect, not a shock or a jar, but a gentle insinuation of reassurance. Nahia's eyes were troubled as she regarded Killashandra, her lips curving upward in a slight smile which blossomed as she felt Killashandra's resistance to her dissipate. Then a little frown gathered at her brows as she became aware of the lingering crystal resonance within Killashandra. It was the crystal singer's turn to smile reassurance and an acknowledgement of what Nahia was: an empath.

Killashandra had heard of such people but she had never en-

143

countered one. The encyclopedia had not hinted that psi talents were an Optherian quality. It could be a wild talent and often was. In Nahia it was combined with unexpected beauty, integrity, and an honesty which few citizens of the Federated Sentient Worlds could project without endangering their sanity. Lars had been correct in his statement that Nahia's especial talents would be a galactic asset. She was Goodness personified.

Nahia looked with gentle inquiry at Killashandra, struggling to identify the elusive contact with crystal. Killashandra smiled and, with a final light pressure on Nahia's fine-boned hand, released her and leaned slightly against Lars.

At this point, the other men stepped forward to greet the newcomers.

"I'm Hauness, Nahia's escort," said the tallest of the three, an attractive man whom Killashandra judged to be in his mid-thirties. His handclasp was strong but not crushing and he, too, exuded a charm and personality that would have been instantly apparent in any group—at least any group that did not contain Nahia. Or Lars. "Believe me, Lars, we had no report of such rough weather when we embarked on this journey but—"

"There are matters we must discuss with you, no matter what the risk." Erutown was the oldest, and bluntest. His manner suggested that he tended to be a humorless pessimist. He gave Killashandra's hand one brief shake and dropped it. "And there was no risk—in the weather—when we started." He hovered, his upper body inclined away from Killashandra even as his feet shifted, as if he wanted to separate Lars from Killashandra and plunge into the "matters to be discussed" as quickly as possible.

"Theach," said the third man, giving Killashandra a brief, self-effacing nod.

He was the sort of nondescript human being, mild mannered, with undistinguished features, who can be encountered almost anywhere in the human population, and promptly forgotten. Only because she had heard of his mathematical abilities from Lars did Killashandra give Theach any sort of an inspection and thus noticed that his eyes were brilliant with intelligence: that he had already assumed she would discount him, indeed, hoped that she would, and was quite willing to accept the sort of dismissal to which he was clearly accustomed.

So Killashandra gave him a saucy wink. She half expected Theach to retreat in confusion as many shy men would, but, smiling, he winked back at her.

Erutown cleared his throat, indicating that now introductions had been made, he wanted to initiate the discussions they had come for.

"I don't know about you, Lars, but I'm starving," Killashandra said, gesturing toward the catering area. "Is it all right to see what's available?" She turned to the others. "May I fix something for you?"

Lars gave her hand a grateful squeeze before he released it. He told her to find what she fancied and he'd have the same but the others demurred, gesturing toward the low table where the remains of a meal could be seen.

The four conspirators didn't know that Killashandra's symbiont-adapted hearing was uncommonly acute. At that distance they could have whispered and she would have caught what was being said.

"They finally sent the message two days ago, Lars." Erutown's baritone was audible above the noises Killashandra was making in the catering unit.

"Took them long enough," Lars said in a low growl.

"They had to search first. And search they did, uncovering a variety of minor crimes and infringements which, of course, slowed them down." Hauness was amused.

"Any one of us caught?"

"Not a one of us," Hauness replied.

"Cleansed us of some very stupid people," Erutown said.

"She is safe, isn't she, Lars?" Nahia asked in gentle anxiety, a graceful gesture of her hand indicating the darkening southern horizon.

"She should be. All she needs is enough sense to climb the polly tree."

"You ought to have contacted us before you acted so impulsively, Lars."

"How could he, Erutown?" Nahia was conciliatory. Then she gave a little chuckle. "Impulsive but it has proved such an extremely effective gambit. The Elders have been forced to reapply to the Heptite Guild."

"They haven't admitted that the crystal singer has been abducted?"

"As no one has confessed to committing such a heinous crime, how could they?" Hauness asked reasonably, his voice rippling with amusement. "Elder Torkes has been hinting dark words about that islander assault—"

Lars let out a burst of sour laughter for which Erutown growled a warning, looking over his shoulder at Killashandra who was well out of sight in the catering area.

"What you don't know, Lars," Hauness went on, "is that the crystal singer had had an altercation with Security Leader Blaz and stalked out of the installation before *any* repair had been accomplished."

Lars emitted a low whistle of delighted surprise. "Is that why she was wandering about Gartertown? I had wondered!"

"Erutown may not approve, and some of the others were appalled at your action, Lars, but there is no doubt," and Hauness overrode Erutown's disapproving murmurs, "that the action will require embarrassing enquiries when the second crystal singer arrives."

"As long as it also requires an appeal to the Council," Lars said. "Now what else brought you here so unexpectedly?"

"As I said, the search for the crystal singer exposed some unsuspected flaws in our organization. Theach and Erutown must ruralize. Have you another suitable island?"

Lars paused, staring at Hauness, and then the others. Erutown scowled and looked away but Theach regarded him with a smile.

"Some of my scribblings were discovered, and as I am already under threat of rehabilitation . . ." Theach shrugged eloquently.

When Lars looked to Erutown for an explanation, the man did not meet his gaze.

"Erutown was denounced as a recruiter," Hauness said. "Not his fault."

"It was, if I was daft enough to recruit such soft-bellied cowards!"

Lars grinned. "Well, I could put you ashore with the crystal singer." Something increased his mirth out of proportion to the joke, though Hauness grinned and Nahia tried to control unseemly mirth at Erutown's expense. "The island's big enough and she might even be grateful for company."

"I would be easier in my mind about her safety if Erutown and Theach *were* there," Nahia said. "The hurricane will have frightened her badly."

"I don't like the idea," Erutown said.

"Actually, if she thinks you've also been kidnapped . . ." Hauness suggested, then gestured to dismiss his notion at Erutown's negative response.

"I wouldn't object," Theach said. "One doesn't know much about crystal singers, except that they heal quickly and indulge in an unusual profession."

"You?" Erutown snorted contemptuously. "You'd probably drown yourself thinking up more theories."

"When I initiate a session of theoretical thinking, I take the precaution of seating myself in some secure and secluded spot," Theach said in amiable reprimand. "An island would suit me very well indeed."

"You'd starve!"

"No one can starve on a polly island." Theach turned for confirmation to Lars, who nodded.

"You have to work at it, though," Lars amended. "For at least a few hours every day."

"Despite a misapprehension current about my absent-mindedness, I have found that intense thought stimulates an incredible appetite. Since eating replenishes both body and the mechanics of thought, I do pause now and again in my meditations to eat! If I have to gather the food myself, I shall also have had that beneficial exercise. Yes, Lars," and Theach smiled at the islander, "I begin to think that an island residence would provide me with all I require: seclusion, sustenance, and sanctuary!" He sat back in the chair, beaming at his circle of friends.

"How many know you and Erutown are in the islands?" Lars asked seriously.

"Nahia has been working very hard lately, Lars," Hauness aid. "She was granted a leave of absence: I took my annual holiday and announced our intention of cruising the coast. There are friends who will vouch for our presence in mainland waters. Besides, who would expect us to brave a hurricane?"

147

"We boarded the jet from the seaside without being seen the night before she sailed," Erutown added. "What Elder would suspect Nahia's involvement with renegades?"

"If they had any sense whatever," Nahia said in a crisp tone that surprised Killashandra with its suppressed anger, "how could they fail to realize that I sympathize deeply with repressions, frustrations, and despairs which I cannot avoid feeling! With injustices not all the empathy in the world will ease."

A moment of silence followed.

"Is your woman to be trusted with any of this, Lars?" Hauness asked quietly.

Suppressing a flare of guilt at her duplicity, Killashandra decided that it was time to join the group before Lars perjured himself.

"Here, this should satisfy, Lars," she said, approaching the others with a purposeful stride. She set before him a generous plate of sandwiches and hot tidbits which she had found in the food storage. "You're sure I can't get anything for you?" she asked the others as she began to gather up the used plates and cups.

Erutown gave her a sour glance, then turned to watch the roiling cloud formations of the approaching storm. Theach smiled absently, Hauness shook his head and settled back next to Nahia who had leaned back in the couch, eyes closed, her beautiful face relaxed.

When Killashandra returned with her own serving, Lars and Hauness were absorbed by the satellite picture of the approaching hurricane, displayed on the vdr. It would be a substantial blow, Killashandra had to admit, but not a patch on what Ballybran could brew.

Storm watching could be mesmerizing, certainly engrossing. Theach was the first to break from the fascination. He reseated himself at a small terminal and began to call up equations on the tiny screen. There was a tension to the line of his back, the occasional rattle of the keys that proved he was still conscious, but there were long intervals of total silence from his corner during the next few hours.

"It's not going to be a long one at its current rate," Lars remarked when he had finished eating. "The eye'll be on us by night."

"Is it likely to make the mainland?"

"No. That is, after all, eight thousand kilos off. It'll blow itself out over the ocean as usual. You only get our storms when they make up in the Broad, not from this far south."

So, Killashandra thought, she was in the southern hemisphere of Optheria, which explained the switch in seasons. And it explained why this group felt themselves secure from Mainland intervention and searches. Even with the primitive jet vehicles, an enormous distance could be traversed in a relatively short time.

It struck Killashandra that if Nahia, Hauness, and the others could travel so far, so could the Elders, especially if they wanted to implicate islanders. Or was that just talk? If, as Lars had admitted, Torkes had set him up to assault her in order to verify her identity and was using that assault now to implicate the islanders, would it not be logical to assume that some foray into the islands would be made by officialdom? If only to preserve their fiction?

Killashandra closed her mouth on this theory for she had gleaned it from information she had overheard surreptitiously. Well, she'd find a way to warn Lars, for she had a sudden premonition that a warning was in order. From what she had seen of the Elders, reapplying to the Guild would be a humiliating embarrassment to their sort of bureaucracy. Unless—and Killashandra smiled to herself—they took the line that Killashandra Ree had not arrived as scheduled. How tidy it could be made, the Elders able to suppress any reference to the reception in her honor. However, Lanzecki would know that she had gone, and know, too, that she would not have evaded the responsibility she had accepted. And there would be computer evidence of her arrival— even the Elders would have a hard time suppressing that sort of trail mark. Not to mention her use of the credit outlet on Angel. This could be very interesting!

She must have dozed off, for the couch had been comfortable, the day's unusual exercise exhausting, and watching the weather screen soporific. It was the lack of storm noise that woke her. And a curious singing in her body which was her symbiont's reaction to drastic weather changes. A quick glance at the screen showed her that the eye of the storm was presently over Angel

Island. She rubbed at her arms and legs, sure that the vibration she felt might be discernible. However, Nahia had curled up on the end of the long couch, Hauness, one arm across her shoulders, was also asleep, head back against the cushions. Theach was still diddling, but Erutown and Lars were absent.

She heard voices and steps on the circular stair and made a dash for the toilet. She distinguished Lars's distinctive laugh, a bass rumble from his father, and a grunt that could be Erutown, and some other voices. Until the eye had passed and the symbiont had quieted, Killashandra wanted to avoid everyone, especially Lars.

"Carrigana?" Lars called. Then she heard him approach the toilet and tap on the door. "Carrigana? Would you mind fixing some hungry storm watchers more of those excellent sandwiches?"

Under ordinary circumstances, Killashandra would have had a tart rejoinder but catering would solve the more immediate problem.

"Just a moment." She splashed water on her face, smoothed back her hair, and regarded the blossoms about her neck. Strangely enough they were not dead, their petals were still fresh despite the creasing. Their fragrance scented her fingers as she opened the crushed flowers and spread them back into their original shapes.

When she opened the door, Nahia and Hauness were making their way toward the catering area.

"They only want to talk weather," Nahia said with a smile. "We'll help you."

The others did talk weather, but on the comunits to other islands, checking on storm damages and injuries, finding out what supplies would be required, and which island could best supply the needs. The three caterers served soup, a basic stew, and high-protein biscuits. In the company of Nahia and Hauness, the work was more pleasant than Killashandra would have believed. She had never met their like before and realized that she probably never again would.

The respite at the storm's eye was all too brief, and soon the hurricane was more frightening in its renewed violence. Though it was a zephyr in comparison to Ballybran turbulence, Killashandra rated it a respectable storm, and slept through the rest of it.

A touch on her shoulder woke her, a light touch that was then repeated and her shoulder held in a brief clasp. That was enough to bring Killashandra to full awareness and she looked up at Nahia's perplexed expression. Killashandra smiled reassuringly, attempting to pass off the storm resonance still coursing through her body. As Lars was draped against her, she moved cautiously to a sitting position and took the steaming cup from Nahia with quiet thanks. Killashandra wondered how the man had been able to sleep with her body buzzing.

Other storm watchers had disposed themselves for sleep about the room. Outside a hard rain was falling and a stout wind agitated the rain forest but the blow had become a shadow of its hurricane strength.

"We had orders to wake people as soon as the wind died to force five," Nahia said and extended a second hot cup to Killashandra for Lars.

"Has there been much damage? Many injuries?"

"Sufficient. The hurricane was unseasonably early and caught some communities unprepared. Olav is preparing emergency schedules for us."

"Us?" Killashandra stared at Nahia in surprise. "Surely you're not going to risk being seen and identified here?"

"These are my own people, Carrigana. I am safest in the islands." Serenely confident, the beauty returned to the catering area.

Lars had awakened during that brief interchange although he hadn't changed his position. His very blue eyes were watching her closely, no expression gave her a hint of his mood. Lazily he caressed her leg. Gradually his lips began to curve in a smile. What he might have said, what thoughts he held behind those keen eyes he did not share with her. Then he touched the garland she still wore, carefully unfolding a crushed petal. "Will you be crew for me? We won't have much time together southbound. Tanny, Theach, and Erutown sail with us, and we'll be dropping off supplies here and there . . ."

"Of course I'll come," Killashandra said eagerly. She wouldn't miss the trip for the world. Only . . . how would Lars take her deception? Would she lose him? Well, she didn't have to admit that she was the crystal singer they had incarcerated on the island!

The winds out of the Back Harbor were brisk enough to be dangerous, but the well laden *Pearl* settled down to her task like the splendid craft she was. Erutown was the nonsailor among them and took to a bunk in the forward cabin until the motion sickness medication had taken effect. Theach had appropriated the small terminal, smiling with absentminded good humor at his shipmates, before he resumed his programming.

Now that Tanny was on his way, he was as cheerful a companion as one could wish. Nor was he impatient with Killashandra as a crewmember. They had set sail once the winds had dropped to force three, one of the first of the larger sailing vessels to leave haven. Others were being loaded and crewed for their relief voyages. After the enforced idleness of the storm, it was good to be physically active. Killashandra didn't mind the wet weather nor the tussle with wind as she and Tanny made periodic checks of the deck cargo.

Fresh water and food were unloaded at the first stop, and some emergency medical supplies. The *Pearl* had carefully motored past the debris floating in the small harbor: roofs, the sides of dwellings, innumerable polly trees, fruit bobbing about like so many bald heads. That sight had startled Killashandra and she had nearly exposed her ignorance of island phenomena to Tanny. The inhabitants had taken refuge on the one highland of the island, but they were already hauling salvageables from the high tide mark and the water. They cheered the arrival of the *Pearl*, some wading out to float the watertight supplies in to shore. The exchange was completed in the time it took the *Pearl* to turn about and head back to the open sea.

And that was the routine at a half-dozen smaller islands. Killashandra had had a long look at the charts and the compass; they were taking a long arcing route, "her" island being the farthest point of their journey to the southwest.

The waters were studded with islands, large, small, and medium. All showed the devastation of the storm, and on most the polly trees were still bent over from their struggle with the hurricane: on some of the smaller islands, the trees had been uprooted. As no one made a comment on this waste, Killashandra could not ask how soon polly would reestablish itself.

In answer to a faint emergency call, they eventually sailed into the harbor of a medium-size island that had lost its communications masts and had been unable to make contact with Angel. Lars and Tanny went ashore there, leaving Killashandra in conspicuous sight while Erutown and Theach remained below. Some of the most urgently needed items could be supplied from the extras on board and Lars contacted Angel for the rest.

As they finally lifted anchor and sailed onward, Tanny's rising excitement was communicated to Killashandra. She could recognize nothing, but if they were indeed near the island of her incarceration, she had swum *away* from nearby help.

As they approached the next landfall, she didn't need Tanny's shout of relief to know they had reached "her" island; the huge polly tree in the center was a distinctive landmark. Not only had the tree survived but also its siblings or offspring, and the little hut she had made in their shelter. Lars had to restrain Tanny from diving into the breakers and swimming ashore in his eagerness to reassure himself.

"I don't see anyone!" Tanny cried as the *Pearl* motored toward the beach. "Surely she could hear the engine!"

"Is this where you want to dump us?" Erutown growled, surveying the uprooted polly, the wind-depressed trunks of more, and the storm debris on the once white sands.

"Oh, you'll be luxuriously situated, I assure you," Lars said. Killashandra had decided that Lars and Erutown were in basic disagreement on too many counts. Lars was delighted to deposit the man out of the way for a while. "We've solar-power units for Theach's equipment, all sorts of emergency camp gear, and plenty of food should you tire of the stuff the island and the sea provide."

"And a hatchet, a knife, and a book of instructions?" Killashandra asked. She was not above priming her surprise.

"There speaks the polly planter." Grinning, Lars flipped the toggle to release the anchor, cut off the engine, and gestured Tanny overboard. He was halfway up the heights to the shelter before the others had made the beach.

"There's no one here, Lars. Ye gods, what shall we do? There's no one here!" Tanny screamed.

Consternation smoothed Lars's features and he set off up the slope at speed. Killashandra followed at a more leisurely pace, wondering whether she would ease their fears. One look at the terror and hopelessness of Tanny's face, and a second one at the shock on Lars's eroded her need for revenge. Erutown and Theach were on the beach, out of hearing.

"You don't know very much about crystal singers, do you, Lars . . ."

He swung around, stared at her, trying to assimilate her words. Tanny reached his conclusion first and sat heavily down among the storm-strewn polly fronds, his expression incredulous.

". . . If you thought I'd just sit here until it suited you to retrieve me."

Chapter 14

Any discussion of *that* would have to be postponed. Theach and Erutown reached the height, looking about them for their fellow exile. Unable to look in Killashandra's direction, Tanny shot one horrified glance at Lars as the latter smoothly invented a note that she had been removed from the island by a passing vessel. He even flourished a piece of paper from his pocket as he commented that he was glad she was safe.

"That tears it," Erutown said gloomily. "We'll all be in trouble."

"I doubt it. A very good friend of ours skippered that ship," Lars replied without a blink. "She can't go anywhere without my knowledge." Tanny made a strangled sound and Killashandra grinned, choking on her laughter. "There's nothing you could safely do without jeopardizing yourself at this point, Erutown. It isn't as if you'll be out of touch," and Lars handed the man a small but powerful handset. "The frequency to use for any contact is 103.4 megahertz. All right? You can listen in on any of the other channels but communicate only on the 103.4."

Erutown agreed with ill grace, hefting the set doubtfully. With a sideways grin at Killashandra, Lars handed over hatchet, knife, and polly book.

"There now, you're completely equipped," Killashandra said cheerfully. "You'll find that a polly island is quite restful." She glanced maliciously at Tanny and Lars. "Everything you require—polly for food, fish in the lagoon for sport and a change of diet, and a fine reef to prevent the omnivorous from dining on

155

you. You're far better off than I was on my polly island, I assure you." Tanny squirmed, noticeably discomfited.

"Oh, we'll do fine, Carrigana." Theach grinned as he began to unpack the solar reflectors.

Lars chuckled, linking his arm in hers, and swinging her down the slope to the beach.

"C'mon, Tanny, I want to be at the Bar Island before sundown."

What with the routine necessary to up anchor and maneuver the *Pearl* through the one gap in the reef, there wasn't time for discussions until they were once again under full sail and beating due north for the Bar Island.

"Tanny, I think you'd better go below," Lars began, signaling Killashandra to join him in the cockpit. "What you don't know won't hurt you—"

"Who says?" Tanny growled.

"Fix us some grub, will you? All this excitement gave me an appetite. So," and once Tanny had slammed the hatch closed, Lars turned expectantly to Killashandra, "could I have some explanations?"

"I rather think a few are due me!"

Lars cocked an eyebrow, grinning sardonically at her. "Not when you must have figured out many of the answers already if you're half as smart as I think you are." Lars slid a finger across the scar on her arm, then he reached for her hand and held it up before her face, his thumb rubbing against the crystal scars. "'I came from the City.' Indeed!"

"Well, I did . . ." she said, deceptively meekly.

"Your best line, you witch, was the one about your having had no choice about coming to the islands!" Lars could not contain his mirth then and tilting his head back, roared with laughter.

"I wouldn't laugh if I were you, Lars Dahl. You're in an unenviable position in my files." She tried to sound severe but couldn't.

His eyes were still brimming with humor when he abruptly switched mood. He touched the garland. "Yes, I am rather. And on Angel Island. For one thing, according to island tradition, this announces us handfasted for a year and a day."

"I had guessed that the garlands signified more than your loving wish to adorn my person." The words came out more facetiously than she meant for she ached with a genuine regret. Lars's steady blue eyes caught her gaze and held it. He waited for her explanation.

"With all the will in the world to continue what we started, I don't have a year and a day here, Lars Dahl." The words left her mouth slowly, unwillingly. "As a crystal singer, I am compelled to return to Ballybran. Had I understood yesterday morning precisely what these blooms meant, I would not have accepted them. Thus does ignorance wound the giver. I am . . . tremendously attracted to you as a man, Lars Dahl. And in the light of what I have been told, heard, and overheard," she gave him a faint smile, "I can even forgive you that idiotic abduction. In fact, it would have been far more humiliating for me to have been caught in a raid on a bootleg brewery. What you cannot know is that I wasn't sent to Optheria merely to repair that organ—I am here as an impartial witness, to learn if restriction to this planet is popularly accepted."

"Popularly accepted?" Lars lifted half out of the cockpit seat in reaction. "What a way to phrase it! It is the most singularly unpopular, repressive, frustrating, discouraging facet of the Optherian Charter. Do you know what our suicide rate is? Well, I can give you hard statistics on that. We made a study of the incidents and have copies of what notes have been left by the deceased. Nine out of ten cite the hopelessness and despair at having no place to go, nothing to do. If you're unlucky enough to be unemployed on Optheria, oh, you're given food, shelter, clothing, and assigned stimulating community service to occupy you. Community service!—Trimming thorn hedges, tidying up hillsides, dusting boulders in the roadways, painting and repainting federal buildings, stuffing the faces and wiping the bottoms of the incontinent at both ends of life. Truly rewarding and fulfilling occupations for the intelligent and well educated failures that this planet throws upon the altar of the organ!"

He had been emphasizing his disgust with blows of his fist to the tiller, until Killashandra covered his hand with hers.

"Which one of our messages got through? It's been like tossing a bottle message into the Broad Sea with precious little hope of its ever floating to the Mainland."

"The complaint originated with the Executive Council of the

Federated Artists' Association, who claim a freedom of choice restriction. A Stellar made the charge, though I wasn't told which one. His principal concern was with the suppression of composers and performers." She gave him a wry grin.

Lars raised his eyebrows in surprise. "It wasn't me who sent that one." Then he seemed to take heart, his expression lightening with renewed hope. "If one appeal got through, maybe others have, and we'll have a whole school of people helping us— And you'll help us?"

"Lars, I'm required to be an impartial—"

"I wouldn't dream of prejudicing you . . ." His twinkling eyes challenged her as he threw his free arm about her shoulders, nibbling at her ear.

"Lars, you're crushing me. You're supposed to be sailing this ship . . . I've got to think how to go on from here. To be candid, I really don't have much more than your word that there is a widespread dissatisfaction, and not just a few isolated instances or personal grudges."

"Do you know how long we've been trying to reach the Federated Council?" Now Lars gestured wildly in his agitation. "Do you know what it will mean to the others when I tell them one message *has* got through, and someone is actually investigating?"

"That's another matter that we have to discuss, Lars. Is it advisable to *tell* them, or would it be wiser for me to continue covertly?" His jubilation subsided as he considered her question. "I suppose the suicide file would be acceptable as valid evidence. Has the restriction matter ever been put to the vote here?"

"A vote on Optheria?" He laughed sourly. "You haven't read that abominable Charter, have you?"

"I scanned it. A boring document, all those high-flown phrases turned my pragmatic stomach." Before Killashandra's eyes rose the vision of tortured architecture coping with "natural formations" so as not to "rape" the Natural World. "So there is no referendum mechanism in the Charter?"

"None. The Elders run this planet and, when one of them keels over and can no longer be resuscitated, a replacement is appointed—by the remaining undefunct Elders."

"No rising from the ranks on merit here?"

"Only in the Conservatory, and for especially meritorious composition and exceptional performance ability. Then one might possibly, on rare occasions, aspire to reach the exalted rank of a Master. Once in a century, a Master might possibly gain an appointment to the Council of Elders."

"Is that what you were after?"

Lars gave her a wry grin. "I tried! I was even willing to assault you to gain favor and show them what a good, useful, boy I was." He snorted at his gullibility.

"Granted, I haven't heard an approved composition, much less yours, played on the sensory organ," Killashandra began in casual accents, "but I was tremendously impressed by your performance the other evening. The musical one."

"The time, the place, the ambiance . . ."

"Not so fast, Lars Dahl. I was a trained musician before I became a crystal singer. I can be a critical auditor . . . and when I heard your music, I didn't know you as well as I do now, so that is an unbiased assessment. If by any chance the Stellar who lodged the complaint with the Artists' Association had had you in mind, I second his concern."

Lars regarded her with a genuine surprise. "You would? What music training did you have?"

"I studied for ten years at the Fuerte Music Center. Voice."

Lars nearly lost his grip on the tiller and before he had altered the course, the *Pearl* yawed in the rough seas, throwing Killashandra against him. "*You* were the soprano that night?"

"Yes." She grinned. "I recognized your tenor at the barbecue. Where did you learn Baleef's *Voyagers*? And the *Pearl Fishers* duet? Certainly not in the Conservatory."

"My father. He'd brought some of his microlibrary with him when he came to Optheria."

"Your father is naturalized?"

"Oh, yes. Like yourself, he didn't come to the islands by choice. If we mention your true identity to no one else—and what *is* your true name? Or don't crystal singers give them?"

"You mean to say you don't know the name of the woman you assaulted and then abducted?" Killashandra pretended outrage.

Lars shook his head, grinning at her with an almost boyish mischief.

"Killashandra Ree."

He repeated the syllables slowly, then smiled. "I like that much better than Carrigana. That was a rather harsh name to say endearingly. The *ell*s and the *sh* are sweeter."

"Possibly the only sweet thing about me, I warn you, Lars."

He pointedly ignored that remark. "My father must know who you are, Killashandra. It will give him new heart for I'll tell you frankly, he was far more discouraged about those arrested in the Elders' search than he let on to the others. Nor"— he paused, only then aware of the water sloshing in the cockpit about their toes—"nor do I like deceiving Nahia. She doesn't deserve it."

"No, she doesn't. Though I have the feeling she already has a good idea that I'm not the island maid I've been portraying."

"Oh? Was she at that reception in the Conservatory?"

"No, but she sensed the crystal resonance." Killashandra stroked her arm explanatorily. Lars caressed her then.

"You mean, that's what I've been feeling whenever we touch?"

Killashandra gave him a reassuring smile. "Not entirely, lover. Some of it is a perfectly spontaneous combustion."

Lars guffawed at that, embracing her once again.

"Shouldn't I bail or something?" she asked as the chill sea water splashed over her toes. His arm restrained her.

"Not just yet." He frowned, glancing off to port, not really seeing the sprouts of islets as he corrected their course a few points easterly. "However, if we tell my father and Nahia who you are—"

"Hauness, too?"

"What Nahia knows, Hauness does, and safe enough in both their hands. But then what? Hard copy on the suicide files is rapidly available. But I should insist that you meet with other groups to prove unquestionably that the arbitrary restriction to Optheria is not popularly acceptable."

"I'm glad you agree to that."

"In doing that, you will also need to avoid the Elders. It wouldn't do for them to discover you blithely treading the cobbles at Ironwood or the terraces of Maitland."

"You never told them you'd kidnapped me, so why couldn't I visit other communities?"

"Because you've now been missing for five weeks. How would

you explain such an absence, much less why you haven't repaired their precious Festival organ?"

"I'd've done that if that wretched security officer hadn't been in his flatulent dotage! My absence is easy to explain. I just don't explain it." She shrugged diffidently.

Lars sniggered. "You don't know how much our Elders dislike mysteries—"

"You have seen me playing a humble island maid, Lars. Try seeing me as a highly indignant and aristocratic member of the Heptite Guild." As she spoke, her voice became strange, disdainful, and Killashandra pulled herself arrogantly erect. Lars started to remove his arm from her shoulders in reaction to the transformation. "I'm *more* than a match for Ampris or Torkes. And they need my services far too much to annoy me again."

"I'm obliged to mention that they've sent for a replacement—"

"I know that."

"How could you?"

Killashandra grinned at him. "Crystal singers have preternaturally acute hearing. You and your little band of conspirators were only across the room from me. I heard every word."

Lars momentarily let the tiller slip but Killashandra grabbed it and steadied the helm.

"A second crystal singer might be all to the good, depending on who they send. But we've time to spare—it'll take nearly ten weeks to get another singer here. I happen to need the contract money so I'll repair their damned organ. Maybe this time, I'll get the kind of help I need." A thought suddenly struck Killashandra. "By all that's holy, I'll get you!" She prodded Lars's chest with her forefinger.

Lars snorted with derision. "I'm the last person welcome in the Conservatory!"

"Ah, but you will be welcome—as the man who rescued this poor abandoned crystal singer from durance vile!"

"What?"

"Well, that would answer why I've been absent. But, of course, I never set eyes on my abductor so I can't say who it might be." Killashandra fluttered her eyelashes in mock horror. "There I was, taking a stroll to compose myself after that horrible confrontation with an officious oaf and *wham! bang!* I'm coshed on the head and wake up, all alone, on a deserted island, heavens know where!" Killashandra got into the part with a faked swoon. "I'm less of a ham with a properly respectful audience, I might add. But there I am. Lost! Who knows who the dastards are— using a plural will suggest a whole group of conspirators, you see— And then you . . ." Killashandra laid a delicate hand on Lars's arm. His eyes were bright with mirth and he had his lips pressed together against distracting laughter. "You—loyal despite your terrible disappointment"—and Killashandra put her hand to her breast and breathed hard"—rescued me and insisted on returning me to the safety of the City, to install the crystal manual so that the priceless organ will be ready for the Summer Festival. Thus currying favor with the powers that be—which, in view of your subversive activities, is a very good idea—and saving them the cost of another expensive crystal singer. We are very expensive to hire, you see. And I have the impression that the Elders are credit-crunchers."

Lars began to chuckle, rubbing his chin as if he was visualizing those moments of triumph.

"If you can be trusted not to overact"—he ducked as she shook her fist at him—"you know, it might work."

"Of course it will work! I was able to gauge audience reactions to a pico. And more than just give you a well-deserved return for their meannesss and chicanery to you, I'll pretend that I'm so very nervous about a repetition of assault and battery that I'll need you by my side *all* the time."

"I think," Lars began, slowly, thoughtfully, "Father and the others will like this plan."

"Oh?"

Lars gave a rueful snort. "I got rather soundly told off for acting in a unilateral fashion when I abducted you, you know. My father is a mild mannered man most of the time—"

"Then let us by all means present this idea to him—them. And by the way, speaking of mild-mannered men, what do you know about Corish von Mittelstern?"

"The man looking for his uncle?"

"That's the one."

"Well, he's not an Optherian agent if that's what you're worried about. We checked him for residue."

"Checked him for what?"

"D'you recall the arc at the shuttleport? That's to prevent Optherians from leaving the planet. The arc is set to detect a mineral residue that is present in our bone marrow. There's absolutely no argument with the port guards if you try to enter the shuttleport. They just shoot."

"And that's activated by any Optherian passing the sensors?"

"Even visitors who've stayed long enough to absorb sufficient trace to be detected." Lars's expression was sour. "Like my father."

Killashandra half heard that comment, as she was thinking back to her exit from the port. Thyrol had been right beside her and the alarm hadn't gone off for them, though it had when the rest of the Optherian quartette had passed.

"Strange, that," she said half to herself. "No, Corish isn't Optherian. He came out on the *Athena* with me. But I've a very good notion that he's an FSP agent of some sort. I mean, what good is just one impartial observer if the object is to change the *status quo* of an entire planet? Even if I am a crystal singer."

"Did Corish know that?"

"No." Killashandra chuckled. "To Citizen von Mittelstern I was a brash and impulsive music student traveling cheap to the Summer Festival!" When Lars gave her a puzzled look, she laughed. "Being a crystal singer entails some rather curious disadvantages which are not relevant to the more important discussion at hand."

"I don't know much about crystal singers—"

"What you don't know won't hurt you," she said, waggling a finger under his nose. "But I'd very much like to know more about Corish, and if there is a missing uncle."

"Why didn't Corish recognize you on the beach?"

"The same reason you didn't. And he didn't know me all that well," she added, a bit amused by Lars's reaction. "He rather obviously, at least to me, cultivated the company of an innocuous and silly young music student. And one or two other anomalies alerted me."

"I'd encountered a few of those creatures recently myself," Lars remarked in a reproving drawl.

"I did the best I could with the background material I had."

Lars pulled her as close to him as the tiller allowed. "Your only mistake, now that I think back on it, were your comments about singing. *Every*one in the islands sings. But voice is not an instrument for real music . . . according to the Masters."

Killashandra began to sputter indignantly. "That in itself proves how stupid they all are!"

Lars laughed in delight at her reaction and then drew his feet up as the water began slopping up their calves.

"Tanny!" he shouted. "On deck, on the double."

The hatch was opened so quickly in response to his call that Killashandra wondered how long the young man had had his ear to the wooden panels.

"Haven't you found us something to eat yet? About time." For Tanny held up two heavy soup mugs. "Give it over and start bailing."

Chapter 15

It took quite a bit of persuading on Killashandra's part to reassure Tanny that she intended no reprisals against him for his very minor part in her abduction. Lars explained that he had managed to sneak her on board the ocean jet with the help of another friend who merely thought Lars's latest girl friend had had a shade too much new brew.

"One for the girls, are you, m'bucko?" Killashandra had asked in an arch tone.

Lars nodded at her garland. "Not any more, Sunny! I've made an honest woman of you!"

That exchange did more to reassure Tanny than any other argument Killashandra had presented. That and the fact that she was perfectly willing to help bail out the cockpit.

Bar Island was reached just before sunset, with enough time to unload the emergency supplies. The Bar Islanders had been directly in the hurricane's path and suffered more damage than any of the other islands on their sweep. Two men, a woman and a young girl had internal injuries which the medical facilities of the smaller settlement could not treat adequately. Lars immediately offered them passage on the *Pearl Fisher*, giving Killashandra a guarded and rueful grin of regret. Nor did they have a chance to be private that night. Everyone pitched in to finish constructing temporary communal shelters, and Killashandra found herself once again plaiting polly fronds, pleased that her deftness caused no questions. When a halt was called at midnight, Killashandra was far too tired to do more than curl up gratefully against Lars on the sand, her head pillowed on his arm, and fall asleep.

At first light of a sullen day, the injured were floated on bladder rafts to the *Pearl*, carefully hoisted aboard, then secured in the cabin bunks. Killashandra was given instructions by the medic for the administration of necessary drugs and care. The patients had been sedated for the voyage, so he expected no problems.

As soon as she could, Killashandra went up on deck. She found care of the sick and injured a distasteful necessity and the faint odor of antiseptics and medicine made her slightly nauseous. She said nothing about her disinclination, uncharacteristically wanting to sustain Lars's good opinion of her. He was bent over the chart display on the small navigational terminal, plotting the most direct course for Angel Island's North Harbor where the main medical facility was situated.

"Tide and wind are in our favor this morning, Killa," he said, reaching his arm about her waist and drawing her in to him without taking his eyes from the display. He tapped for an overlay of the route he had chosen and she could see how it made use of the swift channels between the islands and the fuller morning tide. "We'll be in North before we know it." He made a final correction and laid in the course. Now the display cleared to show him the compass headings and the minimum required tacking to slip into the swift current just beyond Bar Island's western reef. "Is the spinnaker set, Tanny?"

"Aye, aye skipper," the young man called from the bow as Killashandra watched the vivid red and orange sail belling out briefly over the bowsprit before the wind caught it.

There's an exhilaration to sailing a fast, trim ship, with a following wind and a current to assist smooth passage. The *Pearl* slipped into the flow as effortlessly as a slide down a greased pole. The sea was almost calm, and gunmetal green-gray, not quite the same color as the gray sky.

"Lucky it's today instead of yesterday," Killashandra said, settling herself in the cockpit beside Lars. He had the tiller on its upper setting so that he could see forward without the cabin blocking him.

"They're all secure below?"

"Secure and asleep! I'll check on the half hour."

They sat together enjoying wind, sea, and sail while Tanny

coiled lines and set all fair. Then he joined them in the cockpit, maintaining the companionable silence.

Just before noon, sailing smartly on the same westerly current that had nearly defeated Killashandra, they rounded the Toe and tacked eastward to sail right up to the large North Harbor pier at the elbow of the Angel. When Lars had been able to estimate his time of arrival, he had called it in, so medics and grav units were waiting for the injured. Killashandra, dutifully checking every half hour, had had no problems with her patients but it was an immense relief to turn them over to trained medical technicians.

"Father wants a word with us," Lars said quietly in Killashandra's ear as they watched their passengers being trundled away. "Tanny, anchor the *Pearl* at buoy twenty-seven, will you? And keep her ready. Don't know where we'll have to go next. Stay on the page, okay?"

Tanny nodded, his expression rather strained, as if he was relieved to stay on the *Pearl*, whose eccentricities he could cope with and understood.

If the Wing Harbor on the south side of Angel Island had appeared rustic and homely to Killashandra's eyes, North Harbor was the antithesis: that is, within the framework of the Charter's prohibition against raping "a natural world." The colorful buildings set up above the harbor behind sturdy sea walls utilized manmade materials and modernistic surfaces in some sort of tough, textured plastic and a good deal of plasglas so no vista would be hidden from the occupiers. If the architecture lacked warmth or grace, it was also practical in a zone where wind speeds could make a dangerous missile out of a polly branch.

Lars guided Killashandra up a ramp that climbed to the top of the Elbow, where a dormered structure commanded views of the main harbor as well as the smaller curved bay that featured the old stratovolcano that was the Angel's Head. A small sailing craft was tacking cautiously through the Fingerbone reefs at the end of the Hand. From the different colors in the sea, Killashandra could distinguish the safer, deeper channel, but she didn't think she'd like to sail that in a ship as large as the *Pearl*.

To her surprise, the first person they saw as they entered the Harbor Master's office was Nahia. She had been using the terminal and upon their entry she half rose, her expression eager for Lars's news of the stranded crystal singer.

"We needn't have worried ourselves for a moment about our captive, Nahia." Lars strode up to the empath and, before she could protest, kissed her hand.

"Lars, you simply must stop that," Nahia protested, giving Killashandra a worried glance.

"Why? I only do you a courtesy you fully deserve!"

Would Nahia comfort Lars, Killashandra wondered, after she had departed Optheria?

"The woman is all right, isn't she, Carrigana?" Nahia was by no means reassured by Lars's droll comment.

"Never better," Killashandra replied affably. She wondered why Lars was drawing the game out when he had specifically said he didn't wish to deceive Nahia. She gave him a sharp glance.

"Where's Father?"

"I'm here, Lars, and there's trouble on its way," the Harbor Master said, appearing from the front office. "I'm only grateful we had the hurricane, for it slowed down the official transport. There's to be a full search of the Islands. Torkes leads it so it'd be the height of folly to protest or interfere."

"Then isn't it fortunate that the crystal singer has been rescued," Killashandra said.

"She has?" Olav Dahl looked about, even to peering outside, seeking the woman.

Unerringly now, Nahia turned her worried face toward Killashandra, her eyes widening.

"And, Olav Dahl, by your courageous son, who found her abandoned on an island while he was on a hurricane rescue mission in the vicinity."

"Young woman, I—" Olav Dahl began, frowning at her light tone.

"You are Killashandra Ree?" Nahia asked, her beautiful eyes intent on Killashandra's face.

"Indeed. And so grateful to the loyal upright Optherian citizen Lars Dahl that this much-abused crystal singer feels secure only in his presence." Killashandra beamed fatuously at Lars.

Nahia's slender hands went to her mouth to suppress her laughter.

"I presume that in your official capacity you can inform the official vehicle of this felicitous news?" Killashandra asked Olav Dahl, smiling encouragingly at him to coax a less reproving response.

Olav Dahl regarded Killashandra with an expression that became more and more severe, as if he didn't believe what he was hearing, didn't condone her levity, and quite possibly would not accept her assistance. Slowly he sank onto the nearest desk for support, staring at her with amazement. Killashandra wondered that this man could be Lars's father until suddenly a smile of great charm and pure mischief lightened his countenance. He got to his feet, one hand outstretched to her, radiating relief.

"My dear Guildmember, may I say how pleased I am that you have been delivered from your ordeal? Have you any idea at all who perpetrated this outrage on a member of the most respected guild in the galaxy?"

"None under the sun," Killashandra replied, the epitome of innocent bewilderment. "I left the organ loft, rather precipitously, I hasten to add, because of a distressing incident with an officious security captain. I hoped that a stroll in the fresh air might compose my agitated spirits. When all of a sudden—" She brought her hands together. "I think I must have been drugged for a long time. When I finally regained consciousness, I was on this island, from which your son fortuitously rescued me only this morning!" Killashandra turned, fluttering her eyelashes at Lars in a parody of gratitude.

"I find that absolutely fascinating, Killashandra Ree," said a totally unexpected newcomer. Lars half crouched as he whirled toward the doorway framing Corish von Mittelstern. "Evidently your credentials were far more impressive than you led me to expect. So you're the crystal singer who was dispatched?"

"Oh, and have you found your dear uncle?"

"Actually, I have." Corish, his lips twitching with the first real amusement she had seen him exhibit, gestured toward Olav Dahl.

Lars was not the only one who stared at his father. Nahia gave a silvery little laugh.

"It was too amusing, the confrontation, Lars," Nahia said, chuckling. "They were circling the truth like two hemlin cocks. It was all I could do to retain my composure, for, of course, Hauness and I have known Olav's history. It didn't take me very long to perceive that Corish was not looking for the man in the hologram."

"I could hardly brandish Dahl's real likeness in case I jeopardized him. I'd memorized his facial characteristics so I thought I'd recognize him once I did see him." Then Corish turned to Killashandra. "He hadn't altered as much as you had. I didn't recognize you at all, with your hair and eyebrows bleached and a good few kilos lighter. If it matters," and Corish gestured at the matched garlands, "this is an improvement over the mawkish music student."

"So are you Council or Evaluation?" Killashandra shot a triumphant glance at Lars. "Olav's no more your uncle than I am. That inheritance business was very thin."

"For you, perhaps," and Corish inclined his body toward her, and his manner turned starchy at her criticism, "but you'd be surprised at how effective it was. Especially with Optherian officials who might get their percentage out of it." Corish made an age-old gesture with his thumb and forefinger. "Since all off-planet mail is censored, and not always delivered to the addressee, such a problem is peculiarly applicable to Optheria."

"I withdraw my comment." Killashandra nodded graciously and then seated herself in the nearest chair. "Do I also assume that Olav has been a—misplaced—agent?"

"Inadvertently detained," Olav replied on his own behalf, with a nod to Corish. "My briefing was at fault, on a point no one had considered at headquarters. To whit, the mineral residue, which is what trapped me here. And which provides the Optherians with such a simple means of preventing unauthorized departure from this planet. The exile has not been without profit to me," and he smiled warmly at his son, "though my time was not spent in activities of which the Council wholeheartedly approve. 'If you can't lick 'em, join 'em' is useful advice." He winked at Killashandra, who gave a crow of laughter. "However, you appear to be remarkably tolerant of the abuse you have suffered at my son's hands."

Killashandra laughed. "Oh, yes, since it has afforded me the chance to investigate a complaint."

"Oh?" Olav exchanged glances with Corish.

"Lodged by a Stellar of the Federated Artists' Association."

"Really?" Nahia clapped her hands together in delight, grinning at Lars with triumph. "I told you they were a good choice."

Corish had straightened up in his chair. "You . . . were also told to investigate?"

"Oh, yes, but the organ repair should have been the priority!" And she gave Lars a stern glance.

"We can discuss this at a later time," Olav said, raising his hand for silence. "We have a much more immediate problem in the imminent arrival of an official search party."

"I've outlined the way to deal with that, haven't I?" said Killashandra.

"To what purpose?" Olav asked. "Not that I am ungrateful for your forgiving my rascally son . . ."

"I think that would be my preeminent task, Olav Dahl," Killashandra replied with a grim smile. "I don't know which Elder supervises Security on this planet, but from what I have seen, your son is probably first on their list of suspects whether or not they've any evidence at all."

"Oh, I agree, Olav," Nahia said.

"Will Security believe your explanation?" Corish asked skeptically.

"What?" Killashandra rose in a flowing movement, drawing herself up to her full height, in a pose of haughty self-confidence. "Refute the statement of a crystal singer, a member of the Heptite Guild, a craftsman whose services are vital to the all-important tourist season? You must be joking! How, under which ever name you hold sacred, can they challenge what I say? Besides," she said, relaxing and flashing a friendly smile, "I have every confidence in Lars's ability to lend credence to the account. Don't you?"

"I must say, when you assume that pose, Killashandra, I'd hesitate to contradict you." Corish rose to his feet. "But now, I think that Nahia and I had better join Hauness and prepare to disappear. If they credit Killashandra's explanation, they'll not be likely to mount a twenty-five-hour radar watch, will they? So we won't have that problem to contend with."

Nahia had returned to the console, and was taking some hard copy from the retrieval slot. "I've all the charts we need, Olav, and my thanks for your suggestions. Just in case, I think we will take the devious course through the islands and then double back north. Lars, Olver survived the purge and you can contact us through him when you need to." Corish had her by the arm and was drawing her toward a rear exit. "May I hope to see you again, Killashandra?"

"If that is at all possible, officially, yes, of course, and I look forward to the occasion." Abruptly, annoyed at her stilted phrases, Killashandra stepped forward and swiftly embraced Nahia, kissing her on both cheeks. She stepped back, rather surprised at her uncharacteristic effusiveness until she saw the pleasure in Nahia's brilliant eyes and smiling face.

"Oh, you are kind!"

"Don't be ridiculous!" Killashandra replied fiercely, and then smiled with embarrassment. She felt Lars take her elbow and squeeze it gently.

"Should I need to contact you, Killashandra," Corish added, opening the door and all but pushing Nahia out, "I'll leave a message at the Piper Facility. As I already have." The door closed behind them with an emphatic slam.

"Come," Olav said, striding toward his front office. "We'll signal the jet. Fortunately, the return of the *Pearl* has been entered in the Harbor log and not too much time will have elapsed before we inform them of this good news." Olav paused in front of the huge console, frowning slightly at Killashandra. "You are certain you wish to go through with this? It could be dangerous!"

"Far more dangerous for them," Killashandra said with a snort. "To have put me in such a situation in the first place." Then she laughed. "Just think, Olav, with Lars's confession that Torkes and Ampris hired him to 'assault me,' to prove my identity, how they have compromised themselves."

"I actually had not considered that aspect." He turned to the console and began to send out the message.

The jet cruiser responded instantly with a request for visual with which Olav instantly complied.

"Look pleased but humble, Lars," Killashandra muttered before she turned to the screen, once more the haughty and arrogant crystal singer.

"Elder Torkes, I must protest! It is over five weeks since I was abducted from the City—a City, I might add, in which I had already been assaulted though I had been told in unequivocal terms that Optheria was a 'secure' planet, where everyone knew his place, and no unusual activities were condoned or permitted." Killashandra stressed the words as sarcastically as possible, enjoying the shock on the Elder's face. "Yet I could also be insulted by a minor and officious idiot, *and* kidnapped! I could be abandoned on this dreadful world. And it has taken you all this time to come to the islands which you yourself told me were populated by a dissident group. Dissident they might be, but courteous they are, and I have been made to feel far more welcome in these islands than I was during your pompous, ill-provisioned reception. I will also inform you, if you haven't already heard from them, that my Guild will take a very dim view of this whole incident. In fact, reparations may well be required. Now, what have you to say to me?"

"Honored Guildmember, I cannot adequately express our horror, our concern for you during your terrible ordeal." Those in the Harbor Master's office saw the effort which Elder Torkes was forced to make to moderate his own manner. "I don't know how the Council can ever redeem itself in your eyes. Anything we can do—"

"I suggest that you begin by expressing gratitude to the young man who rescued me after that frightening hurricane— Why, I thought I'd be swept to sea and drowned during the night. This is the young man," and ruthlessly Killashandra pulled Lars beside her. Torkes's face was unreadable as he inclined his head in the curtest possible recognition. "He's the skipper of the—what did you say your boat's called, Captain Dahl?"

"The *Pearl Fisher*, Guildmember."

"I might add that he took considerable risk to himself and his vessel to put in to that island. The monsters in the lagoon and all about it were in some sort of frenzy. The storm does that, he told me. But I was so relieved to see another human after all that time . . . Look at me! I'm a sight! My hair, my skin! I'm nothing but skin and bones!"

"Our estimated time of arrival is 18:30, Guildmember. Until that time, the Harbor Master will be able to attend to your comfort to the limits of his facilities." Torkes regained some of his usual repressive manner as he eyed Olav Dahl significantly.

"Begging your indulgence, Elder Torkes, but the Guildmember insisted that you be contacted before any personal comfort was seen to. We are hers to command until your arrival."

The picture was cut off at the cruiser screen. No sooner was it blank than Lars seized Killashandra in his arms, whirling her about the communications room, roaring his approval.

"His face! Did you see how he had to struggle to control himself, Killa?"

"You'll break my ribs, Lars— Leave off! But you can see how easy it is—"

"When you have one of the most prestigious Guilds in the FSP to back you," Olav said, but he was grinning as broadly with satisfaction at the confrontation as Lars was.

"Well, you have the FSP Council—"

"Only if they are in the position to acknowledge me," Olav reminded her, raising a hand in contradiction. "Which they are not, as my mission here was covert. The Council does not interfere with planetary politics when no other planet or system is affected. Optheria could not be approached on an official basis, you know. The FSP had ratified their Charter."

"With you to explain all about the lack of popular acceptance of the restriction, surely—"

"My dear Killashandra Ree, the situation on Optheria cannot be altered by one man's testimony, especially a man who could, by planetary laws to which he is now subject under intergalactic regulations, be tried and convicted of treasonous acts."

"Oh!" Killashandra's elation drained away quickly.

"Don't concern yourself with this problem now, my friend— for I count you one," Olav said, gripping her on the shoulder. "I am grateful for what you have already achieved." He took Lars's shoulder in his other hand, smiling with great affection at his son. "Ever since we saw the cruiser jet on the screen, I'd been wracking my brains on how to protect Lars from interrogation by Torkes. You have scuttled that plan, but do not deceive yourself that all will be fair sailing."

"It was a superb performance, Killa! When I tell the others—"

"Softly, Lars, softly," Olav said. "Torkes has had enough to swallow. Give him no more on your peril. Now, Killashandra, we must do the courteous for you, and lavish you with suitable gifts and personal services—"

"Teradia, of course, Father. And I'll advise her about our visitors—and their preferences." Lars grimaced with distaste.

"Yes, I'll warn her you're coming up and then I'll organize appropriate festivities."

"Why waste a barbecue on Torkes? He doesn't eat!" Killashandra said in disgust.

"But you do, Killashandra, and it's *your* return to civilization that we're celebrating!" Lars squeezed her about the waist.

"One point, Lars," and Olav laid a restraining hand on his son's arm as he reached and removed the garland from his neck. "I am sorry, but these would bring unwelcome questions." He reached for Killashandra's, and she hesitated before giving it to him.

"Not half as sorry as I am." She walked out of the building, Lars following quietly behind her.

Chapter 16

Teradia's house was situated on one of the upper levels facing North Harbor, and as they hurried up the steep, zigzag stairs that linked the terraces, Killashandra saw that much of the debris occasioned by the hurricane had already been removed. Groups of young people were unhurriedly staking polly trees upright and replanting those young pollys which had been entirely uprooted. Others were pruning bushes or restoring bedding plants.

"Are there any snakes in this paradise?" Killashandra asked when they paused at the first level to let her catch her breath.

"Snakes? What are those?" Lars asked, humoring her.

"Normally, a long, slender, legless reptile—only I meant humans with unpleasant characteristics." She made a weaving, sinuous gesture with her hand, and grimaced with distaste. "Surely the Elders make use of informers and spies."

"Oh, they do. Most of whom report themselves to us and pass back such information as we want the Elders to have." Lars grinned as his fingers caressed her arm. "It's not naive of us; islanders stick together. The Elders can give us little that we lack—except the freedom to leave the planet. To be sure, not many of us would leave: it's having the option to do so. And my father has a small detector so that people posing as tourists can be quickly identified. Father has a theory that only a certain type of personality is attracted to such an infamous occupation, and they often give themselves away. Strangely enough, by not singing!" He gave her a mischievous grin. "I was relieved to hear you singing lustily at the barbecue."

"I nearly didn't because, if I could recognize your tenor, you

176

might have spotted me as that midnight soprano. So I sang alto. But, Lars, isn't Nahia in jeopardy for being here? Someone might just slip up and mention her presence?"

Lars took her by the elbows and pulled her against him, unconcernedly stroking her hair. "Beloved Sunny, Nahia would be protected under any circumstances but, as it happens, only my father, you, and the people she came with, know she was on this island during the hurricane. Her party's ocean jet has been secreted in another of the Back caves, unseen by anyone. It's still there and won't emerge until we've had a chance to jam the cruiser's surveillance systems. Nahia and Hauness will use the islands to screen them from any possibility of detection when the cruiser takes you—all right, and me—back to the Mainland. Satisfied? I told you my father is efficient. He is.

"There will also be no one here tonight from Wing Harbor who might inadvertently remember the girl Lars Dahl had as his partner."

"But—"

"No one in Wing will feel slighted: they're all too busy with storm damage. Every building on the waterfront collapsed. And Wingers avoid Elder inspection as they would a smacker school."

Killashandra did feel relieved by his explanations. She was rather pleased, too, as she reviewed her confrontation with Torkes. Nor would she fail to be exceedingly cautious in the presence of any of the elders. Torkes would never forgive her for that tongue-lashing, and she knew that he would do everything he could to rank the others against her if a second confrontation was to occur. Still, she was glad she had launched her frontal assault on the fardling tyrant.

"We shan't leave anything to chance, however, Sunny," Lars went on as they climbed to the last terrace level. "If sun-bleached hair and eyebrows alter your appearance enough to deceive an FSP agent—"

"Corish was not expecting me to be on that beach, any more than you—"

"Then Teradia can restore your beauty. With more sophisticated clothes, and that hauteur of yours, you'll be every inch the crystal singer." Lars halted, swinging her into his arms again. No one was in sight. "Will the impressively beautiful crystal singer still favor her island lover?" He smiled down at her, but tension caught at the corners of his grey-tinged eyes.

"Don't tell me you—who braves hurricanes, Elders, and Masters—feared my ranting?" She soothed the creases from his eyes. "I assumed a role, Lars Dahl, from some opera or other. I play no role with you, no matter under what circumstances. Believe me. Let's not lose a moment of what we have together!"

She stood on tiptoe to kiss him and the hunger they both felt made them tremble.

"How are we going to make out, Killa, on board that cruiser? And back on the Mainland?"

"Oh, citizen!" Killashandra laid her hand gracefully against her bosom, fluttering her eyes, as much to keep back the tears as to embellish her assumed character. "When I trust to you my safety, where else shall you be but with me, wherever I go, even in my bedchamber? And have you seen where they quartered me in the Conservatory? You'll see, Lars. It will all be arranged *my* way!"

By then they had reached an establishment with a modest sign spelling out "Teradia" in graceful lettering. Teradia herself greeted them, a woman as tall as Lars, with a supple, willowy figure, and densely black hair very intricately braided. Her skin was olive and flawless, the pale green pupils of her eyes appeared luminous: she was a superb testimonial to her establishment.

"Olav Dahl wants the very best for you, Killashandra Ree, and I myself will see to your care."

"I'll supervise," Lars interrupted. "The bleaching must be . . ."

With a quick movement, Teradia placed one hand across Lars's chest and eased him away from Killashandra, a look of mild disdain on her elegant features. "My dear boy, clever you may be in some of the ways of pleasing a woman, but this is *my* art . . ." she began to draw Killashandra away with her, "and you will allow me to practice it. Come, Guildmember, this way."

"Teradia, that's not fair." Lars pushed through the door in pursuit. "I'm Killashandra's bodyguard—"

"Here I guard her body, though from the look of her skin and hair, you've done a poor job— Sun-bleached, dry-skinned, waterlogged child."

"Teradia!"

For the first time Killashandra had seen her lover rattled; she looked more keenly at Teradia. There was a twinkle in the woman's eyes, though her expression did not soften at his exasperation.

"It is, of course, as the Guildmember wishes . . ."

"How do you do it, Teradia?"

"Do what?"

"Quell him."

Teradia shrugged delicately. "It is easy. He has been reared to respect his elders."

"What?" Killashandra peered more closely at Teradia's face.

"She's my grandmother," Lars said with a disgusted growl.

"My compliments, citizen," Killashandra replied, trying not to laugh at Lars's discomposure. "I shall have your artistry to support me this evening—"

"And me!" Lars was emphatic.

So, under Lars's eyes and occasionally with his help and company, Killashandra was soaped and bathed and massaged and oiled, and repairs to hair and nail accomplished. Killashandra fell asleep during the massage and later Lars fell asleep while Teradia tinted Killashandra's hair and dyed her eyebrows dark again.

"It does make a considerable difference in your appearance," Teradia said, surveying her handiwork. "I'm not certain which becomes you more," she added thoughtfully. "You are a striking woman in either guise. Now," she went on so briskly that Killashandra did not have to make any reply to this assessment, "we don't have everything back from hurricane storage, but I know exactly where I put several unusual gowns that would suit your style and rank. Come this way, into the dressing room."

Killshandra looked over her shoulder at the slumbering Lars.

"If he fell asleep in your presence, he is far more tired than he would ever admit, Killashandra Ree. We will leave him so until he is needed to escort you back to Olav Dahl."

By the time Teradia had garbed Killashandra to her satisfaction, which had nothing, Killashandra realized, to do with her own, Lars had awakened. He executed a double take at the vision before him, presented a properly stunned expression before he began to smile then nod with approval.

"In there," Teradia said, flicking her fingers to direct him to another dressing room in the shop portion of her establishment. "We can't have a shabby escort. Not that any will notice you."

Killashandra began to frown, then the woman winked slowly and grinned. "That one is too sure of himself by half."

"He'll need it," Killashandra said sadly.

"Oh?"

But before Killashandra could say anything more, an unclad Lars had stormed into the room, waving a heavily embroidered, tissue thin, blue shirt and equally thin blue trousers.

"If you think I'm parading about like a stud on sale! When did I ever have the need to display—"

In one long stride Teradia reached the room, and scooped up a pair of blue briefs that had evidently fallen to the floor. She flourished them under his nose and then pushed him back into the room.

"Well, if that's the case . . ."

Killashandra stifled her giggles.

"You only wanted to take the limelight . . ."

He poked his head around the door. "Not when I know Torkes's proclivities. Then again," he paused in the act of withdrawing his head, "he probably has the cruiser packed with his boys so I'm safer here than in City."

"Who needs the bodyguard then?"

"Shall we have a mutual assistance pact? I read those were once very popular."

"Done!"

Lars slammed open the door, strode across the room, and gathered her into her arms, beaming down at her.

"If you spoil her dress or make-up . . ." Teradia's mock anger subsided as she became aware of the atmosphere between them.

Lars ached to kiss Killashandra as badly as she wanted to have his lips on hers. He sighed deeply and let her go. "You look regal, Killashandra! But I think I liked you even better on the beach at Wing! Then you were mine alone to enjoy!" His voice was low, his words meant for her, his sentiment unhindered by his grandmother's presence. "You have outdone yourself, Teradia." He pulled the woman close, and kissed her cheek.

Killashandra felt relief that there would be another sane and well-adjusted person to help Lars when she had returned to Ballybran.

"Now we had better go, Killashandra. The cruiser will have docked!"

Killashandra thanked Teradia as warmly as she could, wishing that the woman did not dismiss so casually her genuine gratitude.

As they started to retrace their steps to the Harbor Master's residence, Killashandra was instantly aware of an alteration in the ambiance. Far below the squat bulk of the cruiser jet did much to explain the change, looming as it did, gross and menacing, its white ovoid hull diminishing the graceful fishing vessels. The slanted superstructure, the little nodules of its armaments, and the sprouting whiskers of its communications and surveillance equipment added to its menacing presence.

Killashandra unconsciously hugged Lars's arm. "That is a very deadly looking machine. Do they have many of those?"

"Enough!"

"Can Nahia and Hauness escape it?"

Lars chuckled, relieving his own tension and reducing hers. "The *Yellowback* is smaller and faster, highly maneuverable and could slip through reefs that would ram the cruiser. Once they're away, they're well away."

Killashandra could see the coming and going on the ramp leading to Olav's—people bearing tables, chairs, seating cushions, baskets of fruit, bowls of fruit, jars, several men staggering under loads of provender. Killashandra had been expecting another beach barbecue, with its pleasant informality. It had not occurred to her that there might be no beach at North Harbor, nor would the Elder have been entertained in the casual setting she had so much enjoyed at Wing. She groaned.

Lars squeezed her hand. "What's wrong?"

She gave a gusty sigh. "State occasions! Formality! Scrapes and smiles and total boredom."

Lars laughed. "You'll be surprised. Pleasantly."

"How will your father get away with it?"

Lars grinned at her. "You'll see."

What she first saw was the disposition of guards, lining the route up from the harbor, spaced neatly and stiffly about the Residence, and armed. She had seen very few stun rifles in her life but she could recognize them.

"What was he expecting? Civil war?"

"Elders usually travel with a considerable entourage. Especially in the islands. We are so aggressive, you see." Lars spoke with deep sarcasm and she took in an anxious breath. "Oh, don't worry, Killa. I'll be circumspect. You'll not even recognize me as your impetuous lover."

She cocked an eyebrow at him. "I'll expect a return of that lover as a reward for my evening with Torkes. And why is it Torkes? I thought he was in charge of Communications."

Lars choked back a loud laugh, for they had neared the first sentry. "Elder Pedder is afflicted with motion sickness."

The sentry who had been watching them approach from the corner of his eye suddenly pivoted, ported his weapon, and stared with impartial malevolence at them. "Who goes there?"

"The crystal singer, you fool," Killashandra replied in a loud and disgusted tone. "With her bodyguard, Lars Dahl." When Killashandra would have proceeded she was stopped by the weapon. "How *dare* you?" She darted forward, grasped the weapon by its muzzle, and levered it forcefully to the ground. The surprised young sailor panicked and relinquished his weapon. "How *dare* you threaten a crystal singer? How dare you threaten *me*?"

Killashandra was seized by a violent surge of real anger at the archaic and inane formality. She didn't hear Lars trying to soothe her; she barged past two more sentries who came to assist their mate; she would have gone through the officer who came hurrying up the ramp, flanked by three additional guards on either side. She paused momentarily, seething at this additional obstacle. The officer had either encountered Elders in a tearing fit or he instantly recognized an elemental force. He barked an order, and the barricade suddenly became an escort which fell in behind the officer and Lars, who had managed to keep at Killashandra's heels as the enraged crystal singer stormed forward to the Residence, seeking the initiator of this additional affront.

Here Lars took the lead, adroitly indicating the way. She heard an exchange of urgent shouts. She had a confused vision of more guards snapping to attention, and another pair hastily opening the elaborately carved wooden doors—which despite her involvement in anger, she recognized as magnificent panels of polly wood. Then she was in the formal reception antechamber of the Residence, and she rememberred thinking that the tip of this iceberg was the business end. She continued her angry progress right to the shallow tier of steps that led down to the main level. With an alert and wary expression, Olav was half way across the floor to greet her. Behind him Elder Torkes was seated on a high wooden chair, members of his staff standing about the room, conversing with several islanders.

Automatically, Killashandra gave the assembled one quick glance before she proceeded toward Torkes. "Did I spend weeks on a deserted island to be stopped and questioned by an *armed* minion? To have a *weapon* thrust in my face as if I were an enemy? I"—and Killashandra nearly bruised her breast bone as she thumped herself with rigid fingers—"I am the one who has been assaulted and abducted. I am the one who has been at jeopardy and you—" Now she pointed an accusing finger at Torkes, who was regarding her in a state of shock. "You have been safe! Safe!"

Afterwards Lars told her that she had been magnificent, her eyes visibly emitting sparks, her manner so imposing that he had been breathless with astonishment. What operatic role had she been using?

"I wasn't," she'd replied with a rueful smile, for the effect of her dramatic entrance had more than satisfied her rage. "I've never been so angry in my life. A *weapon*? Pointed at *me*?"

Torkes heaved himself out of his chair, his expression that of a man confronting an unknown and dangerous entity and uncertain which course to take. "My dear Crystal Singer—"

"I am not your dear anything."

"Your experiences have unnerved you, Guildmember Ree. No aggression was intended against you, merely—"

"—Your wretched, suffocating need for protocol and an irrelevant show of aggression. I warn you"—and she waggled her finger at him again—"I warn you, you may expect the most severe retribution"—she caught herself; in her rage, she had been on the point of revealing too much to Elder Torkes—"from my Guild, reparation for the callous and undignified way in which I have been treated."

Torkes regarded her finger as if it were some sort of deadly weapon in itself. Before he could assemble a suitable reply Olav was at Killashandra's elbow, offering a glass of amber liquid.

"Guildmember, drink this . . ." His baritone voice, so soothing and conciliatory, penetrated her ranting. She knocked back the drink, and was rendered momentarily speechless. The shock of the potent beverage effectively restored her to discretion. "You are understandably overwrought, and have been needlessly upset, but you are safe here, now, I do assure you. Elder Torkes has already initiated the most thorough investigation of this terrible outrage and personally supervised your security here on Angel Island."

Olav's tactful reassurances gave her the time to regain use of her throat and vocal cords. Her throat was on fire, her stomach throbbing, and her eyes watered. Which seemed a good cue to develop. She allowed her tears to flow and reached weakly for Olav's hand to support her. Instantly she felt Lars take her right arm, and the two men led her to the other elaborate chair in the chamber, seating her as if she were suddenly fragile.

"I am overset. Anyone would be, enduring what I have," Killashandra said, using her sobbing to purge the last dregs of anger, for she estimated that she'd worked that pitch long enough. "All alone, on that wretched island, not knowing where I was, if I'd ever be rescued. And then the hurricane . . ."

A second glass was proferred. When she glared at Olav, he winked. Nevertheless, she sipped cautiously. Polly wine.

"Please accept my apologies, Elder Torkes, but that ridiculous weapon was the last straw." Her voice died away but she managed to sound reasonably sincere. Then she smiled weakly at the nonplussed Elder, and fluttered her eyelashes at his attendants. They seemed afflicted by some sort of paralysis. It afforded Killashandra considerable satisfaction that she had managed to confound an entire Optherian crew. They had stood in great need of such a lesson. She relaxed into the cushioned back of the chair.

"There isn't an islander in this Archipelago who would do you any injury, Guildmember," Olav continued, now offering her a finely stitched handkerchief. "Especially after the news of your devoted nursing of the Bar Island injured. When I consider how unselfishly you volunteered to assist, and you only an hour away from being rescued, why, we are all in your debt."

Shielding her face from Torkes with the handkerchief, Killashandra looked up at Olav. She blotted the last of the tears she could manage to squeeze out. She had received his message. She gave a sniff, then exhaled in a huge sigh.

"What else could I do? Their need was far greater than mine for I had suffered no real physical injury. It was excellent therapy," and she managed that on a rush of breath, "for me to tend those less fortunate than I. And I do feel safe with you, Harbor Master, and with Captain Dahl!" She touched each man on the arm, favoring them with a tremulous smile. Lars managed to give her shoulder an admonitory pinch which, she felt, indicated that she had milked this scene for all it was worth. "I hope you didn't encounter that ferocious storm on your way here, Elder Torkes?"

"Not at all, Guildmember. In fact," Torkes cleared his throat nervously, "we didn't set out until sure that the hurricane had dwindled. I ought to have listened to Mirbethan's representations, Captain"—he turned to the senior officer behind him—"for she offered to accompany us, Guildmember, on the slim chance that we would discover you here."

"How very kind of her."

"She would have been an ideal companion to settle your nerves, Guildmember."

"Yes, she was most considerate but, though I appreciate her willingness, I now insist on someone . . ." she waved a negligent hand in Lars's direction, "who is capable of managing himself in difficulties. I have seen Captain Dahl in action, fighting to bring his ship close enough to take me off that island, and in dealing with high seas, and injured people." And that should be the end of that notion. Had it been Mirbethan's? Or Ampris's? From whichever source, she'd not spend credit on it.

"If I may suggest it, Guildmember, would you be feeling recovered enough to dine now?" Olav asked, deftly changing the subject. "Or should Captain Dahl escort you to the quarters prepared for you here in the residence?"

"Why, yes," Killashandra said, extending her hand to Lars and smiling graciously at Olav, "I think that perhaps hunger is at the root of my deplorable temper. I'm not usually so easily upset, citizens." Now that the scene had been played, she *was* ravenous and hoped that Olav's hospitality would be to the standard she expected. It was, and she was seated on Olav's right at the beautifully appointed banquet table. Torkes was opposite her, Teradia appearing at his right hand. Evidently she had merely had to change her gown. Killashandra did wonder how she had arrived so promptly. Other charmingly dressed ladies partnered the officers of Torkes's retinue and from some discreet corner delicate music wafted to the diners' ears.

The food was sumptuous, a feat, considering the island had so recently been in the throes of a hurricane. As Killashandra sampled the many dishes presented, she realized that the components were not as varied as the manner in which they had been prepared. Polly—fruit, pulp, and heart—was the basis of nine dishes. Smacker was served as a chowder, boiled, broiled, fried in a delicious light batter and in a rich piquant sauce. The largest yellowbacks she had yet seen had been lightly broiled with slivered nuts. A succulent mollusc was offered, grilled with a dollop of some flavor enhancer. There were salads of greens, moulded salads of some jellied vegetable, fruit, and fish.

From the way in which Torkes's officers filled their plates, and refilled them when the dishes were presented a second time, they weren't used to eating. Torkes was abstemious by comparison although a fair trencherman away from Elder Pentrom's dietary regimen. He did not refuse the wine, either, though his two senior captains did.

When the first hunger was appeased, Torkes addressed Lars, his expression far too bland to be as affable as he sounded.

"Just where did you discover the Guildmember, Captain Dahl?"

"On a polly islet slightly east of Bar Island. I don't normally pass by for it's a bit off the regular trade route, but with the higher tides to give me clearance over the reef in that area, I could take a bit of a short cut to Bar, which I aimed to reach before sunset."

"Do you have this islet marked on your charts?"

"Of course, Elder Torkes. I will show you its location immediately after dinner." Lars had one hand on her thigh under the table and gave her a reassuring squeeze. Had his father tipped him off as he had her? "As well as the entry in my log which verifies the position."

"You keep a log?"

"Of a certainty, Elder Torkes. The Harbor Master is most insistent on such details which are, in my view, an integral part of responsible seamanship."

Farther down the table, an officer nodded his head in agreement. Torkes returned to his meal.

"What is this delicious fish, Harbor Master?" Killashandra asked, indicating the smacker.

"Ah, that is one of the island delicacies, Guildmember," and Olav launched into an amusing description of the habits of the tropical behemoth and the dangers of capturing it. In his tale he managed to touch on the strength and bravery of smacker fishermen and their dedication to an unenviable task. Much of the smacker catch went to feed the Mainland.

With such innocuous tidbits and discourse, the meal finished. Immediately upon rising from the table, Elder Torkes told Lars Dahl that now was the time to show him the islet.

"We can call up the information right here," Olav said, going to the elaborate sideboard of the dining room. One section of its flat surface immediately transformed to display a terminal while the island seascape above slid to one side exposing a large screen.

Killashandra, watching Torkes obliquely, saw him stiffen until Olav merely gestured for Lars Dahl to retrieve what documents he needed. Within a moment, a small-scale chart of the entire Archipelago dominated the screen. Lars tapped keys and the chart dissolved to a larger-scale one of Angel Island, then flowed left toward Bar Island, slightly upward, and in another adjustment, magnified the chosen islet, complete with its protecting reefs, quite isolated from other blobs of polly-treed islands.

"Here, Elder Torkes, is where I discovered the Guildmember. Fortunately, whoever abandoned her left her where there is a good fresh spring." He now magnified the islet so that its topographical features were apparent.

"I'd a bit of a shelter on the height," Killashandra said.

"Here," Lars agreed and pointed.

"And mercifully I was high enough there to be out of reach of the hurricane tides—just barely—I fished in this lagoon, and swam there, too, because the larger things couldn't pass over the reef. But, as you can see, gentlemen, I could not even have swum to an occupied island for help!"

One of Torkes's officers noted the longitude and latitude of the islet.

"Just thinking about it again distresses me." Killashandra

turned to Olav. "That was a magnificent dinner to be served so soon after a hurricane, Harbor Master. And it was such a pleasure, for me especially," and she graciously gestured, "to have so much variety to choose from and enjoy. Now, I would like to retire."

"Guildmember, there is much to discuss—"

"We can discuss it just as easily in the morning, Elder Torkes. It has been a long and exhausting day for me, remember. We left Bar Island with the injured at dawn and it's now midnight." She turned from the Elder now to Olav. "I am quartered tonight in the Residence?"

"This way." Olav and Lars immediately escorted her to the inner wall where a lift door slid aside. "Let me assure you that this is the only way into the living section of the Residence. This will be guarded well tonight." He peremptorily gestured for the guard to be posted.

"Elder Torkes, this is the first time that we have been privileged to entertain members of the Council," Teradia said, her deep voice tinged with awe as she took Torkes's arm and began to lead him back to the reception room.

Olav bowed over Killashandra's hand, smiling as he came erect and gestured her into the lift. The door slid shut on Killashandra and Lars and, with an exaggerated sigh of relief, Killashandra leaned against him.

He made a quick sign with his hand, his eyes busy on the ceiling pane.

"I am totally exhausted, Captain Dahl." So, Torkes had had the area monitored. That would make it exceedingly awkward for her and Lars.

The lift made a brief, noiseless descent and then the door slid open to a scene that caught her breath. The wide window gave onto moonlit harbor. An aureole of bright light illuminating the ancient stratovolcano as a second moon rose behind it. Of one accord, they stood for a long moment in appreciation of the beauty.

As Lars led her down to the short corridor toward two doors at its end, he glanced at the chrono on his wrist. Killashandra had time to notice the grin on his face before all the lights went off. Simultaneously she saw three short blue flashes, two along the corridor and a third one at the first door.

"What—" she began in alarm, but then the lights came on and Lars took her in his arms.

"Now we're safe!"

"You blew the monitors?"

"And his ship's systems. Father's got a way with electronics and . . ." he swung her into his arms and impatiently strode toward the first door, which slid open at their approach, "I'm about to have my way with you."

Which, of course, was exactly what Killashandra had been hoping for.

Chapter 17

A breakfast tray in hand, Teradia appeared early the next morning. Killashandra found she was in a large room brightly lit by sunlight reflected from the surface of the harbor. How the woman maintained her perfect grooming and serene composure Killashandra would have given much to know. Perhaps it had something to do with the experiential tranquillity of advanced years, although "old" in the physiological sense did not seem to apply to Teradia.

"And what of the day, oh bringer of delights?" Lars asked, settling pillows behind Killashandra. "Olav didn't miss a trick last night, did he?"

"He's still playing them this morning." Teradia smiled faintly. "May I compliment you on last night's performance, Killashandra? You were spectacular. I don't think anyone on Torkes's staff had ever witnessed its like."

"I was consumed with righteous wrath," Killashandra replied. "Imagine, someone pointing a weapon at me! A crystal singer!"

Lars soothingly stroked her arm and poured out the steaming morning beverage. "What's Olav up to today then?"

Teradia seated herself on the edge of the wide bed, folding her hands together in her lap, the faint smile still tilting the corners of her full lips. "As you surmised, the power failure effectively crippled the cruiser, since Olav had so courteously suggested that they hook up to the land facilities and spare the cruiser's batteries. When it went, Torkes was quite upset, worrying about you, Guildmember, and thinking this was another attempt on your safety. Of course, the lift wouldn't operate, and an inspection party quickly discovered that this apartment cannot easily be scaled

190

from the ground, so they posted guards on the waterfront. That's why your sleep was undisturbed." She lowered her eyes briefly. "Olav worked with the cruiser's engineers all night, to discover the trouble in our generators which, as you might suspect, had suffered previously undetected damage from the hurricane. All is now restored, except, of course, the units which were over-loaded!" She pointed out the several char marks where walls met the ceiling. "And, of course, the blown chip was discovered to be water damaged. Your father has a genius in that area. But I think you had both better put in appearances shortly. There are suitable garments for you both in the dressingroom and I have been re-quested to deliver necessities for you to the cruiser, Killashandra."

Teradia rose in one lithe movement, hesitated, and then moved to Killashandra's side. "You can have no idea how I enjoyed seeing an Elder rendered speechless. An excellent strategy on your part. Keep them off balance and guessing. They don't have any expe-rience with that!" Then Teradia laid her soft, fragrant cheek against Killashandra's and before the crystal singer could react, had glided out of the room and closed the door.

"You *have* made an impression," Lars said. "I'll tell you about Teradia's experience with the Council and you'll understand what she meant. I never would have thought of complaining about that sentry nonsense," and Lars gave an exasperated sigh, "but then, I'm used to it. It must be . . ." He searched for the appro-priate word, shrugged when he couldn't find it. "How remarkable not to need weapons or guards. Is it the case only in Ballybran, or did that felicitous state exist on your Fuerte, too?"

"Both. On Fuerte for lack of aggression, and on Ballybran be-cause everyone's too busy in the Ranges cutting crystal. We know our place and are secure in it," she paraphrased, mimicking Am-pris's voice. "Lars, how are we going to fuse the monitors at the Conservatory? They'll have installed them, I know."

"You could always throw another tantrum."

"No, thank you. Fits of temper are exhausting."

"Oh, is that truly why you're tired today?"

"Pleasure never tires me. Now let's eat and dress. I've just been attacked by a case of circumspection."

A few minutes later they emerged onto the reception floor with no further delays. An officer immediately leaped to his feet at their arrival, stammering queries about Killashandra's rest, apologies for any inconvenience caused by the power failure, and obsequiously requesting Killashandra and Captain Dahl to join the Harbor Master and Elder Torkes in the communications room.

Olav Dahl looked tired but there was a merriment in his eyes as he asked if all her needs had been satisfied. She reassured him, then turned to Torkes and affected surprise at his evident fatigue, fussing at him graciously.

"If the Guildmember is agreeable, I should like to depart immediately," Torkes replied, when the amenities were completed. He eyed her as if he expected her to demur.

"I left unfinished—even unstarted, to be totally candid—" she said, "the task which brought me to Optheria. I am more eager than you can imagine to complete the organ's repair and depart. I'm sure we will all feel relieved when I'm safely homebound."

Patently Elder Torkes could not be more in agreement, although he kept throwing skeptical glances at Killashandra as he made his farewells to Olav Dahl. Lars kept in the background. Meanwhile sailors in Council uniform had formed up into a guard of honor all the way from the Residence down to the pier where the cruiser's boat awaited its distinguished passengers.

Just as she reached the top of the steps, Killashandra looked up at the terraces, at the polly trees, the dwellings, at the old volcano on the Head, at the fishing skiffs serenely clearing the harbor, and she didn't want to leave Angel Island. Someone touched her arm and there was Olav with two garlands in his hand.

"Indulge me in an island custom, Guildmember." He draped the fragrant blossoms about her neck. Killashandra had just recognized the blooms as those with which Lars had handfasted her, when she saw Olav bestow one on his son. "Discharge your duties assiduously to the protection of the Guildmember's person, my son, and return to us only when you have seen her safely to the shuttle port!"

Before Killashandra could say anything in acknowledgment, Olav had stepped back. So, she could only smile her gratitude for his vote of confidence and proceed to the waiting boat. Impatiently she brushed aside the tears in her eyes before anyone could notice, and took a seat under the awning amidships. She was not surprised when Lars did not elect to join her for she could well imagine that he had been equally astonished by Olav's farewell.

She sat staring at the squat bulk of the cruiser, and liked it less the nearer she got to it. Nor did her opinion change during the three-day voyage back to the City. The Captain, a dour man named Festinel, was waiting at the top of the gangplank and escorted her himself to her cabin, explaining that her bodyguard would be quartered in the next cubicle, within hearing distance. She did not groan but saw this trip would be a repetition of the Trundomoux voyage. Well, she had survived that, too. Lars came along the companionway at that point and was greeted almost effusively by Captain Festinel.

During the evening meal, it was apparent from Festinel's deference to Lars that the man had been impressed by the islander's seamanship, or rather, the false account of his rescue of Killashandra from the dangerously positioned islet of exile. Killashandra added only her physical presence to the officers' mess. She was tired. She could feel muted crystal resonance in her body, though it was insufficient to raise the hair on those nearby. She was pleasant when addressed but limited her answers, contenting herself with enigmatic smiles. Elder Torkes kept shooting her wary, surreptitious glances but did not engage her in conversation. Which satisfied her. Keep him guessing about her, and off balance. Only how were she and Lars to have any sort of normal relationship if her quarters in the Conservatory were monitored?

On the crowded cruiser there was no way for them to have a private word or even the chance of a caress. Abstinence after the feast did nothing for her temper. So, preoccupied, she didn't notice the subliminal whine until the second evening, when she twitched all through dinner, rubbing at her neck and ear. Something was wrong.

"You're very unsettled tonight, Guildmember," Lars said finally, having endured her contortions throughout dinner. He spoke quietly, for her ears only, but his voice carried.

"Nerves— No, it's not nerves. Does this cruiser use a crystal drive?" She spoke in a loud, accusing tone, looking to Captain Festinel for her answer.

"It does, Guildmember, and I regret to inform you that we are experiencing some difficulty with it."

"It urgently needs to be retuned. As soon as you're in port. The way it sounds right now, it'll be broadcasting secondary sonics by morning."

"The engineer has been monitoring an uneven drive thrust but it should see us safely to the Mainland."

"You have reduced speed?"

"Of course, Crystal Singer, the moment the instrumentation recorded resonance."

"What is the matter with the cruiser?" Elder Torkes asked, only then aware of the nature of the discussion.

"Nothing for you to worry about," Killashandra said curtly, without glancing in his direction, for she was rubbing that side of her neck. She felt Lars stiffen beside her, and heard the tiny intake of her left-hand partner's breath. "I hope." She rose. "The whine is subsonic but highly irritating. Good evening, gentlemen."

Lars followed her and for a miracle they were alone in the companionway as he escorted her to her cramped quarters.

"Is it monitored?" she asked him in a low voice. He nodded.

"Do you require any medication to sleep, Guildmember?"

"Yes, if you can find some polly wine, Captain."

"The steward will bring a decanter to your quarters."

With a bottle of that inside her, Killashandra slept in spite of the increasingly audible distortion. The next morning, the noise was almost audible. Even Lars was affected. She was relieved when Captain Festinel requested her presence on the bridge. And concerned when she was shown the drive print-out. Festinel and his engineering officer were justifiably concerned.

"We were due for an overhaul when this emergency came up, Guildmember. The Broad Sea had more turbulence than we had anticipated, putting a strain on the compensators as well as the stabilizers, especially at speed." The Captain was flatteringly deferential so Killashandra nodded as he made his points, and frowned wisely at the print-out as if she knew what she was seeing. Fortunately the bridge was buffered against crystal noise as the rest of the ship was not, giving her a respite from the sound.

Until she put her hand on the bulkhead and felt it coursing through the metal.

"The drive is losing efficiency," Killashandra said, recalling the phrases which Carrik had used at the shuttle port on Fuerte, and obscurely pleased with herself that her memory remained lucid for that period, now so completely divorced from her present life.

"Frankly, I'd prefer heaving to and having a good look at the crystal drive, but our orders are to proceed with all possible speed to the Mainland." The Captain shrugged and sighed.

Killashandra decided against reassuring him. The drive was souring: she didn't need the printout to tell her that. But she had only the one experience on which to base an opinion and had no intention of ruining the image she had projected by a bad guess.

Then Captain Festinel asked hesitantly, "Do you really *hear* crystal resonance?"

Killashandra was aware of the expectant hush in the bridge as junior and senior officers, not to mention Lars at her side, waited for her reply.

"Yes, indeed. Like a dull ache from my earbones to my heels. If it were any louder, you'd find me asking for a life raft!"

"We know so little about your profession . . ."

"It is one like any other, Captain, with its dangers, its rewards, an apprenticeship to pass, and then years of refining one's skills." Killashandra was conscious, as she spoke, of one set of ears listening more keenly than others. She dared not look at Lars. "One facet of my training was retuning soured crystals." She made a rueful grimace. "Not my favorite occupation."

"Are there any prerequisites for the profession?" the older engineer asked, as he looked up from the print-out.

"Perfect and absolute pitch is the one essential."

"Why?" Lars asked, surprised by that unexpected condition.

"We're called crystal singers because we must tune our subsonic cutters to the dominant pitch of the crystal we cut from the ranges. A dangerous and exhausting task." She held out her hands so that all could see the fine white scars that crisscrossed the skin.

"I was told," Lars said in an amused drawl, "that crystal singers have amazing recuperative powers."

"That is quite true. Crystal resonance apparently slows the degenerative processes and accelerates the regenerative. Crystal singers retain their youthful appearance well into the third century."

"How old are you, Guildmember?" a brash young voice asked.

Frowning, the Captain turned about to seek the source of such insolence but Killashandra laughed. "I am a relatively new member of the Heptite Guild, and in my third decade."

"Are you able to travel anywhere you wish?" Did she detect a note of yearning?

"All crystal singers travel," she said with commendable restraint and then realized that her statement was hardly politic on Optheria. She had shown few examples of the tact for which Trag had chosen her. "But we always return to Ballybran," and she tried to make it sound as if going home was more desirable than traveling far away. No sense in arousing hopes on Optheria, especially in the presence of the cruiser's senior officers. "Once a crystal singer, always a crystal singer!"

In the same instant the printer extruded an impatient sheet, Killashandra felt a stab of crystal shock travel painfully from her heelbone to her ears.

"Kill the drive," she shouted as the Captain was issuing the command.

Breathless from the unexpected peaking, Killashandra sagged against Lars. "Congratulations," she said, hoping the sarcasm would hide the pain in her bones, "you have just lost one of your crystals. What are they? Blues?"

"Greens," the Captain replied with some pride, "but the same crystals since the cruiser was commissioned."

"And Optheria will spring credit for organ crystals with considerably more alacrity than for plebeian greens, huh?" Festinel nodded solemn affirmation. "Engineer, I request permission to inspect the crystal drive with you. My apprenticeship in tuning crystals may be of some use here."

"Honored, Guildmember." He strode to the comunit. "Damage report!"

"Sir," came the disembodied voice from the bowels of the cruiser, "casing blown, foam applied, no injuries."

"As you were!"

An acrid stench, a combination of odors arising from the intense heat on the crystal casing and on the foam, was still being exhausted by fans when Killashandra, Engineering Officer Fernock, and Lars reached the drive deck. The captain had hurried to inform Elder Torkes of the delay. Killashandra winced as she caught residual echoes from the other crystals of the drive. Or perhaps more than one element had blown. That could happen.

Fernock quickly directed his men to sweep up the now hardened foam and remove the cover. The durametal had been fractured by the explosion and came off in pieces.

"See if stores have a replacement." Fernock's expression suggested this was unlikely. "I'd not want to drive unshielded crystal."

"There'd be no problem so long as the remaining brackets are secure," Killashandra said, reasonably sure that she was correct. After all, there was no shield at all around black crystal. And they generated far more power than greens.

Suction was used to clean foam from the intact blocks but both Killashandra and Fernock warned the seaman to stay away from the fragmented shaft.

"Bracketing came adrift," Killashandra announced, remembering her manners enough to look to Fernock for confirmation.

"You're right. See, here?" Fernock pointed to the lopsided bracket at the green's base. "Now how could that happen?"

"You said the seas were turbulent. And that you were overdue an overhaul. Doubtless the discrepancy would have been seen and corrected. No fault of yours, Officer Fernock."

"I appreciate that."

"All right, then . . ." Killashandra squatted by the drive, reached for the shattered green crystal.

"What are you about, Guildmember?" Fernock grabbed her wrist and Lars moved forward.

"Well, until this crystal is moved, we won't." And she again reached for the crystal.

"But you've no gloves and crystal—"

"Cuts clean and heals quickly. For me. Allow me, Fernock."

The man continued to protest, but he made no further attempt to stop her. The first splinter did not cut her. Fortunately the broken bracket also made it easier for her to lift out the pieces. She pointed to a metal oil-slop pail and when it was fetched, she laid the crystal in it. She removed the remaining portions with only one slice, when the final fragment resisted her initial pull. She held up her bleeding hand.

"Behold, before your marveling eyes, the incredible recuperative powers of the crystal singer. One of my professions' few advantages."

"What is another?" Lars asked.

"The credit!" She reached for the suction device. "This won't be good for anything, and *no one* is to touch it on its way to the disposal unit." She depressed the toggle and made sure that the few loose slivers were cleared. "I'll check all the brackets to be sure none are loose. More problems are caused by faulty bracketing than anything else."

That was a tedious enough process but it was her own safety she was ensuring, hers and Lars's. With Fernock and Lars handing her the appropriate tools, she released each bracket in turn and reseated the five squat crystal shafts remaining. Then she struck each in turn for tone. They were all *G*s, of course, in a crystal drive, and to her intense relief, each emitted a pure unblemished tone. She glanced up at Lars, once, to see him nod at the true *G* she had just sung. He had not been the only one fascinated by the process. There had been a constantly changing if discreet audience on the catwalk above the drive floor. As well. This would only enhance the image of the crystal singer. And it might just safeguard her against any more nonsense from the Elders.

"There now, Mr. Fernock," she said at last, arching her back against the crick caused by awkward positions. "I think you can safely proceed with reconnections. I don't think there's any danger if the load is properly apportioned. A five-shaft drive should generate enough power to get us to the Mainland." She held up the hand that had been profusely bleeding an hour before. "See? All better."

"Guildmember, do you know how long it would have taken me and my men to make such repairs?"

"I couldn't begin to guess, Mr. Fernock, but do get on with the job." She smiled at the disconcerted officer and then, with Lars a step behind her, retraced her steps to the upper deck.

"Citizen, you're too much for this island boy."

"Huh! I was showing off . . . again," and, leaning backward on one hand, kissed him lustily. Just in time to avoid the exchange's being witnessed by Captain Festinel, who was hurrying to check on repairs. "You were a very deft assistant, Captain Dahl. I must ask for your help with the organ repair." She sedately continued her ascent.

"Surely, just perfect pitch—" Lars began as they returned to the wardroom.

"—Perfect and absolute—"

"—As you say, isn't the only requirement for your profession?"

"The major one. Ballybran is a Code Four planet—"

"What does that mean? I'm an island lad from a iggerant planet," and Lars' voice was rich with contempt.

"Dangerous. Singing crystal is rated a 'highly dangerous' profession, limited to Type IV through VIII bipedal humanoids . . ."

"Are there any other kind?"

"Don't alien life forms come for the Festival? The Reticulans are avid musicologists though I could never come to terms with their croons as music."

"Are they the ones that look like an assembly of twigs on a barrel?" The wardroom was empty and Lars swung her into his arms, kissing her passionately, stroking her body, murmuring endearments. But knowing that they could be interrupted at any time inhibited Killashandra's response, even as she yearned for more. At a scraping sound, they broke apart, Killashandra sliding breathlessly into the nearest chair.

"What a delightful description of Reticulans! The barrel is mostly windbag but I've never been close enough to discover which of their pseudopods are the pipes."

Lars stopped pacing, for the noise in the companionway had ceased, and he came back to fondle her.

"A candidate for Guild membership has to pass Physical Fitness Test SG-1, Psychological Profile SG-1—which you'd never pass if you continue to do *that*, Lars—and Education Level 3."

"I'm not applying to the Guild, only applying a member . . ."

This time the footsteps stopped and the door was slid back. Mr. Fernock entered, smiling broadly when he saw the occupants.

"We'll be underway in ten minutes, Guildmember, thanks to

your invaluable assistance. And we'll be able to make a reasonable enough speed on five shafts to reach our destination on time."

"How marvelous," Killashandra said in a languid drawl. Marvelous was not really the way she felt, considering the inner turmoil Lars's caresses had stimulated. She couldn't get to the City and the Conservatory fast enough.

Chapter 18

Fortunately Lars was equally frustrated by their lack of privacy and made no further overtures. Perversely, Killashandra missed them. The cruiser had broken out flags and a full honor guard for the ceremonial and triumphant return. Killashandra steeled herself for yet another protocologically correct reception. She reflected on what scene she could produce to shorten the tedium, and debated whether or not a scene would produce any advantage. She had made several points. Unless she had sufficient provocation, she decided to leave well enough alone. For now. She might need to produce an effect to gain privacy within her suite.

For she was determined to enjoy Lars without any surveillance for whatever time remained to them. She could, of course, stretch out the organ repair as long as she wished. Or her instruction of technicians. She could include Lars in that program. He had the perfect—and absolute—pitch to tune crystal as well as the strength and manual dexterity required. She must do everything she could to make him indispensable to the Elders, for whatever protection that could provide him, since he didn't seem at all interested in leaving Optheria. Even if that were possible.

"We're near enough for you to have a spectacular view of the City Port," Lars said, interrupting her reflections.

"A 'natural' port?" She smiled.

"Completely, though not nearly as good a natural harbor as North."

"Naturally."

"Captain Festinel awaits your arrival on the bridge."

"How courteous! Where's Torkes?"

"Burning up a few communication units with orders. He was incensed that you had to bloody your hands on the drive of a mere cruiser."

"Doesn't he value his skin as much as I do mine?"

Her entry rated salutes, rigid attention from the seamen and a smile and a warm handshake from Festinel. She politely accepted his effusive thanks and then pointedly turned to watch the rapidly approaching shoreline.

The City Port bustled with activity: small water taxis skipping across the waves, larger barges wallowing across their swells, and coastal freighters awaiting their turn at the piers which, with their array of mechanical unloading devices, were anything but "natural." The cruiser's velocity had moderated considerably now that it was in congested waters. Ponderously it approached the Federal docking area, where sleek courier vessels bobbed alongside two more squat cruisers.

Killashandra had no difficulty identifying their berth—it was crowded with a welcoming committee, all massed white and insipid pale colors, blurred faces turned seaward, despite the glare of the westering sun, which was full in their eyes. The cruiser swung its bow slightly to port and the drive was cut, momentum carrying the big vessel inexorably to the dock and the grapples clanked against the hull, bringing it to a halt with a barely perceptible jolt.

"My compliments on a smooth docking, Captain Festinel—and my thanks for an excellent voyage." Killashandra made gracious noises to all the bridge staff and then swept out to get the rest of the tedious formalities over.

"Ampris!" Lars grunted as they reached the portal. Beneath them the gangway was extruding the few meters to the dock.

"Of course, and my quartette lined up like the puppets they are. I think I am developing a splitting headache. All that crystal whine, you know." She raised her hand to her forehead.

"See what line Ampris takes first." Lars's face was set, his nostrils flaring a little as he settled his respiratory rate.

Killashandra suppressed a perfectly natural surge of repugnance for a man who had ordered an assault on her, then hypocritically assured her that the culprit would be punished . . . How could she punish Ampris? The method she had employed with Torkes would not work; Ampris was too wily.

The gangplank had locked in place, the honor guard was arranged, Elder Torkes appeared, the welcoming committee began to applaud and, every inch the gracious celebrity, Killashandra descended. Mirbethan took a step forward, anxiously scanning Killashandra's face for any sign of the "ordeal." Thyrol, Pirinio, and Polabod all bowed low but permitted Elder Ampris to do the honors.

"Guildmember Ree, you cannot imagine our elation when we learned of your safe deliverance—" Then Ampris caught sight of Lars, whom he was patently not expecting.

"This is Captain Lars Dahl who rescued me so boldly, and at no small risk to himself and his vessel. Captain Dahl, this is Elder Ampris." Killashandra took the plunge, pretending ignorance of any previous contact between the two men. "I am forever indebted to Captain Dahl, as I'm sure the Council of Elders must be, for delivering me from that wretched patch of nowhere."

Lars saluted crisply and impassively as Elder Ampris executed the shallowest of acknowledgments.

"The Harbor Master at Angel Island has detached him from duty there to be my personal bodyguard." Killashandra gave an elegantly delicate shudder. "I won't feel safe without his sure protection."

"Quite understandable, Guildmember; however, I think that you'll find *our* security measures—"

"I felt quite secure within the Conservatory, Elder Ampris," Killashandra said demurely. "I seem to be only at risk when I leave its sanctuary. I assure you I have no desire to do that again."

"Security Leader Blaz—"

"I'll not have that officious oaf near me, Elder Ampris. He's the reason I was put in jeopardy. The man has no intelligence or tact. I don't trust him to spit in the right direction. Captain Lars Dahl is in charge of my personal security at my personal insistence. Have I not made myself clear?"

For a second Elder Ampris looked about to argue the point, but the moment passed. He inclined his head again, forced his face into a grim smile, and then gestured toward the waiting vehicle.

"Why this vast throng?" Killashandra asked, smiling graciously about her.

"Some of the winning composers and prospecive performers for this year's Festival and final-year students."

"All waiting for the organ to be repaired?"

Elder Ampris cleared his throat. "Yes, that is true."

"Well, I shan't delay them any longer than necessary. Especially since Captain Dahl proved so capable in assisting me with the cruiser drive."

Ampris stopped midstride and stared first at her, then incredulously at Lars.

"Yes, weren't you informed that the cruiser had drive difficulties this morning? One of the crystals shattered. I still have a slight headache from the distortion. Naturally the ship could not proceed without emergency repairs. And while that was merely a matter of removing the shards and resetting the brackets on the undamaged crystals, it does require steady hands, a keen eye and ear. Captain Dahl was far more adept than the cruiser's engineer. And he has the perfect and absolute pitch required. I think he will prove an admirable assistant, one in whom I certainly repose complete trust. You do agree, I'm sure." They had reached the vehicle now. "You first, Captain Dahl, I shall want Elder Ampris on my right."

Lars complied before the Elder could blurt out a protest and Killashandra settled herself, smiling as warmly as possible at Ampris, just as if she hadn't delivered a most unpalatable request.

The quartette settled itself in the seats behind them and the vehicle left the dock area. Ports required much the same facilities throughout the galaxy. Fortunately nature had conspired in favor of human endeavors, so warehouses, seamen's hostels, and mercantile establishments were not quite so tortuously situated in City Port as in the City proper. The Music Conservatory on its prominence was visible as soon as the Port gave way to an agricultural belt. From this approach, Killashandra could see the lateral elevation of the Festival auditorium and the narrow path that led to the suburb Lars had called Gartertown. She wondered if there'd be a new brew soon. Maybe Lars could collect a few bottles for her?

The drive was in the main a silent one, with Ampris stewing beside her and Lars stiffly silent. The strained atmosphere began to affect her, causing her to wonder if she really were doing the right thing for Lars. Yet if she hadn't taken pains to divert suspicion from him, he'd be running with a threat of rehabilitation hanging over him. Had she erroneously assumed that he was as eager to continue their relationship as she was? Olav had wreathed them both with the handfast garlands. Surely that act held significance. She'd best have it out with Lars as soon as possible.

After what seemed a long time, they drew up at the imposing entrance to the Conservatory.

"I dispensed with the formality of a welcoming throng, Guildmember, in the interests of security." Elder Ampris got out of the car and turned to give her a steadying hand.

"I have no fear of a second assault, Elder Ampris," she said, taking his dry clasp and smiling ingenuously at him, "with Captain Dahl beside me. And, you know, after the courtesies I received at the hands of the islanders, I'm beginning to think that that attack, as well as my abduction, were made to seem island-instigated. I can't imagine an islander being jealous of anything on the Mainland."

Lars had emerged from the car, but his expression was devoid of reaction. The skin on Ampris's face was taut with the effort of controlling his. "With your comfort in mind, Guildmember, perhaps you might prefer to eat in your suite this evening?"

"That is so thoughtful, Elder Ampris. Resetting a crystal drive is an exhausting process. So many fiddling things requiring fine muscle coordination and complete concentration." She sighed wearily, turing slightly to smile apologetically at Mirbethan and the others. "I want to be well rested to attack that repair tomorrow. Oh, Thyrol? With Captain Dahl to assist me, I won't need any other helpers."

She took Lars's arm and ascended the shallow steps to the main entrance. She felt him quivering but for which of several reasons she couldn't have told without glancing at his face. And she didn't dare do that. "Do you know the way to my quarters, Captain Dahl?"

"If I may just escort you," Mirbethan answered, hastening to lead the way.

"I was never in this part of the Conservatory, Crystal Singer" Lars said as they entered the imposing main lobby.

"You've been to the conservatory, Captain Dahl?" Killashandra asked.

"Yes, Guildmember, I studied here for three years."

"Why, Captain, you have unexplored capabilities. Are you then a singer?"

"Vocal music is not taught at the Conservatory: only the organ."

"Really, I would have thought the planet's main Conservatory would exploit every musical potential. How odd!"

"Do you find it so, Guildmember?"

"In other parts of the FSP, vocal arts are much admired, and a Stellar soloist highly respected."

"Optheria places more value on the most complex of instruments." Lars's tone was of mild reproof. "The sensory organ combines sound olfactory and tactile sensations to produce a total orchestration of alternate reality for the participant."

"Is the organ limited to Optheria? I've never encountered one before in all my voyaging."

"It is unique to Optheria."

"Which certainly has many unique experiences for the visitor."

Mirbethan's pace, and her erect back, seemed to reflect at once her approval, and shock, at their conversation.

"Why, then, Captain Dahl, if you have studied to use the organ, are you sailing about in the islands?"

"Because, Guildmember, my composition was ah . . . not approved by the Masters who pass judgment on such aspirations, so I returned to my previous occupation."

"To be sure, I am selfishly glad, Captain—for who would have rescued me had you not been in those waters?" Killashandra sighed deeply just as they turned the corridor into the hall she did recognize. "Mirbethan?"

The woman whirled, her expression composed though she was breathing rather rapidly.

"By any chance, I mean, I know I've been gone a good while, but I do hope that those beverages . . ."

"Your catering facility has been completely stocked with the beverages of your choice."

"And the chimes have been turned off?"

Mirbethan nodded.

"And the catering unit instructed to supply proper-size portions of food without requiring additional authorization?"

"Of course."

"Thank you. I, for one, am starving. Sea air, you know." With a final smile, Killashandra swept through the door Lars held open.

By the time he had shut it, she had discovered four ceiling surveillance units in the main salon. "I am quite weary, Captain."

"With due respect, Guildmember, you did not eat much of the evening meal, perhaps a light supper—"

"The variety on the catering unit seems geared to student requirements . . . unless you, having spent time here, can make a suggestion."

"Indeed I would be delighted to, Guildmember." Lars located several more as they moved through the suite to the two bedrooms. He peered into the first bathing room and grinned broadly at her. "May I draw you a bath?"

"An excellent idea." She strode to what was evidently the one room that had been left unmonitored.

Lars began filling the tub, having turned the taps on full.

He reached into his tunic and extracted an innocuous metal ball. "A deceiver, Father calls it. It distorts picture and sound—we can be quite free once it's operating. And when we leave the suite,"—he grinned, miming the device returned to his pocket—"it'll drive their technicians wild."

"Won't they realize that the distortion only works when we're here?"

"I suggest that tomorrow you complain about being monitored in the bedroom. Can we cope with just one free room?" He began to undress her, his expression intense with anticipation.

"Two," Killashandra corrected him with a coy moue as the bright and elegant overall Teradia had chosen for her fell in a rainbow puddle at her feet.

It was, of course, thoroughly soaked with the water displaced when Lars overbalanced her into the tub.

When they had sated their appetites sufficiently, Killashandra idly described wet circles on the broad expanse of Lars's chest. "I think that with the best motives in the world, I have placed you in an awkward situation."

"Beloved Killashandra, when you sprang that," and he aptly mimicked her voice, "'I have no fear of being assaulted with Captain Dahl beside me,' I nearly choked."

"I felt you quaking, but I didn't know if it was laughter or outrage."

"And then suggesting that someone else had instigated the attack to implicate islanders—Killashandra, I wouldn't have missed that for anything. You really got mine back on the flatulent fardling. But watch him, Killa. He's dangerous. Once he and Torkes start comparing notes . . ."

"They still have to get that organ fixed in time for all those lucky little composers to practice their pieces. I'm here and even if a replacement is coming, it's the old bird-in-the-hand."

"Yes, and they've got to have done all the Mainland concerts to ensure a proper Optherian attitude toward visitors."

"Proper attitude? Mainland concerts? What do you mean?"

Lars held her slightly away from him in the capacious bath, reading her face and eyes.

"You don't know? You don't really know why that organ is so important to the Elders?"

"Well, I do know that the set-up will produce an intense emotional experience for the listener. It verges on illegal manipulation."

Lars gave a sour laugh. "Verges? It *is*. But then you would only have seen the sensory elements. The subliminal units are kept out of sight, underneath the organ loft."

"Subliminals?" Killashandra stared at Lars.

"Of course, ninny. How do you think the Elders keep the people of Optheria from wanting any of the marvels that the visitors tell them about? Because they've just had a full dose of subliminal conditioning! Why do you think people who prefer to exercise their own wits live in the islands? The Elders can't broadcast the subliminals and sensories."

"Subliminals are illegal! Even the sensory feedbacks border on illegality! Lars, when I tell the FSP this—"

"Why do you think my father was sent to Optheria? The FSP

208

wants proof! And that means an eyeball on the illegal equipment. It's taken Father's group nearly thirty years to get close enough."

"Then you weren't here just to learn to play that blasted thing?"

"Playing the blasted thing is the only way to get close enough to it to find out where the subliminal units are kept. Comgail did. And died!"

"You're suggesting he didn't suicide?"

Lars shook his head slowly. "Something Nahia said during the hurricane confirmed my suspicion that he hadn't. You see, I knew Comgail. He was my composition tutor. He wasn't a martyr type. He certainly wanted to live. He was willing to risk a lot but not his life. Nahia mentioned that he'd asked Hauness to provide him with rehab blocks. A good block—and Hauness is the best there is—prevents the victim from confessional diarrhea and a total loss of personality. Comgail had been so above reproach all the time he'd been at the Conservatory that not even a paranoid like Pedder would have suspected him of collusion with dissidents. But, for shattering the manual, Comgail'd automatically be sent to rehab. He had prepared himself for that. He wasn't killed by a crystal fragment, Killa, he was murdered by it. I think it was because he had found the access to the subliminal units."

"Subliminals!" Killashandra seethed with horror at the potentially total control. "And he found the access? Where? All I need is one look at them—"

Lars regarded her solemnly. "That's all *we* need—once we find them. They've got to be somewhere in the organ loft."

"Well, then"—Killashandra embraced him exuberantly— "wasn't I clever to insist that you and I handle the repairs all by ourselves."

"If we're allowed!"

"You've the jammer." She rose from the deep bath, Lars following her. "Say, if your father's so clever with electronics, why hasn't he figured a way to jam the shuttleport detection arch?"

Lars chuckled as she dried him, for once more interested in something other than his physical effect on her.

"He's spent close to thirty years trying. We even have a replica of the detector on Angel. But we cannot figure a way to mask that residue. Watch out for my ears!" She had been briskly towelling his hair.

"Does the detector always catch the native?"

"Infallible."

"And yet . . ." She wrapped her hair in a towel. She pointed to the jammer and then proceeded to the salon. Lars followed, the jammer held above his head like a torch, a diabolical gleam in his eye as he waved it at each of the monitors he passed. "Yet when Thyrol came out right with me, the detector didn't catch *him*. And passed me."

"What? No matter how many people pass under it, it will always detect the native!"

"It didn't then! I wonder if it had anything to do with crystal resonance."

"You mean in you?"

"Hmmm. It's not exactly something we can experiment with, is it? Prancing in and out of the shuttleport."

"Hardly—and we're half a world away from the only other one."

"Well, we can worry about that later. After we've found the access and after we've repaired that wretched organ! Now," and she opened the doors of the beverage store with a flourish, "what shall we drink with our supper?"

Chapter 19

Killashandra woke before the chimes, which did not sound in her suite but were nevertheless audible from the adjacent sections of the Conservatory. She woke refreshed and totally relaxed, and cautiously eased herself away from Lars's supine body so that she might have a better view of his sleeping form. She felt oddly protective of him as she propped her head on one hand and minutely inspected his profile. Thus she noticed that the tips of his long eyelashes were bleached and the lid itself was not as dark as the surrounding skin. Fine laugh, or sun lines, fanned out from the corners to the temple. The arch of his nose just missed being too high, too thin, being balanced by fine modeling and length. His cheeks wore a dusting of freckles which she hadn't noticed before. And several dark brow hairs were out of line as the brow curved around the eye socket. Several hairs bristled straight up at the inner edges of brows that would almost meet when he frowned.

She liked best his wide lips, more patrician than sensual. She knew the havoc they could raise with her body and felt they were perhaps his best feature. Even in sleep, the corners raised slightly. His chin was rather broader than one was aware when his face was mobile, but the strong jawline swept back to well-shaped ears, also tan, with a spot of new sunburn about to peel on the top skin.

The column of his neck was strong and the pulse beat in his throat. She wanted to put her finger tip on it and almost did before retracting her hand. He was more truly hers when asleep, untouched by stress, relaxed, his rib cage barely moving.

She loved the line of his chest, the smooth skin clothing smooth

211

pectoral muscle, and once again she had to repress the wish to run her hand down the shape of him, to feel the fine crisp hair on his chest. He was not hirsute and she found that much to her preference as well, his legs and arms having only a fine dusting of blond hairs.

She had seen handsomer men but the composition of his face pleased her better. Lanzecki—now that was the first time she'd thought of him in days—actually was the more distinguished in looks, heavier in build. She decided she preferred the way Lars Dahl was put together.

She sighed. It was easier to be philosophical about Lanzecki. Would she have been as easily resigned to that loss if she hadn't met Lars Dahl? She had broken off with Lanzecki for his own good, but she hadn't "lost" him, for she would return to Ballybran. Once she'd left Optheria . . .

For a moment her emotions hovered above a new abyss of despair and regret. And for the first time in her life, the thought of bearing a man's child crossed her mind. That was as much an impossibility as remaining with Lars, but it emphasized the depth of her emotional involvement with the man. Perhaps it was just as well that no child was possible, that their liaison would end when this assignment was over. She surprised herself! Children were something other people had. To feel that desire was remarkable.

Optheria, for all its conservatism and alleged security, had unexpected facets of danger. Not the least of which were her adventures so far. She could hardly fault Trag, or rail at the *Encyclopedia Galactica*. Facts she had had. What couldn't have been foreseen were the astonishing predicaments which had entangled her. And the fascinating personalities.

More extraordinary still, she remembered all too vividly, and with just a trace of chagrin, her rantings and ravings and desperations when she'd left Ballybran, a sacrifice to the Guild for Lanzecki's good. Now, when contemplating a much deeper and irreversible loss, why was she so calm, fatalistically resigned, even philosophical. How very strange! Had her loss of Lanzecki inured her to others? Or was she mistaking her feelings for Lars Dahl? No! She'd remember Lars Dahl for the rest of her life without benefit of data retrieval.

The second chimes rang faintly across the open court outside the windows. Faint but sufficient to waken Lars. He was as neat on wakening as he was in sleep. His eyes opened, his right hand searched for her body, his head turned and his smile began as he located her. Then he stretched, arms above his head, back arching toward her as he extended his legs and then on the top of his extension, suddenly retracted himself, drawing her against him, to complete a morning ritual which included the exercise of their intimate relationship. Each time, they seemed to discover something new about themselves and their responses. She particularly liked Lars's capacity for invention, stimulating as it did heretofore unsuspected originalities in herself.

As usual hunger roused them from these variations.

"Breakfast here is the heartiest meal," Lars said cheerfully, striding quickly for the catering unit. "You'll like it."

Killashandra saw that he had left the jammer behind him, and she followed him at a quick trot, holding the device up to distort anything else he might say.

He laughed. "We'd best leave them something to hear. A discussion of breakfast must be sufficiently innocuous."

Killashandra settled in one of the chairs near the catering unit, swiveling her hand as she looked at the little jammer. If only some way could be found to mask that mineral residue in Optherians! Blank out the detector.

"You know," Killashandra said as they ate, sitting companionably together on the elegant seating unit, "I simply cannot understand this concentration on one instrument—albeit a powerful one—but they're wiping out more than ninety-nine percent of the FSP's musical traditions and repertoire, as well as stultifying talents and potential. I mean, your tenor is formidable!"

Lars shrugged, giving her a tolerant side glance. "Everyone sings—at least in the islands, they do."

"But you know *how* to sing."

Lars cocked an eyebrow at her, still humoring what he felt was her excessive fascination with a minor ability.

"Everyone knows how to sing—"

"I don't mean just opening the mouth and shouting, Lars Dahl. I mean, projecting a voice, supporting it properly on the breath, phrasing the music, carrying the dynamic line forward."

"When did I do all that?"

"When we did that impromptu duet. When you sang on the beach, when you did that magnificent duet from *The Pearl Fishers*."

"I did?"

"Of course. I studied voice for ten years. I—" She shut her mouth.

"Then why are you a crystal singer instead of one of these famous vocal artists?"

A surge of impotent fury, followed by a wave of regret, and then a totally incomprehensible loathing of Lars for reminding her so acutely of the interview with Maestro Valdi—the moment that had changed her life—rendered Killashandra speechless.

Lars watched her, his mild curiosity turning to concern as he saw the emotions in her stormy eyes and face. He put a hand on her bare thigh. "What did I say to distress you so?"

"Nothing you said, Lars." She dismissed all that from consideration. It was over and done with. "I had all the requirements to be a Stellar, except one. A voice."

"Ah, now." Lars pulled back in indignation.

"I'm quite serious. There's a flaw, a noticeable and unpleasant burr in the voice that would have limited me to secondary roles."

Lars laughed now, his white teeth gleaming in his tanned face, his eyes sparkling. "And you, my beloved Sunny," he kissed her lightly, "would never settle for being second in anything! Are you first among crystal singers, then?"

"I don't do badly. I've sung black crystal, which is the hardest to find and cut properly. In any event, there aren't degrees among singers. One cuts to earn enough credit for the things one needs and wants." Now why wasn't she being totally honest with Lars? Why didn't she confess that the sole aim of most crystal singers was sufficient credit not to have to sing crystal—to leave Ballybran for as long as possible?

"I wouldn't have thought crystal singers are so much like islanders," Lars surprised her by saying. "Well, you cut for what you need and want, much as we fish or plant polly, but all we really need is available."

"It's not quite the same thing with crystal," Killashandra said slowly, glad she had been less than honest. Why disillusion Lars needlessly? On so many worlds, in so many minds, there were so many misconceptions about crystal singers, she had not realized how much a relief it was to find an unbiased world—at least one unbiased with respect to her Guild.

"Cutting crystal seems more dangerous than fishing." He stroked her scarred hand. "Or learning polly."

"Stick to fishing, Lars. Crystal's hazardous to your health. Now, we'd best apply ourselves earnestly to fulfill my Guild contract with these fardling fools. And maybe shake them out of their organic rut!"

They dressed and then Killashandra entered the number Mirbethan had given her. The woman seemed immensely relieved to accept the call and said that Thyrol would be with them directly.

"D'you suppose he slept in the hall?" Killashandra murmured to Lars as she answered the polite scratching on the hall door. Lars shook his head violently, then held up his hand while he deactivated the jammer and pocketed it. "Good morning, Thyrol. Lead on." She gestured peremptorally, smiling at Thyrol before she noticed two burly men in security uniforms. "I have no need of them!" she said coldly.

"Ah . . . they will not interfere, Guildmember."

"I'll make sure of that, Thyrol. I will need the duragloves—"

"Everything you requested before your unfortuante disappearance is in the organ loft."

"Oh, very well then. It's gathered dust long enough. Lead on!"

Once again the instinctive reaction to tiptoe and maintain silence affected Killashandra as they emerged onto the stage of the Festival auditorium. She glanced at Lars to see if he was similarly affected. He grimaced slightly and she noticed that his active stride perceptibly altered. She did not miss the almost covetous way he frowned at the covered organ console. And wondered what she could do about *that*! She had been entranced with the music he played on the twelve-string instrument, and she was eager to hear it with organ amplification. Or would that be too cruel an imposition?

As Thyrol used his keys on the panel to the loft, Killashandra wondered if among them were the keys that would allow access to subliminal mechanisms. All three on that ring were apparently needed to open the loft door. Or would someone of Thyrol's rank even know about such a refinement? She presumed it was limited to Elder rank only, or maybe a Master or two. They'd need someone with a hefty dab of imagination and energy to create subliminal images. Unless the subliminals reflected the inflexibility of the Elders' attitudes toward everything, which was also logical— Why search for a template when one was oneself the ultimate role model?

The necessary equipment was indeed in the loft, neatly stacked against one side of the long wall. Lars maintained an attitude of casual indifference after giving the room a sweeping glance. Killashandra noted the monitor buds, caught Lars's glance and gave him a nod. She waited until his hand disappeared into his pocket and then bent over the open console and the glittering shards of crystal.

"Lars Dahl, grab a mask and some gloves, and bring that bin over here. And a mask and gloves for me. I don't fancy inhaling crystal dust in those close quarters." Then she looked up at the burly men taking up so much space in the loft. "Out!" She flicked her fingers at them. "Out, out, out, out! You're taking up space and air."

"This room is well ventilated, Guildmember," Thyrol began.

"That is not the point. I dislike observers peering at my every move. There's no need for *them*. Certainly no one can get in or out of here. They can stand on the other side of the door and repel boarders! In fact, Thyrol, without meaning offense, your absence would oblige."

"But—"

"You'll only be hovering. I'm sure you have more important duties than hovering! And you're a distraction— Or, are you one of those I'm to teach crystal installation?"

Thyrol drew back, affronted by the suggestion and without further protest retired from the loft.

"Now," Killashandra began, not even watching the man leave, "the first thing we must do is clear the shards. Stick to the larger pieces, Lars Dahl. My body deals with cuts more easily than yours. Hand up that lid. We'll put the pieces on that before transferring them to the bin. Crystal has a disastrous habit of spraying shards when it bounces . . . Shouldn't want unnecessary accidents to mar this procedure."

"Why'd you want the jammer on in here? Guild secrets?" Lars's voice was muffled by the mask.

"I just want them to understand that monitors won't work around me. I was brought up on a planet that respects privacy and I'm not allowing Optherians to violate that right. Not for all the sensory organs on this narking world. Besides, how else can we search for the access? It would look far odder if suddenly their scanners don't work, than if they haven't worked from the start. Now, let's do what we came for."

It was slow work, especially once Lars had cleared the larger pieces. The extractor could be used only in short bursts; continued suction expelled tiny splinters right through the bag. For that reason, the bag had to be emptied and brushed out after each burst.

"It'd be easier with two of these, wouldn't it?" When Killashandra nodded, Lars strode to the door panel, slid it open, and issued the request. Killashandra heard a murmured reply. "Now, I said! We don't have time to wait for the request to go through Security. By the First Fathers! Does everything have to be authorized by Ampris. Move it! Now!"

Killashandra grinned at him. Lars's return grin was pure satisfaction.

"If you knew how often I've wanted to bark at a Security man—"

"I can't honestly imagine you making meek—"

"You'd be surprised at what I'm willing to do for a good reason." He gave her a singularly wicked look.

A case of the extractors was delivered in half an hour by an officer whom Lars later told Killashandra was Blaz's second in command, but not a bad fellow for all of that. Castair had been known to look the other way during student romps which Blaz never would have permitted.

"Guildmember," Castair began, as Lars took the case from him, "there's some problem with the monitoring system in here."

"There is?" Killashandra straightened up from the console, glancing about her.

Castair indicated the corner nodules.

"Well, I don't want someone distracting me while I'm doing this. Your repairs can wait. We certainly are not damaging anything!"

"No, of course not, Guildmember."

"Then leave it for now." She waved him off, bending back to the tedious cleaning before he had left.

"Perfect pitch is not the only talent required to sing crystal." Lars's comment startled Killashandra as she finally stood erect, arching her back against tight muscles.

"Oh?"

His expression was a mixture of respect and something else. "A crystal singer has total concentration and an absence of normal human requirements—such as hunger!"

Killashandra twisted her wrist to look at the chrono and chuckled, leaning against the unit behind her. It was mid-afternoon and they had been working steadily since nine that morning.

"You should have given me a nudge."

"Several," Lars said drily. "I only mention it now because you're looking a bit white under your tan. Here." He thrust a heatpak at her. "I do not have your dedication so I sent for food."

"Without authorization?" Killashandra broke the seal on the soup, aware that she was very hungry indeed.

"I took a hint from your manner and pretended they had no option but obedience." He shook his head. "Are all crystal singers like you?"

"I'm pretty mild," she said, sipping carefully at the now heated soup. Lars passed her a plate of small sandwiches and crackers. "I only act the maggot when circumstances require. Especially with this lot of idiots." She lifted and rotated one shoulder to ease back muscles. Lars came to her side, pushing her away from her perch, and began to massage her back. His fingers unerringly found the tension knot, and she murmured her gratitude. "I hate this part of working in crystal so I'd rather get it over and done with as fast as possible."

"How crucial is the clean sweep?"

Killashandra sang a soft note and the crystal shards answered in a nerve-twitching dissonance.

Lars shook convulsively at the sound which, in spite of being soft, took time to die away. "Wow!"

"White crystal is active, picks up any sound. Leave so much as the minutest particle of crystal dust and it'll jam the manual and produce all kinds of subharmonics in the logic translator. It'd really be easier to start with a brand new manual case but I doubt they'd have spare parts. Which reminds me—the ten brackets that I've cleared are all spoiled." She picked one up, turning the clamping surface so that the scratches picked up the light. "Tighten one of these on a new crystal and you'd create uneven stresses through the long axis of the crystal, introducing spurious piezoelectric effects and probably a flaw in next to no time."

Lars took the bracket from her, hefting it in his hand. "They're no problem. Olver can do them."

Instinctively Killashandra looked up at the monitors as Lars mentioned his contact. She dragged at the fabric of Lars's sleeve and pointed to the surveillance buds, where traces of black had mysteriously appeared to make an aureole about each unit. "Now what did that?"

Killashandra chuckled and pointed to the white crystal. "A secret weapon for you when I leave. Sing white crystal to whatever room you're in and blast the monitors." She reached for one of the larger pieces Lars had cleared away and hefted it. "We'll just save some of this for you. I wonder if Research and Development know about this application of white."

Suddenly Lars had his arms about her, his face buried in her hair, his lips against her neck. She could feel the tension in him and caressed him with gentle hands.

"Oh, Sunny, must you leave?"

She gave him a twisted, rueful smile, gentling the frown from his face with tender fingers. "Crystal calls me back, Lars Dahl. It's not a summons I can ignore, and live!"

He kissed her hungrily and as she responded they both caught the slight sound, swiveling away from each other, as the door slid open.

"Ah, Elder Ampris," Killashandra said, "your arrival is most opportune. Show him the bracket, Lars Dahl," and when Ampris regarded this unusual offering with amazement, "run your fingers over the clamping edge . . . carefully . . . and feel how rough it is. We're going to need some two hundred of these, for I'm not about to trust new crystal in old brackets. All I've removed so far have been scratched just like that one. Will you authorize the order—and designate it as urgent?"

Killashandra snapped her mask back over her face and picked up the brush. Then she swore.

"I could also use a handlight of some sort. Some of this wretched stuff is like powder."

Elder Ampris peered in and she heard his intake of breath. She straightened, regarding him passively, seeing the stern accusation in his eyes.

"Let me demonstrate, Elder Ampris, the need for meticulous care." She hummed, more loudly than before, and took great delight in its effect on the man. "Sorry about that." She resumed work.

"I came to inquire, Guildmember, how soon the repairs would be completed."

"Since the idiot who smashed the manual put his heart in the destruction, it's going to take a lot more time than it did for me to remove one shattered crystal from the cruiser drive—if that's the comparison you were using." Killashandra sighed, and looked disconsolately at the crystal ruin. "It's slow going because of the nature of crystal and because, as you perceived, every smidge-idgin has to be cleaned out. That's all we've achieved today . . ."

Elder Ampris shot a sour glance at Lars. "More helpers?"

Killashandra gave a bark of laughter. "Just find me a vacuum capable of sucking up crystal dust and we'd clear this in an hour. Or, supply me with a brand new case!" And she gave the one before her a dismissive slap with her hand. Crystal pinged, Lars and Ampris winced. "Gets to you, doesn't it? Well, Elder Ampris, that's where we stand. Now, if you'll excuse me, the nitty gritty doesn't get done by talking about it." She picked up her brush but Ampris cleared his throat.

"A dinner and concert have been arranged for your enjoyment this evening," he said.

"I appreciate the courtesy, Elder Ampris, but until I have finished this, I wouldn't feel right about taking any time off for mere entertainment. If you'll send us in some more food—"

"Guildmember," Lars interrupted, "with all due respect, Elder Ampris is not . . . I mean, it is hardly his responsibility . . ."

"What are you trying to say, Captain?"

Ampris, his eyes glinting with the first glimpse of the humor she had seen from him since that long-ago reception, held up his hand, relieving Lars of the necessity of explanation.

"If the Guildmember is willing to forego pleasures to complete her task, I feel I may serve as messenger for her requirements."

"Apparently everything I require has to be authorized by you anyway. Seems silly to waste time with all those intermediate stages." Killashandra grinned at Ampris without a sign of remorse. "Would you not have a word with them out there, or Thyrol? Speed things up tremendously. Oh, and don't forget, I need two hundred of those brackets. And the handlight. Lars, you go with him and get it, will you? It has to be small enough not to hamper sight, and I'd prefer a tight beam."

They left and she returned to work. When Lars came back with several handbeams, his eyes were bubbling with humor.

"Your wishes are his commands, Oh mighty Guildmember, Oh sweeper of the white crystal specks! Orders were issued to all the boys out there," and he jerked his thumb at the closed door panel, "that anything you request is to be secured as fast as possible."

"Hmmm. Bring one of those lights to bear on this corner, will you, Lars?" She flicked the brush and disclosed tiny granules that glittered in the light. "See? The fardling things are pernicious! I'll get 'em, every last speck!"

When the sumptuous dinner was wheeled in to them some time later, she grumbled but stopped working.

"Is crystal singing some kind of disease?" Lars asked conversationally.

"You sail. Do you call a halt in the middle of a storm? Do you leave off fishing in the midst of a school to nap?"

"It's not quite the same thing—"

"It is to me, Lars. Be of good cheer. The bracketing will be relatively easy and you can help me do that."

Despite her protests, Lars carried her out of the organ loft just before midnight. When they reached her suite, she insisted that they had better have a good soak, to be sure none of the crystal dust had penetrated their clothing. In the bath, he had to hold her head above water, for she kept falling asleep.

It took nearly four days to ensure that no speck of crystal dust remained in the case. By the time they arrived each morning, new monitor buds had been installed. So the first thing that Killashandra did on entering the organ loft was to hum a happy tune, charging the white crystal shards to do their duty and blast the fragile sensors.

On the third day, the new brackets were delivered and Killashandra set Lars Dahl to checking each one under a microscope. Fourteen were rejected for minor flaws. After the visit of Elder Ampris, they had no visitors. Thyrol would conduct them every morning to the loft, unlocking it and inquiring after their needs. Excellent meals were delivered at the appropriate hours. Assured of uninterrupted privacy, with easily disabled monitors, Lars had the freedom to undertake a very patient examination of the room, searching for the location of the subliminal equipment.

On the fourth morning, as Thyrol led them across the stage, Killashandra noted a curious discrepancy. The loft room did not extend the entire length of the stage behind the organ console. She silently counted her paces to the door. When Thyrol had closed the panel and Lars had activated the jammer, she paced out the width of the room.

"In-ter-est-ing," she said, her nose against the far wall. "This room is only half the length of the stage, Lars. Does that suggest anything to you?"

"It does, but there is no corresponding door on the other side of the console!" He joined her in her scrutiny of the blameless wall. "The subliminals have to be linked to the main frame data bases. I wonder . . ."

She followed his inspection of the cables that festooned the ceiling, pausing where they ran alongside to the wall.

"Just a little minute," he said, his eyes wide with discovery, and he spun one of the impervo tubs to a position just under the cables.

He had to crane his neck, half stooped against the ceiling, but he gave a low and triumphant whistle. When he jumped down, he gathered Killashandra in his arms and whirled her about, crowing with exultation.

"The wall drops—how I don't know, but there is just the slightest gap at the top, where no one would think to look for it. And three very heavy cables go through the wall."

Lars replaced the tub before he began to inspect the corner joint. Once again he gave an exultant *yip*.

"The whole wall must move, Killa—but how?"

"That large a mass sinking into the floor might be a touch noisy."

"If we knew the mechanism . . ." He felt along the corner, then the floor, pressing and tapping.

"That's far too obvious, Lars. Stupid they are but never obvious. Try for an extrusion on one of the units, underneath 'em, inside . . ." She ran searching fingers under the one nearest her, finding nothing but a rough edge on one corner which produced a gouged finger. "*Ach*, I haven't the patience for this sort of nonsense right now. You go ahead. I'll finish this last bit of cleaning."

By the time their lunch was brought in, Lars had found nothing more. The units that could be opened had been opened with no result. Lars stewed and fussed all through the meal at his inability to resolve the problem.

"What sort of form do the security measures generally take on Optheria? Bureaucracies tend to find a reliable mechanism and stick with it," Killashandra suggested, with only half her attention on that part of the problem since she was so close to clearing the manual case for the next task.

"I can find out. Would you mind being left alone this evening?" He grinned at her, stroking her arm gently. "You'd be a mite conspicuous where I want to go."

"And where would that be?" she asked with an arch glance of mock disgust.

"I've got to acquire a few more clothes," and he twitched the fabric of his shirt, not as gaudy as that of most island designs but certainly noticeable amid the drab garb of the city dwellers. "Talk to a few people. Lucky for us, it's nearing the time of year when the subliminals wear off and normal student appetites revive. I might be late, Killa,"—he made a grimace of regret—"We don't have as much time together . . ."

She kissed the pulse in his throat. "Whenever you return then. That is, of course," and she had to add a light touch to relieve the tension in her throat, "if the guards pass you in."

Chapter 20

"And?" Killashandra prompted Lars the next morning as they breakfasted. Despite a valiant effort to stay awake, she had been asleep when he returned and he was showering when she was awakened by the distant chimes.

"I got clothing, all right enough," Lars admitted with a frustrated sigh. "The Elders' search and seizure for you was far more comprehensive than our visitors," and despite the jammer he was taking no chances, "had led us to believe. Or perhaps knew. Anyone—anyone who has been booked even for a pedestrian offense—was drawn. Half a dozen students were sent on to rehab without benefit of Inquiry."

"Olver?"

Lars ran his fingers through his hair, scratching his head vigorously as if to erase his despondency. "How he escaped I don't know and neither, I gather, does he. We didn't exchange more than a few signs." Lars propelled himself from his chair, pacing, head down. "It could very well be that the Elders have marked him and are playing a waiting game."

"Are Nahia and Hauness safe?"

Lars gave her a quick and grateful smile for that concern. "They were holding clinics in Ironwood," he waved his hand to the north, "at the time of your disappearance. The City, Gartertown, and the Port took the brunt of search and seizure. And Security then used your disappearance as an excuse to take known dissidents in protective custody."

"How many are?"

"In protective custody? My dear Guildmember, such figures are never made public."

"An informed guess? Suicide is one form of social protest, the size of the p.c. population another one."

Lars shook his head. "Hauness might be able to find out," and Lars resumed his head shaking, "but I wouldn't risk getting in touch with him right now."

Killashandra stared at Lars Dahl for a long moment, a sinking sensation that had nothing to do with hunger cramping her guts.

"And I have made you as vulnerable as any of those already in p.c., haven't I?"

Lars shrugged and grinned. "If you hadn't named me your rescuer, I'd be tucked away in a rehab cubicle right now spinning out my brains."

"After I've gone?"

Lars shrugged again, then gave her an impudent wink. "All I need is a half-day's start on 'em. And once I've made the islands, there isn't an S & S team that can find me if I don't wish to be found."

He sounded so confident that, for a moment, Killashandra almost believed him. As if he sensed her doubt, he leaned over her in the chair, his eyes more brilliantly blue than ever, his lips upturned in a provocative half smile.

"Beloved Sunny, if it wouldn't sound mawkish, I'd say that meeting you has been the high point of my life so far. And confounding Elders Torkes and Ampris are adventures to lighten my darkest hour—"

"Which might yet be in a rehab booth!"

"I know the risk, and it's been worth it, Killa!" He kissed her then, a light brief touch of his lips to hers but it set her blood ringing as quickly as crystal.

"Speaking of Elders," she began in an attempt to shake off her anxiety, "we begin to bracket crystal today." She rose from the chair with a determined effort, then saw his expression. "All right—I grant you, learning to bracket and tune crystal won't advance you in the Elders' files, but those are useful skills anywhere else in the FSP."

Lars laughed. "Had we but worlds enough and time—"

Killashandra let out a great guffaw. "Malaprop!" But outrageous humor made a better start to a tricky day than gloom.

Lars was every bit as quick to learn and adept in the use of his strong hands as Killashandra had thought he'd be. To set the white crystal in the brackets, she asked Thyrol the height of the stroke of the padded hammers. They already had six in place by the time Elder Ampris appeared in the loft, Thyrol hovering anxiously behind him in the open door. Killashandra noticed, first, the breath of sweet fresh air and she flicked a quick glance at the intruders as they stood there. Lars was holding the crystal dead still.

"You'll feel just the slightest surface tension and a slippery, almost electric, tension when the clamps are tight enough. Tell me when you do."

She tightened the brackets, keeping both little fingers under the crystal so that she could sense that surface tension.

"Now!" Lars said.

"Right on!" She struck the crystal with the tone hammer, and the rich deep note spun through the air, drifting out and causing the two door guards to risk a quick peer into the loft. A muted and discordant response came from the covered tubs of crystal shard. Then she straightened up and turned to the observers. "And that's how it's done, Elder Ampris."

Ampris's bright brown eyes glittered as he arranged his mouth in a smile which she took to mean approbation.

"The lower octave is always easier, for some reason, to set and pitch," Killashandra went on affably. "We're making excellent progress."

"And?"

Killashandra heard a curious vibration in that single word. Elder Ampris was overly eager to have this installation completed and it could not be simply to allow performers practice time. He also exhibited an uncharacteristic nervousness; his fingers rubbed against his thumb.

"I think we'll have the entire manual finished by tomorrow evening. Set the next pair of brackets, will you, Lars Dahl, while I watch." Killashandra stepped away from the cabinet, stood next to Elder Ampris. "He's quick and deft and once I'm sure he's doing it right, we'll work both ends against the middle."

Ampris regarded her with a blink, his mind evidently jumping to another application of that phrase. His stiff and pleased smile forewarned her. "You will then perhaps be delighted to have trained assistance."

"Trained?" Killashandra glanced at Lars who had also suspended motion, catching the smugness in Ampris's dry tone.

"When we could not find you anywhere in the City, Guildmember, we apprised your Guild of your disappearance. And requested a . . ." Ampris's smile took on a faintly apologetic twist, "replacement. Our need, as I'm sure you appreciate, is urgent."

"It takes nearly ten weeks to get from the Scoria system to the Ophiuchian."

"Not by FSP courier ship." Ampris inclined his head briefly. "Your Guild values you highly, Killashandra Ree . . ."

"Surely you've communicated news of my rescue?"

Ampris spread his hands deferentially. "But of course. But we did not then know how promptly the Heptite Guild would respond. The courier ship has entered our atmosphere and at this very moment is landing at the shuttleport."

"Trag!" And there was no doubt at all in Killashandra's mind that that was who had been dispatched.

"I beg your pardon."

"Lanzecki would have sent Trag here."

"This man is capable?"

"Eminently. However, the more we can do now, the sooner Trag and I will finish. If you'll excuse us, Elder Ampris?" And Killashandra signaled Lars to continue. "One last request of you, Ampris,"—although Ampris had not yet stirred from his vantage point—"those tubs of crystal shard could now be removed to wherever I—or Trag—will be instructing the trainees. Some of the larger pieces can be useful but they are a considerable nuisance sounding off in here."

"Yes, we should want to restore the monitors within this room, Guildmember, now that the organ is so nearly repaired." Ampris flicked his hand at Thyrol who then issued the appropriate order to the guards. Killashandra did not dare glance in Lars's direction.

"Don't bounce the tubs about," Killashandra warned, as the guards shuffled out with the first one.

"There now," Killashandra said when the door had slid shut, leaving them alone, "the shards'll be more accessible to us now. We can purloin the ones we want. Can you get your hands on a small plasfoam pouch?"

"Yes. Who's this Trag?"

"The best person they could possibly have sent. Lanzecki's Administration Officer." Killashandra chuckled. "I'd rather him than an army, and certainly I'd rather him than any other singer they could have chosen. And a courier ship. I am flattered."

"Somehow Ampris is too pleased with this development."

"Yes, and fretting with impatience." Killashandra mimicked his hand gesture and Lars nodded grimly. "Is it just that he wants the organ done? Or us out of the loft for good?" She swiveled slightly so that she was facing the wall they could not shift. "Why?" She bit one corner of her lip, trying to solve its mystery. Then, with an exclamation, she ran her hands around the casing of the manual, picked up the lid and examined it closely.

"What are you looking for, Killa?"

"Blood! Did you see any discoloration on the shards you handled?"

"No— If Comgail was killed by," and he gestured at the newly placed crystal spires, "there would have been blood somewhere here!"

"Was there only the official version of Comgail's end?"

"No. I had a chance to speak with one of the infirmary attendants and she said that he was covered in blood, crystal fragments had pierced eyes, face, and chest."

"With a little help, perhaps? But do you know for certain that it was Comgail who shattered the manual?"

Lars nodded slowly, his eyes gray and bleak, his face expressionless.

"And he had mentioned earlier that he knew the access to the subliminal units was through the organ loft?"

Again Lars nodded and both stared at the wall.

"Comgail did all the maintenance on the Festival organ?" At Lars's impassive nod, Killashandra scrubbed at her face with one hand. "Did Ampris ever compose or perform?" she asked in angry exasperation.

The look of total surprise on Lars's face gave her the answer.

"No wonder he's been bouncing about here," Lars cried, seizing Killashandra and hugging her with the excess of his jubilation. "No wonder he's been so eager to get the manual repaired. He can't get to the subliminal units until it is. He can't alter the subliminals for this year's concerts. Oh, Killa! You've done it."

228

"Not quite," Killashandra said with a laugh. "I'm only hypothesizing that the manual provides the unlocking mechanism. We've no idea what sort of music key he'd use. It could be anything—"

"No, not anything," Lars cried, shaking his head and grinning, his eyes vividly blue again. "I'd stake my life I know what he'd use—"

"I wish you wouldn't use a phrase like that," Killashandra murmured.

Lars gave her a reassuring grin and went on. "Remember what you said about bureaucracy finding one mechanism that suited them? Well, Ampris's one and only Festival offering utilizes a recurrent theme."

"But everyone on the planet would know it then."

"What difference would that make? You'd still have to have access to this manual, wouldn't you?"

"True. What's the theme?"

"It's a real thumpety-dump," and he da-da-ed the notes to Killashandra's utter amazement.

"Not only is it thumpy-dumpety-dump, it's complete and utter plagiarism. Ampris lifted that theme from an 18th Century composer named Beethoven."

"Who?"

Killashandra lifted her hands in exasperation. "Enough of this idle speculation, Lars, we've got to finish the organ as fast as possible."

"What about Trag?"

Killashandra shook her head. "Trag is no threat to us. If we could just get the bass notes finished, we'd have something to show him. I hope." She dropped a set of brackets into Lars's hands and took another for herself. "You wouldn't happen to know the signature of Ampris's composition?" When Lars shook his head, she cursed briefly and then began to chuckle. "We'll just try the original one!"

Because they were rushing, nervous with anticipation and hope, hands sweating from tension, it seemed to take three or four attempts to place each of the next three crystals. Lars was muttering imprecations by the time Killashandra could test the third one.

No sooner had she struck the crystal than the door panel slid open and the aperture was filled by Trag's bulky figure.

"Trag, I bless your timely arrival. We're both fingers and thumbs trying to set this manual. A fresh hand and a sane mind will work wonders!"

Trag gave her a nod of his head and stepped inside, giving Lars a cursory glance before his attention was completely taken by a critical appraisal of their endeavors. Killashandra ignored the entrance of Ampris, Torkes, Thyrol, and Mirbethan, who filed slowly into the room in Trag's wake. Trag picked up the tuning hammer and struck each of the crystals.

Trag merely nodded his head. Lars made a noise of protest but Killashandra shot him a warning glance. The fact that Trag had no comments to make was all the approval she required, knowing better than to expect overt praise from him, For a *very* fleeting moment, however, she was seized with a totally irrational desire to throw her arms about Trag's neck, a notion which she quickly suppressed without revealing it by so much as a grin.

Elder Torkes, resembling the scavenger bird more faithfully than ever, seemed about to step forward, then, apparently, changed his mind as if aware of how Trag's bulk diminished his stature to insignificance.

"You have only just arrived, Guildmember, and as it is now midday, refreshment has been prepared for you," Torkes began with scant courtesy.

Trag dismissed the offer. "You gave the Guild to understand the matter was of the most urgent."

"We need to eat," Killashandra said tartly. "Just send us in some food, please, someone," and she picked up more brackets as Trag removed the next crystal from its bed of plasfoam. "We might even finish this today if given the chance to work without interruption."

"Not quite," Trag amended in his deliberate fashion as he held the crystal up for inspection in the ceiling light. Satisfied he lowered it, his gaze traveling beyond to the fascinated observers. "If you please?" And he extended his hand toward the door.

Killashandra, her eyes on Lars's blank face, had to fight not to chortle at the aura of dismay, fury, and shock emanating from the four high ranking Optherians. But her hands were free of both sweat and tremble and, with Lars carefully tightening the matching bracket, they were ready to fasten it the moment Trag inserted the crystal in place. The door panel *whoosh*ed over the rectangle of sunlight. Killashandra tightened her bracket just as Lars finished his. Trag took up his hammer for the ceremonial tap and the *D*, mellow and clear, broke the silence of the room.

"Just two more, Trag, and I believe we'll have something to show you," Killashandra said, reaching for more brackets. "This is Lars Dahl."

"A lover posing as a bodyguard! A young man with highly suspicious credentials," Trag said bluntly, his hooded stare fixed on Lars.

Killashandra held up a hand to restrain any understandable outburst from Lars but he only smiled, inclining his head in brief acknowledgment of the description.

"According to Elder Ampris or Torkes?" Killashandra asked, grinning at Trag as she faced him squarely.

Trag focused his attention on her. Had she not been so positive of her own righteousness, she would have been hard pressed to maintain her composure beneath that basilisk stare.

"I will hear your explanation, then, for I warn you, Killashandra Ree, the Guild looks with disfavor on a member who abrogates her contractual obligations for whatever personal reasons obtain . . ."

Killashandra stared at Trag incredulously.

"I was given two assignments here, Trag, by you—"

"The secondary assignment was considerably less important than the primary—" Trag's big hand indicated the unfinished installation.

"The two are more closely linked than you or Lanzecki imagined when the Guild accepted that contract. But then abduction ought not to be a high-risk-factor on well-ordered, conservative, secure Optheria. Right? Ever aware of my primary obligation," Killashandra allowed some of her outrage to color her voice, "I swam dangerous channels from one island to another in order to escape the one I was dumped on. Confounding all parties and managing thus to return to my primary contractual obligation."

Trag merely raised his eyebrows.

"Tell me, Trag, what is your opinion of subliminal conditioning?"

Trag's bleak eyes widened fractionally. "The Council of the Federated Sentient Planets has declared any form of subliminal projection morally criminal and punishable by expulsion from the Federation."

"Then if I were an Elder," Lars said in a quiet, faintly amused tone, "I wouldn't be so quick to accuse anyone else of having highly suspicious credentials."

"If you will assist us to install the next two crystals, Trag, I believe we may be able to prove our allegation," Killashandra said.

"If you cannot prove this allegation, Killashandra Ree, you are liable to severe discipline and censure."

"Then isn't it convenient that I'm right?"

"Guildmember, I have been subjected to subliminal conditioning," Lars said, as if he sensed her minute uncertainty. Trag turned his penetrating stare on the islander.

"The insidiousness of subliminal conditioning, Lars Dahl, is that the victim is totally unaware of the bombardment."

"Only if he is unprepared, Guildmember. My father, late an agent of the Federated Council, was able to safeguard me, and other friends, against electronically induced subliminals. Which, I might add, are particularly adaptable to the heavy emotional experience of the sensory organ."

"Late an agent?" Killashandra fancied she saw some diminution of Trag's intractability.

"Trapped here by the same restraint which keeps Optherians from competing in galactic enterprise," Lars replied. "Contact with the Federated Council has only just been reestablished after nearly thirty-three years—"

She and Trag heard the minute sound at the same instant and assumed suitable poses of interrupted labor when the door panel slid open. Mirbethan escorted the lunch table which the security guard wheeled in.

"If you'll just leave it there, Mirbethan," Killashandra gestured with a hand full of brackets while Trag and Lars bent over an already sited crystal, "we'll take a break shortly."

"Not the one they expect, either," Lars murmured when the door panel had closed. Trag favored him with another unnerving stare. Lars returned it equably, with a slight bow toward the manual case. "After you, Guildmember."

"Why three more crystals?" Trag asked.

"This loft is half the size of the available space behind the organ console on stage," Lars said. "We think the subliminal programming equipment is hidden behind that wall, and accessed by a musical key activated from this manual. We have reason to believe that Comgail, who is alleged to have smashed the crystal," Trag's eyebrows raised, "was killed because he had discovered that musical key, not because he was injured by the shards or because he had destroyed the manual. That would have only got him sent to rehab."

"Who is responsible for the subliminal programming?"

Lars grinned maliciously. "My own personal candidate is Ampris; he is musically trained."

"It wouldn't take musicality to strike notes in the right sequence," Trag said.

"True, but he knows as much about the organ as every performer must and he became head of the Conservatory about the time the subliminal conditioning started. It began shortly after my father arrived, and he was here to investigate the first request for the revocation of the planet-bound restriction. Then, too, Torkes has always favored the propaganda control of population. But what one Elder does, the others invariably condone. And subliminal conditioning sustains them in their power."

"Arrange for me to meet your father, Lars Dahl."

Lars grinned. "His credentials are as suspicious as mine, Guildmember. I doubt we could reach him. In any event, we are here, close to the damning proof of what we suspect. Surely a bird in hand—"

"Bird?" The word exploded from Killashandra, a result of the tension she felt and a combination of surprise and respect for Lars's sterling performance under Trag's unnerving scrutiny.

"Perhaps the analogy is wrong," and Lars shrugged diffidently. "Well, Guildmember? Have I my day in court, too?"

"Three more crystals?" Trag's manner gave no indication of his thoughts.

"Two more," Killashandra said, "if we are using the original key."

Trag made a barely audible grunt at that comment before he reached for the next crystal and motioned Lars to place his bracket.

Killashandra could not keep her mind entirely on the task at hand for she suddenly realized just how much rested on the truth of the dissidents' contentions. Had she indeed allowed a sexual relationship to cloud her judgment? Or favorable first impressions from Nahia, Hauness, and the others to color her thinking? And yet, there was Corish von Mittelstern, and Olav Dahl. Or was that convoluted situation carefully contrived? She might be out on a limb, the saw in her own hand, she thought as she delicately tightened the bracket on the second crystal. She didn't dare look at Lars across the open case as they straightened up.

Expressionless as ever, Trag handed Lars the tuning hammer. Lars gave Killashandra a rakish and reassuring grin and then tapped out the sequence: da da da-dum, da da da-dum. For one hideous moment, nothing happened and Killashandra felt the last vestige of energy drain from her body with the groan she could not stifle. A groan that was echoed by a muted noise and a slight vibration in the floor. Startled, she and Lars looked down but Trag remained with his eyes fixed on the ceiling.

"Clever!" was his comment as the wall sank slowly and, to their intense relief, noiselessly apart from the initial protest. "Clever and utterly despicable." As soon as the descending wall reached knee height, Trag swung over it, Lars right behind him.

For a heavy man, Trag moved with considerable speed and economy of motion. He did a complete circuit of the room, his eyes sweeping from one side to the other, identifying each bank in the complicated and extensive rack system, and the terminal which activated the units. He completed his circuit at the three heavy cables that provided the interface between the two sets of computers.

"No one has been in here for some time," he said finally, noting the light coating of dust on the cabinets.

"No need, Guildmember."

"You may address me as Trag."

Lars grinned triumphantly at Killashandra, where she stood, resting her ear against the door panel. Nothing must interfere at this so critical moment.

"Trag. The yearly dose for Optherians occurs shortly before the Festival season begins, and the tourists arrive. All Optherians are given the 'opportunity and privilege,'" and Lars's voice was mildly scornful, "of attending the preliminary concerts for the current year's Festival selections. The Mainlanders get their dose then, to keep them contented while the tourists are here. Then, the tourists get theirs, which includes sufficient Optherianisms to prevent them from accepting messages from strangers for posting once they return to their homes. Some don't, you know, having fallen for the vastly superior and secure Optherian natural way of life."

Trag dropped his gaze from the fascinating cable. "How many escape these conditioning sessions?"

"Not many Mainlanders, though there are a few who independently discovered the subliminal images." Lars turned to Killashandra. "Nahia, Hauness, Brassner, and Theach. Over the last ten years, they've been able to warn those they felt could be trusted."

"Do the Elders know that some escape?" Killashandra asked.

"There is a head check at the concerts which simultaneously registers with the Central Computers."

"But islanders don't go to the concerts, do they?" Killashandra said with a chuckle. It was a relief to know that she had occasion to be amused. It had looked very grim for a bit there, with Trag coming on strong as Guildmember.

"I think it is time to end such pernicious subjugation," Trag said. He took from his biceps pocket a hand-unit of the sort used to check programming systems, and placed it on the nearest cabinet. "It should be a simple matter of reprogramming the master sensory mixer to bypass the subliminal generator. That would inhibit the subliminal processor, yet leave no physical trace of alteration." Taking from the same pocket a heavy compound knife of the kind favored by crystal singers for field use, he opened the heaviest cutting blade. He sliced carefully at the plastic cable cover, peeling it back to expose the multicolor flex package.

Killashandra watched as Trag set the system checker against the flex, taking a preliminary reading. As he pondered the results, she could not restrain a glance at the subliminal room. The devices were so repugnant to her, abusing every precept of the individual privacy which had been her birthright on Fuerte, that she felt besmirched just looking at them.

"If there's no power . . ." Lars began, his hand half-raised in caution.

"I have had sufficient experience with this sort of equipment, Lars Dahl." Trag entered instructions on the hand unit, noted the display on the rectangular vdr, and a muscle twitched in his cheek. "The subroutine of the subliminal will function on any dummy test, and indicate the programming modes selected under their program listing, but I am placing a security lock," and with those words he put the device firmly against the thick red-coded cable and depressed the main key, "on it now. I don't have the equipment necessary to generate a program for propaganda detoxification."

"That's too bad," Killashandra said with heartfelt dismay.

"There!" Trag said. "And unless they know exactly what I've done to inhibit the subliminal processor, the alteration can't be reversed. Let the Optherians program that computer for whatever images they wish. None will reach the minds of the people they intend to pervert!" Trag pulled hard on the plastic coating and then pressed it firmly back around the cables. Killashandra could not see where the cable had been entered.

"And you'll bear witness to the Federated Council?" Lars was taut as he eagerly awaited Trag's reply.

"We shall all bear witness to the Council, young man," Trag replied.

Lars nodded but his smile was wry. "It will be the crystal singers's word that will be credited, Guildmember Trag, not that of an islander whose motivations are suspect."

"Even if he could leave the planet, Trag," Killashandra said. "Remember the arc at the shuttle port? Didn't it glow blue and erupt guards with weapons?"

Trag nodded. "Except when I passed under it."

"That arc detects a mineral deposit in Optherian bones," Lars said, "and in those of anyone here for more than six months. Which is what caught my father originally."

Trag dismissed that difficulty with a flick of his hand. "I have a warrant in my possession to arrest the party or parties responsible for the Guildmember's abduction, which would take you past their reprisals."

"You came well prepared, Trag," Killashandra said with a rueful smile. "But you'd have to bring the entire population of the Archipelago if you named Lars Dahl abductor."

When Trag turned to Lars for affirmation, he nodded. "I hadn't planned on leaving Optheria," Lars said, with a slightly embarrassed grin, "and I'm sure my father is more than willing to, but you'd need an entire liner to remove those who'd be vulnerable. The Optherian Elders have been waiting for years for an excuse to search and seize the adult population of the islands. They'd all end up in rehab. Unless, of course, you also have the authority to suspend every government official on this charge."

Trag was silent for a long moment, regarding Lars steadily. Then he exhaled slowly. "I was given broad powers by the Federated Council but not that broad." His lower jaw jutted out slightly. "Had there been any suspicion of this . . ." He paused, his contempt for once visible in his expression. "Let us not reveal this knowledge prematurely."

Carefully they removed every trace of their entry. Neither man had touched the cabinets or files, so covering their tracks took little time. Meanwhile Killashandra repositioned herself at the door panel, listening for sounds of approach.

Trag reexamined the cables he had clipped, checking from all angles to be sure the incision would escape all but the most critical inspection. He gave the room a thorough survey and then, apparently satisfied, looked expectantly at Killashandra and Lars.

"Well, close it!"

Killashandra gave a burst of puzzled laughter, more shrill than amused.

"How?"

Lars chuckled as he took the hammer from her nerveless hand. "Find something he likes . . ." He tapped out the Beethoven sequence again. The wall immediately responded by closing, giving the barest *thunk* as the panel met the ceiling. Trag gave the cable housing a final glance and dismissed it with a shrug.

"I suggest you eat something, Killashandra. You're too pale. Probably the effect of combining both assignments for your Guild. Lars Dahl, set the next bracket."

Chapter 21

It was well that they had com-
pleted their investigations, for Elder Ampris returned twice, the
first time issuing an unrefusable invitation to a quiet dinner with
several of the Elders who were most anxious to meet the
Guildmember.

"Which means you'd better eat before you go," Killashandra
told Trag when Ampris had left them. "Especially if Elder Pentrom, a medical man with interesting views on nutrition, is attending." She made a very small circle—thumb and forefinger
overlapping—to indicate the size of the portion. "Trag, do you
drink?"

Trag peered up at her. "Why?"

"The worthy Elders, Pentrom in particular, are currently under
the impression that members of our profession must daily con-
sume alcohol in substantial quantities to assist their unusual
metabolism."

Trag slowly straightened from the manual. His expression bordered on the incredulous. "Oh?"

"They are so frail, these Elders of Optheria"—Lars made a de-
rogatory comment—"that I should dislike causing any of them
distress. Prematurely, that is."

"Or exposing yourself as a calculating fraud?" Lars suggested.

"Occasionally it is useful to spawn a helpful myth about our
profession. Otherwise we'll be stuck with water which, despite
its high mineral content, is not purified because of the Optherian
lust for nature untampered. It tastes as if it was decanted from
the tank of the first long-range starship. The beer here is not bad."

A flicker crossed Trag's usually inscrutable face. "Yarran beer?"

"Unfortunately no." Trag's preference raised him further in her estimation. "The Bascum brew is potable while the better beer is illegal." She shot a knowing glance at Lars who grinned back at her.

"They generally are. Your advice is timely, Killashandra," Trag said, then appropriately sounded the B-flat.

Thirty-four crystals were in place when Elder Ampris appeared for the second time late that afternoon. There was no disguising the elation in his eyes at their progress. He was seething with the most excitement she had yet seen an Elder exhibit. Had he despaired of running up this year's dose of indoctrinal conditioning on his subliminal program?

"We will finish this tomorrow," Trag told Elder Ampris, "with a further day to tune the new manual into the system, and to check the other three manuals for positive feedback. One minor detail on which Killashandra was unable to reassure me: Was the organ in use when the manual was destroyed?"

"I believe it was," Ampris replied, his lids dipping to conceal his brown eyes. "I will of course confirm this. After the deplorable desecration, I myself conducted an inspection of the other manuals to be sure they were undamaged."

"Elder Ampris, Killashandra Ree and I would consider ourselves derelict in our Guild obligation to Optheria if we failed to assure ourselves, and you, that your Festival organ is in full and complete working order."

"Of course," Ampris managed through clenched teeth. Then, in an abrupt alteration, he smiled tightly. "Most thorough of you."

"Can we turn on the main organ console from here?" Killashandra asked, wondering what had caused Ampris's sudden change. "I admit that I am quite eager to hear it in all its glory."

Ampris regarded her for a long moment before his thin lips widened in the original smile.

"For you to appreciate fully the versatility of the Festival Organ, you need some measure of comparison. Therefore I am delighted that you are able to attend this evening's concert which will be performed on the two-manual Conservatory instrument."

"Yes, of course." Killashandra let pleased affability ooze through her voice. "Now that this installation is nearly completed, and with Trag here, I realize how much tension I've been under. It is always so much easier to share responsibilities, isn't it, Elder Ampris?" she added gaily.

He murmured something and withdrew. Trag looked at her expectantly.

"When the inevitable can no longer be avoided, it is always wise to accept it gracefully." She grimaced. "Though I have to admit I *despise* student concerts."

Lars grinned. "Oh, you won't be getting the students tonight, Killa. And in view of what you told me of the origin of Ampris's party piece, I eagerly await your critical appraisal. Are you at all musical, Guildmember?" he asked Trag.

"Frequently." Trag carefully replaced the tools in their case, gestured for Lars to close the crystal container. Killashandra covered the manual, and taking a hair from her head, wet it and laid it carefully across one corner of the lid. Trag gave a snort that she translated as approval.

"Hair of the dog that bit?" Lars asked.

"Where do you get these sayings?" Killashandra demanded, rolling her eyes in exaggerated dismay. Then she pointed to his pocket.

"I'd like to have a close look at that device," Trag said. Lars withdrew the little jammer.

"Trag, I'm trying to get them to believe that it's me distorting their monitors."

Trag surprised Killashandra by placing his hand flat against her shoulder blade. "Not any more. But I would qualify. Sensible of you."

"How many of the myths about crystal singers are derived from sensible precautions?" she asked Trag. "Or survival techniques?" Trag shrugged indifferently.

Lars deactivated the device as Killashandra opened the door panel and the three left the loft. Killashandra watched Trag to see if the acoustics of the Festival auditorium affected him. Trag did not so much as alter his firm stride or respond to the echoes his vigorous pace produced. The guards had to scurry to keep up with them.

Once inside the guest suite which Trag was to share with them, Lars switched on the jammer before he passed it over to Trag.

"They've been replacing the monitors in the organ loft every day but a trill of crystal and they shatter," Killashandra told Trag as she made her way to the beverage counter. "A cold glass of the Bascum, Trag?"

"Please." Trag returned the jammer to Lars. "What sort of detector do they have at the shuttleport?"

"Isotope scanner," Lars said with a grimace. "The popular theory is that the detector is set off by a rare isotope of iron peculiar to Optherian soil. Once the residue of the isotope builds up in the bone marrow, it tends to be self-perpetuating. There've been unsuccessful attempts to neutralize the isotope and jam the scanners but nothing works." Then he scowled. "All the guards are rehabs and never miss. Trying to get past them is an effective form of suicide. There is also a stun field that operates in the event that another concerted attempt is ever made to gain entry to the port."

"I was met by four Optherians . . ." Trag began.

"Who had been passed in. Oh, authorized personnel come and go but they are very careful to display their authorization to the guards."

Killashandra had punched up sandwiches which she now passed to the men.

"We don't have much time before dinner and the concert, and I need a bath," she announced, her mouth half full of sandwich.

"So do I." Lars followed Killashandra, taking the jammer with him after an apologetic nod to Trag. "'Trag is no threat to us, huh?" Lars murmured sarcastically, once they were in the unmonitored bathroom.

Killashandra shrugged and grimaced. "I didn't think he'd cut up that stiff, but then, neither of us knew what lies the Elders were spinning. And the Guild does have a reputation to maintain, especially if they had to call in the FSP to get a cruiser for a fast trip here. But," she added, rather pleased, "it means they cared."

"I felt I was talking to a brick wall, Killa, until it came down." Lars ran his fingers through his thick hair. "What would you have done if it hadn't, Killa?"

"Well, it did and Trag has been converted. Now all we have to do is get word to your father. Just how many people would we

241

have to get to safety? I mean, if Trag has that warrant for party or parties . . ."

Lars framed her face with his hands, grinning down at her. "No matter how broad that warrant, Killa, it wouldn't extend to all those who really need our protection. Nahia, Hauness, Theach, Brassner, and Olver are just the most important. Why—"

"Couldn't some just disappear into the islands?"

Lars shook his head.

"Then we'll have to hold tight somehow until Trag reports the subliminal conditioning to the Federated Council. The Fleet Marines would land, in force, and the Elders would be sampling rehab. You're safe as long as I'm here—and stop shaking your head. Look, Trag can return, now that the organ is repaired and I'm unabducted—"

"Is the cruiser still here?"

"Oh, I rather doubt it."

"Then unless he can recall it, he's surfaced on Optheria until the next liner and that's not due for at least two weeks."

"Two more weeks!" Killashandra realized that she had taken for granted the same constant space traffic that frequented Shanganaugh Moon Base.

"What? Have my charming presence and inspired coupling worn thin now that you have a fellow crystal singer to pair you?"

"Trag? You think—Trag and I? Don't be funny! Listen to me, young man, there's a lot you don't know about crystal singers!"

"I'd like the time to find out." His reply was wistful even if the kiss he gave her was not. And her response to his embrace temporarily suspended less urgent matters, even the bath.

Fortunately, by the time Trag knocked peremptorily on the bathroom door, they were both dressed.

"Coming," Killashandra responded in a trill, bestowing one last kiss on Lars before she hauled open the door. Sweeping dramatically into the main room with Lars a step behind her, she was delighted to see Trag, a half-empty glass of beer in his hand, in the company of Thyrol, Mirbethan, and Pirinio. Facetiously wondering if Polabod had been loaned to another quartette, she greeted them graciously, exclaiming her eagerness to attend the evening's concert and, at long last, hear an Optherian organ.

Dinner was served in the same chamber that had charmed Killashandra. The charm was enhanced this time by the fact that Elder Pentrom was missing from the guest roster. Trag was monopolized at one end of the table by Elders Ampris and Torkes, who engaged him in very serious discussions, while Mirbethan did her best to introduce unexceptional topics into conversation at the other. Thyrol, Pirinio, and two very meek older women instructors completed the buffer between the Elders and the distinguished and newly arrived Guildmember Trag.

"Elder Torkes," Trag said in a well-pitched voice that carried to every part of the dining room after he had sipped the beverage in his glass, "my metabolism requires the ingestion of a certain quantity of alcohol daily. What have you to offer?"

After that, Killashandra didn't bother straining her ears to hear what information, or misinformation, might be exchanged. Fortunately the portions served them were considerably more generous, if unexciting to the palate, than her first dinner there, so that hunger was assuaged.

There was no reason to dally at the festive board so, immediately after the sweet course was finished, Mirbethan led the way to the Conservatory Concert Hall. Those already assembled rose to their feet at the entrance of the distinguished visitors.

"Like lambs to the slaughter," Lars whispered in her ear.

"Wrong again!" she whispered back, then composed her features in a gracious expression. Until she had a good look at the seating.

The organ console, of course, dominated the blue and white stage. Golden curtains were richly draped to complete the frame which was bathed in a gentle glow of diffused light. They walked up a slight ramp to the orchestra floor where Mirbethan smilingly turned and gestured toward their chairs.

Bloody inquisition, Killashandra thought to herself. Upholstered in a mid-blue velvety fabric, the chairs were bucket shaped, semirecumbents equipped with broad arm rests, sculptured to fit wrist and hand for proper sensory input. Killashandra did not expect to find an easy repose for over each seat was a half hood, no doubt containing additional sensory outlets. As Lars might remark, the occupants of the seats were sitting ducks.

Nevertheless, and because it was consonant with the role she had adopted, Killashandra expressed delight over the "ambiance

243

of the hall," the charming decor, and the unusual seating. She counted fifteen rows extending up and into the shadows behind her, all of them filled. She counted the front-row seats on her side of the entrance as fifteen so that some four hundred and fifty people, the complement of the Conservatory, were about to be entertained.

She took her seat but because of the tilt and the arm rest, the only part of her that could touch Lars was her foot. She angled so that she could touch his. She felt a return pressure which gave her far more reassurance than she should need or had expected to gain from such a minimal contact.

The house lights dimmed and Killashandra was filled with a perturbation she had never experienced before at what was usually the most enjoyable, anticipatory moment of a performance.

A woman swirled out onto the stage, her robes flowing out behind her. She bowed quickly to the assembly and took her place at the organ console, her back, with its pleated draperies, illuminated by the spotlight. Killashandra saw her lift her hands to the first manual and then all the lights went out as the first chord was played.

Killashandra all but kicked Lars as she recognized the music. In most Conservatories, a man named Bach would have been credited with its composition. On Optheria it was unlikely that any sheep safely grazed. Then the sensory elements began their insidious plucking. It was well done, the scent of new grass, spring winds, tender green, soothing color, bucolic fragrances and then— Lars's foot tapped hers urgently but she had already caught the image of the "shepherd," a glamorized Ampris, a kindly, loving, affectionate, infinitely tender shepherd, gazing for that one moment upon the members of his "flock."

Had Trag failed? Disappointment and a keen flare of apprehension suffused Killashandra. She forced herself to recall that first glimpse of this smaller theater. There had to be a second subliminal generator behind this organ console. Indeed, there was probably one attached to every one of these insidious instruments. How would they disconnect them all? A second image, of a grieving Ampris, saddened by a misdemeanor of his flock—saddened but infinitely tolerant and forgiving—capped her disgust with the entire exercise.

Killashandra caught all of the images that were broadcast, as sharp and as clear as if a hologram had been suspended for inspection on a tri-d screen. The subliminals seemed etched on her retina. Something to do with her symbiont's rejection of this superimposition?

When the lights came up, Killashandra elected to seem to be affected by the performance as she should have been.

"Guildmember?" Mirbethan asked in a soft but eager voice.

"Why, it was charming. So soothing, such a lovely scene. I declare that I could smell new grass, and spring blossoms." Lars tried to step on her toe. She struggled up out of the clutch of her seat and peered around at him. "Why, Lars Dahl, it is everything you told me it would be!" He tapped twice, getting her message.

A second performer strode out on the stage, his manner so militant that Killashandra laid a private bet with herself: one of the Germans or an Altairian, if Prosno-Sevic's bombastic compositions had been composed before the Optherians had settled this planet.

The music was an uninspired melange of many of the martial themes, each new one buffeting the captive audience so that she found herself twitching away from the onslaught of the music, and wondering if she would survive the subliminals. She did, but her eyeballs ached with visions of Torkes and an improbably robust Pentrom urging the faithful onto the path to victory and planetarianism, defending the credo of Optheria to the death.

An audible sigh—of relief?—preceded the applause this selection engendered. So the audience was being soothed to trust, encouraged to resist subversive philosophies: now what, Killashandra wondered?

An alarmingly thin and earnest young man, swallowing his Adam's apple convulsively as he crossed the stage, was the next performer. He looked more like a wading bird than a premier organist. And when he took his seat and lifted his hands, they splayed to incredible arachnoid lengths, making the soft opening notes ludicrous to Killashandra's mind, especially when she recognized the seductive phrases of a French pianist. The name escaped her momentarily but the erotic music was quite familiar. She held her breath against the first image and choked on the howl of laughter as the subliminal image of Ampris-the-seducer was superimposed, in reds and oranges, on the viewers' abused senses. Fortunately, the notion of Ampris making love to her, or anyone, was so bizarre that the eroticism—even magnified by scent and sensory titillation—failed to achieve its full effect. Lars's continual tapping—was he succumbing to the illusion, keeping the beat, or trying to distract her from the powerful sensuality—against her toe kept reminding her how perilous their position was at the moment.

Bolero! The name returned to her as the lights came up. And fury at this arrant manipulation set a flush in her cheeks that matched those in Mirbethan's as the delighted woman turned to inquire breathlessly how Killashandra had enjoyed the concert.

The seats were all tilting forward, releasing their occupants once more into the cold cruel world of reality.

"I have never so totally experienced music before in my life, Mirbethan," Killashandra said in ringing, heartfelt tones. What she felt in her breast was not what the performance was expected to generate. "A balanced and professional performance. The artists were magnificent. Excellent adaptations to the Optherian organs."

"Adaptations? Oh, no, Guildmember, this was the first performance of three brilliant new compositions," Mirbethan said and Killashandra could only goggle at her.

"That music was totally original? Composed by the performers?" Killashandra's surprise was misinterpreted by Mirbethan as the proper expression of awe. Lars squeezed her arm warningly and she managed to contain her outrage.

"A truly brilliant concert," Trag said, joining them as the audience was dispersing. "An experience I would not willingly have foregone."

Never having heard so much warmth in his voice, Killashandra looked sharply at Trag. Surely, if her symbiont had protected her . . . Now she stared at Trag's flushed face, his bright eyes, and noticed that a smile had reshaped his lips. Killashandra grabbed at Lars's arm and, before anyone else could see her dismay, she pulled them both into the crowd, away from Trag and the two Elders who escorted him.

"Easy, Killa," Lars murmured in her ear. "Don't give it away. Not now!"

ANNE McCAFFREY

"But he—"

His hand twisted her fingers cruelly, reminding her of the danger they were in.

"That last piece will send them all to their beds, alone if necessary," Lars continued, breaking up the sentence into quick short phrases as he hurried her away from the hall. "No one is expected to linger. Not after that dose of eroticism." They turned a corner, Killashandra accepting Lars's direction. "Trag's coming."

"Don't you understand? No one here composed that music. It was all stolen!"

"I know, I know."

"Yours wasn't stolen. It was original. The only bloody original music I've heard on this fardling mudball!"

"Shush now, Killa. Only one more corridor and we're home safe and then you can rant and rave."

"I get the cold shower first."

"What and waste the music?"

She tried to kick him but they were walking so fast she would have lost her balance if she'd succeeded.

"I will not be manipulated . . ." and the last word she roared in the privacy of their suite. She was hauling the Beluga spider-silk kaftan over her head as she reached the bathroom door and, flipping on the cold water, stood in its frigid torrent until she could feel her flesh shriveling. Lars pulled her out, handing her a towel as he took her place.

"I think it's a shame to waste all their hard work and effort—"

"Did you want to go to bed with an image of Ampris?" she demanded at the top of her voice.

"Oh, I saw Mirbethan," Lars said ingenuously, toweling himself dry.

"Mirbethan?"

"Yes, didn't you know that was why she was included in your welcoming committee? She's bi—"

"What?" Killashandra screeched that at the top of her lungs.

"Compose yourself, Killashandra Ree," said the cool voice of Trag from the doorway. "You and Lars Dahl are in every bit as much danger as you thought. We must talk."

247

Chapter 22

"First," Trag said as Killashandra and Lars joined him in the main room, and he pointed to the monitors. Lars held up the jammer. "Very good. Secondly, I need to hear an account of your adventures here, Killashandra. Then I can separate the fact from the fiction presented by Ampris and Torkes. Both are clever men."

"A drink, Killa?" Lars asked and his voice was rough with either anger or anxiety.

"I would appreciate something stronger than that tasteless beer, please, Lars Dahl," Trag said.

"My pleasure, Trag."

Killashandra could feel the tension release in her belly and she let out a lungful of air as Trag's courteous request gave her a reassuring measure of his attitude. She took a quick pull at the polly liqueur which Lars handed her before he sat on the couch, not touching her but with one arm protectively along the back. She began with her arrival on the *Athena* and her suspicions about Corish. Nor was she any less than candid about the fit of pique with Optherian bureaucracy which had led her to leave the Conservatory grounds, her subsequent kidnapping, escape, and her second meeting with the young islander. She was as forthright about Lars's effect on her sexuality as she was about the impact Nahia, Hauness, and Theach had had on her sympathies. Crystal singing tended to peel off unnecessary veneers and conditioned attitudes, not that she had been afflicted by many, having been raised on Fuerte.

During her recitation, Trag had sipped his drink, any reaction hidden by his hooded eyes. He finished the last of the polly liqueur which Lars had elected to serve him as she concluded the summary and he gestured politely to Lars for a refill.

"They are clever, those old men, but they have not dealt with crystal singers before," Trag said. "They have outsmarted themselves this time. Whom the Gods would destroy, they first make mad."

Killashandra regarded Trag in mild astonishment and then Lars, wondering if his habit was contagious. But Trag's adage was eminently applicable.

"Or think themselves impervious to the slings and arrows of outraged fortune," Lars said with a mischievous grin. Killashandra groaned in protest.

"Tomorrow I shall offer to realign the Conservatory instrument," Trag said. "I distinctly heard a burr—the first sign of a souring crystal."

"Will they permit you?" Killashandra asked.

"They are greedy. And they have no qualified crystal tuner until we have trained some. I have already resolved the point that the Guild contracted to supply the crystals and technical assistance, without reference to the number of appropriate technicians supplied. Therefore no further sum is to be paid by them. Until they received that reassurance from me, they were trying to make out that you were in breach of contract—"

"In breach? Me? When they placed me in jeopardy? First by hiring an assailant to prove my Heptite origination? Then they hinder me in the execution of my assignment? And they malign my competence?" Killashandra quickly switched to malicious amusement. "Not that they will really appreciate the level of competence we have exhibited! Nor the caliber of the technical assistance they've bought!" She grinned at Trag. "So, what other knotty problems did you solve at dinner?"

"Your incorruptible dedication to your Guild."

"What!" Killashandra's irritation rekindled. "Of all the—"

Trag held up his hand, a gleam in his eye that suggested to Killashandra that he was enjoying her discomfiture. Firmly she controlled herself. It didn't help to notice, out of the corner of her eye, that Lars was struggling to suppress his own amusement.

"Coming as I do from Guildmaster Lanzecki's office, I am," Trag paused unexpectedly, shooting a glance at Killashandra which she could only interpret as sly, "above reproach. I am also male. Apparently the Elders trust few women in any but the most traditional or subordinate capacities. I assured them that not only were you Guildmaster Lanzecki's first choice for such a delicate and crucial installation, but you were mine as well."

Killashandra sniffed but gave him a long hard look, to remind him exactly why Killashandra Ree had been Trag's first choice.

"Your praise, Guildmember, is only surpassed by your concern for the welfare of the Guild," she said demurely.

"In a matter affecting the Guild reputation, I am, too, incorruptible," Trag replied, neatly parrying her thrust.

"So tomorrow are Lars and I permitted to continue with the Festival organ?" Trag nodded. "And you will reorganize the second instrument?"

"In the best interests of the guiding precepts of the Federated Sentient Planets Council, yes, I certainly shall. Otherwise I assure you that these Elders would not receive unreimbursed and gratuitous services from the Heptite Guild."

"Bravo!" Lars called.

"Their greed blinds them," Trag said. "So, following a recent example, we shall take the opportunity that is presented," he added, nodding toward Lars who returned the compliment. "Basically they have trite minds. Security, pride, and sex! Imagine! Inflicting such prurience on tonight's audience."

Killashandra regarded Trag with mild astonishment. The man was positively garrulous, volunteering comments not to mention uncontracted services. Or was he simply responding to the backlash of that maladroit rendition of the *Bolero*? She'd have thought Trag made of sterner stuff, especially since he'd been forewarned of the subliminals.

"Oh, that's a common diet for the Conservatory," Lars said. "For the masses, they have other themes, sometimes so indigestible I wonder how they can be swallowed, even conditionally. Mainlanders are often subjected to a spectrum ranging from xenophobia," Lars began ticking the subjects off on his fingers, a fear of races in their own territories, to claustrophobia to nip any budding interest in space-faring, to fear of disobedience, fear and disgust of acts that are 'unnatural,' fear of committing an illegal action, rational or not. They've even constructed a negative-feedback loop to inhibit thinking along lines the Elders have suddenly decided are subversive. A dislike of the color red was achieved a year or so ago.

"Then," and Lars was really warming to his subject, "the tourists get a different menu: love of the simple life, very little eroticism—which would follow, wouldn't it? All sorts of nebulous goodnesses to be obtained by staying on here. Immense credit balances are constantly flashed luringly at the most bizarre moments. Naturally the disadvantages aren't mentioned at all."

"No lecture on Full Disclosure?" Killashandra shot Trag a glance but he ignored her.

"Have you a reliable contact in the Conservatory, Lars?" Trag asked him.

"I wouldn't dare contact any of them after tonight's subliminal messages. I could try the marketplace—"

Trag shook his head. "It was politic to agree with Ampris and Torkes that you, Killashandra, have undoubtedly fallen under this young man's insidious spell." He raised his hand at Killashandra's guffaw. "Neither of you are to be allowed to leave the Conservatory without escort. For your safety, of course, Killashandra."

"Of course!"

"What works in your favor, though, in this infatuation—"

"Trag!"

"I'm not Ballyblind, Killashandra," Trag said in a stern voice, "and, if the Elders consider you two self-absorbed to the exclusion of other, more treacherous activities, it is a safeguard, however tenuous. At least while we are still on Optheria." Trag turned to Lars. "Once we leave, Lars Dahl, you are in grave jeopardy."

Lars nodded and, when Killashandra closed her fingers about his, he smiled down at her. "All I need is a half-day's start on any pursuit; no one will ever find me in the islands."

Trag managed to look skeptical without changing a muscle in his face. "Not this time, I think. This time the islanders are to be disciplined to a final and total obedience to the Optherian Council."

"They have to catch us first," Lars said calmly, although anger flared in his eyes and his fingers tightened on Killashandra's. In an abrupt change he shrugged. "The threat of wholesale reprisal is scarcely new."

"Trag has that warrant . . ." Killashandra suggested but caught the obstinate set of Lars's face.

"May I remind you, Killashandra," Trag said, "that a Federated Council warrant is not a writ one exercises with impunity. If I am forced to use it, Lars, and whoever else it includes, would be charged with your abduction and subject to the authority of the FSP Council."

"If I don't press charges, once they're off Optheria—"

"If you perjure yourself in a Council Court, Killashandra Ree, not even the Heptite Guild can rescue you from the consequences."

"I repeat, and listen to me this time," Lars interrupted firmly, jiggling Killashandra's arm for her attention, "I only need a head start and there isn't a captain on this planet who could catch me. Look, Trag, it's not your affair, but if you're willing to disorganize the Conservatory projector, would you consider doing others? There are quite a few two-manual organs on the Mainland. To have two sabotaged will already be a considerable boon, but the more Mainlanders who are freed from subliminal manipulation, the more chance we'd all have of surviving until the Federated Council moves.

"The Elders can blandly puff on about disciplining islanders, but first they have to jizz enough Mainlanders up to the point of a punitive action. Mainlanders are a passive bunch, after so many years of the pap they've been subjected to." He grinned maliciously. "You saw last night which of the three pressures the audience responded to the most— Not the martial pride! So, psyching a punitive force up would take time, a clever program, and sufficient audience saturation. The smaller the net the subliminals cast, the longer it will take the Elders to mount any sort of expedition to the islands.

"Now," and Lars leaned forward urgently, "you and Killa have to make a report to the Federated Council? Well, I would find it hard to believe that any Council acts fast. Right?"

Trag nodded. "Speed is determined by the physical threat to the planet involved."

"Not to the population?" Killashandra asked, surprised at Trag's emphasis.

Trag shook his heavy head. "Populations are easy to produce, but habitable planets are relatively scarce." He indicated that Lars should continue.

"So, your report will be considered, deliberated upon, and then?"

"It may indeed take time, Lars Dahl, but the Federated Council has outlawed the use of subliminal conditioning. There is absolutely no question in my mind that action will be taken against the Optherian Elders. A government which must resort to such means to maintain domestic satisfaction has lost the right to govern. Its Charter will be revoked."

"There's no danger that you and Killashandra will be restrained from leaving?" Lars asked abruptly.

"Why should we be? Can they have any suspicion that someone knows that they maintain control by illicit means?"

"Comgail did," Killashandra said, "even if he was killed before he could pass on the information. Whoever killed the man must wonder if Comgail had accomplices."

Lars shook his head positively. "Comgail's only contact was Hauness and Hauness didn't reveal that until after Comgail's death. I knew that some drastic measure was planned. Not what it was."

"Tell me, Lars," Trag asked, "does any one suspect that you are aware of the subliminals?"

Lars shook his head vigorously. "How? I always pretended the correct responses after concerts. Father didn't warn me until I was sent to the Mainland for my education. His warning was accompanied by a description of the retribution I would suffer, from him as well as the Council, if I ever revealed my knowledge unnecessarily." Lars grinned. "You may be sure I told no one."

"Besides your father, who knows?" Trag asked. "Or don't you know that?"

Lars nodded. "Hauness and his intimates. As a trained hypnotherapist, he caught on to the subliminals but had the sense to keep silent. It is quite possible that others in his profession know it, but if they do, they don't broadcast it either. What could they do? Especially when I doubt that many Optherians know that subliminals are against Federation Law!" The last was spoken in a bitter tone. "Who would suspect that music, the Ultimate Career on Optheria, can be perverted to ensure the perpetuation of a stagnant government? Then there was the almost insoluble problem of trying to get word off Optheria, to someone with sufficient status to get Council attention. Complaint from people who could be considered a few maladjusted citizens— and every society has some—carries little weight.

"It was Hauness who devised a way to get messages off Optheria for us. Posthypnotic requests—yes, yes, I know, and don't think it was an easy matter for him to violate his ethics as a physician-healer, but we were getting desperate. A suggestion to receive and later mail a letter from the nearest transfer point seemed a minor infraction. I am certain that Hauness only capitulated because Nahia was suffering so much distress. She had to cope with such a devastating increase of suicide potentials. She's an empath, Trag—"

"You must encounter Nahia, Trag, before you leave Optheria," Killashandra said, twining her fingers reassuringly about Lars's. He gave her a quick and grateful glance.

"That's why, if you would go to Ironwood to check out the organ there, you would surely encounter Nahia and Hauness," Lars said eagerly.

"I would?" Trag asked.

"Quite likely, if you were suddenly taken ill."

Trag regarded him steadily. "Crystal singers do not succumb to planet-based diseases."

"Not even food poisoning?" Lars was not to be deterred.

"And that's a likelihood if you eat often with the Elders. Or do I mean starvation?" Killashandra remarked.

"That way, you can warn Nahia and Hauness, and they can alert others." Lars leaned forward, eagerly waiting for Trag's decision. "I couldn't save myself at the expense of my friends."

"How large a group do you have, Lars Dahl?" Trag asked.

"I don't know at the moment. We had about two thousand, and more were being investigated. The Elders's search and seize to find Killashandra reduced our ranks considerably." Regret for having provoked the Elders to such action colored Lars's expression. He squared his shoulders, accepting that responsibility. "I fervently hope more sacrifices will not be required."

"Do your islanders perpetrate many outrages on the Mainland?"

"Outrages on the Mainland?" Lars burst out laughing. "We leave the Mainland to stew in its own juice! If you wish to punish an island child, you threaten to send him to a Mainland school. What crimes were being laid on our beaches?"

"Crimes hinted at darkly but never specified, apart from the attack on Killashandra—"

"Ampris instigated that—" Killashandra said angrily.

"And her abduction."

"And I have laid that firmly on the shoulders of unknown malfeasants. I thought they'd bought that."

"They might have if the attachment between you and Lars Dahl was not so apparent, almost as if you were in resonance with each other. However," and Trag went on quickly, "Torkes contended that young Lars Dahl could scarcely have found you so conveniently if he had not known where you were. The islands being so numerous and widespread he does not accept coincidence."

"I think Torkes is in for a large surprise on the mechanics of coincidence," Killashandra said in her most caustic tone. She had poured another stiff drink for herself, trying to dull anger and indignation. "Trag, I don't see why the Federated Council cannot act expeditiously—"

"This planet is not threatened by destruction."

"Our much vaunted Federated Council is not much better than the Elders Council, is it?"

"I will do everything in my power, Lars Dahl, to ensure the physical and psychological integrity of your adherents," Trag said. "And if that includes servicing every instrument on this planet, I will do that, too." A slight shift of the alignment of his lips gave him an appearance of smiling. "Greed provokes me. And all this talk has made me thirsty. What is this?" he asked, obliquely requesting a refill.

"The fermented juice of the ubiquitous polly fruit," Lars said, serving him. "The Elders may complain about the islands but they are its best customers."

"Tell me again about the security arrangements at the shuttle port," Trag went on. "A liner is due in two weeks' time. I should like to have you both on it."

"There's more chance of sailing a straight course in the islands, Trag," Lars said, shaking his head discouragingly. "If anyone had been able to discover a flaw in the security curtain at the shuttle port, it would have been done. My father had the unique honor of adjusting the screens to prevent a mass attack. Father came here on a short-term contract to provide security micro-units for the Optherian Council. Father was co-opted by the Federated Council because of his expertise with microchip installations. The Federation wanted him to find out why another agent had never reported back to them. But, while he was installing the chips, he didn't have much luck with the covert assignment. So when the Optherians offered him the shuttleport contract, he took it. No one mentioned the fact that three to four months was the longest it was safe to stay on Optheria without getting trapped. When he realized that he was, and even he couldn't get past the shuttleport curtain, he talked himself into his position as Angel Island Harbor Master. Far enough away from the shuttleport to satisfy the Elders, and far enough away for him to feel safe from them."

"How is cargo transferred?" Trag asked.

"What little there is is unloaded through the main passenger lock, which is operated by the shuttle pilots, true and loyal, uncorruptible citizens of Optheria. The only way into the shuttleport is past the detector's arc. And if the detector is set off without first presenting the right pass to those rehabbed guards," he made a popping sound, "you're dead."

"Ah, but Thyrol was right beside me as we left the port, Lars," Killashandra said. "And the arc did not go off. Yet you say that it goes off whenever the mineral residue is detected."

"Crystal resonance might mask or confuse the detector," Trag remarked, choosing his words slowly. "For the same thing occurred, and with Thyrol beside me, when I exited the port."

"Why don't we just boldly go under the fardling arc then? Both of us with Lars between."

"You no longer resonate, Killashandra," Trag said.

"Besides, that only helps me, Killa. I won't leave the others vulnerable to the Elders's reprisals."

"Impasse!" Killashandra threw her hands out in disgust but she had to admire Lars's stand. "Wait a minute. I may not resonate, but white crystal does. Trag, they blow out the monitors at the sound of an *A*. Won't crystal resonance affect other piezoelectrical equipment? I know it'd be folly to try to blow out the shuttleport detector . . ."

"That's been tried, too, Killa." Lars interrupted her with a rueful grin.

"Trag?—If crystal resonance provides a mask . . ."

"I should not like to put it to the test and fail."

Killashandra turned to Lars. "You said something about your father being able to detect Council agents. Does he have a unit?"

"A small one."

"If we had it, we could test crystal resonance with it. We've got all those crystal shards, Trag, and you know how interactive white is."

"First we have to contact my father," Lars said with an ironic laugh, "then get him and the device here. Oh, it's not large but certainly not something you carry bare-faced through City streets." But, even as Lars spoke in pessimistic terms, it was clear to Killashandra that she had revived his hopes. "All the more reason, Trag, for you to get to Ironwood and make contact with Nahia and Hauness. They've got the oceanjet. They could discreetly bring Father and the device as far as Ironwood."

"There are no other embarkation clearances at the shuttleport?" Trag asked.

Lars shook his head slowly. "No other beside the security curtain has ever been needed. You forget, Trag, that loyal, happy, natural Optherians have no desire to leave their planet. Only tourists, who can buy tickets anywhere, so long as they've enough credit."

"Then," and Trag got to his feet, carefully putting the glass down on the nearest surface, "patently I must oblige both you and the greedy Elders. Good night."

Killashandra watched, wondering if the polly had got to the impervious Trag but his step was as firm and unswerving as ever. She saw that Lars was watching his progress, a very thoughtful expression on his face.

"If this idea works, Killa," he said, taking her in his arms, his eyes on that distant prospect, "is there enough crystal to get six or seven people off Optheria?"

"Don't hope too hard, Lars!" she cautioned him, her head against his shoulder, her arms about him. "Nor can we schedule a mass exodus on the next liner without giving the whole scheme away. But if crystal resonance fools the scanner, the most vulnerable people will get free. The Festival season hasn't even started. When it does, a few one-way passengers could go out on each flight." She looked up and caught the bleak look on his face. "Lars, dance with me?"

"To a distant drum?" he asked with a rueful grin, but he shortly sloughed off depression.

The next morning Killashandra woke to the second chimes and to an interesting idea.

"Lars, Lars, wake up."

"Why?" and he attempted to pull her back down on the bed, murmuring suggestions.

"No, I'm serious. We responded to the subliminals last night, didn't we? How long are they supposed to be effective?"

"Huh? I dunno. I've never . . . Oh, I see what you mean!" And he sat up, linking his arms about his raised knees and considering the implications. "We never took last night's performance into our deliberations, did we?" He rubbed his chin thoughtfully, then grinned at her. "I'd say we could work this to our advantage. Security, pride, and sex, huh!" Lars began to laugh, a mirth which developed into such a paroxysm that he fell back on the bed and hauled his knees up to his chin to relieve the muscular cramp of uncontrollable laughter.

Trag appeared in the doorway, pointed to the ceiling monitor and, when Killashandra pointed to the jammer on the table, he came in and shut the door, regarding Lars expressionlessly.

"We got conditioned last night, Trag," Killashandra said by way of explanation as she hauled her coverall on. "I don't think I should overdo it, but if Lars wants to act disaffected with me, it will lull Ampris and Torkes into thinking their programming's effective. Even on a crystal singer. Trag, I could even stay on here . . . not want to leave Optheria. I'm a musician. If last night is the best they can do, just lead me to a keyboard! I'll show 'em some sensory music that'll knock 'em in the aisles."

Trag shook his head slowly from side to side. "Risky for any number of reasons which I shouldn't have to enumerate."

Brushing laugh tears from his eyes, Lars was still grinning broadly as he reached for his clothes.

"So what was so funny?" Killashandra asked.

"Mirbethan as a sex image when I have you!"

"I'm not sure I needed to know that!" Killashandra stalked into the main room and up to the catering unit. She punched out her selection so hard that the tab stuck and a succession of beverage cups paraded out. Fortunately the mechanism was programmed against excessive use and the emergency panel flashed "quota" at her as the depressed button snapped out again.

"Put Ampris in my place and what do you have?" Lars wanted to know and his voice was just a shade repentant.

"Nausea." She handed him a cup from the plentiful supply waiting on the catering facility.

Chapter 23

They had just finished eating when the comunit blipped. Killashandra flicked open the channel. Mirbethan appeared, looking both annoyed and hesitant. Killashandra schooled her face to courteous inquiry.

"My apologies for disturbing you so early, Guildmember . . ." she did not continue until Killashandra had murmured reassurance, "but a citizen has been most persistent in trying to contact you . . . We have assured him that you are not to be disturbed by trivia. He insists on speaking with you personally and his attitude borders on the insolent." Mirbethan closed her mouth primly on the verdict.

"Well, well, what's his name?"

"Corish von Mittelstern. He says that he met you on board the *Athena*." Mirbethan obviously doubted this.

"Indeed he did. A pleasant young man who knows nothing of my Guild affiliation. Put him through."

Corish's image immediately replaced Mirbethan's. He was frowning but his expression cleared into a broad smile once he saw Killashandra.

"Thank Krim I got you, Killashandra. I was beginning to doubt that you even existed, with that Conservatory playing it so cosy. I never heard of a Conservatory monitoring the calls of a student."

"They're very careful and they prefer your complete dedication to your studies here."

"You mean, you've been allowed to play on one of those special organs?"

Killashandra affected a girlish giggle. "Me? No. But I heard the most marvelous recital on the Conservatory's two-manual sensory organ last night. You wouldn't believe how versatile it is, how powerful, how stimulating. Corish, you've simply got to get to one of the concerts before you leave. The public ones will be starting soon, they tell me, but I could see if it's possible to get you to one here at the Conservatory. You really have to hear the Optherian organ, Corish, before you can possibly understand what it's like for me." Someone pinched her arm. Well, maybe she was overdoing it a trifle but enthusiasm was not out of order. "Have you found your uncle yet?"

Corish's expression altered from the skeptical to the dolorous. "Not yet."

"Oh, dear, how very disappointing."

"Yes, it is. And I've only two more weeks before I'm scheduled to leave. The family is going to be upset about my failure. Look, Killashandra, I know you're studying hard, and this is a chance of a lifetime for you, but could you spare me an evening?" Killashandra gave Corish full marks for a fine performance.

"Oh, Corish, you sound so discouraged. Yes, I'm sure I can wangle an evening out. I don't think there's a concert tonight. I'll find out. I'm not a prisoner here."

"I should hope not," Corish said stiffly.

"Look, where can I reach you?"

"The Piper Facility," Corish replied as if there were no other suitable place in the City, "where you *said*," and he emphasized the word, "that you'd leave a message for me. I was concerned when there'd been no word at all from you. Food's not bad here but they won't serve anything drinkable. Typical traveler hostel. I'll see if they can recommend some place a little more Optherian. This isn't a bad world, you know. I've met some sterling people, very helpful, very kind." Then his expression brightened. "You check and leave word at the Facility only if you can't make it. Otherwise, come here at seven thirty. You have enough funds for ground transport, don't you?" Now he was the slightly condescending, well traveled adult, older sibling.

"Of course I do. You sound just like my brother," she replied cheerfully. "See you!" And she broke the connection, turning to Trag and Lars. "That sort of solves one problem, doesn't it?"

"Does it?" Trag asked darkly.

"I think so," Lars replied. "Corish has an unlimited travel pass, issued by Elder Pentrom. His credentials must have come from very highly placed Federationists for that kind of assistance."

"More likely, 'his uncle' is due to inherit a sizable hunk of credit of which the Optherian government will get its own share." Killashandra suggested. Lars nodded. "And if his cover has been that good, it's unlikely the Elders have tumbled to his true identity so he could get in touch with anyone we need, including Olav Dahl! Or Nahia and Hauness."

"What concerns me," Lars said, his eyes clouded with anxiety, "is why he's getting in touch with you right now. He must have come back to the City from Ironwood—and Nahia and Hauness. Maybe they're in jeopardy. So many people were picked up on the search and seize . . ."

Killashandra put a reassuring hand on Lars's arm. "I think somehow Corish would have managed to intimate that."

"I think he did by not admitting to finding his uncle."

"If he admitted to having found this uncle," Trag said, unexpectedly joining forces with Killashandra to reassure Lars, "he would no longer have any need to use that travel pass, and if he's as good a Council agent as he seems to be, he wouldn't surrender that option."

Lars accepted that interpretation with a nod of his head and pretended to be reassured.

"We'll know soon enough," Killashandra said kindly.

"Well, when you meet Corish this evening," Lars said, "walk to whichever restaurant he's been recommended. That way you have some chance of open talk. The Piper is certain to recommend The Berry Bush or Frenshaw's. Neither are far from the Piper, but both restaurants are run by Optherians, loyal and true to the Elders, so you'll be under observation. The food's pretty good." Lars gave her an encouraging grin.

"Then I'm taking the jammer, too. Got to keep them thinking it's me that causes the static. Well, they should have had enough time to digest Corish's innocuous conversation." So Killashandra tapped out a sequence on the comunit. "Mirbethan, is there a concert tonight? I shouldn't want to miss any but von Mittelstern has invited me to dinner tonight, and I've accepted. I don't want him to come charging up here and discover I'm more than the simple music student he thinks me, so I'll settle his doubts."

Whatever Mirbethan thought was disguised by her reassurances that no concert was scheduled.

"Then please arrange transport for me this evening. By the way, when is the next concert? I'm fascinated by the organ effects. Fabulous concert last night. The most unusual one I've ever attended."

"Tomorrow evening, Guildmember." Mirbethan's reply was gracious, but Killashandra noticed the slightly smug turn to the woman's faint smile.

"Good." Killashandra broke the connection. "Offense is the best defense, Guildmember," she added, turning to Trag. "You didn't have to promise the Elders that you'd discipline me for my emotional aberration, did you? Well, then, it's business as usual for me in a normal fashion which means I come and go, whether they trail me or not. Right? And since I'm disaffected with you," and Killashandra kissed Lars's cheek, "I'll go alone. Unless, Trag, you want to come and meet Corish."

"I might, at that," Trag said, half-closing his eyes a moment.

"That gives me the chance to moon after Mirbethan," Lars said slyly.

Killashandra guffawed and wished him luck.

"Now let us attend our duties," Trag said, gesturing for Killashandra to precede them to the door.

When they reached the Festival Auditorium, a large contingent of security men was loosely scattered about the stage, concentrated near the organ console, which was open. Two men were fussing about the keyboard but Killashandra couldn't tell whether they were dusting or adjusting the keys. Suddenly Elder Ampris detached himself from the gaggle and took a few steps forward to meet them.

"Don't overdo it, Killa," Lars murmured at her, aiming a slightly fatuous grin at the Elder.

"After last night, Elder Ampris, I wonder at my audacity in suggesting that I play on any Optherian organ," she said, and felt Lars's admonitory pinch on the tender inside flesh of her arm. Unnecessary, she felt, since she had forced herself to employ a meek and sincere tone of voice.

"You enjoyed the concert?"

"I have never heard anything like it," she said, which was no more than the truth. "Truly an experience. Mirbethan tells me there'll be another one tomorrow evening. I do hope that we'll be invited?"

"Of course you are, my dear Killashandra," Elder Ampris replied, his eyes glittering almost benignly at her.

She limited herself to a happy smile and continued on to the organ loft door.

"A word with you, Elder Ampris," Trag began, his anxious frown attracting the Elder's instant attention.

Killashandra and Lars continued into the organ loft.

"You pinched far too hard!"

"You wouldn't fool me, Killa!"

"Well, I did fool him," and hiding her gesture from observation, she pointed to the hairless corner of the manual cabinet.

"Jammer on?" she asked.

"The moment I finished pinching."

"Brackets, please!"

They had already positioned the first of the final slender crystals when Trag and Elder Ampris entered.

"Only five more crystals and this installation is complete," Trag was saying to Ampris. "I know that Killashandra is well aware that these upper register notes require the finest tuning." Killashandra nodded, receiving his tacit message. "I will check the brackets on that sour crystal in the Conservatory organ and be back here in time for the tune-up."

Killashandra was hoping that Elder Ampris would leave them to the task but he elected to remain, observing every movement. Killashandra hated to be overseen under any circumstances, and to have Ampris's gimlet eyes on her made the hairs on the back of her neck rise. She was annoyed, too, because Ampris's presence put a damper on any conversation between herself and Lars. She had enjoyed the bantering exchanges which relieved the tedium and tension of this highly precise work. So she felt doubly aggrieved to be denied a morning of matching wits with Lars Dahl. They would have so little time left to enjoy each other's company.

Therefore, it gave her a great deal of vicarious pleasure to spin out the last final bracketings, giving Trag ample time to make his alterations on the Conservatory program. And deliberately irritating Elder Ampris with her persnickety manipulations. He was in a state of nervous twitch when she and Lars tightened the last bracket.

"There!" she said on a note of intense satisfaction. "All right and tight!" She picked up the hammer and, seized by a malicious whimsy, struck the first note of the Beethoven motif. Out of the corner of her eye, she saw Ampris start forward, one hand raised in protest, his face drained of all color. She went up the scale, and then, positioning the hammer on the side of the crystal shafts, descended the 44 notes in a glissando. "Clear as the proverbial bell and not a vibration off the true. A good installation, if I say so myself."

Killashandra slid the hammer into its space in the toolbox and brushed her fingertips lightly together. She released the damper on the striking base of the crystals and replaced the top. "I don't think we'll fasten it just yet. Now, Elder Ampris, the moment of truth!"

"I would prefer that Guildmember Trag—"

"He can't play! Doesn't even read music," Killashandra said, deliberately misinterpreting Elder Ampris. Lars pinched her left flank, his strong fingers nipping into the soft flesh of her waistline. She would have kicked back at him if she could have done so unobserved. "But I suppose you would feel more secure if he was to vet the completed installation," she added, giving Ampris a timorous smile more consonant to someone in the thrall of subliminal conditioning than her previous declaration.

Trag's reappearance was fortuitous.

"Just as I suspected, Elder Ampris, a loose bracket on the middle G. I checked both manuals thoroughly."

Ampris regarded Trag with a moment's keen suspicion. "You don't play," he said.

"No."

"Then how can you tune crystal?"

Killashandra laughed aloud. "Elder Ampris, every would-be crystal singer has perfect and absolute pitch or they can't get into the Heptite Guild. Guildmember Trag doesn't need to be a trained musician. Guildmaster Lanzecki isn't, either. One of the reasons I was chosen for this assignment is because I am—and trained in keyboard music. Now, Trag, if you will inspect the installation?" She and Lars lifted off the cover.

Trag was not above giving Ampris a second fright for he tapped out three of the Beethoven notes in the soprano register before altering the sequence to random strikes. Then he did each note in turn, listening until the exquisite sound completely died before hitting the next crystal.

"Absolutely perfect," he said, handing her the hammer.

"Now, with your permission, Elder Ampris," Killashandra began, "I would like to use the organ keyboard." When she saw his brief hesitancy, she added, "It would be such an honor for me and it would only be the sonics. After last night's performance, I would be brash indeed to attempt any embellishments."

Bowing stiffly to the inevitable, Elder Ampris gestured for her to proceed from the loft. Not that she could have done anything to damage the actual organ keyboard, and live, with so many security guards millimeters from her. As she took her seat, pretending to ignore the battery of eyes and sour expressions, she decided against any of the Beethoven pieces she remembered from her Fuertan days. That would be risking more than her personal satisfaction was worth. She began to power up the various systems of the organ, allowing the electronic circuits to warm up and stabilize. She also discarded a whimsical notion to use one of Lars's themes. She flexed her fingers, pulled out the appropriate stops, and did a rapid dance on the foot pedals to test their reactions.

Diplomatically she began with the opening chords of a Fuertan love song, reminiscent of one of the folk tunes that she'd heard that first magical night on the beach with Lars. The keyboard had an exquisitely light touch and, knowing herself to be rather heavy handed, she tried to find the right balance, before she began the lilting melody. Even playing softly and delicately, she felt, rather than heard, the sound returning from the perfect acoustics of the auditorium. The phase shield around the organ protected her from the full response.

Playing this Festival organ was an incredible, purely musical experience as she switched to lowest manual for the bass line. For her as a singer, keyboards had been essential only as accompaniment, tolerated in place of orchestra and choral augmentation. She might have been supercilious about the Optherian contention that an organ was the ultimate instrument, but she was willing to revise her opinion of it upward. Even the simple folk song, embellished with color, scent and "the joy of spring," she thought sardonically, was doubly effective as a mood setter when played on the Optherian organ. She was sorely tempted to reach up and pull out a few of the stops that ringed the console.

Abruptly she changed to a dominant key and a martial air, lots of the bass notes in a sturdy thumpy-thump, but half-way through she tired of that mood, and found herself involved in the accompaniment to a favorite aria. Not wishing to spoil the rich music by singing, she transferred the melodic line to the manual she had just repaired, taking the orchestra part in the second manual and the pedal bass. The tenor's reprise naturally followed, on the third manual, mellower than the soprano range. From that final chord, she found herself playing a tune, filling in with a chorded bass, and not quite certain what tune it was when she felt someone pinch her hip. Her fingers jerked down the keys just as she realized that it was Lars's melody she was rehearsing. She made the slip of her fingers into the first music that came to mind, an ancient anthem with distinct religious overtones. She ended that in a flourish of keyboard embellishments and, with considerable reluctance, lifted her hands and feet from the organ, swiveling around on the seat.

Lars, being nearest, took her hand to ease her to the ground from the high organ perch. The pressure of his fingers was complimentary, if the arch of his eyebrows chided her for that slip. It was the surprise on Elder Ampris's face that pleased her the most.

"My dear Killashandra, I had no idea you were so accomplished," he said with renewed affability.

"Woefully out of practice," she said demurely, though she knew that she had struck few wrong notes and her sense of tempo had always been excellent. "Almost a travesty for someone like me to play on that superb organ, but I shall remember the honor for the rest of my life." She meant it.

There was a general sort of highly audible reshuffling as the security men permitted a handful of hesitant new arrivals closer to the console. Some nervous clearings of throats and foot scufflings also echoed faithfully about the auditorium.

"Balderol's students," Elder Ampris murmured by way of explanation. "To practice for the concerts now the organ is repaired."

At a glance, Killashandra decided there must be nine security men for each student. She smiled kindly, then noticed out of the corner of her eye that a solid line of the biggest security men stood shoulder to shoulder in front of the door to the organ loft. Were they glued to their posts?

"Well, let's leave them to it," she said brightly. "Don't you have some students for Trag and myself? To learn crystal tuning? They must have perfect and absolute pitch, you know," she reminded Elder Ampris as they left the stage. Her voice sounded dead as her final words were spoken in less resonant surroundings.

"That is not scheduled until tomorrow, Killashandra," Ampris said, mildly surprised. "I had thought that you and Guildmember Trag should take this opportunity to see the rest of the Conservatory."

That was not high on Killashandra's list of priorities but since she was momentarily in Ampris's good graces, she should make an effort to stay there. She was not best pleased when Ampris turned the projected tour over to Mirbethan, excusing himself on the grounds of urgent administrative duties. Instead of proving to Ampris that sublimation worked on crystal singers, she had to watch Lars proving it to Mirbethan while she tried to attach herself to Trag. At first Trag remained his inscrutable self but suddenly altered, attentive to her explanations of this classroom, that theory processor, when the small theater had been added, and which distinguished composer had initiated what ramification on the Festival Organ. Had Lars brazenly pinched the impervious Trag? As she trailed behind the trio, now inspecting the cheerless and sterilely neat dormitories, she would have been glad enough to receive Lars's pinch.

If she had herself been more receptive, she would have been impressed by the physical advantages of the Conservatory for it was exceedingly well organized and equipped in terms of practice and classrooms, library facilities, processing terminals. There was even a library of books, donated by the original settlers and subsequent visitors. The actual Conservatory had been designed as a complete unit and built at one time, only the Festival Auditorium added on at a later date although included in the original plans. In design it was a complex far superior to Fuerte's Music Center, which had sprawled in extensions and annexes with no basic concept. There was, however, more charm in a corner of Fuerte's Music Center than in any of the more elaborate and pretentious chambers of Optheria's Conservatory.

"The Infirmary is this way." Mirbethan's unctuous voice broke through Killashandra's sour reflections.

"I've been there," she said in a dry and caustic tone and Mirbethan had the grace to look embarrassed. Then she gave Lars a penetrating look which he returned with an impudent wink. "And I'm hungry. We didn't eat any lunch in order to get the installation completed."

Mirbethan was full of apologies and, when both Trag and Lars said they were sure the Infirmary was of the same high standard as the rest of the premises, she led them back to their quarters.

Once inside, Lars ostentatiously activated the jammer and Killashandra heaved a sigh of relief. She hadn't realized how tense she'd become.

"I'm hungry, that's all, I'm hungry," she told herself as she made her way to the caterer.

"Where did you find the subliminal unit, Trag?" Lars asked, pausing at the drinks cabinet.

"Under the stage, but keyed by the same motif. For clever men, the Elders can be repetitive."

Killashandra gave a contemptuous snort. "Probably can't remember anything more complicated at their advanced ages."

"Don't make the mistake of underestimating them, Killashandra," Trag said solemnly as he poured himself a brew.

"Let them have that privilege," Lars added. "Sententious bastards. We're down to Bascum, Killa."

"Well, that goes well with the fish, which seems the only thing left on today's menu."

Lars guffawed. "It always is. Take the soup instead," he said in a tone that suggested dire experience. "And don't, Killa, play my music again in the Conservatory," he added, waggling a finger at her. "Balderol heard me practice often enough."

"I won't say I'm sorry," Killashandra replied. "It just happened to develop from the previous chord. It's probably the most original music ever played on that organ if what we heard last night is standard."

"They don't want originality, Killa," Lars said with a twist to his smile. "They want more of the same that they can orchestrate to mind-penetration. Trag, what did Ampris say about your doing the provincial organs?"

"I haven't suggested it. Yet. There has been no opportunity."

Lars looked anxious. "I'm the one who's greedy now. Disabling their program in the City is a big step forward because so many provincials make the trek here in order to say they've heard the Festival Organ, but *they're* not the ones who'd be recruited to Ampris's punitive force. So they're the ones we want to keep unaffected this year."

"Who else has access to the organ lofts?" Trag asked.

"Only . . . Ah!" Lars's expressive face altered to triumph. "Comgail never got the chance to make his annual inspection of the other facilities. And maintenance is Ampris's responsibility, not Torkes. He'll have to use you and Killa, Trag. He hasn't anyone else. And he certainly wouldn't entrust maintenance to the puff heads you're supposed to initiate into the art of crystal tuning."

"Especially not you, Lars," said Killashandra with a laugh.

"Let's not continue that part of the farce, Killa," Lars said.

"Why not?" asked Trag. "I think you must realize that we will not leave you on this planet, no matter how cleverly you could hide yourself amid your islands, Lars Dahl. Crystal tuning is a universal skill."

"So is sailing, Trag."

"But let us continue as we have started. Farce or not, it keeps you in our company and safe."

"Trag, are you recruiting?" Even to herself, Killashandra sounded unnecessarily sharp.

Trag turned his head slowly to look at her, his heavy features expressionless. "Recruiting is not permitted by the FSP, Killashandra Ree."

She snorted, "Neither is subliminal conditioning, Trag Morfane!"

Lars looked from one to the other, grinning at this evidence of unexpected discord. "Here, here, what's this?"

"An old controversy," Killashandra replied quickly. "If all the provincial organs need at least basic maintenance, then you and I, Trag, are the only qualified technicians on Optheria. Ampris will have to ask you, for I can't see him asking me, and that solves that problem, doesn't it?"

"It should," Lars replied, grinning at her for her change of subject and the facile solution.

"We shall see," Trag added, rising to refill his glass.

"I need a bath," Killashandra said, rising. "After a morning spent with Ampris, I feel unclean!"

"Now that you mention it," Lars murmured and followed her.

A stolid security man drove the small ground vehicle that evening. Its plasglas canopy gave her an unobstructed view of the City in its tortured sprawl as she was driven sedately down from the Conservatory prominence. The spring evening was mild and the sky cloudless. Quite likely, Killashandra thought, she was seeing the City at its best, for spring growth hazed most of the vegetation with a delicate green, gold, or fawn brown, providing some charm to the otherwise sterile buildings. The residential dwellings often sported vines, now sprouting a bright orange leaf or blossom.

Most of the traffic was pedestrian, though a few larger goods-carrying vehicles intersected their route through the winding streets of the City. There seemed to be no visible roadway controls but her driver slowed to a complete halt at several cross streets. At one, she received incurious glances from the several pedestrians also halted on the footpaths. Doubtless all good Optherians were at home with their families at that hour, and the few people that Killashandra did pass looked glum, anxious, or determined. It occurred to Killashandra that she missed the light-hearted islanders with their ready smiles and generally pleasant behavior. She'd seen very few genuine or lasting smiles in the Conservatory: a perfunctory movement of the lips, a show of teeth but no genuine delight, pleasure, or enthusiasm. Well, what else could she expect in such a climate?

She spotted the Piper Facility before the driver turned up the broader thoroughfare to it. It hung, block-square and utilitarian, like hostels anywhere, even Fuerte. She had once thought the native orangy-red sandstone of Fuerte garish and common but she could feel almost nostalgic for its hominess. Certainly the relaxed and random designs of Fuertan architecture were a patch above Optheria's contorted constructions.

The timepiece above the entrance of the Piper Facility flashed a big 1930 as the driver reduced the forward speed of the vehicle. Precisely then, the main door slid aside and Corish, looking tanned and expectant, emerged. Immediately he saw Killashandra, he smiled a warm and enthusiastic welcome.

"Right on the dot, Killashandra, you've improved!" he said, giving her an unnecessary assist out of the vehicle.

"Thank you, driver," Killashandra said. "I really need to stretch my legs, Corish. Let's walk to the restaurant if it isn't far. I felt awfully conspicuous where so few people use ground transport."

"Have you paid him?" Corish asked, reaching into his belt pouch.

"I told you I could," she began in a sulky voice and made shooing gestures at the driver. The man reengaged the drive and the vehicle slid slowly away. "I'm being monitored, Corish, and we need to talk," she said, cocking her head up at him with an apologetic expression on her face.

"I thought so. I'm told to try the Berry Bush so I expect it's got monitors in the utensils. This way." Corish cupped his hand under her elbow, guiding her in the right direction. "It's not far. I'm only just back from Ironwood."

"Lars is in a swivet about Nahia and Hauness."

"They're all right . . ." and Corish's tone of voice added *so far*, "but the search and seize continues! Hauness is convinced that the Elders mean to rouse a punitive expedition against the islands. In spite of your safe return."

"Torkes doesn't believe in coincidence. More important . . ." and Killashandra broke off, stunned by the look of pure hatred on the face of a woman passing by. Killashandra glanced around but the woman had not paused or accelerated her pace.

"More important?" Corish prompted, his hand impelling her to keep pace with him.

With an effort, Killashandra redirected her attention, but an afterimage of the intensity of that expression burned in her mind.

"The Elders use subliminal conditioning."

"My dear Killashandra Ree, that is a dangerous allegation." Corish tightened his fingers on her arm, shocked by her statement. He looked about, to see if any of the few passers-by could have overheard.

"Allegation, fardles! Corish. They blasted last night's audience with it," she said, only barely able to keep her intense indignation at the conversation level. "Security, pride, and sex was the dose. Didn't Olav mention subliminals to you? He knows about them."

Corish set his mouth in a grim line. "He mentioned them but he could provide me with no proof."

"Well, I can swear to it, and so can Trag. He disconnected the processor on the Festival Organ yesterday—while we had the chance—and the Conservatory instrument today." She cast him a snide sideways glance. "Or should we have waited until tomorrow night so you'd have firsthand experience?"

"Of course I trust Trag's evidence . . . and yours." He added the last in an afterthought. "How were you able to find the equipment? Wasn't it well hidden?"

"It was. Shall we say a joint effort—the murdered Comgail, Lars, and Trag. It wasn't crystal that killed Comgail, and I never could see how it had, but a desperate man. Probably Ampris. There'll be enough witnesses to testify before the Federation Council. Nahia and Hauness, too, if we can get them out."

"You'll never get Nahia to leave Optheria," Corish said, shaking his head sadly. He gestured for them to make a right turn at the next junction. The smell of roasting meats and frying foods greeted their nostrils, not all of it appetising. But this was clearly a catering area. Open-front stalls served beverages and a pastry-covered roll—with a hot filling to judge by the expression of a man cautiously munching one.

"If we could get anyone out," Corish said gloomily. "They're all in jeopardy now."

"Which is why we want you to contact Olav and get him and . . ."

A change in air pressure against her back gave Killashandra only a second's warning but she had turned just enough to deflect the long knife descending to her back. Then a second knife caught her shoulder and she tried to roll away from her assailants, hearing Corish's hoarse cry.

"Lars!" she shouted as she fell, trying to roll away from her attackers. *"Lars!"* She had become too used to his presence. And where was he when she really needed him? The thought flitted even as she tried to protect herself from the boots kicking her. She tried to curl up, but hard rough hands grabbed at arms and legs. Someone was really attempting to kidnap her, even with Corish beside her. He was no bloody use! She heard him yelling above the unintelligible and malevolent growls of the people beating her. There were so many, men and women, and she knew none of them, their faces disguised by their hatred and the insanity of violence. She saw someone haul back a man with a knife raised to plunge into her, saw a face she knew—that woman from the street. She heard Corish howling with fury and then a boot connected with her temple and she heard nothing else.

Chapter 24

Of the next few days, Killashan-
dra had only disconnected memories. She heard Corish arguing
fiercely, then Lars, and under both voices, the rumble of Trag who
was, she thought even in her confusion and welter of physical
pain, laying down laws. She was aware of someone's holding her
hand so tight it hurt, as if she didn't have enough wounds, but
the grasp was obscurely comforting and she resisted its attempt
to release hers. Pain came in waves, her chest hurt viciously with
every shallow breath. Her back echoed the discomfort, her head
seemed to be vibrating like a drum, having swollen under the
skull.

Pain was something not even her symbiont could immediately
suppress but she kept urging it to help her. She chanted at it,
calling it up from the recesses of her body to restore the cells with
its healing miracle, especially the pain. Why didn't they think
about the pain? There wasn't a spot on her body that didn't ache,
pound, throb, protest the abuse that she had suffered. Who had
attacked her and *why*?

She cried out in her extremity, called out for Lars, for Trag who
would know what to do, wouldn't he? He'd helped Lanzecki with
crystal thrall. Surely he knew what to do now? And where had
Lars been when she really needed him? Fine bodyguard he was!
Who had it been? Who was the woman who hated her enough to
recruit an army to kill her? Why? What had she done to any
Optherians?

Someone touched her temples and she cried out—the right one
was immeasurably sore. Then pain flowed away, like water from
a broken vessel, flowed out and down and away, and Killashandra

sank into the gorgeous oblivion which swiftly followed painlessness.

"If she had been anyone else, Trag, I wouldn't permit her to be moved for several weeks, and then only in a protective cocoon," said a vaguely familiar voice. "In all my years as a physician, I have never seen such healing."

"Where am I going? I'd prefer the islands," Killashandra said, rousing enough to have a say in her disposition. She opened her eyes, half-expecting to be in the wretched Conservatory Infirmary and very well satisfied to find that she was in the spacious bed of her quarters.

"Lars!" Hauness called jubilantly. His had been the familiar voice.

The door burst inward as an anxious Lars Dahl rushed to her bedside, followed by his father.

"Killa, if . . . you knew . . ." Tears welling from his eyes, Lars could find no more words and buried his face against the hand she raised to greet him. She stroked his crisp hair with her other hand, soothing his release from uncertainty.

"Lousy bodyguard, you are . . ." She was unable to say what crowded her throat, hoping that her loving hand conveyed something of her deep feeling for him. "Corish was no use, after all." Then she frowned. "Was he hurt?"

"Security says," Hauness replied with a chuckle, "he lifted half a dozen of your assailants and broke three arms, a leg, and two skulls."

"Who was it? A woman . . ."

Trag moved into her vision, registering with a stolid blink that her hands were busy comforting Lars Dahl. "The search and seize stirred up a great deal of hatred and resentment, Killashandra Ree, and as you were the object of that search, your likeness was well circulated. Your appearance on the streets made you an obvious target for revenge."

"We never thought of that, did we?" she said ruefully.

The movement to her right caused her to flinch away and then offer profuse apologies, for Nahia was moving to comfort the distraught Lars.

"So you took the pain away, Nahia? My profound thanks," Killashandra said. "Even crystal singers's nerve ends don't heal as quickly as flesh."

"So Trag told us. And that crystal singers cannot assimilate many of the pain-relieving drugs. Are you in any pain now?" Nahia's hands gently rested on Lars's head in a brief benison, but her beautiful eyes searched Killashandra's face.

"Not in the flesh," Killashandra said, dropping her gaze to Lars's shuddering body.

"It is relief," Nahia said, "and best expressed."

Then Killashandra began to chuckle, "Well, we achieved what I set out to do in meeting Corish. Got you all here!"

"Far more than that," Trag said as the others smiled. "A third attack on you gave me the excuse to call a scout ship to get us off this planet. The Guild contract has been fulfilled and, as I informed the Elders's Council, we have no wish to cause domestic unrest if the public objects so strongly to the presence of crystal singers."

"How very tactful of you." Belatedly remembering caution, Killashandra looked up at the nearest monitor, relieved to find it was a black hole. "Did the jammer survive?"

"No," Trag said, "but white crystal, in dissonance, distorts sufficiently. They've stopped wasting expensive units."

"And . . ." Killashandra prompted, encouraging Trag since he was being uncharacteristically informative.

He nodded, Olav's grin broadened, and even Hauness looked pleased. "Those shards provide enough white crystal to get the most vulnerable people past the security curtain. Nahia and Hauness will organize a controlled exodus until the Federated Council can move. Lars and Olav come with us on the scout ship. Brassner, Theach, and Erutown are to be picked up by Tanny in the *Pearl Fisher* and leave with Corish on the liner—"

"Corish?" Killashandra looked about expectantly.

"He's searching most thoroughly for his uncle," Hauness said, "and attending the public concerts which have been hastily inaugurated, to soothe a disturbed public."

"What's the diet?"

"Security, pride, reassurance, *no* sex," Hauness replied.

"Then you didn't get to the other organs, Trag?"

"Corish suggested that some should be left in, shall we say, normal operating condition as evidence, to be seen by the Federal Investigators."

"What Trag doesn't say, Killashandra," replied Nahia, a luminous smile gently rebuking the other crystal singer, "is that he refused to leave you."

"As the only way to prevent the Infirmary from interfering with the symbiont," Trag said, bluntly, disclaiming any hint of sentiment. "Lars thought to send for Nahia to relieve pain."

"For which I am truly grateful. I've only a tolerable ache left. How long have I been out?"

"Five days," Hauness replied, scrutinizing her professionally. He placed the end of a hand-diagnostic unit lightly against her neck, nodding in a brief approval of its readings. "Much better. Incredible in fact. Anyone else would have died of any one of several of the wounds you received. Or that cracked skull."

"Am I dead or alive?"

"To Optheria?" Trag asked. "No official acknowledgment of the attack has been broadcast. The whole episode has been extremely embarrassing for the government."

"I should bloody hope so! Wait till I see Ampris!"

"Not in that frame of mind, you won't," Trag assured her, repressively stern.

"Nor more of us for the time being," Hauness said, nodding significantly to the others. "Unless Nahia . . ."

Killashandra closed her eyes for a moment, since moving her head seemed inadvisable. But she opened them to warn Hauness from disturbing Lars, who was still kneeling by the bed. He no longer wept but pressed her hand against his cheek as if he would never release it. The door closed quietly behind the others.

"So you and Olav can just walk into the scout ship?" she asked softly, trying to lighten his penitence.

"Not quite," he said with a weak chuckle, but, still holding her hand, he straightened up, leaning forward, toward her, on his elbows. His face looked bleached of tan, lines of anxiety and fear aging him. "Trag and my father have combined their wits—and I'm to be arrested by the warrant Trag has. Don't worry," and he patted her hands as she reacted apprehensively, remembering Trag's remarks about using the warrant. "Carefully worded, the warrant will charge me with a lot of heinous crimes that weren't actually committed by me, but which will keep Ampris and Torkes happy in anticipation of the dire punishment which the Federated Courts dispense for crimes of such magnitude."

Killashandra grabbed tightly at his hands, ignoring the spasm of pain across her chest in her fear for him. "I don't like the idea, Lars, not one little bit."

"Neither my father nor Trag are likely to put me in jeopardy, Killa. We've managed a lot while you were sleeping it all off. When we're sure that the scout ship is about to arrive, Trag will confer with Ampris and Torkes, confronting them with his suspicions about me—in your delirium you inadvertently blew the gaff. Trag is not about to let such a desperate person as me escape unpunished. He has held his counsel to prevent my escaping justice."

"There's something about this plan that alarms me."

"I'd be more alarmed if I had to stay behind," Lars said with a droll grin. "Trag won't give the Elders time to interfere, and they'll be unable to protest a Federal Warrant when a Federation scout ship is collecting me and you and Trag. The beauty part is that the scout's the wrong shape to use the shuttle port facility. Its security arrangements require open-space landing anyhow. That way my father has a chance of boarding her."

"I see." The scheme did sound well-planned, and yet some maggot of doubt niggled at Killashandra—but her unease could well arise from her poor state of health. "How did Olav get invited here?"

"He'd been called in by the Elders on an administrative detail. Why so few islanders attend concerts!" Lars had regained considerable equilibrium and he rose from his knees, still holding her hand, to sit beside her on the bed.

"Who did attack me, Lars?"

"Some desperate people whose families and friends had been scooped up by that search and seize. If only I'd been free to get into the marketplace, Olver would have warned me of the climate of the City. We'd have known not to let you walk about."

"As Corish and I left the Facility, a woman who gave me such a look of hatred—"

"You were spotted long before she saw you, Sunny, driving down from the Conservatory. If only I'd been with you . . ."

"Don't fret about *ifs*, Lars Dahl! A few aches and pains achieved what the best laid plans might have failed to do."

Lars's face was a study in shocked indignation.

"Do you know how badly you were hurt? Hauness wasn't kidding when he said you could have died from any one of those wounds, let alone *all* of them together." He held her hand in a crushing grip. "I thought you were dead when Corish brought you back. I . . ." A sudden look of embarrassment rippled across his stern face. "The one time you really needed a bodyguard, I wasn't there!"

"As you can see, it takes a lot to kill a crystal singer."

"I noticed, and don't wish to ever again."

Unwittingly he had reminded them both of the inescapable fact that their idyll was nearly over. Killashandra couldn't bear to think of it and quickly evaded further discussion of that.

"Lars," she said plaintively, "at the risk of appearing depressingly basic, I'm hungry!"

Lars stared at her in consternation for a moment but he accepted her evasion and his understanding smile began to replace the sadness in his eyes.

"So am I." Lars leaned foward to kiss her, gently at first and then with an urgency that showed Killashandra the depths of his apprehension for her. Then, with a spring in his step and a jaunty set to his shoulders, he went in search of food.

Killashandra did have to endure the official apologies and insincere protestations of the Elders, all nine of them. She made the obligatory responses, consoling herself with the thought that their days were numbered, and she would shorten that number as much as possible. She pretended to be far weaker than she actually was, for once the symbiont began its work, her recovery was markedly swift. But, for official visits, she managed to assume the appearance of debility so that her convalescence had to be supervised by Nahia and Hauness, skilled medical practitioners that they were. This gave the conspirators ample time to plan an orderly and discreet exodus of people in jeopardy from Elderly tyrannies.

Olav had smuggled his miniature detector unremarked into the Conservatory as a piece of Hauness's diagnostic equipment. At first they had been bitterly disappointed when it responded to

Lars's proximity, despite his pockets being full of white crystal shards. If Trag approached with Lars, the device remained silent, so Killashandra's theory that crystal resonance confused the detector was correct. But her resonance was gone and, with the imminent arrival of the scout ship, there would be no chance for Trag to usher a few refugees past the security curtain at the shuttleport arch.

Fortunately Lars also remembered that Killashandra had disrupted the monitors by singing the crystal fragments. These, resonating discordantly as the wearer hummed, fooled the detector. It was then only a matter of experimentation to discover just what quantity of crystal provided adequate shielding. Perfect pitch was actually a handicap, the more out-of-tune the note, the more the white crystal reacted, and deluded the detector.

A week after the attack, Olav had no further excuse to stay at the Conservatory, and left, it was said, for the islands. He had been able to convince the Elders of his determination to send more islanders to the public concerts. Actually, he stayed in the City and made a few minor but important alterations to his appearance. The next day, he reported to Hauness and Nahia in Killashandra's suite, bearing documents that proved him to be the qualified empath whom Hauness and Nahia had drafted from their clinic to attend Killashandra. Now that Killashandra was recovering, they wished to return to their other patients in Ironwood.

"Nahia's the one who ought to be leaving," Lars had bitterly objected. "She's the most vulnerable of us all."

"No, Lars," Trag had said. "She is needed here, and she needs to be here, for reasons which you might not understand but for which I esteem her."

Trag's unstinted approval of the woman did much to placate Lars but he told Killashandra that, in leaving, he keenly felt himself the traitor.

"Then come back with the Revision Force," she said, more than a little irritated by Lars's self-reproach on this and other issues. She immediately regretted the suggestion at the look of relief in Lars's face. But it was a solution which could resolve many of Lars's doubts, especially when she knew he loved his home world and would be happy enough sailing the *Pearl Fisher* around the islands. She was somewhat relieved that Lars would be happy on Optheria once the government had been changed. "The Federation will need people with leadership potential. Trag says it usually takes a full decade before a new provisional government is appointed, much less ratified by the Federation. You might even end up a bureaucrat."

Lars snorted derisively. "That's the most unlikely notion you've had. Not that I wouldn't like to get back here unprejudiced. I'd like to make sure the change is going to be beneficial."

"And ensure that you had official permission to sail about in your beloved islands." She managed to keep the bitterness out of her voice for she could think of many things that a man with Lars's abilities and talents could do, once free to move about the galaxy. It rankled that her body was not sufficiently mended to add that argument to verbal ones. Lars was treating her as if she were fragile. He was gentle and affectionate. His caresses, though frequent, were undemanding, leaving her frustrated. He was so solicitous of her comfort that she was frequently tempted to wreak a bit of violence on him. Although her jagged, red scars looked more painful than they were, a lover as considerate as Lars had always been would be reluctant to approach her. The symbiont couldn't work fast enough for her. But would it have repaired her *before* the scout ship brought them to the Regulus Federation Base? She tried hard to overcome her desire for Lars and to ignore the fact that time was running out for them both.

It was too soon and not soon enough when Mirbethan communicated the imminent arrival of the scout ship, the CS *914*. Then she was called upon to witness Trag's confrontation of Lars, in the presence of the astonished, and delighted, Elders Ampris and Torkes as the Guildmember, imposing in his righteous indignation and wrath, accused Lars Dahl of infamous acts against the person of Killashandra Ree, and displayed the Federal Warrant. Against Killashandra's loud cries of distress and disillusionment over her erstwhile lover's felonies, Ampris and Torkes struggled to contain their exultation over the arrest.

Trag's timing was superb and his manner so daunting that, with the Federal Scout ship landed in the shuttleport valley, the Elders were left with no option but to permit the arrest and the deportation of their erring citizen. There was no doubt they were delighted, though deprived of the joy of punishing him, that the Federal justice due to be meted out to Lars Dahl would be far more severe than their Charter allowed them. Among the others vindicated by this unexpected climax was Security Officer Blaz, who clamped restraints on Lars's wrists with undisguised satisfaction.

What was supposed to have been a dignified farewell to their auspicious guests was hastily cancelled by Ampris, waving off the various instructors and senior students gathered on the steps of the Conservatory. Presently only Torkes, Mirbethan, Pirinio, and Thyrol were left.

Lars was strong-armed by Blaz into the waiting transport and it was difficult for Killashandra not to react to that treatment. Or deliver an appropriate parting shaft at the officious Blaz. But she was supine on the grav-stretcher guided by the disguised Olav and she had to concentrate on looking sufficiently ill to require the services of an empath.

When Torkes stepped forward, obviously about to say something which would nauseate her, she forestalled him. "Don't jostle me when you load this floating mattress," she irritably warned Olav.

"Yes, let us not unnecessarily prolong our leave-taking," Trag said, giving the float a little push into the ground transport. "Scout pilots are notoriously short-tempered. Is the prisoner secure?" Trag's voice was the cold of glaciers as he glanced back at his prisoner, and Security Captain Blaz growled a reassurance. He had insisted on personally turning over this felon to the scout captain.

It was a silent journey, only Blaz enjoying his circumstances. Lars affected an appropriate dejected, fearful pose, not looking up from his hand restraints. From her position, Killashandra could see nothing but the upper stories of buildings and then sky, and they passed so fluidly she experienced motion sickness; she spoke severely to her symbiont until the reaction disappeared. Trag was staring stolidly out the window on the seat in front of her, and Olav was beyond her view. Rather an ignominious departure to all appearances. And yet, a triumphant one, considering what she and Trag and Lars had accomplished.

She contented herself with that reflection but it was with considerable relief that she saw the spires of the shuttle port appear, approach, and pass by as the transport was driven to the landing site of the scout ship. It was on its tail fins, ready for take-off; the mobile scout pilot waited for her passengers by the lift on the ground.

"There is no way I am going up that," and Killashandra pointed to the lift, "in this," and she slapped the grav-stretcher.

"Guildmember, you have been—" Olav began firmly.

"Don't 'Guildmember' me, medic," she said, raising up on her elbow. "Just get me off this thing. I'll leave this planet as I got on it, on my own two feet."

The transport stopped and Trag and Olav were quick to get her float out.

"Chadria, Scout Pilot of the CS *914*," said the trim woman in the Scout Service blue, walking forward to lend an unobtrusive hand. "My ship's name is Samel!" A smile lurked in her eyes but fled as Security Officer Blaz hauled Lars unceremoniously out of the transport and roughly propelled him to the lift.

"Where do I stow the prisoner, Scout Pilot Chadria?" he said in an ill-tempered growl.

"Nowhere until the Guildmembers are settled," Chadria replied. She turned to Killashandra. "If you're more comfortable on the float—"

"I am not!" Killashandra swung her legs over the side of the float, and Olav hastily adjusted its height so that she only had to step off it to be erect. Lars moved forward but was hauled back to Blaz's side and she could see him tensing in rebellion. "Trag!" The man supported her around the waist. "Permission to come aboard, Chadria, Samel!"

"Permission granted," scout and ship replied simultaneously.

The unexpected male voice, apparently issuing about his feet, startled an exclamation out of Blaz. A small, superior smile twitched at Lars's lips, hastily erased but reassuring to Killashandra.

She let herself be conducted to the lift by Trag and the medic, wondering how Olav would be able to stay if Blaz continued in his officious manner. There was no hint of uncertainty in either man's face so she decided to let them worry about such a minor detail. She remembered to salute the ship as she stepped aboard.

284

"Welcome, Killashandra, Trag. And you, gentle medic." The ship spoke in a baritone voice which rippled with good humor. "If you will be seated, Chadria will be up in just a moment."

"How are we going to get rid of Blaz? And keep Olav?" Killashandra whispered urgently to Trag.

"Watch," Samel said and one of the screens above the pilot's console lit up, displaying a view of the lift.

"I'll take control of this fellow, now," Chadria was saying as she pulled a wicked little hand-weapon from her belt. "I was told to secure quarters aboard. And there's nothing he can do to escape a scout ship, Officer. Get on there now, you."

The observers could see the conflict in Blaz's face but Chadria had pushed Lars onto the lift and stepped on the platform with her back to Blaz so that there was no room for him to accompany them, and no way to dispute this arbitrary decision with someone's back. That maneuver confused Blaz just long enough. The lift ascended quickly, Blaz watching uncertainly.

"Permission to board?" Lars said, grinning in at Killashandra.

"Granted, Lars Dahl!" Samel replied, and Chadria stepped beside Lars in the airlock, punching out control sequences. The lift collapsed and secured itself, the airlock door closed, Lars and Chadria stepped into the cabin while the inner door slid shut with a final metallic *thunk*. An alarm sounded.

On the ground, Blaz reacted to the claxon, suddenly aware that the medic was still on board and not quite sure if that was in order. The transport driver shouted at him as the ship's drive began to rumble above the noise of the take-off alarm, and Blaz had no recourse but to retreat to safety.

"Oh, that was well-done!" Killashandra cried and, finding her legs a bit unstable in reaction to the final moments of escape, she sank onto the nearby couch.

Trag thumbed the bar that released the restraints on Lars's wrists and Lars stumbled to enfold Killashandra in his arms.

"Everyone, take a seat," Chadria warned, sliding into the pilot's gimballed chair. "We were told to make it a fast exit," she added with a grin. "Okay, Sam, they're secure. Let's shake the dust!"

Chapter 25

Killashandra's complacency about their confrontation with the Federated Council on Regulus Base altered drastically as the CS *914* began its final approach to the landing strip. The building which housed the administrative offices for that sector of the Federated Sentient Planets covered an area slightly more than twenty klicks square.

Chadria cheerfully informed her passengers that there was as much again in subterranean levels as above ground, and some storage areas delved as much as a half a klick below Regulus's surface. Monorail lines connected the sprawling offices with the residential centers thirty and forty klicks away, for most of the workers preferred the nearby valleys and the many amenities available there. Regulus was a good post for everyone.

From a distance, the profile was awe inspiring. The random pattern of rectangular extrusions above the mass of the complex was silhouetted against the light green early-morning sky. Even Trag was impressed, a reaction which did nothing to assuage Killashandra's growing sense of doubt. She inched as close to Lars as possible and felt him return the pressure in an answering need for tactile reassurance. But he was nowhere near as tense as she was. Perhaps she was just hypersensitive due to her recent ordeal. As they approached, the building dominated the landscape to the exclusion of any other features on Chinneidigh Plain. Skimmers could then be seen landing and taking off at the myriad entrances, each embellished with official symbols depicting the department housed within.

"We're cleared to land at the Judicial Sector," Chadria said, swinging about in her gimballed chair. "Don't look so worried."

She grinned up at the three. "They don't leave you hanging about here for weeks on end. You'll know by midday. It's anticipation that gets to you, and waiting!"

Killashandra knew that Chadria meant to reassure them, for both brain and brawn partners had been excellent hosts, with stories scurrilous and amusing, and stocks of exotic foods and beverages in the scout ship's well-stocked larder to tempt every taste. With exquisite tact, the others had left Killashandra and Lars to enjoy their own company for the week in which the CS 914 hurtled from one corner of the sector to the Regulan planet at its center. Courtesy, however, had dictated to both Lars and Killashandra that they join the others at mealtimes and for evening conversations, and the occasional rehearsals of Lars's defense against the warrant's charges. Trag and Olav had begun a friendly competition over a tri-dimensional maze game which could last up to a day between well-matched players. Chadria and Samel had teamed up against the two men in another contest, one of multiple-choice, which could be expanded to include Lars and Killashandra whenever they chose to play.

There was a strange dichotomy about that journey: the tug between learning more of each other's minds and sating their bodies and senses sufficiently to cushion the imminent parting. On the final day, it was more than Killashandra or Lars could endure to make love: instead they sat close together, one pair of hands linked, playing the maze game with an intensity that bordered the irrational.

Now Chadria swung back to the screens as their progress to the landing site closed with the linear diagram Samel displayed on the situation screen. Killashandra could not restrain the small gasp nor her instinct to clutch at Lars's hands as the two positions matched and the scout ship settled to the ground.

"Here we are," Samel said in a tactfully expressionless tone. "Ground transport is approaching. Glad to have had you all aboard and I hope that Chadria and I will meet you again."

Chadria lifted her long frame from the chair, shaking hands with each one in turn, clasping Killashandra's with an encouraging smile and giving Lars an impish grin before she kissed his cheek in farewell. "Good luck, Lars Dahl! You'll come out on top! Feel it in my bones."

"Me, too," Samel added, and opened the two lock doors.

Killashandra wished that she felt as positive. Then, suddenly, there was no way to evade the inevitable. They picked up their carisaks and filed out. Trag and Olav took the lift down first, permitting Lars and Killashandra a few moments privacy.

Killashandra didn't know what she had expected but the ground transport was a four-seat skimmer, remote controlled, the purple-gold-and-blue emblem of the FSP Judiciary Branch unobtrusively marking the door panel. She took in a deep breath, looking off to the massive tower of the entrance. As she had done for several days, she repeated to herself that "justice would prevail," that the much edited wording of the warrant would support their hopes. And that the disclosure of subliminal conditioning would result in the swift dispatch of a revisionary force to overthrow the Elders' tyranny on Optheria.

But one Killashandra Ree, one-time resident of the planet Fuerte, barely four years a member of the Heptite Guild, had had no encounters at all with Galactic Justice, and feared it. She had never heard or known anyone who had been either defendant or plaintiff at an FSP court. Her ignorance rankled and her apprehension increased.

Silently the four settled into the skimmer and it puffed along on its short return journey. It did not, as Killashandra half expected, stop at the imposing entrance. It ducked into an aperture to one side, down a brightly lit subterranean tunnel, and came to a gentle stop at an unmarked platform.

There a man built on the most generous of scales, uniformed in the Judicial Livery, awaited them. In a state of numbness, Killashandra emerged.

"Killashandra Ree," the man said, identifying her with a nod, not friendly but certainly not hostile. "Lars Dahl, Trag Morfane, and Olav Dahl." He nodded politely as he identified each person. "My name is Funadormi, Bailiff for Court 256 to which this case is assigned. Follow me."

"I am Agent Dahl, number—"

"I know," the man said pleasantly enough. "Welcome back from exile. This way." He stepped aside to allow them to enter the lift which had opened in the wall of the platform. "It won't take long."

Killashandra tried to convince herself that his manner was re-assuring if his appearance was daunting. He towered above them and both Lars and Trag were tall men. Killashandra and Olav were not many millimeters shorter but she had never felt so diminished by sheer physical proportions. The lift moved, stopped, and its door panel slid open to a corridor, stretching out in either direction, pierced by atriums with trees and other vegetation. Gardens seemed an odd decorative feature of a Judicial building but did nothing to buoy Killashandra's spirits. She rearranged her fierce grasp on Lars's fingers, hoping that Funadormi did not see it and that he did, to show this human representative of the Courts that Lars Dahl had her total support.

Funadormi gestured to the left and then halted their progress at the second door on the left, which bore the legend "Grand Felony Court 256."

Killashandra reeled against Lars Dahl, Trag behind him placed a reassuring hand on his shoulder, and Olav straightened his lean frame against the imminent testing of a scheme that had been entered rather lightheartedly.

Funadormi thumbed open the panel and entered. It was not the sort of chamber Killashandra would have recognized as judicial. She did recognize the psychological testing equipment for what it was, and the arm-bands on the chair beside it. Fourteen comfortable seats faced that chair and the wall screens and a terminal which bore the Judicial Seal. A starred flag of the Federated Sentient Planets bearing the symbols indicating the nonhuman sentient species was displayed in the corner.

The door panel *whoosh*ed shut behind them and Funadormi indicated that they were to be seated. He faced the screen, squared his shoulders, and began the proceedings.

"Bailiff Funadormi in Grand Felony Court 256, in the presence of the accused, Lars Dahl, remanded citizen of the planet Optheria; the arresting citizen, Trag Morfane of the Heptite Guild; the alleged victim, Killashandra Ree, also of the Heptite Guild; and witness for the accused, Olav Dahl, Agent Number AS-4897/KTE, present at this sitting. Accused is restrained under Federal Sentient Planet Warrant A-1090088-O-FSP55558976. Permission to proceed."

"Permission is granted," replied a contralto voice, deep and oddly maternal, definitely reassuring. Killashandra could feel her muscles unlock from the tenseness in which she had been holding herself. "Will the accused Lars Dahl be seated in the witness chair?"

Lars gave her hand a final squeeze, smiled with a cocky wink at her, rose, and took the seat. The Bailiff attached the arm cuffs and stepped back.

"You are charged with the willful abduction of Heptite Guild-member Killashandra Ree, malicious invasion of the individual's right to Privacy, felonious assault, premeditated interference with her contractual obligation to her Guild, placing her in physical jeopardy as to shelter and sustenance, deprivation of independent decision and freedom of movement, and fraudulent representation for purposes of extortion. How do you plead, Lars Dahl?" The voice managed to convey an undertone of regretful compassion, and an invitation to confide and confess. Highly sensitized to every nuance, Killashandra wondered if, by some bizarre freak, the Judicial Branch might actually be guilty of a subtle use of subliminal manipulation in that persuasive voice.

"Not guilty on all counts." Lars answered quietly, and firmly, as he had rehearsed.

And, Killashandra reassured herself, he was not, by the very wordage that Trag and Olav had cleverly employed.

"You may testify on your own behalf." The request was issued in a stern, uncompromising tone.

Although Killashandra listened avidly to every word Lars said in rebuttal and in explanation, tried to analyse the terse questions put to him by the Judicial Monitor, she was never able to recall the next few hours in much detail.

He was completely candid, as he had to be, to discharge the accusations. He explained how Elder Ampris, superior to Lars Dahl, student in the Conservatory and as a ruling Elder of the Optherian Council, had approached him, citing the dilemma about Killashandra's true identity and the request to wound her, resolving the quandary. His reward was the promise of reconsidering Lars's composition. The point that Lars had been coerced to perform a personally distasteful act by an established superior was accepted by the Court. To the charge that the abduction was premeditated, Lars explained that he had come upon the victim

290

unexpectedly in an unprotected environment and acted sponta-
neously. He had, it was true, rendered her unconscious but without malice. She had not even suffered a bruise. She had been
carefully conveyed to a place of security, with tools and instructions to provide daily food and shelter, so that she had been in
no physical jeopardy. As she had left the premises of her own
volition, she obviously had not been denied independence of decision and movement. He had not fraudulently represented himself as her rescuer for she had not required rescue, and she had
requested his continued presence as a safeguard against further
physical violence from any source on Optheria. He had not premeditated any interference on her contractual obligation to her
Guild for he had not only assisted her in repairing the damaged
manual, her preemptive assignment, but he had also provided her
with conclusive evidence to resolve the secondary assignment.
He therefore restated his innocence.

After Lars gave his testimony, Killashandra was called to the
chair and had to exercise the greatest degree of control to suppress
signs of the stress she felt. It didn't help to know that the sensitive
psych equipment would record even the most minute tremors
and uncertainties of its subject. That was its function and the
results which the Monitor then analyzed against the psychological profile of each witness. Objectively she was pleased that her
voice didn't quaver as she supported Lars's testimony on each
count, managing to publicly absolve him from felonious assault
as he was, in fact, acting even when he abducted her in her best
interests, contractually and personally. She kept her answers con-
cise and unemotional. Subjectively she had never been so terrified
of any experience. And the equipment would record that as well.

Trag and Olav had their turns in the witness chair. Each time
the subliminal manipulation was mentioned, there was a significant pause in the flow of questions, though there was no hint of
how this information was being received and analyzed by the
Judicial Monitor, since, in point of law, this part of everyone's
testimony was irrelevant to the case at hand.

When Olav resumed his seat between Trag and Lars, the Bailiff
approached the screen. They could all see the activity of the terminal but the pattern of its flashing lights disclosed nothing. Kil-

lashandra, holding Lars's hand, jumped an inch above her chair when the contralto voice began its summation.

"With the exception of felonious assault, the charges against the accused, Lars Dahl, are dismissed." Killashandra swallowed. "Criminal intent is not apparent but disciplinary action is required by law. Lars Dahl, you are remanded into the custody of the Judicial Branch, pending disposition of the disciplinary action. You are further remanded for examination of the charge of subliminal manipulation against the Elders of Optheria. Olav Dahl, you are seconded to assist these investigations, which have now been initiated. Trag Morfane, Killashandra Ree, have you anything to add to your recorded testimonies on the charge of subliminal manipulation by the Elders of Optheria?"

Having already been as candid as possible, neither crystal singer could expand on the information already on record. And Killashandra did not quite understand the matter of disciplinary action for Lars and the remand orders.

"Then this session of the Grand Felony Court of Regulus Sector Federation is closed." The traditional *crack* of wood against wood ended the hearing.

Perplexed by the legal formulas, Killashandra turned to Lars and his father.

"Are you free, or what?" she demanded.

"I'm not quite sure," Lars said with a nervous laugh. "It can't mean much. Everything else was dismissed, wasn't it?" He looked to Olav and was sobered by his father's solemn expression.

"He has been remanded," the Bailiff explained kindly, taking Lars by the arm. "I interpret the judgment to mean that the Court has dismissed all charges but Lars Dahl's physical assault on you in the matter of your abduction. Disciplinary action is always short term. On the second remand charge, the Court requires further discussion of the allegations about the use of subliminal conditioning by the Optherian government. If these are proved correct, then it is likely that the disciplinary action will also be suspended. I can give you hard copy of the precedents involved, indeed of the entire trial, if you wish." When Lars nodded a perplexed affirmation, "Then I shall program them for your quarters. If you gentlemen will come with me?"

A panel at the back of the seating area opened and it was toward this that Funadormi gestured Lars and his father.

"Come with you?" Lars cried, trying to break from the Bailiff's grip.

Shock and surprise briefly immobilized Killashandra and before she could make a move to reach Lars, the Bailiff, securely holding her lover, had him nearly to the open door.

"Wait! Please wait!" she screamed, falling over the chairs in her haste.

"You two have been dismissed. Justice has been served! Arrangements for your transport have been made and the ground vehicle programmed to take you to the appropriate site."

"But—Lars!" Killashandra's cry of protest was made to the immense back of the Bailiff which was disappearing through the aperture, totally eclipsing Lars. Olav hurried anxiously after, adding his protests. "*Lars Dahl!*" she screamed, every fear alerted to his unexpected departure. The panel closed with a final *thuck* just as Killashandra reached it.

"Justice has been served?" she shrieked, beating the wall with impotent fists. "What justice? What justice! LARS DAHL! Couldn't they let us say good-bye? Is that justice?" She wheeled on Trag who was trying to silence her tactless accusations. "You and your foolproof verbiage. They've charged him after all. I want to know why and what does disciplinary action mean for a man who's put himself on the line for a whole benighted fardling useless planet?"

"Killashandra Ree," and both crystal singers turned in astonishment as the voice issued unexpectedly from the wall. "During your evidence, your psychological reactions exhibited extreme agitation and apprehension—unusual when compared to your official profile—which have been interpreted as fear of the accused, despite your generous testimony to his actions against you. Disciplinary action will prevent the accused from any future acts of felonious assault."

"WHAT?" Killashandra could not believe what she had heard. "Of all the ridiculous interpretations! I love the man! I *love* him, do you hear, I was frantic with worry *for* him, not against him. Call him back. There's been a dreadful miscarriage of justice."

"Justice has been served, Killashandra Ree. You and Trag Mor-

fane are scheduled to leave this Court and this building immediately. Transport awaits."

The silence after that impersonal order provoked a thunder of
tinnitus in her skull.

"I don't believe this, Trag. This can't be right. How do we
appeal?"

"I do not believe that we can, Killashandra. This is the Federal
Court. We have no right of appeal. If there is one available to Lars,
I am certain that Olav will invoke it. But we have no further
right. Come. Lars will be taken care of."

"That's what I'm fardling afraid of," Killashandra cried. "I know
what penalties and disciplines the Judicial Branch can use. I had
Civics like any other schoolchild. I can't go, Trag. I can't leave
him. Not like this. Not without any sort of a . . ." Tears so choked
her that she could not continue and a sudden disastrous inability
to stand made her wobble so that Trag only just kept her from
falling.

She didn't realize at first that Trag was supporting her out of
the room. When she found them in the hall, she tried to wrench
herself out of Trag's grasp but there was someone else by then,
assisting Trag and between the two of them, she was wrestled into
the lift. She struggled, screaming imprecations and threats, and
although she heard Trag protesting as sternly as he could, she was
put in padded restraints. The ignominy of such a humiliating
expedient combined with fear, disappointment, and her recent
physical ordeal sent Killashandra into a trembling posture of aggrieved and contained fury.

By the time they reached the shuttle transport to the Regulus
transfer moon, she had exhausted her scant store of energy and
crouched in the seat, sullen and silent, too proud to ask for her
release from the restraints. She let Trag and the medic lead her
where they would, and didn't protest when they undressed
her for immersion in a radiant fluid tank. Legitimate protest and
recourse denied her, she submitted to everything then, despairing
and listless. Over and over she reviewed her moments in the witness chair, when her body, the body which had loved and been
loved so by Lars, had betrayed them both with false testimony.
She was appalled at that treachery, and obsessed by the horrifying
guilt that she, herself, her anxieties and idiotic presentiments,

had condemned Lars on the one count which had not been dismissed by the Court. She could never forgive herself. Somehow, sometime, she would be able to face Lars, and beg his forgiveness. That she promised herself.

All the way back to Ballybran, she said not a single word to anyone, nodding or shaking her head in answer to the few questions that were put directly to her by officials. Trag supervised her meals, immersed her in radiant fluid whenever such facilities were available, and remained by her side during her wakeful hours. If he resented her silence or interpreted it as an accusation, he gave no indication of regret, remorse, or penitence. She was too immersed in her obsession with the outrageous circumstance of Lars's betrayal to try to explain the complexities of her depression.

By the time she and Trag had completed the long journey to Ballybran's surface, Killashandra was completely restored to physical health. She paused only long enough in her quarters to check, as she had begun to do toward the end of the trip, with galactic updates. There was no further word on the Optherian situation beyond the original bulletin announcing the arrival of Revision troops on the planet to "correct legislative anomalies." She refused to consider what that statement might mean for Lars. Dumping her carisak, she changed into a shipsuit. Then she headed for the Fisherman's bailiwick and, with a voice grown gruff from disuse, demanded her sonic cutter. While waiting for him to retrieve it from storage, she checked with Meterology and, with a twinge of satisfaction, learned that the forecast predicted a settled period of weather for the next nine days.

She backed her sled out of its rack herself, though she could see the wild protesting signals of the duty officer trying to abort her precipitous departure. As soon as she was clear of the Hangar, she poured on the power and, in an undeviating line, fled for the Ranges.

It was all part of the miserable web of ironic coincidence that she found black crystal again in the deep, sunless ravine in which she had hoped to bury herself and her grief for the reason and manner of her parting with Lars Dahl.

Epilogue

Stolidly Killashandra watched, arms folded across her breasts, as Enthor reverently unpacked the nine black crystal shafts.

"Interstellar, at the least, Killashandra," he said, blinking his eyes back to normal vision as he stepped back to sigh over the big crystals. "And this is all from that vein you struck last year?" Killashandra nodded. Not much moved her to words these days. Working the new claim, she had quickly recouped her losses on the Optherian contract; Heptite rules and regs had required her to part with a percentage of that fee to Trag. She accepted that as passively as she had accepted everything since that day in Court on Regulus. Not even Rimbol had been able to penetrate her apathy, though both he and Antona continued their attempts. Lanzecki had spoken pleasantly to her after her first return from the Ranges, complimented her on the new black crystal vein but their early relationship could never have been revived even if Lanzecki had persisted.

She didn't see him. She saw no one but Lars, a laughing Lars, garland-wreathed, his blue eyes gleaming, teeth white in his tanned face, his bronzed body poised on the deck of the *Pearl Fisher*. She woke sometimes, sure she felt his hand on her hip, heard his voice in the whisper of the wind in the deep ravine, or in the tenor of warming crystal at noon, when the sun finally touched the cliff. She made two attempts to succumb to crystal thrall but each time the symbiont had somehow pulled her back. Not even that enchantment was powerful enough to break through her emotions, obsessed as she was by the guilty betrayal of her body in the witness chair on Regulus.

She had kept informed of the situation on Optheria and often, on the nights brilliant with crystal song, she composed letters to Lars, asking to be forgiven that betrayal. She wrote imaginary letters to Nahia and Hauness, knowing that they would be compassionate, and intercede for her with Lars. In her better moments, common sense dictated that Lars would not have held that bizarre psychoanalysis against her for he, of them all, knew how much she treasured and admired him. But he had not heard her impassioned plea to the Court, and she doubted if "I love you" had been included in the hard copy of the hearing transcript. And he had other plans for the rest of his life.

She frequently entertained the notion of returning to Optheria to see how he was getting on, even if she never made actual contact with him. He might have found another woman with whom he could share his life on Optheria. Sometimes she returned from the Ranges, full of determination to end her wretched half-life, one way or another. She had more than enough credit for a fiercely expensive galactic call: ironically through some of the black crystal she had herself cut. But would she reach Lars on Optheria? Maybe, once he had completed that disciplinary action and his subordination to the Federal investigation of Optheria, he had found another channel for his abilities and energies. Once he discovered his freedom to travel the stars, they might have won him from his love of the sea.

At her most rational, she recognized all the ifs and ands and buts as procrastinations. Yet, it was not exactly an unwillingness to chance her luck that restrained her: it was a deep and instinctive "knowing" that she must remain in this period of suspension for a while yet. That she had to wait. When the time was right, action would follow logically. She settled down to wait, and perfected the art.

"You're in early, too, you know," Enthor was saying to her. "Storm warnings only just gone out."

"Aren't those good enough?" Killashandra asked. "No need to risk life and limb, is there?"

"No, no," Enthor hastily assured her.

Killashandra had, in fact, answered the storm warning her symbiont had given her. She was used to listening to it because it so often proved the most accurate sense she had.

"You've enough here to spend a year on Maxim," Enthor went on with a sly sideways glance. "You haven't gone off in a long time, Killashandra. You should, you know."

Killashandra shrugged her shoulders, glancing impassively at a credit line that would once have made her chortle in triumph. "I don't have enough resonance to have to leave," she said tonelessly. "I'll wait. Thanks, Enthor."

"Killa, if talking would help . . ."

She looked down at the light hand the old Sorter had put on her arm, mildly surprised at the contact. His unexpected solicitude, the concern on his lined face nudged the thick shell which encased her mind and spirit. She smiled slightly as she shook her head. "Talking wouldn't help. But you were kind to offer."

And he had been. Sorters and singers were more often at loggerheads than empathetic. The northeaster which her symbiont had sensed swept a fair number of singers in from the Ranges to the safety of the Complex. The lift, the hall, the corridors were crowded but she wended her way through, and no one spoke to her. She didn't exist for herself so she didn't exist for them.

The screen in her quarters directed her to contact Antona. There usually was a message from the medical chief waiting for her. Antona kept trying to make a deeper contact.

"Ah, Killa, please come down to the infirmary, will you?"

"I'm not due for another physical?"

"No. But I need you down here."

Killashandra frowned. Antona looked determined and waited for Killashandra's acquiescence.

"Let me change." Killashandra brushed at the filthy blouse of her shipsuit.

"I'll even give you time to bathe."

Killashandra nodded, broke the connection and, unfastening the suit as she made her way to the hygiene room, switched on the taps. Though once—fresh in from the Ranges—she might have done, she didn't luxuriate in the steaming water. She made a quick but thorough bath, and put on the first clean clothes she found. Her hair, close cropped for convenience, dried by the time she reached the Infirmary Level. Her nostrils flared against the smell of sickness and fever, and the muffled sounds reminded her of her initial visit to Antona's preserve. A new class must be passing through adjustment to the Ballybran symbiont.

Antona came out of her office, her color high with suppressed excitement.

"Thank you, Killa. I've a Milekey Transition here whom I'd like you to talk to, reassure him. He's positive there's something wrong." Her words came out in a rush, as she dragged Killashandra down the hall, and thrust her through the door she opened. Impassively, Killashandra noted the number: it was the same room she had so briefly tenanted five years before. Then the occupant rose from the bed, smiling.

"Killa!"

She stared at Lars Dahl, unable to believe the evidence of her eyes for she had seen his phantom so often. But Antona had brought her here so this vision had to be real. Avidly she noted each of the tiny changes in him: the lack of tan, the gauntness of his shoulders under the light shirt, the new lines in his face, the loss of that twinkle of gaiety that had been a trademark of his open, handsome expression. He had subtly aged: no, matured. And the process had brought him distinction and an indefinable air of strength and the patience of strength and knowledge.

"Killa?" The smile had dropped from his face, his half-raised hand fell to his side as she failed to respond.

Imperceptibly she began to shake her head, and tentatively, certain that he would vanish if she admitted to herself that he was flesh, bone, and blood, her hands began to lift from her sides. Inside her body the cold knot into which all emotion and spirit had been reduced began to expand, like a warm draught through her veins. Her mind reverberated with one exultant conclusion: he was there, and he wouldn't be if he hadn't forgiven her.

"Lars?" Her voice was a whisper of disbelief but sufficient reassurance to propel him across the intervening space. Then, as if he found their reunion as incredible as she, he folded her carefully into his arms.

Momentarily she lacked the strength to return the embrace but burrowed her head into the curve of his shoulder and neck, inhaling the smell of him, and exhaling into the tears she had kept bottled for the eternity in which they had been parted.

Lars swept her up in his arms, and carried her to the chair, where he cradled her, appalled at the wildness of her sobbing and comforting her with kisses, caresses, and strong embracings.

"That fardling machine that served justice was never told we were emotionally attached, the one piece of information that no one but us would have thought relevant," he said, releasing in talk the tension he had endured all through the process of getting to this point when he would be ready, and able, to meet her again. "Then Father found out what had happened and he moved the entire Department to revoke that judgment on the basis of misinterpretation of your psychological response. Poor sweet Sunny, so worried about me she messed us both up." To her surprise, he chuckled. "You didn't know that the only reason that disciplinary action was entered against me was the Court's attempt to satisfy what they took to be a suppressed desire for revenge in you. Justice was being served, blind as it was. Father finally reached a human in authority, swore blind to half a dozen psych-units that he himself had handfasted us on Angel Island and got the action revoked. D'you know, that Court Bailiff was a narding construct! No wonder I couldn't move when he grabbed me. Then, when we did understand our rights, Trag had already departed with you."

"I guess you were pretty upset."

At such a massive understatement of fact, she managed to nod, trying to laugh at the absurdity, but she couldn't stop weeping. It had built up quite a head and it ought to prove conclusively to Lars, if he needed any, just how much she had missed him. She had waited so long to be in his arms, to hear his rich and pleasant tenor voice, and the sort of nonsense he was likely to speak. He could have been speaking gibberish and she'd have been content to listen. But he was also telling her the things she would have asked about him, what she needed to know to put some color in the past dreadful year.

"Then Father, Corish, and I spent two months processing material for the Council. Theach, Brassner, and Erutown had come out with Corish and they got assigned to the Revision Corps until someone in the Council took a closer look at the equations which Theach was idly calling up on his terminal." Lars smiled tenderly as he delicately blotted tears from her cheeks, then kissed her forehead for such an un-Killashandraish display of sentimentality.

"So he landed on his feet, as usual. Five more people, including the brewmaster of Gartertown, whom you might remember," he added, tapping her nose as he teased, "got out on the next liner and are being resettled. What had worried Nahia and Hauness was what refugees would do once they got off Optheria, but there seems to be a resettlement policy. Not that Optherians have all that many skills to offer the advanced societies.

"Father and I got drafted to brief the actual Revision Force. You see, right after that infamous hearing, several more agents were sent in to play tourist during the Summer Festival. Good job we left some two-manuals intact. They came back, reporting that they were subjected to blatant subliminal conditioning at public concerts in Ironwood, Bailey, Everton, and Palamo. One thing Father and I emphasized was that the Revision Forces had better wait until after The Festival or they'd have a bankrupt planet as well as a disorganized one. So Optheria got its annual chance to acquire revenue," and Lars grinned with great satisfaction, "and the Elders hadn't twigged to the fact that no subliminal messages were going out on either of the big Conservatory organs. Leaving the mainlanders quite willing to accept anything said about them.

"When we've spare time, I've got some tapes of the actual landing and the takeover. Four Elders had fatal seizures but Ampris, Torkes, and Pentrom will answer to the Supreme Judiciary for their infamous, felonious, malicious, premeditated, and illegal manipulation of Optherian loyalties.

"The Revision Forces are well installed now on Optheria . . ." He looked out with the unfocused gaze of someone imagining a scene and his smile was briefly sad. He bent to kiss Killashandra again, noting that her tears had abated and her breath was no longer taken in ragged gasps.

"Why didn't you go with them?"

"Oh, I was given many arguments why I should. Even a rather complimentary commission. Father returned, but I rather thought he wouldn't leave Teradia for long. To my surprise, Corish went, and of course Erutown and Brassner. I had other plans."

Killashandra shook her head in sad rebuke. "If I'd known what you planned to do . . ." Her gesture included all that his presence in the Infirmary signified.

Lars hugged her tightly to him. "That's why I didn't mention them. Besides," and he gave her a raffish look, "I hadn't really made up my mind."

"How did Trag recruit you then?"

Lars raised his eyebrows in surprise. "He didn't. It is illegal to recruit citizens for the highly dangerous Heptite Guild. Didn't you know? Candidly, my beloved Sunny, I was much impressed by Trag's integrity. It was refreshing to find an honorable and trustworthy man. It was yourself who did the recruiting, Killa. You were the embodiment of the undeniable advantages of being a crystal singer. Your vibrant youth, charm, invulnerability, indefatigable energy, and resourcefulness. Then all those diversified assignments, space travel, credit, not to mention the chance to see a Galaxy I had been denied all my reckless youth—"

"You're mad." Vitality returned to Killashandra in the form of exasperation with his flamboyance, and such relief that she was once again in its presence. "Did you listen to one word I told you about the *dis*advantages? Didn't you pay attention to any of the details in the Full Disclosure, and that isn't the half of what does happen? As you'll find out. How could you be so blind?"

"None so blind as will not see, eh, Killa, my lovely Sunny? My pale Sunny, my beloved. Is there no sun on this planet that you are so wan?" He began to kiss her in a leisurely fashion. "I admit I did hesitate. Briefly." His eyes sparkled with his teasing. "Then I ran the entry on Ballybran itself. That decided me."

"Ballybran? Ballybran decided you?" Killashandra wriggled about in his arms, astounded. Not that she understood why she had such ambivalent reactions to his decision in the first place. He was here! How had she, and that conniving symbiont of hers, known that he would come? Because she didn't dare think that he wouldn't? Long absent, she felt the caress of crystal along her bones.

"Of course, Sunny. Now if you'd thought to mention earlier on that Ballybran has seas—"

"Seas?" Killashandra put a hand on his forehead. He must be feverish. "Seas!"

"All I've ever needed for perfect contentment is a tall ship and a star to sail her by." He held her as her temper began to rise, though she didn't know if he was mauling that obscure quotation or not. "And then, too, Ballybran has you, beloved Sunny!" His tenor voice dropped to an intense and passionate whisper, his eyes were an incredible brilliant blue, dominating her immediate vision. His arms encompassed her in a grip that reminded her of sun-warmed beaches and fragrant breezes and— "Show me, crystal singer, all that Ballybran has to offer me."

"Right now?"

About the Author

Born on April 1, Anne McCaffrey has tried to live up to such an auspicious natal day. Her first novel was created in Latin class and might have brought her instant fame, as well as an A, had she attempted to write in the language. Much chastened, she turned to the stage and became a character actress, appearing in the first successful summer music circus at Lambertville, New Jersey. She studied voice for nine years and, during that time, became intensely interested in the stage direction of opera and operetta, ending this phase of her life with the stage direction of the American premiere of Carl Orff's *Ludus De Nato Infante Mirificus*, in which she also played a witch.

By the time the three children of her marriage were comfortably at school most of the day, she had already achieved enough success with short stories to devote full time to writing.

Between appearances at conventions around the world, Ms. McCaffrey lives at Dragonhold, in the hills of Wicklow County, Ireland, with two cats, two dogs, and assorted horses. Of herself, Ms. McCaffrey says, "I have green eyes, silver hair, and freckles; the rest changes without notice."